D0390461

About the author

I grew up in the Elands River Valley, Eastern Cape, South Africa and in many ways, I had a magical childhood where I had freedom to be a child against the backdrop of apartheid. My father and mother were British ex-pats who were appalled by apartheid.

While working in Uitenhage after matriculating, thinking about my future, I became aware of gunshots and wounded and screaming people streaming past the shop where I worked. That was the day of those terrible killings in Langa.

Since then, Langa has niggled and nudged at me for over thirty years. Now living in the shadow of Stonehenge in Wiltshire, I finally feel able to tell this story. As I walk and roam through Wiltshire, even here in the lush green countryside, I hear them beg me to tell their story.

CLOUD CUCKOO LAND

LOUISE STRADLING

CLOUD CUCKOO LAND

Vanguard Press

VANGUARD PAPERBACK

© Copyright 2021
Louise Stradling

The right of Louise Stradling to be identified as author of
this work has been asserted by her in accordance with the
Copyright, Designs and Patents Act 1988.

All Rights Reserved

No reproduction, copy or transmission of this publication
may be made without written permission.
No paragraph of this publication may be reproduced,
copied or transmitted save with the written permission of the publisher, or in accordance
with the provisions
of the Copyright Act 1956 (as amended).

Any person who commits any unauthorised act in relation to
this publication may be liable to criminal
prosecution and civil claims for damages.

A CIP catalogue record for this title is
available from the British Library.

ISBN 978 1 80016 205 1

*Vanguard Press is an imprint of
Pegasus Elliot MacKenzie Publishers Ltd.*
www.pegasuspublishers.com

First Published in 2021

**Vanguard Press
Sheraton House Castle Park
Cambridge England**

Printed & Bound in Great Britain

Dedication

This book is dedicated to those who lost their lives at Langa and their families.

This is a work of fiction. Names, characters, businesses, places, events and incidents are either the products of the author's imagination or used in a fictitious manner. Any resemblance to actual persons, living or dead, or actual events is purely coincidental.

Acknowledgements

As with any book there are always many people who need to be acknowledged. So here goes: firstly, to my friend David Ashforth, thank you so much for reading this book — you were the first English person to read this — my family are from South Africa so it was always going to be hard to gauge how people from a different community would connect with this book. You gave me excellent advice and worked so hard on the book through lockdown, and I really appreciate it.

Secondly, my family — they must be sick of listening to scenarios by now. My mother, who read it (more than once) and who has been so encouraging. My sister Emma who was instrumental in getting it published — going to extraordinary lengths to motivate me and help me with the selling part. She knows me so well — selling is not something I do well. Emma, you also kept telling me to believe in the project and you were right. Then the rest of the cheerleading team, Claire, Connor, Dan, Nina and Sam (although very far away), you have always believed in me. Then there is Claire Groeneveld who so painstakingly and thoroughly went through the final edits. Thank you so much, what a boon - having such a brilliant editor in the family! Finally, I cannot thank the family without mentioning you again, Mom. You always encouraged and believed in me. You never stopped and without you none of this would ever have been completed. Thank you mom and we all miss you so much.

Anna Olson who painstakingly edited this book, without this essential service very little of it would have made sense.

Then there is of course the production team, without which, a project like this could never ever be completed. The entire team at Pegasus — too numerous to name individually — and Vicky Gorry who took me patiently through the whole process without ever losing it despite my idiotic questions.

Prologue

Combat units were ready and waiting. Eight camouflaged men squeezed into the cramped quarters of the back of the *buffel*. Shoulder to shoulder, weapons ready, loaded. Two extra men up front — a driver and the *kommandant*. That made ten men, all armed, all dangerous: a fighting action team.

Identical soldiers; police playing at soldiering. Police-camouflage issued to little boys to look like soldiers. All masked with thick grey scarves drawn up to their eyes despite the heat. They were ready and primed — fingers on triggers. Trigger-happy.

Hours before in the early morning briefing, their orders had been succinct. They knew where, when, and had long ago made up the why. Today someone would pay the price for challenging the regime. Someone would pay the ultimate price and the nameless, fearless men on this mission were determined to make them pay. They had taken the trouble to dress up like soldiers to perform a soldier's duty — the patriotic duty of every white South African in the fight to preserve the world as they knew and understood it to be.

Outside the *buffel*, dawn was creeping over the distant mountains of Alexandra Township, thick and brooding with a seething silence. There was no movement. Only the godless and forsaken were awake at this hour. The A team was there to make a deadly noise like an alarm breaking the virgin silence.

Suddenly the back door of the *buffel* was yanked open by a camouflaged arm. The signal for the mission had been given.

Inside the tin shanty, it was stifling. The small man, stripped to the waist, lay in the only room against the corrugated wall on the small low bed. His skin shone with sweat. His breathing was so shallow he could have been dead. The tiny woman, at first invisible next to the man, had one arm thrown over her eyes. She too was stripped to the waist and her skin wore a thin sheen of glistening sweat making her skin silver black in the dim light of the room. The woman's face in repose was beautiful like a doll. A thin bed sheet spotted with tiny black flecks was kicked to the bottom of the bed.

Two little boys lay on a mattress on the floor. Like puppies they were intertwined, naked and deep in sleep. The stink of wood smoke hung in the tiny room like a tangible living thing. Last night's supper pot lay overturned near the door. The walls were papered with old newspaper articles now faded and outdated yellow. Pictures of long-gone public figures and places of interest looked down on the family as if from an alien world.

It was very dark in the tiny, stifling hut and it would be mid-morning before the sun penetrated the hovel. Somewhere outside a dog began to bark but was suddenly and mysteriously stopped.

Suddenly the door exploded inward and huge violent hands yanked the half-woken man to his feet as if he weighed nothing at all. The noise, in contrast to the utter silence of before, was deafening and unfathomable; it was impossible to make out individual words or where it was all coming from. It seemed like an army of a thousand soldiers were in the tiny room. A large foot stomped on the woman's chest, and she lay winded and helpless on the floor next to her screaming children. The man in the hands of two uniformed men flopped back and his head rolled like a rag doll.

The terrified children clutched each other and added to the mindless noise, screaming with huge tears smearing their faces.

The man was hurled through the open door into the soft morning air where he landed on the hard red clay, his knees jarring on the dry path that could have been solid concrete. A rifle muzzle was shoved into his face, a cold grey metal bruising and cutting his cheek. Shouted, unintelligible words battered his head so that he swayed and threatened to fall on his face. But cruel hardened arms held him upright so that he faced the horrible nightmare looking directly into the muzzle of the rifle. He put his hands on his head and stared intently at the barrel, hardly even daring to breathe. He could hear his whimpering wife and the screams of his small boys, his beautiful children. But he could not turn, could not do anything. That's when he started to pray.

There were similar scenes enacted all along the haphazard street as men were ejected into the swollen air. Men stripped to the waist, some even naked, their skin as dark as the retreating night, kneeling in the African dust while the A team screamed and slapped their way into their lives, into their very souls. In their identical uniforms of blue anonymity, they ordered the shivering, shaking black men to stay where they were kneeling on the hard unyielding clay while the women and children helplessly wailed.

Chapter 1 — Langa

Near Uitenhage 1984

In the hot, steaming township there was no peace. No place to be alone. No place to listen, to stop and hear the birds. In fact, there were no birds, no insects trilling in the punishing sun. It was a strange, solemn aloneness amongst the clamouring, heaving, striving masses. It seemed so very odd that despite the broiling masses the township could be the loneliest place on earth.

In the township people turned hard, looked hard, their faces set in a grim façade that pretended to keep defeat at bay. An unreadable but unmistakable mien of desperation hung about the visage of every person. And the children born into this place were instantly old and streetwise. The children of this place had to grow up quickly in the harsh dark reality of the township. In this place, childhood was sacrificed at the altar of segregation because they were born into a world that was unfair, unjust and unkind. It was a world of brutality and dog eat dog. It was a world that ate up the weak and mild, and spat out the bones and moved on carelessly to the next victim.

Survival was a matter of ingenuity coupled with sly cunning that had nothing to do with intelligence and everything to do with an innate desperation borne out of poverty. And this heaving mass of human degradation was a place that some people called home. Outsiders stayed away and only spoke of the place in the hushed tones of those who were not forced to live there. And every day ordinary people were forced out of the countryside and into the depths of the townships up and down the land and they adapted or died.

So it was that Winston, drawn with grief and shrunken with dread, came to the township, hoping, against everything that he had been told, that he might recapture the joy of his childhood.

But as the bus set him down on the hard orange clay, he could see that the stories had not been exaggerated. Despite the small coil of dread in the pit of his stomach, Winston stepped forward and was instantly sucked into the heaving mass of people. The dry orange dust frolicked around his tatty feet. The dust of Langa Township, so unique, yet so very common. And he was the only person not moving.

He pulled his small, worn bag — a leftover from a white boy's school days — onto his shoulder and then round under his arm for protection. Looking after his meagre possessions in a place like this was an instinctive reaction borne out of the stories that he'd assimilated and what he now saw in all its sordid reality before him. The bag contained little enough — one white shirt and some small pieces of underwear and a pair of socks so full of holes that Winston knew he'd never wear them. But he had stuck them deep into the bag, spurred on by his mother's watery, pleading eyes.

Masses of indistinguishable men, grim and grey, shuffled past in a cloud of thick pungent tobacco smoke, jostling and jarring him so that he held the bag even more tightly to his chest, conscious that he must look every inch the outsider. Nothing could have forced him to relax even though his brain screamed at him to do so. The tangible shock and dismay held him even more tightly and he no longer cared that all of these men could see he was new. Despite the warnings he'd received from friends and family, he could do nothing to blend in with this bustling alien crowd. Tired and dusty and desperately needing something to drink. His head buzzed with a ringing that crowded out all sensible thought and running his thick tongue over his teeth he wondered when last he'd had a drink.

But no one molested him or even spoke to him. When eyes did rest on him, dark sullen eyes, they flickered away quickly as if embarrassed by his alienness. His bag was after all, small and worthless and he wondered if he had become invisible on the journey, as if insignificance had caused him to disappear.

The Xhosa voices came rapidly, like an explosion of gun fire, and even though it was his language, he couldn't understand what they were saying, as if stress and doubt had rendered him incapable of understanding. The township had made him a foreigner. He felt small, too, although on the farm he'd always been one of the biggest boys. These were real men, not boys, and even though most were scrawny and wiry they were in a strangely inexplicable way strong and bullish. It was in the way they walked and sauntered, wasting no energy and pushing inexorably onwards.

He twisted the well-worn paper through his fingers; he'd been too afraid to put it in his pocket. He'd kept it in his hand for the entire bus journey and now it was soft and supple from too much handling. It was inscribed with his aunt's address in thick red crayon, which was all they had (a leftover from a donation to the school from some far-off country). The paper had been folded over and over again so that it had little tears at the corners. It had been carelessly ripped from a newspaper and was frayed almost to illegibility, but it had taken on the mantle of a good luck charm. He could not part with it if his life depended on it.

The aunt had been old and almost forgotten but remembered at last when Winston was desperate and needed to escape. He could remember the moment his mother had taken a piece of the newspaper from the wall and asked his uncle for the address. It seemed so strange that he could remember irrelevant little details but nothing important.

His mother had watched in her small bird-like way as Winston scrawled the address onto the paper in between the newsprint. She had descended into smallness and weakness after Doda had died and her clothes in imitation had become worn and patched. Even her voice wavered, and Winston had noticed with dismay how old she had so suddenly become. Old before her time.

Her eyes were finally dry — they had not been so for months — when she waved her son away as if her whole body had dried up and her once-dark hair was now peppered with grey and thinning in a way that Winston had not noticed until he was on the bus looking down at her. As the bus rolled away, throwing out clouds of gritty dust, he turned in his seat and watched her standing on the side of the road, unmoving and fading until she was a tiny speck. He turned to look forward but could not get the small bald patch at the top of his mother's head out of his mind.

Winston felt the futility of his quest now that he was faced with Langa — a sprawling township with no signs and no one to ask for help. He quailed at the thought of approaching any of the men that were still hurrying away from him. A strange feeling forbade him from moving to ask directions, as if in that action he might disturb his own invisibility and once he was noticed he would expose himself to an unnamed but terrible danger. This last batch of men were the stragglers and seemed in an even greater hurry than those that Winston had first encountered. These hollow-eyed men seemed even more menacing, as if lateness made them angry and bad-tempered. And while he dithered, they had hurried off, paying him no attention.

Winston wondered why his uncle and then later his mother had thought it would be so simple. His uncle had explained that he was young and strong, and it would not be long before he found work and then he could help his mother and the others. His sisters and helpless, sweet Melikhaya.

His uncle's words had been so seductive. He, the eldest surviving son living at home, needed to provide for his mother and the younger children now that Doda was no longer there. It was this thought that, as nothing else had, prompted him to move.

He imagined the little money he had left. There was enough left to return home, but he knew that he could not return, not yet. Probably not for a long, long time. Probably, if he were honest, he would never return. Winston, young and naïve, had clutched at this new opportunity and was glad to be away from the cloying sadness that had gripped his once happy childhood home.

There had been a faint glimmer of hope when the expedition to Langa was first mooted. There was hope even on the desperate dusty bus ride. There was hope right up until he stepped from the bus and was faced with the hideous reality of Langa on a Wednesday workday morning, smouldering and seething with bitterness and indignation.

Where was he to start in finding the aunt he did not know and had never met? It was a mystery that overwhelmed him and threw him into despair. With a desperate, sinking feeling, he knew that he would not find her. How could he? Where would he begin?

On the bumpy diesel-fumed bus journey, he'd rehearsed little words of introduction. She would not be expecting him. How would she even know him? Even if he could have written, he was not sure that she could read; so many of her generation had never learned. Even if she could have read the letter, he had no idea how to explain what had happened. He had no idea how to even begin. Did she even know of the sad story that had befallen her family so very far away in the country?

Mama, becoming increasingly confused and bewildered over the last few months since Doda's death, had not been able to remember the connections to her long-lost sister and often segued into thoughts about her own long missing eldest daughter. There were times when her daughter and her sister became the same person. When Winston was little, he had not really listened properly to his mother's stories about her family. He was, once again, a small boy with a whole world that was invisible to his mother just as her world was invisible to him.

Winston had never dreamt that he would need an aunt to run to. Had never dreamt that he would leave his beloved valley behind. Most of his family lived and stayed in the valley their entire lives. The only two people he knew who had left, his sister and his aunt, had become entirely lost to the family. Never in all his musings for the future had Winston ever imagined himself in such a place as this.

Even when he eventually galvanised himself to start looking for the street name jotted on the piece of newspaper, his reluctant feet seemed to understand the futility of it more than his bewildered uncomprehending brain. He walked first one way, following a group of men who seemed to have a sense of determination, as if by latching on to them he too could have a purpose. But then he changed his mind and walked back to the bus stop. Then he tried to walk against the tide of people but gave up; it was too difficult.

Back at the bus stop, a group of ragged street children started shouting and calling to Winston who did his best to ignore them. After a while, he could no longer keep looking at the inadequate piece of paper, nor stand the increasingly jeering nature of the children. He began to look around and his eyes eventually lighted on a street trader. The old man was looking straight at him, his rheumy eyes watering. The man, impossibly ancient, was sitting on a wooden crate, his wares, meagre as they were, spread on the ground at his feet; tobacco and matches spread out like rare jewels.

The old man looked at the paper Winston held out to him but shook his head. He couldn't read. When he spoke, his open mouth revealed shreds of rotting black teeth. Winston said the name of the street and the old man grinned again. Yes, he knew the street. It was *lappa* side, he said, pointing behind him at the mass of tin houses sprawling unordered and endlessly into the distance. He told Winston, in elaborate animated gestures, how to follow a track which would take him where he wanted to go.

It was little more than a pathway. It would though, the old man assured him, lead to the place that he wanted. Winston asked about his aunt, calling her by the name that they used on the farm, but the old man laughed as if names were meaningless. The old man, perhaps noticing something about this boy so out of place, stopped grinning. 'Go there.' He pointed. 'You will find her.' He nodded optimistically and turned to sell some matches to a dirty dishevelled woman with black nails.

Winston, quelling his disappointment, assured himself that the man couldn't possibly know all the people that he saw — there were just too many. Also, he was not unkind, and Winston began to recapture some of the hopeless optimism that he'd felt on the bus. He turned away, reluctant to leave the old man but now the ragged children had come dangerously close, and the old man flicked a wrinkled hand to shoo them away. It was clear that the old man did not trust them. For the first time that day Winston smiled, a small timid smile. The children were not above stealing matches and cigarettes and Winston recognised remnants of himself in the small cheeky boys.

They retreated giggling and, surprised, Winston saw how very young they were. He bought a cigarette from the old man even though he didn't smoke and put the cigarette behind his ear where it would not stay for long, falling into the street like a discarded thought. Someone would gleefully find it and declare that this was their lucky day.

The street, obscurely situated and not even signposted, proved to be nothing more than a small gravel path. That he even knew it was the correct street was only due to two gossiping *mamas* who insisted that it was the place he was looking for. Winston, dazed into apathy, wandered hopelessly down the track gazing at houses leaning precariously together as if holding each other up in drunken agreement. Built of tin, they reflected the midday sun, turning the lane into a boiling cauldron. Dizzy now with thirst and hunger Winston stared into the steaming pack of houses but it was quiet and deserted like a graveyard.

The hard-faced people on the path, for even in this small place there were people, too many people, scowled and turned away. No one had heard of Auntie Cansi. Although it was still early and a long way from the dark, Winston began to feel a frisson of fear lick at the edges of his heart. Although his uncle had portrayed the township as a place of opportunity, Winston could only remember other stories of a wild, unpredictable township and this brought a frown to his forehead.

During the long summer evenings in the country when the sun had dropped out of the sky like a bullet and evening came on with loud crickets, the children, sitting on the outskirts of the fire, told each other horror stories of the townships. There were many stories, but they all followed the same theme — tales of murder and death. All the wild stories involved misguided adventurers who were never heard of again. When Winston reflected on those stories, even though they were told by children, he knew that some of the horror was true. After all, his own sister had disappeared into the township. Never had they heard from her again and he knew that Mama was afraid that she was lost to them forever.

With a sense of unreality, he too was now in this place where people went to be lost. Now, when he least wanted to, he remembered those horror stories from around the fireside. And it was all he could do not to sit down with his head in his hands and weep. All the people who moved to the townships were surprisingly similar to how Winston was now: lost and desperate.

The fear, real and tangible, licked around the fringes of his mind like a hungry wolf. Around the fire at night in the open country after their supper these wild stories of the townships had thrilled him and his friends. Stories that were the stuff of myth and intrepid adventure had now become a reality for Winston. And there wasn't any thrilling adventure to be found, only gnawing desperation and despair.

The children around those country fires were hardly recognisable to Winston now. How they'd revelled in the tales, never imagining that any of them would find themselves in the middle of just such an impossible tale.

This much Winston knew to be true. Hadn't his sister gone to the township in Port Elizabeth? Hadn't his sister been missing now for nearly five years? There was no way of knowing what had happened to her and now she was one of those grisly fireside stories. Most of these stories involved night-time miseries and now that Winston was actually in the township he began to fret. Worry now became bigger than his thirst and hunger and he lurched wildly down the haphazard street and breathed heavily like a gasping swimmer. When he looked down, he saw that his shoes were coated with orange dust and his shirt was wet with a fearful sweat. He could smell his own fear and shame which mingled together and settled about him.

Winston said a silent thanks to God that his two younger sisters had not come with him, as they had begged to do. They were better off with his uncle in his valley home. This was most definitely not a place for young girls.

Not finding his aunt was something that had never entered his head. Perhaps it was that he couldn't fit it in with all the other concerns that had occupied him over the last few months. He hadn't even given it a thought — that his auntie, who he'd never met, would not be there — would not be there to help him. Mad, desperate thoughts began to enter his head. Of days and nights spent in terror in the ditches and alleys of the township.

Those alleys, not deep but filled with effluence and unspeakable waste, were not places that Winston cared to think about and now he skipped over one and tried not to look too closely into its depths.

His money was small and very precious. He knew that it would only last for a very short time and he'd already wasted precious cents on a useless cigarette. The money was safely embedded in the toe-tip of his shoe — sewn there by his youngest sister. He felt the hard little nub as he walked — like a comforting little reminder of all his worldly wealth which had felt vast at home and now felt tiny. Now that he was finally in the township, he realised how small and puny his money, extra shirt and tatty pieces of underwear were. He knew he would not eat when the money was gone.

Then out of the orange clingy dust and shambolic, dishevelled houses came a piece of great good fortune.

Chapter 2 — Kobus Jonker

Pretoria, Johannesburg, 1984

Resistance, as the popular saying went, was useless. In fact, this saying was more valid than most people realised because of crusaders like Danie J. Swanepoel and others, zealots and action men (for they were all men) who were keeping the country safe from the *swart gevaar*. These people, and there were many of them, held a hard, implacable line that endeared them to the regime and rendered their opponents helpless and impotent in the holocaust of their beliefs. This small elite band of men were keeping that *swart gevaar,* the black and present danger, at bay. They were holding the huge rage of the indigenous people back through violence, murder and assassination.

And they had many followers — people who had become disillusioned and despondent in the face of the people, the huge raging masses that simply could not be held back any longer. These people were, without exception, white and driven by a fearful disease that made them cruel and desperate. They were happy to put their trust and futures into the hands of the hidden security organisations that had sprung up all over the country. And the most interesting thing about these organisations? They didn't officially exist.

Kobus Jonker was one of the followers. And for many years he considered himself a lucky man. Why was he lucky? He was lucky because he met a leader called Danie J. Swanepoel. But that was only later when he truly knew Danie. At first Kobus was disappointed that when he met Danie there was no thunderbolt of commonality. There was no instant connection, but only a dingy office and piles of dishevelled papers. The office was dark and smelled of disuse and neglect, musty with something unpleasant and long forgotten. The office was so small and cramped that Kobus could take three or four steps and travel its whole length and breadth.

Kobus had been told by his commanding officer that he was needed downtown but that was all he knew. Battling the downtown Johannesburg traffic, thick like molasses, Kobus followed instructions as he had been doing all his life. It had never occurred to him to ask for more information. Kobus, used to obeying, never having been a leader, did simply as he was told never thinking for one second that this was why he'd been chosen to meet Danie. He'd long ago come to the painful realisation that he would never be the commanding officer himself. When he looked into the faces of his family, his father, mother and even his own wife he realised that they too had realised this — long before he ever had. Kobus knew what it was to be a failure.

So, it was a despondent and disheartened Kobus who entered the office which was clearly a hastily assembled meeting place. Danie was casually perched on the end of the battered desk leafing through a folder which he immediately threw down to rest amongst the other discarded files on the table. The file was pale blue, one of the files that the police force used to record all the details of every policeman recruited. Kobus realised with a jolt that it was his file, his name on the spine sliding sideways onto the desk.

And immediately Danie had struck a chord, something that ignited that old almost forgotten flame, and Kobus had felt the stirrings of a reawakened, sluggish zeal and he smiled. For the first time in a long time, a real smile.

Then with a jolt Kobus realised that he was being interviewed. It was certainly not like any of the other interviews he'd ever attended with a stream of standard questions and official forms.

Danie, dressed in faded blue jeans that buckled just below his protruding stomach, was at once casual yet strangely compelling. His eyes, while not quite meeting Kobus', sparkled with an intensity that Kobus was to learn meant Danie was focussed and would get what he wanted. His not-quite-white shirt was crumpled and stained, an unidentifiable mess that he'd attempted to clean, still clinging to the front just below the pocket. His rolled-up sleeves revealed tanned arms and a brown V-shape at his throat. The window was open and as they were on the ground floor, the air was tinged with the curry odour of the Indian take-away nestling in the filthy alleyway across the road.

It was uncomfortably warm, like moving through water, as was usual for January, and unsightly sweat stains had appeared under Kobus' arms. Danie, fancying himself as a dynamic and engaging speaker, had started speaking, rising from his perch on the desk and immediately rushing forward to clasp Kobus' hand, switching his glowing cigarette to his left hand. Danie's voice was surprisingly high for such a large person.

'Hello Kobus,' he said. The cigarette, more than half smoked, dripped ash on the floor, mingling with the unidentifiable debris of many anonymous meetings. Kobus would learn that it was typical of Danie to maintain a sense of casual informality that gave the illusion that they were old friends.

And Danie had launched straight into an impassioned speech as if continuing from another earlier conversation. 'Remember there are hordes of these people!' His lip curled on the word 'people', and he took a drag on his cigarette which had burned down almost to his fingers. He flicked the cigarette out of the window where it fell to the street unnoticed among the pavement traffic.

'We've got no choice; they are everywhere, and we have to stop them by any means.' Kobus had heard it all before but from Danie the words seemed invested with a new and exciting earnestness that reminded him of childhood. Danie's voice was like thick warm molasses that spilled over Kobus so that the words struck a long-lost chord of yearning that he'd thought was irretrievably gone. Years later, if asked, Kobus would say that Danie had sounded like a welcome preacher, a saviour.

While he never quite met Kobus' eyes, his faded light-blue eyes never left Kobus' face and Kobus began to feel, for the first time in his life, that this man and he were talking a language only they understood. Kobus had been feeling empty and lost for so long that he felt as if he'd awoken from a dark nightmare into a bright cool day.

The previous night's dreams had been filled with his father — he hadn't thought of the old man for so long — he was young again (possibly a teenager) holding out a hand with tears streaming down his face. The old man had turned away and he awoke with the echo of tears oddly mixed with fading laughter. He marvelled at the dream, how young he'd felt and looked and when he awoke, for a few moments, he forgot that he was a grown man in his late forties. He knew then he'd never forget that elation of youth that had not yet been driven away by the dream wrecker of middle age.

Meeting Danie had been a shining beacon of hope.

Danie took Kobus around the shoulders — Kobus was a large man, but Danie made him feel small — and led him to the paper-littered desk. Here he indicated a chair for Kobus and seated himself behind the desk as if he were lowering himself onto a throne. He rested his eyes on Kobus and they never left him. Danie had a way of pinning people down with his eyes that suggested they were the only person on earth, and it worked. Kobus was caught.

'You know it's one set of rules for those *kaffirs* and another for us. They bomb us with roadside bombs and then the whole world goes mad when we shoot them. Our boys, some as young as seventeen, are sent to the Caprivi Strip and slaughtered because the whole world supports these *kaffirs*. Well, I for one have had enough. We are going…' here he pointed to himself and then Kobus, 'to put a stop to it.' He lit another cigarette and threw the spent match on to the desk where it continued to smoke disconsolately as if thinking of setting fire to the papers. He flicked the ash from his shirt and stared at Kobus. No one had ever looked at him like that. With hope and something else. That something was the thing that Kobus had missed for a very long time. A thing that was hard to name but it made Kobus swell as if he could fill the world. He thought that finally he'd do something useful like he'd always wanted.

And those words that Danie had spoken would not leave Kobus. Like stray dogs they hungrily stayed with Kobus all through the next day. It was strange because the words were not new. These words were spoken in the pubs at night lifted high in the air like trophies. The words were spoken at *braais* over roasted meat where they mingled with the smells and became legendary. In fact, anywhere a white person went, the words lingered like old memories. But when Danie spoke those words, they took on a new zeal, a new importance and Kobus was listening.

'So, we can play the game by their rules or by our own. I think that you, like me, want to play the game by the rules that will help us win.' Kobus nodded. These too were words that Kobus had heard many times before. Barroom talk, his wife called it, but now coming from Danie it became real, as if shortly to be followed at last by actions. And in the end, all it had taken was a nod of the head and Kobus was part of the team. Danie had sprung up from the desk and grabbed for his hand and shook it vigorously as if he could never have envisioned doing any of this on his own without Kobus.

They were in it together and he made it sound like a matter that was of vital importance to all of them. A matter of life and death. Danie had further turned the screw by making it sound like he never gained personally from any of the work that they did. Danie was the original self-sacrificing messiah of counterinsurgency in South Africa. And Kobus had been drawn by a religious fervour (even mania, he later realised) into the arms of the saviour. His saviour.

It wasn't until later when he thought about it, when it all went horribly wrong, that he remembered the horrible truth had been there all along. Why would they, all of them, do anything at all for Danie? It was as if Danie had touched some hidden nerve that made them forget the rules themselves. Made them trust him when he'd done nothing to deserve that trust.

Kobus knew too that if he had asked what it was that made people follow Danie, none of them could have answered. When it came to describing Danie, words became trapped in his mouth. Danie was always dishevelled and carried around with him a distasteful smell of cigarettes and something else that was stale and unidentifiable. Kobus could not remember a time that he hadn't seen Danie without a cigarette. Even when in the middle of one of their raids Danie had a cigarette jammed into his mouth. He said that he couldn't stand the smell of the townships and *kaffirs* and that only cigarettes helped to quell the rising bile. And yet despite all of this Kobus (and the others) felt strangely compelled by him, drawn like moths to the light.

The old, jaded message suddenly took on a new energy that must have been borne out by his larger-than-life persona. A huge, booming person who was impossible to ignore and more impossible to dislike. Even so, there were many dynamic personalities that did not command the same blind adoration as Danie. In the end it was pointless brooding over it all. The truth was that they'd followed Danie blindly into the jaws of hell.

Kobus supposed he blocked it all out as if throwing his memories into a deep dark well. What was the point in living in the past? But when he

27

thought about Danie, he was amazed at how he had been drawn in like an unsighted man with his hands outstretched.

And suddenly Kobus was thrown into the A team with Danie like water absorbing sugar. Danie had dominated at the *braais* he held in his backyard. Of course, he had a grand house with a gleaming pool and shining tennis court. He wore the house like a huge medallion, shining and gleaming. The proud possessions paraded together with his wife and two boys, on show like a screaming accolade of his success.

A wife very like Kobus' own matronly wife. Mrs Swanepoel (Kobus could never bring himself to call her by her first name) looked a lot older than her forty-two years. Marta, Kobus' wife, had been friendly with Mrs Swanepoel in a standoffish formal way like two spitting cats forced to live in the same vicinity. Later, much later when Kobus and Marta bickered, she'd thrown Mrs Swanepoel at him like a bad smell, hotly adamant that she would never have been friends with such a woman if not for Kobus.

It was yet another failing that piled up against Kobus like hard bricks. Marta, it was plain, did not approve of the Swanepoel's. Although she never reproached Kobus, she became quiet and withdrawn whenever they visited and then she'd drawn her own children around her, holding them close. Kobus had thought it amusing that Danie had a whistle with which he summoned his wife as if she were a dog. And she'd come too with an earnest marital look in her eye and her cheeks reddening. When Kobus laughed out loud, he caught his wife's eye and turned rapidly away at her thinning lips and lowering eyes.

Danie was at his best at these endless sunny *braais* where he cooked piles of gruesome chunks of leaking meat on an open fire. The smells of burning wood and meat lingered on the air with Danie's words and the meat-streaked red juices into the spitting fire. Cowering servants, like dark shadows, brought out platters of food, salads dotted with red tomatoes and wilting lettuce, and placed the trays on tables on the lawn while Danie gestured with his *braai* tools, spraying the guests with meat sauces.

The children — there were always nameless pale children — frolicked in the pool and the women sat under the palm trees hiding themselves in the shade. Now when Kobus remembered these stories, he could hear Danie, the hero of yarns and adventures spraying the words like he did the offal from the *braai* tongs. The stories were tall and long like the shadows that would creep into the end of the day. And the more alcohol he consumed, the more exaggerated the tales became. While Kobus never actually saw Danie drunk or *dronkverdriet,* the piles of empty bottles that were swept away by nearly invisible servants were like an affront to the sober. At these times he would glance at Marta hearing her words, 'bar-room talk,' and frown at her and feel his palms itch.

That Marta was not captivated by Danie made her different to all the others. It was a joke at the precinct that Danie could utter the most outrageous claims and make them sound commonplace and ordinary. He also had an uncanny way of making bold statements in a way that suggested that everyone agreed with him. And Kobus was later surprised to think of how many times he did not actually agree with Danie. How many times he must have ignored the cold voice of reason and succumbed to the hot joys of Danie's charm.

It was true that everyone who worked for Danie soon learnt to agree with him. In fact, no one ever disagreed with Danie. This was because he stated opinions (his own) as if they were facts and never invited discussion. If anyone had disagreed with him it would be like saying that Paris was not the capital of France. When finally, the world turned against Danie, the whole universe tilted, and Kobus could never quite find his footing again.

For a while it all seemed so perfect. Danie would say at one of his endless *braais*, 'You know what? Other countries have apartheid, they just don't call it that. It's everywhere.' He'd always stand with his chest puffed out as if apartheid was a matter of language only. As if the dispute was over a name rather than a government policy.

He helped them; Kobus realised. He helped them all because now they could say that the problem was not with them but with the name apartheid. If it had been called anything else, then South Africa could be like all the other countries all over the world. It would mean they could keep the perfectly logical segregation, which was, after all, only natural and all this ridiculous fighting would go away. In fact, Danie was convinced, the rest of the world envied South Africa its honesty and would very much like to be like South Africa. Furthermore, he urged, just look at what happened when you let *kaffirs* run their own countries. What an unholy mess the rest of Africa had proved to be. No, if only South Africa had called apartheid something else, then none of the world's enmity would be holding back his beloved country.

It all seemed so very simple to Kobus. Morally, physically and in a thousand different ways, the white man was superior. For a while, the small group of men that had helped Danie to form his counter-insurgency unit rode high on euphoria and elation. They had Danie to thank for a renewed feeling of pride because Danie made it happen. He had the gift of the gab. He was able to separate all the bullshit from what was important. It was good, those few years, very good. It could hardly last — all that bombast — it was just all too logical. Danie had hinted at it many times. He would be sacrificed, like all messiahs. He said this with a tight little smile like a moral clinging to his face for all the men to see.

But it was when things started to go wrong that Kobus started to notice all of the little blunders that the team had made and all the little glitches that Danie had glossed over. All the mistakes that were paved over with the thinnest of concrete. It wasn't that things hadn't gone wrong before but Kobus hadn't noticed in those early days. He'd been blinded by euphoria. Kobus couldn't for the life of him tell why they had gone wrong. It wasn't as if Danie had changed or even that Kobus had changed.

Danie was too difficult to manage. The authorities must have known this. The situation could be likened to letting a vicious, feral dog off the lead before thinking about how to gain back control.

It was true that Danie began to drink more and more; especially brandy — neat and strong. Klipdrift was his favourite. He drank it like other men drank coffee. Also, a coolness between his and Danie's wife developed and deepened until it could not be ignored. And the *braais* became less frequent. It was difficult to enjoy a *braai* when all you were ever allowed to listen to was Danie. When you'd heard all of his stories before. No one dared tell a story of their own or even express an opinion even if it did coincide with Danie's. Opinions were real living things that Danie could not allow to survive in other people.

Kobus marvelled at how much he had longed to be part of Danie's family. He'd even had a ridiculous fantasy that his young daughter Sissie might make a connection with one of Danie's golden boys. Both boys, like twins, were tall and lanky and Danie's joy. Danie said that they were just like he had been at that age. It was hard to see the likeness in these thin, athletic boys and the man who had gone to fat, but it didn't seem to matter. There was a charm, a relic, that was a reminder of those boys and it clung to Danie still.

The eldest was destined for the army, the younger still at school. The schoolboy wore his hair long which was a never-ending source of aggravation to his father. But the boys had kind and gentle faces, not yet hardened by their father's dogma. Not yet drawn into a world where every person that didn't agree with them was trying to kill them. A world where opponents were trying to destroy everything that the white man held sacred. A world of tumultuous hatred that would surely harden and distort even these golden boys.

Danie liked to say that he was close to his boys, but he was gruff and sometimes mean to them like a snarling dog. Shouting at the younger boy about his hair and chastising the elder for never doing anything right until the boy's hands shook and his lips trembled. When these things happened, the others, including Kobus, looked away and waited for the storm to end.

Kobus' own son, in his early teens, a small puny disappointment with his mother's nondescript brown hair, stayed in the shade and shadows and never swam and hardly ever spoke to the other children. He fell below the notice of Danie for which Kobus was both grateful and disappointed. Marta would sometimes put her arm around the thin, frail boy who looked close to tears during Danie's rage and Kobus would feel an unnameable embarrassment and wish her and her son a hundred miles away. As if the boy's weakness could be cured by their banishing. But those days in the golden sun with laughter and raillery made it hard to imagine that it would, one day, all go so horribly and spectacularly wrong.

And although Danie as a leader appeared to be accidental and irregular, he had a zealot's understanding of leadership. To maintain the loyalty of his team, Danie reiterated his beliefs again and again, mostly in the morning before the brandy blurred his outer edges. During these rhapsodies, Kobus could see real tears in the man's faded blue eyes. In any other man this would have been ridiculous. Especially such a huge ramshackle bear of a man as Danie. None of his physical attributes helped inspire his men's respect. His shaggy dirty blond hair always needed cutting and his rough chin always needed shaving. But that was to his credit; despite these shortcomings, his followers adored and worshipped him.

It was truly remarkable that Danie could produce anything other than scorn dressed as he was in shabby jeans and shirts that needed cleaning but somehow it all added to the myth of the man. But the one thing that was guaranteed to make Danie emotional, his voice thickening like hot tar, was his commitment to the state and the ideal of apartheid.

Apartheid was the thing that he could present to anyone in a believable package that even the most ardent detractor could not destroy. Those bleeding-heart liberals, as Danie called them, were ridiculous and easily polished off. After all, Danie only had to sneer down at them, he was bigger and stronger than most of those women, and it was always women. Also, they used the English version of his name which set them at an immediate disadvantage.

'Not Danie,' he'd say his voice dripping with sarcasm and scorn. 'Daaanie,' he'd reiterate, dragging out the a into an 'aah' sound. This was an expert way to draw the women away from the real argument and then put them at a disadvantage. These women were lovely and nice, like English summer days. Danie used that word nice as if he could not be bothered to think of anything more imaginative. When they thought that they had your name wrong, they were immediately drowning in apologies and that was a mistake. Because that meant they never saw it coming. The sucker-punch that would be a political point. A point so sharp it could pierce any bleeding-heart liberal and make their very breath seep away.

Danie was proud to say that he didn't engage in political conversation with any blacks. He joked that the black people he met were either servants and little more than animals, or terrorists and one didn't negotiate with terrorists. That made him a fervent supporter of Margaret Thatcher who also didn't negotiate with terrorists. This was the one international line that he brought into conversation. The one international thought that was not ridiculed.

Kobus had a memory of another type of woman. Molly Goldburn A woman who had the measure of Danie, who had made Danie look small for a little while.

Kobus remembered her because Danie had been looking for her for a very long time. She was famous in the townships. A rare white woman who was welcome in Soweto like a pearl passed amongst very poor people. A woman who was kind and gentle and loved by all. All except Danie. Molly had been arrested along with three other women who had stationed themselves in protest in the middle of a busy, Johannesburg road. The road, a dual carriageway with storming constant traffic, had a grassy island running down the middle. At a set of traffic lights, they'd positioned themselves with signs. Their signs read: APARTHEID IS MURDER!

Three women in the middle of a busy road with harmless signs were hardly worth Danie's notice. If anything, this kind of protest brought on one of his rare laughs like a staccato of barking. Danie liked nothing better than laughing at other people. Especially when they were hurt or humiliated. And Molly and her fellow protesters were humiliated because ordinary white South Africans did not like to see opponents of their system so boldly displayed. They did not like it at all.

On the day of her arrest, Molly was covered in spit and urine thrown from passing cars, and then as if that were not enough, she and her compatriots were taken to Danie. Offered up like prized pearls. The policemen held her at arm's length as if her ideas were a contagious disease. She was tiny, like a small, bedraggled child, between two giants.

Molly, pale and small, in a stained patterned dress, looked as if a strong wind might blow her away. Danie was bored. He had been walking around the grey office like a caged man all day. He was used to action, doing things. The A team did not even officially have an office, so they avoided long spells in the unwelcoming cramped space that served as a temporary base while they waited for instructions or opportunities.

Why this woman had been brought to them no one knew. The other two women had been quickly arraigned and sent home to their beautiful homes in the white suburbs. Molly, though, was a thorn in the side of the local police. She was never sent to jail, or when she was it was not for long and then she was out again. Perhaps this time they thought to scare her properly by putting her in touch with a counter-insurgence officer. Perhaps he could talk some sense into this nuisance of a woman. They lived in a system that did not need constant reminding of the iniquities of apartheid. It was bad enough quelling the enemy without your own side sabotaging the effort!

Molly was calm and quiet, like a small pale shadow. She was seated on the plain wooden bench by the wall and the office fell silent. The men previously engaged in aimless talk and laughter stopped. The sound did not drop away at once but slowly dipped like fading light as they realised that a woman was in the office. Kobus watched her and Danie, like a cat licking his lips, smiled that small tight smile he kept for interrogation.

The woman ignored the men and opened her bag, a canvas bag with bamboo handles, and took out her knitting. She began to knit, concentrating on her stitchery as if there was no one else in the room. The APARTHEID IS MURDER sign leant drunkenly against her left leg and the red letters bobbled slightly as she knitted as if they were alive. The only sound in the room was the clacking of her needles. Danie began to walk towards her.

'So, at last we meet.' His voice was edged with deliberate offence. She looked up but did not stop her work. To Kobus' surprise, she smiled at Danie and raised an eyebrow in inquiry. Danie did something that he never did — he sighed and sat down next to her knocking the sign to the floor. Danie preferred to loom over his victims — he liked to intimidate — but so sure as he was of his dominance now, he forgot his golden rule.

'Why do you do it, eh?' He spoke in Afrikaans and the woman kept knitting. Danie shifted uncomfortably, as if realising the mistake of sitting rather than standing. Even though she was small and stank of urine and even though she was nothing, she remained strangely in control. And even though she did not acknowledge him, he continued to stay seated. He was bored and his boredom made him underestimate her. He thought to play with her rather as a cat does with a mouse. As she continued to ignore him, a deep red flush spread above his shirt collar and the other men looked quickly away.

'You have a nice house,' Danie said in English, his tongue clumsy with the unfamiliar round words.

She looked up, surprised. 'How do you know about my house?' Her voice was deep for such a small woman, cultured and surprisingly warm.

Danie settled into the bench and leaned against the wall, the colour fading a little from his face like a retreating tide. This was more like it. 'We know all about you, Molly Goldburn. Your husband is a doctor, and you have two sons. But what we don't know,' here he turned to the rest of the men with his sly grin, 'is why a woman with everything should stand in the middle of the road where people can throw urine at her.' Here he reached out for the damp sleeve on her dress and let it fall to her tawny freckled arm. She continued to knit still with that smile as if Danie had said something pleasant and amusing.

'Do you know how dangerous it is for a lady such as yourself to put herself in such a place? And what does it achieve? Nothing,' he answered his own question. '*Niks*,' he added for good measure in Afrikaans and now the grin was huge and satisfied as he looked at his companions. But that was where he made another mistake. He was about to launch into the speech that always got them, the words like bullets exploding. The speech about his men and men like him keeping her stupid white arse safe in a world where every black man wanted to rape her and her children. Sometimes he would be graphic too, why not? These white women needed to appreciate what men like Danie were doing to keep them safe.

But before he could start the woman spoke quietly and without taking her eyes off her knitting.

'Well sir, I feel sorry for you. If you think that urine is bad, I can assure you that urine is nothing compared to the iniquity of apartheid. And if I have made one person today think about it, then I have achieved something.' Her knitting progressed as the silence filled the room and the colour began to creep into Danie's face. He opened his mouth to speak.

Here it comes, thought Kobus with a quiet satisfaction. The speech, the standard speech that would make the woman regret everything she believed in. Make her regret her very life.

She held up a hand. A tiny hand that could have belonged to a child.

'No sir, I've heard it many times. Also, there are worse things than urine and I've had *that* thrown at me many a time.' Her voice dropped and her lips twitched, and she said very quietly. 'Can you phone my husband please? He will be worried. He will pick me up as soon as you contact him.' And then she went back to her knitting as if Danie was not even in the room. And he had no choice, bar taking her by the shoulders and shaking her and that he could not do. He stood and adjusted his trousers, taking his time, but she did not look up from her knitting. Danie retreated that day, but he never did again, and he never made the mistake of trying to reason with unreasonable white women.

By the time her husband came, her knitting had reached her lap in a crimson tide and one of the men had asked her what she was making. She told him in faultless Afrikaans that it was a blanket for her forthcoming grandchild. Danie's face darkened as he bent over his paperwork with a devotion that it had never before enjoyed.

When her husband came, a kindly man who helped his wife to her feet as if she were the most precious thing in the world, the office was mostly empty. The man ignored everyone except his wife and escorted her out into the now darkening evening. If Danie ever referred to the instance again, Kobus had not heard him. But he always referred to the women, the Black Sash they called themselves, he called them bleeding bloody hearts, all of them. And their husbands were even worse, *Kaffir boeties*. That's what they were and Danie could not think of a single thing that was worse. Well, he could, and that was a full-blown terrorist, and he had more respect for them because at least they didn't go around with signs, wringing their hands. At least he could legitimately shoot a terrorist.

After that, with increasingly visible opposition, it became essential that people like Kobus and Danie lay down their very lives and save South Africa from terrorism. Kobus knew that every man in the team would do exactly that only because their hero Danie had asked. Although later Kobus knew that this must have been an illusion because Danie was curiously unemotional and careless when he spoke. He was lazy too, using the same analogies. Even after bad raids Danie had at the most shown the signs of boredom and indifference on his face. It was a wonder that any of them had ever followed Danie with such blind devotion. But they had.

Surprisingly for a law officer it was astonishing how much Kobus' life teetered at the edge of the law. Myriads of little lies and transgressions had built up until it was hard to tell the difference between the truth and the lies. He always knew that working for the A-team would be treading a fine line between what most people understood would be the truth and what would be necessary to quell terrorism. The mantra 'fight terror with terror' would necessarily ensure some lawlessness and most of the time it seemed so simple — especially at the beginning. So finally, after all his time working for the A-team he felt no sense of achievement, only a hopeless, pathetic relief that he'd got away with it — in some miraculous way — survived it.

Somewhere buried deep inside, he knew that he would probably be found out and had lived with that knowledge for so long that he no longer remembered life without guilt. Guilt travelled with him wherever he went just as his arms and legs went with him. He could no longer see the vision, feel the depth of mission that he'd once felt. In truth, Kobus was lost like a little boy in a deep, dark forest. And despite his apprehensions, he'd never really expected the lie of his life to be exposed. Not a man for self-reflection, he'd put the lie to one side and hoped that one day he'd retire, and it would all go away. After all, there were countless examples where this had happened. In fact, he reasoned, some of them were rewarded with medals and money.

The closer he got to retirement, the more reasonable it seemed that all of the A-team blunders would merely go unnoticed. So, when exposure came, it was as shocking and unexpected as accidental gunfire in a safe room. And yet it felt oddly familiar because it was always going to end this way. It wasn't a big dramatic revelation of all the lies but a slow painful unravelling of everything that he'd once held sacrosanct... A gradual creeping realisation that the sands had shifted, and he was left stranded all alone with his hollow existence.

Of course, the biggest disaster was the suppurating wound that gnawed and chafed at him the most. But many years had passed, and they'd all sunk into a sense of complacency and the longer the time went on, the more it faded into insignificance. Kobus allowed himself to be swept up into Danie's careless memory and so the illusion continued.

And so, it continued, until one day into the beginning of the fourth year — it all exploded into the open like a messy petrol bomb scattering horrible, hideous debris everywhere. And even though they didn't know it, Kobus and the others were in freefall. His entire life's work — destroyed in a matter of hours.

Chapter 3 — The Politics of Langa

Langa, near Uitenhage, Eastern Cape, South Africa 1984

Even though Winston had only been in the township a matter of hours, he felt the weight of the place pushing him down like a boxer's punch. His steps slowed as his feet had begun to lose hope and his mind became a morass of despair and longing. The strange half-broken houses squeezed together showed him empty windows like blank eyes. The money, so carefully sewn into his sock, pressed against his big toe, working a suppurating blister, and he felt the small lameness in his step. He stopped and leaned his aching head against the peeling bark of a lone tree which offered little in the way of shade. The trunk was spindly like a puny childish arm, but it felt cool to Winston's hot brow.

And in that moment the people, the endless rushing people, faded into the background and Winston felt as alone and stranded as he'd ever felt in his entire life.

Then out of the bewildering rush of people Winston could hear music and singing, laughter too. Like a memory of a time long past. The voices became clearer as if an invisible hand had turned up the sound. They were the voices of people using a language he recognised, not the strangled language of the old man with the cigarettes. A strange feeling curled around his heart, a dangerous feeling that he recognised as hope — these were the voices of young people like him.

He edged closer and closer, stealthily, like a spy. Already he'd learned the lessons of caution and distance. On the edges of the dilapidated buildings stood a separate house, standing proud and alone as if not needing the support of other lesser buildings. It was also bigger and grander than the others.

And in the open front yard he counted seven, no eight, young men. Hardly daring to breathe, as if that simple action would make them vanish, he moved forward. Here were the urbane, sophisticated young men he'd heard so much about, yearned for. And although they were certainly the same age as him, they looked and spoke like men while he was reduced to the position of a spying boy.

Winston hovered on the fringe of the group, not advancing but unable to retreat as if some invisible elastic drew him to the strange exotic group. The men laughed and drank from smoky seductive bottles. One played an old guitar. A monotonous tune with only a few chords repeated over and over again. Yet despite the monotonous unchanging tune, a slim woman wearing old, faded jeans danced.

She danced slowly and at times hardly moving, using her hands to create a mosaic of complex, mesmeric movements. And she was the most beautiful woman Winston had ever seen. He wondered how the other men could continue talking and drinking with such an angel in their midst. He wondered why they did not stop and fall into revered silence.

And on and on she danced. Winston did not know how long he stood there. Forgetting time, forgetting his thirst and hunger.

Suddenly a discordant shout, like a false note in a song, broke the spell. One of the young men, the one wearing a fedora hat at a smart angle, had broken away from the group and was coming towards him.

'Hey comrade! Why are you standing there? What do you want?' Winston turned to the young man with the smile still lingering on his face like a forgotten thought. The slim young man, not quite as tall as Winston, had stepped forward and then stopped. He held out his hand as if to take Winston by the hand, but he only waited for a reply. With one last look at the still dancing woman, Winston turned to go.

But a warm brown calloused hand on his arm stopped him. 'No, comrade, come, come. You look like a friend.' The man turned back to the others, showing white teeth. 'You must come, comrade.' The others hardly seemed to notice Winston and the man indicated a small drum in the semi-circle. Winston had after all been noticed because the others had shifted to make space.

Slowly the man led Winston, gently as if he were a wild skittish animal and sat him silently and obediently in the free space in the semi-circle. The laughter had stopped, and the woman no longer danced, and Winston felt a twinge of loss. Winston focussed his eyes on the ground and showed his teeth, but no one spoke. The friendly man produced a smoky bottle and gave it to Winston. Then the cautionary voice of his uncle came to him. 'Beware of the places of sin.' And in that moment, it seemed to Winston that the trouble came in a smoky dark bottle.

This was a *shebeen* — a place of sin and degradation. His heart beat so hard that he could not believe that the other men could not hear it. This was a place of drinking and unknown terrible sins and Winston began again to feel the same alienation that he'd felt when first stepping off the bus into the heart of Langa. He hardly dared breathe and held the bottle down between his knees, his hands trembling, and hoped that the sin would not find him even as he did not understand what any of it meant.

Slowly the conversation began again, and the musician plucked at the guitar and Winston was able to raise his eyes like the slow creeping of the morning sun. He noticed in confusion that these faces were not hard and careworn at all. They were not shuttered and drawn but open and beginning to smile. Slowly even the laughter returned and the man on the guitar began to strum more forcefully, and they relaxed into a general chatter that washed over Winston like cleansing rain.

And all the while the smoky, cold bottle seeped cool condensation between his fingers, but still, he did not drink. At last, he allowed his eyes to return to the woman but quickly looked away again. As if of their own accord, his eyes returned to her again and again, and with a jolt he noticed her drink from a smoky bottle like the one he held. She, looking at him with a smile full of understanding and gestured with her bottle towards his. 'Drink, comrade.' Her voice reminded him of home, like the honey he collected from the angry bees. He shook his head and she laughed. Not a hard, unkind laugh — a large warm laugh, an embrace. 'Drink, comrade. It's ginger beer. The best ginger beer in Langa. Probably the best ginger beer in the whole of Africa.' And as if to prove it she took a long drink from her smoky bottle. 'My *gogo* makes it.' She smacked her lips. Her throaty laugh seemed to fill the afternoon and stretched on into the whole sky.

He drank like a man dying of thirst. The ginger beer was tart and bitter and so strong that it made him cough but he did not care. He joined the laughter. It had suddenly become easy as if the ginger beer had made him impossibly drunk.

'My *gogo* is good for nothing,' she said, turning to the others holding the empty bottle to her chest. 'But what can we do? She is an old lady now and we have to keep her for her ginger beer.' The smart man with the fedora hat scolded her, telling her that she should respect the elderly, but she turned back to Winston with a smile that told him she did not believe her own words. Her laughter tinkled into the late afternoon sun like jewels. It felt good to be part of something silly and inane. It felt good to laugh again.

Soon, the men, hardly looking at him, drew him in — a question here, an observation there, and suddenly he was part of the story of the group, like he belonged. The smart man said, 'Tell us, where are you from?' But Winston shook his head. He could only answer that his name was Winston. The smart man laughed. 'We all have stories,' he said as if life were not real. But suddenly seriously, the laughter temporarily gone, he said, 'We all have secrets, too, comrade.' That made Winston think of his own secrets. Secret dark places that could never be revealed.

The others nodded but still did not look at Winston and slowly, as if testing the words, Winston said, 'I am looking for my aunt.' He was surprised how easily it had slipped out as if it meant hardly anything at all. The simple sentence held the group and they nodded as if they could hear the echo of past griefs and it was enough to tell them of his search for his aunt. They understood.

Now for the first time in such a long age it felt good to have someone else to share the burden. Now that they knew that he had no home and no place to stay it no longer seemed to matter. In fact, he had laughed more in this one afternoon than he had laughed in the last twelve months.

He was told the names of the people, in an informal way that suggested that it did not matter if he could not remember. 'I am Looksmart,' the man with the fedora hat declared and showed a lopsided smile with two front teeth missing. 'These others,' he said, sweeping his arm over the others sitting in the circle with their smoky bottles and slow conversation, 'do not know how to dress. They also don't know,' he said, raising his voice over their objections. 'They don't know that image is everything.' Here the others booed like a good-natured football crowd and there was no venom in their jeering, only laughter.

And all through the teasing and laughing, Winston waited and burned to know the name of the beautiful woman. At last, rising from her seat, she said, 'My name is Cleva.' The laughter stopped. 'Only because it makes the white man squirm whenever they have to call a black woman clever.' Then the laughter echoed through the afternoon like fluttering butterflies.

Sometime in the late afternoon, the conversation turned like a man travelling from safety into danger. They started to talk of politics. At home they never spoke about politics. His father would sometimes talk about the trouble in the cities and express his satisfaction that they were not part of it. His mother, too timid and too busy, spoke of hardly anything at all. His uncle might have engaged with politics if he wanted but then Uncle Mukeseli was successful on his own and why did he need to worry about change in the big white cities? After all, Uncle Mukeseli was doing well operating as he did just under the eye-line of the white oppressor.

But here all the men and Cleva too, spoke, their words like little steel bullets peppering the air. Winston was the only silent one, sitting in a hail of words, in shaking, bewildering excitement. Somehow, to his delight, Cleva had moved her way around the circle so that she now sat next to him. 'Most conversations here come to politics. There is, after all, nothing else to talk about. Nothing else is relevant.' Then she raised her voice and shouted something back into the crowd of busy words. Winston looked at her lips, full and smart like the words she uttered.

And as the slow darkening day descended into evening, she became more vehement as if the descending night goaded her. 'I would rather die than clean a white bitch's house.' Winston felt the words hard and sharp like a double-bladed knife. And she made no effort to lower her voice and Winston felt a new emotion. He felt shame and a fissure of electricity that he could not identify. Then his thoughts went back to his gentle mother — a lifetime of working, cleaning and cleaning and cleaning. A bent, small woman as if work had made her double over and shrink.

This woman, this Cleva, was like no other person he had ever met before and now that the evening was tiptoeing into the night it was with sadness that he could hardly make out her face.

Lucas, a tall man, began to talk and the others fell silent. He spoke clearly but softly so that the others leant forward to catch his words. 'We should work for the white man. That way every day we can fight them. The only way. In the factories we can see the white man and fight him because that is where the money is. That is the only thing that will hurt the white man. Money!' He stopped and his gaze swept over the men, his words hanging like butchered meat.

There was Paulus, a small, light brown man, a man that was not properly Xhosa, a mulatto — a man the white regime called coloured. He reminded Winston of the Zulu man who had come to live in the valley. A man who had never quite fitted in. An outsider living on the inside.

Paulus the outsider spoke Xhosa and talked to them all like he belonged, and the others listened. Paulus spoke softly too, with a slight lilt that pointed to his foreignness. 'We are in charge of our own destiny,' he said, pointing to the sky like a preacher. He surveyed the company and settled on Winston who shifted awkwardly on his seat. Where he came from words such as these were never uttered. Men did their jobs and thought only of rest and how they would tackle the next day. It felt strange, this outspokenness, this strange logic that resounded in his head and made his heart pound.

Now many voices rose as if in a chanting song and Winston turned his head this way and that, his eyes large and open wide. They spoke in earnest, seriously and with feeling. The darkening evening fell softly and unheeded.

Then Looksmart said suddenly and clearly, that it should be 'One settler, one bullet.' He chanted it again and again, hitting the fist of his right hand into his left hand, like it was a harmless joke, but the laughter was forced. Now Looksmart's expression changed, and he shifted as if ready to leave. As if he'd become bored. The others fell silent, and the darkness grew black like spilled paint. Winston looked around uneasily, surprised at the dark for the first time.

Suddenly Cleva spoke out, her voice fresh as if only just awakened. 'Why do you work for the white man? Don't do his work for him, leave him and soon he will realise that he can't run this country.' She spoke into the air as if it could take up her words and make cudgels of them. The darkened faces murmured but no one spoke for a moment and again Winston shifted. Deep in the bottom of his stomach he wished that he could join this talk. But he was too new and like Paulus — an outsider, someone who did not really belong. The others spoke clearly and slickly as if the words were not new and shiny but old and tarnished.

'Oh, Cleva, how will we live? We will starve.' A new voice had joined the conversation — Sydney, who wore no shoes and had asked Winston earlier, hopefully, if he had any socks in his bag. His feet were covered in dust and his heels so crusty and thick they looked like the tread of a shoe. Winston knew this to be so because this was a man who had walked all his life without shoes as he himself had done. Cleva bridled and Winston sensed that she did not like this man. 'But we are dying anyway. People are dying every day. If we are going to die, then we should die from starvation and then maybe the world will listen.'

Looksmart spoke quickly. 'But they won't listen! They never listen — what is one more black death to the world? They don't care about us. We must help ourselves. We must work and then we must take our money and organise for the resistance.'

'Or you can run away and join *uMkhonto we Sizwe*.' The words floated on the air like dust. Of course, he knew about *Umkonte*, everyone did, but only in a mythical way like stories about heroes fighting dragons. A mythical army ready to face the white man on his own terms — a story so fabulous that only children could really believe in it.

'Yes, yes, we can join the fight, do something real. But we mustn't just die for nothing.' The speaker had a deep voice, a voice that carried authority and the others listened. And now the music stopped — only in it stopping did Winston realise that someone was playing — and the sky fell into a starless darkness and cooking fires flickered as night stampeded over the mountains down onto Langa.

Chapter 4 — The Sacking

They came for Danie first. A laughing mocking Danie sitting on Kobus' desk in the middle of a story about his eldest, golden son. Over the years, Danie had told many such stories and surrounded as he was by smiling faces, always became expansive and even more loquacious and that is why he didn't see the two men. It was the sunglasses that drew Kobus' attention — sunglasses indoors like an exaggerated scenario from a bad film. Both were dressed in identical black tailored suits, and they did not smile. Gradually Danie's listeners lost their own grins and Danie talked on, his voice now loud in the silent room.

Finally noticing the waning attention and the drifting silence, Danie stopped talking.

No longer the centre of attention, he turned slowly and stiffly to face the two men. He looked down at the men even though he was still seated. He had a way of doing that, looking down on people. There was that trademark sneer turning up the corners of his cruel, red, glistening mouth. One of the men said in a flat, expressionless tone, '*Meneer* Swanepoel?'

Danie relieved, once more, returned to the centre of attention, got up from the desk, hitching his trousers up and then straightening his tie and faced the two men. The small smirk still lurked on his lips, and he was enjoying himself once again. He sneered, 'You must mean *Kaptein* Swanepoel. And if you do mean *Kaptein*,' he drawled, curling his lip in an exaggerated style. 'If you do mean *Kaptein* Swanepoel, then that is me.' He turned his back on the two men to face his own men, his A-Team, his blue eyes sparkling and dirty blond hair falling rakishly over his forehead. With a broad smile he stretched out his arms, pleased with himself. His whole life had been the work of wresting attention away from others and he was good at it. Very good.

One of the men stepped forward. '*Kom* Swanepoel, you are coming with us.' He held his arm out in an old-fashioned gesture of politeness, but his tone was foreboding with icy doom. It had been a very long time since his team had heard him referred to by his surname only. Danie always insisted on his full title. In a moment Danie had been subdued and quelled. That was the last time Kobus laid eyes on Danie Swanepoel.

In an instance he was gone. Not even allowed into his office to fetch his jacket. Simply gone with the two men forming a guard on either side of him. The jacket, like an affront, hung forlornly on the back of his office chair.

Two hours later, only one of the men returned for Kobus — in a moment of ridiculous churlishness Kobus felt a stab of chagrin that he did not warrant the escort of two men. They knew there would be no trouble from him. Amazingly, when Danie had been taken, no one had spoken in the office even though there were at least eight men seated awkwardly at their desks pretending to work. A strange feeling of oppression had settled over the office. Kobus could not shrug the feeling of doom from his shoulders.

And in the end, he did not even have the distraction of paperwork to subdue his wild thoughts. Only a little pale desk and memories. Memories that he'd never give up. He felt a strange sense of crippling relief when the man came for him. While he walked the steel grey and deserted hallways, his mind was suddenly and surprisingly empty. It was not anything like he'd thought it would be. His heart beat as it normally did, and his mind lay dormant like a little hibernating creature.

The *Kolonel's* office was eerily large with an enormous desk more suited to a businessman. The polished brown surface ran away towards the window as if in a futile attempt at escape. The desk was unashamedly devoid of any paperwork, pens, pencils or any other blemish to clutter the shining surface. *Kolonel* Meiring was standing at the window which looked out onto the police car park. Several vans sporting the words *Polisie* and black-and-white panels were parked carefully in bays. There were two battered and dented Land Rovers, and as if in counterpoint to the cars, they were parked in a haphazard fashion, suggesting a hurried arrival.

Meiring was broad and solid and what he lacked in height he made up for in breadth. He wore his uniform, which looked as if it hardly touched his body, as a sort of affront as if it did not belong to him. In fact, he looked like a large cardboard cut-out. Several medals glinted in the artificial light as Meiring put his arms behind his back. This had the effect of pushing his chest out and emphasising the medals. He also wore his braided police cap which was not a good sign. This was a formal meeting.

Danie took an absurd pride in the A-team not wearing any uniform other than camouflage trousers and jackets when out on special missions. Danie himself wore the camouflage fatigues day after day and they were often badly in need of a clean. Danie made a virtue of his dirt-encrusted clothes. As if they testified to his hard work and graft. Kobus had once admired this about Danie. The informality and the ability to do his job without uniform constrictions used to be something to admire, but now faced with Meiring it seemed like a foolish, childish action.

Kobus was rudely brought back to the present by Meiring clearing his throat.

'I've long ago given up getting the truth out of Danie Swanepoel. And you...' He paused as if he'd like to say more but unsure on how to do so. Kobus made to speak but Meiring waved him away. 'I no longer care, Jonker. All I know is that I have a missing *kaffir* and several other *kaffirs*,' he almost spat the word, 'who are claiming that their comrade was murdered!" He sneered and turned to look blindly out of the window.

'You can't believe these *kaffirs*...' Meiring turned back, and Kobus was annoyed to note that his own voice shook and quavered. With what? Anger?

'Listen, Jonker. You're not a fool, you must know that we don't care about this *kaffir*.' He waved his hand as if to dismiss the discussion but then stubbornly continued. 'But Amnesty International has got the story. Fucking Amnesty International, full of liberal idiots. They have power though and now the minister wants to show that we are doing something to curb this kind of thing.' He waved his hand as if referring to nothing more than a spilled drink.

'You have to understand, Jonker, this has been going on for too long now. What is it? Two, maybe three years. We have to do something.' He paused and swallowed, his Adam's apple bobbing up and down. Then he continued almost in a monotone as if reading from a script. 'We are breaking up the A team,' he said, and walked up to and stood at the empty desk as if that settled it. The huge *Vierkleur* was pinned on the wall, hanging slightly crooked. Kobus was sure that the flag had been hung upside down. Wasn't there a law against hanging the nation's flag upside down?

His mouth moved but the words would not come, so inadequate they seemed. He struggled to get his mind back on to the subject. He knew it was serious, but it still seemed so unbelievable. The feeling from earlier, like a hangover, had him moving as if in a dream. It felt more important to Kobus that this little self-important turkey fix the flag.

And here it finally was — the A team was to be dismantled. It seemed somehow laughable considering that officially they didn't exist. In the end he asked about Danie, not himself. 'Danie Swanepoel has gone, Jonker. Gone for good. He's a loose cannon and he's become a liability. So, he's gone.'

'You've thrown him to the wolves then.'

'Don't be so *blerry* dramatic, Jonker. He's only going to pastures new. He'll probably join the mercenaries in Sierra Leone.' A short bark of laughter like a gunshot. 'I've spoken to the minister, and you should thank your lucky stars. We will save your career. You've got what? Ten years and then you retire. You keep it all, retirement fund, a real job. You will be in charge of a proper legitimate police unit. No more raids though. Just normal police work.'

'What's the catch?'

'There's no catch. I've stuck my neck out for you, Jonker. It will be your own unit. No interference from above and no terrorist work. But still your own unit.' Kobus suspected that the government minister that Meiring was so eager to blame had never heard of any of them. Danie had been sacrificed for Meiring's career.

'Like I said, Meiring. What's the catch?'

'Your new post is in Uitenhage.' There was a resigned note in Meiring's voice.

'Uitenhage! Where in the hell is that?'

Meiring ignored him and sat in the chair, a hundred miles away from Kobus.

Kobus had not moved since entering the office, still rooted in the doorway hardly in the office at all. Bloody hell. The A team was gone. Stopped. And Danie was gone. He could hardly get past the news that

Danie was gone before he realised that he was saved. But saved for what? Uitenhage. He'd never heard of it. That made it bad, very bad.

Then, just like that, he was angry. The anger rose up his neck. He could feel it like a blush, and he was so angry that he was afraid he might explode. Explode in an angry red ball all over the spotless office. But before that happened, he had to get away, far away from this stifling clean office. Had to hold on to the things that he still had. Like Meiring had said, he had only nine years. Nine years and he could probably get away with less. That meant that he was very close to it all being over. Those nine years reared up in front of him like a high impenetrable wall.

'You can't just get rid of me like that, you know,' he declared in a voice that he hardly recognised as his own. He hadn't meant to sound so much like a child.

'Oh, Jonker.' Meiring was using the voice that he employed for young children. 'How many government ministers do you know, hey?' Meiring waited while Kobus floundered, a little smile on the corner of his overly red mouth. 'I didn't think so.'

Kobus clenched his fists and raged inside. Raged and floundered and churned over his thoughts, handling them carefully as if they were hand grenades. Then Meiring was speaking again. 'I don't know the truth about that bloody *kaffir,* and I don't want to know, Jonker. But I am telling you now, there is a very big stink about it. Very big. I'm not even going to ask you about it because all I get is a lot of bullshit. It doesn't matter anyway. The minister wants to tell Parliament that it has been dealt with and then it's over.' Then after a pause, he said, 'And that's what I want as well. I want to get back to normal and forget about the whole thing.' *And forget about you and Danie* echoed in the air although he did not utter the words. There was now a note of implacability in Meiring's voice.

Kobus turned to go but Meiring stopped him. 'You're not going back. The MPs want you out now.' Again, Kobus' mouth worked but no words came. Suddenly the two faceless men were in the room. Summoned as if by magic and there was no more time for anything else.

Kobus left the office and was surprised to find his anger still raging, a boiling slow burning anger that would simmer, he knew, for hours. Maybe later, when it was too late, he'd think of something to say. Think of a pertinent reply. But not now. Now he was too angry to even think straight, and the dream-like quality had evaporated, and it was all real. He wondered fleetingly where Danie was and then watched the cold grey road rush past and stewed in his own broiling rage as there was absolutely nothing else he could do.

They dropped him at his home. A low sprawling building that his wife treasured second only to her children. How would he explain everything to her? He wasn't in the habit of explaining himself to anyone. Especially his wife.

And he was right — after a few hours of pacing he thought of ways that he might have been able to work on Meiring. Ways to get to a better deal. After all his years of loyal service and this is what he got! He had a map of South Africa in his study. A gloomy little room off the living room. Uitenhage was not even marked on the map. He phoned directory enquiries and a robotic voice told him that it was not far from Port Elizabeth in the Little Karoo. Bloody hell, the place was in the middle of nowhere. In the back of beyond. Kobus had once heard of a little *dorp* as being described as a boil on the arse end of the world. *Uitenhage*, he thought, *you could bet your last Rand, was that boil.*

In the wild turmoil of his thoughts that day, he ranged from Danie, the A-team and then bizarrely to Meiring. He scrolled through his memories of Meiring as if watching a film. He, like all the others (Danie included although he would not admit it), wanted to be noticed by Meiring. Meiring was the key to the top. He was the top. But it wasn't the memories of police work that Kobus thought of. It was Meiring's wife that he thought about.

Meiring had an English wife. Helen Slasenger, like the sports company without the 'z.' Kobus remembered meeting her when she'd told him about the 'z' as if it were important. And he had never forgiven her for that. The moment he met her; he could tell she was different from all the other women he knew. Fragrant, slim and tall, very tall. Taller than most of the men in the room. Taller than her husband, but that wasn't much because it was a standing joke at the station that Meiring was a short shit. And Helen was elegant too.

The men rushed around her like moths to a flame. She treated them all charmingly. The other wives, a mass of floral print and resentment at the other side of the room near the tables laden with snacks and drinks, glowered and whispered together. There was something exciting in that — something exciting in being noticed by Helen and that the other women did not like her.

Then there was the incident with the moth. A moth, clearly attracted by the bright light of the luxurious living room had come in through the elegant French doors. A huge colourful moth, a night-time butterfly, swarmed in through the doors and fluttered helplessly near the ceiling lights before falling onto Helen. She erupted with feminine screams as the bewildered moth clung to her scooped neckline and became entangled in the expensive olive-green material. With her waving arms she was very difficult to assist, although several men attempted to dislodge the moth. Eventually the moth was dislodged and flew miraculously out into the fragrant summer garden where it promptly drowned in the glittering dark pool.

For a full three quarters of an hour, Helen Slasenger had to be cajoled and tempted to re-join the party. Fussed over and cosseted, she eventually returned to her duties as hostess with more men than ever fussing around.

Marta, Kobus' wife, remarked on the incident later that night when they were getting ready for bed. What a fuss she'd remarked, over a simple, harmless moth. English women, she maintained, were pathetic.

Yes, Meiring's English wife was a mistake and, in some quarters, a horrible blight. But Kobus would be going to Uitenhage. Using the English wife to stop Meiring was the stuff of a fictional story only.

Chapter 5 — Looksmart

In the end it had been easy to let the others, his new friends, pick him up and carry him along. And Cleva had talked to him in a low soothing voice as if to a wild bewildered animal and although it shamed him, surprisingly it helped. He told her about the valley. Not the stuff about Doda and his mother, but he told her about the valley, the river and his sisters. He told her of his auntie and the hope that he might find a job and suddenly there came a tremble in his voice, and he stopped talking, embarrassment and a bone weariness overwhelming him into silence. She only smiled and gestured to Looksmart. He followed her arm to Looksmart, a smudge in the darkness.

And when he looked at the smudge, he remembered Looksmart's words from earlier and felt a little stirring of hope. He was a man of the future, not someone stuck in the past.

Winston felt the little nub of money in his shoe that had worked a blister on his toe like ballooning torture.

Now with the descending dark and the pale moon he stood up abruptly, cutting off the loud speakers arguing, and turned sharply. Cleva laid an arm on his.

'Hey comrade...' He shrugged off her light hand, his apologetic face hidden in the deep darkness.

'*Hayi*, comrade, you have nowhere. You told us that you could not find your auntie, hey?' He sat slowly, dismayed that he had revealed so much in such a short time. He had thought that they had done all the talking. That they (these friendliest of people) had laughed and scorned, and he had only been on the edges. A willing outsider. Now he saw that he was in the very centre. She laid her arm on his again and whispered, 'Don't worry, comrade, we will look after you.'

He remained mute with an equal measure of chagrin and delight.

The voices fell silent and the quiet of deep night now settled over them all and some of the men began to leave. Still Winston sat on and then he became aware of Looksmart sitting on the ground next to him. He had a dark blanket from somewhere and he wrapped it around his shoulders with his knees bent so that his legs in their skinny trousers looked like those belonging to a spider.

Winston was uncomfortably aware that Looksmart spoke to him in much the same way as an older protective brother and Cleva like an elder sister. She bustled around, clearing away bottles and chatting to Looksmart and Winston, who were the only ones remaining in the dark shattering night.

And so it was that Winston, after all the worry and uncertainty, became a part of the township in the most unlikely and unexpected way, a working, bustling part. It made him want to laugh and then he would turn to Mama or one of his sisters to tell them, only to remember that there was only Looksmart with his shiny shoes and his clean, pressed clothes. Sometimes they would see Cleva and talk as they did on his first day in Langa but mostly he just worked. Worked and worked like a slave and he lost that feeling of being an outsider and became like the others.

Looksmart still would not let him walk around Langa on his own. He said that the place was wild and unpredictable, especially after dark. And although Winston had only been in the township for two weeks, he felt both insulted and pleased that Looksmart still looked after him.

It had been surprisingly easy to fall into the life that Looksmart gave him. His little shack, no more than a tin room haphazardly thrown together, was squeezed into a row of other houses that were all the same. Looksmart, or someone, had painted the blistered wooden door green, and this gave the shambolic building a rakish air. As if the house was proud of its door. Winston learnt after a while that this helped Looksmart to identify his own home in the mass of similar shacks. The roof — with its rusted tin, sloped down to the back and Winston knew that he would not be able to stand upright at the back of the house where the roof sloped close to the ground.

Inside it smelt strongly of wood smoke. The floor was dirt with a little pile swept into the corner. Neither Looksmart nor Winston cooked here. They ate breakfast in the morning on the way to work, stopping at a local shop to buy what they needed. Then later they ate lunch at work. In any case, there was no place to cook unless the outside charred remains of sticks and stones were ever used. A fire was lit sometimes but only for light and warmth.

On that first evening in the dark, Winston knew that if he were ever left here in the rabbit warren of huts, he would never escape but be doomed to wander for the rest of his life in the foul-smelling darkness of Langa. But after a week he had begun to work out a crazy kind of logic to the hopeless mishmash of streets and lanes that made up Langa. Suddenly he had begun to think of it as home even though he had sworn when he left the valley that he would never be at home anywhere else.

Looksmart's bed frame, placed on bricks with a thin mattress, was the only furniture. The walls were covered in newspaper print. Yellow and fading, the articles told of a mayoral opening of the Uitenhage Town Hall and stories of white people's dogs and cats. A murder story was half covered with adverts for a magazine and an agony aunt column giving advice on how to keep your man interested. The faces that peered out of the yellow sepia were white and out of place in the tiny hut.

Looksmart spoke suddenly into the small room, making Winston jump. 'We will have to sleep head to tail.' Winston nodded, too tired to speak and too tired to care and fell into a deep sleep almost the moment his head hit the mattress.

'Come on,' Looksmart said at the end of his first week, smoothing his shirt and then flattening his hair with a small amount of oil making his palms glisten.

'Where are we going?' Winston asked and wondered if he could spend the day with Cleva sitting in the sun and letting his tired muscles ease. The work had been hard and bewildering and Winston wanted nothing more than to spend the weekend quietly resting.

Winston turned and surveyed him and then shrugged. 'We are going to buy clothes,' he said, and they left the house. Outside it was already warm and although it was busy with people despite the early hour there was a different atmosphere on a Saturday morning. The people were softer and less pinched. Even the children were like the children in the valley, laughing and playful. Winston trailed his new friend who was greeting people in a loud voice like a popular preacher on the way to worship.

Looksmart was dressed in a black suit that left him sweating and glistening in the increasing, creeping heat of the day.

Leaving Langa was always a surprise with its suddenness and Winston marvelled at the way that the township dropped away. Suddenly they entered the tarred roads of the town of Uitenhage with dirty brick buildings and real shops to line the roads.

Also here were cars shooting out of nowhere with blaring horns and flickering lights causing him to feel slightly unbalanced. There were still many black men and women hurrying around on the pavements and darting across the roads between the cars like ants. Looksmart did not speak to the others here, but he walked a little straighter and Winston could see the tension in his ramrod straight back and moved a little closer.

There was an inexplicable feeling of something here — what was it? Winston felt it every time he came into the town. A feeling of temporality as if they knew they would not be long in this place and that they needed, in some urgent and fervent way, to hurry home to the safety of Langa.

The warehouses situated on the industrial estate where Looksmart shopped for his clothes were tucked away out of the main shopping area and Winston, becoming overwhelmed by waves and waves of people, felt relieved to be away from those hordes of anonymous people. He smiled to himself — he remembered this feeling when he first came to Langa and in a short time Langa had become a normality. He doubted if he would ever feel a sense of belonging in Uitenhage itself. It was so cold and hard as if the white man had rubbed off his own soul onto the place.

The warehouse, a curious mess of clothing piled high on tables in a jumble sale of jackets, coats, shirts, trousers and waistcoats and rails of hanging suits which appeared overstuffed, bulging vulgarly, smelling of damp and something unnamed and unsavoury. The warehouse also sold shoes piled in their boxes up against the stained walls in huge towers that wobbled slightly, looking as if they would fall and crush the shoppers below. White and coloured salesmen, wearing snappy suits as advertisements, bore down on Looksmart and Winston. Looksmart, clearly a regular, laughed and joked with the salespeople, adopting his manner of Langa now that they were off the streets. One man, a thin light-skinned man, grabbed a colourful shirt and held it up against Looksmart. 'Hey this suits you; you know. You should buy it.' His voice was high and shrill, and he laughed as if he had told the funniest joke imaginable.

Looksmart proved to be a discerning shopper and the salesman moved away as if in a well-rehearsed ritual, letting the young man decide for himself. There were other salesmen who looked briefly and hopefully at Winston but when he did not pick up any of the clothing, they moved away to other customers.

Looksmart danced down the isles as if invigorated by the piles of clothes, towards the end of a row where a large wooden stand filled with hats and caps of every colour skulked. Looksmart tried several on, looking at himself in a tiny, pitted wall mirror. Besides the mirror was a rack of sunglasses. Although Looksmart donned the caps and hats, one after the other, laughing, Winston did not laugh. Looksmart's expression suggested that this was something that he took seriously and something that meant a great deal to him.

For Winston, who had only ever worn old hand-me-down clothes donated by white people who no longer needed them, found the place bewildering and he felt unbalanced and off-kilter, just like he felt in the streets of Uitenhage.

His clothes were always out of shape, old and often frayed at the edges. Sometimes at Christmas Winston would receive a pair of shorts and once, memorably, a pair of skin-tight black, shiny trousers that only fitted for a month. Winston had wanted very badly to keep the trousers. Lord knew that in January there was very little chance to wear them in the dry heat of the summer. But soon the trousers had found their way to Melikhaya his little brother, who wore them until they fell apart and his mother cut them up for rags.

For Winston to see so many clothes in one place felt strangely uncomfortable and unsettling, as if he had trespassed into the white madam's home and looked into the white *baas*' wardrobe. Winston's household had never owned a wardrobe, wearing as they did all of their clothes during the day. They would put their daytime clothes on the bottom of the bed during the night ready to be donned for the daytime.

His father's green overall hung inside the door on an old nail that had been knocked into the frame for that purpose. Boots, dirt encrusted and dusty, had stayed outside unless it rained and then they came in. Besides, his father was the only person in the house who regularly wore shoes. They were needed for the hard labour performed on the farm, although not everyone was lucky enough to have a pair. There was no need for a child to ever have shoes — better to develop their feet into hard calloused ridges that would serve just as well as any shoes.

His mother wore clothes donated from the white madam and these were big and had to be gathered in at the back so that they did not drown her. This had the effect of making his mother look as if she had been very ill and lost a lot of weight. This made Winston always feel a vague sense of fear around his mother, that she would somehow be totally overwhelmed by the donated clothes one day. Winston could never remember his mother ever wearing clothes that were actually meant for her and her alone.

Looksmart had a small rail in the musty room that he had so willingly shared with Winston. The rail leaned precariously so that it had to be propped against the wall, otherwise it would surely fall and spill all the contents on the ground. All the shoes Looksmart owned were arranged under the rail and although they were small in number, to Winston they seemed to be a vast amount and bewilderingly unnecessary. Looksmart had spoken about the clothing warehouse the evening before, and he had urged Winston to accompany him. When he spoke of the shop, his voice changed and there came a longing and small excitement that betrayed a yearning that went beyond mere clothes.

Looksmart was surprisingly uninquisitive about Winston's life before Langa. To Looksmart, it was as if Winston had arrived in Langa without a life outside of the township. He was not as well versed with life in Langa yet to know that no one probed into another man's business. Winston sensed without having to be told that there were too many sad stories and tragedy, and unnecessary talk did not solve anything. In a rare moment of clarity, Cleva had told him that most people in Langa wanted to escape from something bad and there was no solution to probing a rotten aching tooth. After that, as if embarrassed, she had laughed and then returned to her singing and dancing.

Winston was brought out of his reverie by Looksmart sporting a brown velvet cap that was too big and made him look small like a little lost boy. 'What do you think?' he said, and Winston shook his head. Looksmart turned away, preferring the smiling sycophancy of the salesman.

With a jolt, Winston realised that he had been in Langa for two weeks. Two whole weeks that felt both like a lifetime and a mere moment.

Looksmart, having discarded his jacket, was talking to a shop assistant, bargaining and laughing and enjoying himself. He clearly knew the shop assistant whose Xhosa was good but faulty as if being instantly and directly translated from another language so that the words were not quite in order. Looksmart put the hat down and paid for the shirt and the shop assistant put the money in an old box under the counter. The two spoke a little longer but the man shook his head and Looksmart joined Winston, still smiling but under the smile Winston thought that he saw a little hurt lingering in eyes that did not smile.

The shirt was wrapped in brown paper, and he thrust it at Winston who was so surprised that he took it. 'What is this?'

'A gift. I see that you don't have a shirt, so this is for you.' Winston could not speak because his throat had filled, and he was afraid of what would happen if he tried.

'You know one day I want to work there in that shop. That is the job for me.' They walked for a moment in silence, a warm wind stirring the dirt around their feet and Winston noticed how old and crumpled his shoes looked. The first pair he had ever owned. They hurt his feet, unused as they were to being thrust into shoes.

'You know what that man said?' Looksmart burst out suddenly, stopping in the road. The smile was gone. Winston, surprised, stopped too.

'They only employ coloured people. They don't employ blacks.' He spat. 'Can you believe it?' He held out his hand brown and shining. 'Do I look any blacker than them?' Then suddenly he laughed but it was not a joyful sound.

They continued walking and Winston felt a great sadness for his new friend. Despite their brief connection already, he felt that Looksmart was his closest friend and it produced in him an unexpected pang.

'Every time I go to this shop I ask. Are there jobs? They always say, don't worry, come again. They promise me. But today...' He stopped and swallowed. 'They finally tell the truth. I am Xhosa so I can't work there.' He clicked his tongue and shook his head and great sadness settled over them both.

Looksmart turned abruptly and began to walk with his small brown packet tucked under his arm. Slowly his gait changed, and he began to saunter and soon, to Winston's relief, a small part of the swaggering man came back as they made their way home.

'Let's go back by the river,' Looksmart said and began to weave his way through streets that were less populated and spattered with houses. Houses that the white people inhabited. A man in blue jeans and a big white belly peeking out from under his T-shirt glared at them but Looksmart ignored him.

'Hey, *kaffir*, there is no work here,' he yelled angrily, kicking at something Winston could not see. Looksmart laughed, showing his large white teeth and looking for all the world like he was enjoying a good joke. Then he turned to Winston and said something in Xhosa, and this made Winston smile, but the man walked to the little white wall that separated his lawn from the road.

'Hey *kaffir, voetsek,* you don't belong here. *Voetsek* before I call the police.' He brandished his fist like a mallet and then turned and hurried up the path to his front door.

Not by a flicker of his eyes or twitch in his face did Looksmart show any reaction. He kept walking and smiling until they emerged from the houses onto the main road that divided downtown Uitenhage with the beginnings of Langa.

Looksmart pointed. 'There. That's the river.' A swirling, surly black river wound its way under the bridge where they stood.

'All day in the summer we played here when I was little.' He was silent for a moment and then turned. He slid between the end of the bridge and a wire fence that had been pulled back revealing a short little dirt path that led down to the water. When Winston caught up with him, Looksmart had already abandoned his shoes and pulled up his trousers and was paddling in the shallows and Winston sat on a rock that was warm in the late morning sun. Looksmart's voice was dreamy and quiet.

'Did your mother not worry about you in the river?' Winston looked down at Looksmart's legs. They ended just above his ankles. The water covered his feet as if they had been amputated.

'No, man, she was away, and we only saw her very late in the night and she did not know about the river. The river was only for us children.'

Winston shook his head to banish his own memories of his uncle who lived on the river where children and adults were always together, and the river was the life of them all. Adults kept an eye on the children because they were there in their adult world of tasks that overlapped their children's life. Also, the river that Winston knew was blue and clear, not like this dark, angry water.

Looksmart came out of the river and sat next to his friend. 'You should go in — it's very good. Cool.' Winston shook his head and turned his face to the sun.

'You know I am the only black man who buys my clothes from that place.' He looked into the distance as if pondering why this was so. 'Levy's Clothing Warehouse. You know Cleva says that I am a sell-out.' Winston sat up at the mention of Cleva's name.

'Why does she call you a sell-out?' Winston's voice was soft as if he were saying something else altogether.

'Well, it's because they will take my money. Let me buy things you know? But they won't give me a job. But she's wrong. One day, you will see. They will understand that I can sell clothes and look at me.' Here he waved his hands at his own body. 'I am a very good advert.' He smiled and the immodesty caressed them both and made Looksmart the comedian again.

'Anyway, I told her, shopping and politics don't mix. It's no good losing respect for people just because they want to spend their money where they like.' Looksmart looked off into the distance again. Winston thought about that for a while and then decided that he would probably want Cleva's respect more.

'Besides, she knows that I am the best-looking man that she knows.' Looksmart preened.

Winston sighed at the hopelessness of it all. Looksmart had small dreams but in this place even small dreams were unattainable.

Chapter 6 — Uitenhage

Uitenhage, Eastern Cape 1984

Seething with wronged indignation and a sense of paralysing helplessness, Kobus started his long journey to exile. He hardly noticed the long unchanging road out of the city, black and slick in the heat. A feeling like a sack being pulled over his head muffled the sound and obscured and distorted the first part of the journey so that his head felt curiously empty, as if it was all happening to somebody else. The pick-up truck, a long-ago symbol of prosperity, had seen better days but it still ate up the miles with a satisfying monotony.

At times he came back to himself. He supposed that he couldn't remain suspended in a state of nothingness forever, lost in his impotent thoughts. He became aware of the rough brown country of Pretoria giving way to the lush green outskirts of Natal and then plunging into the brown and dusty and dry countryside of the Orange Free State. The pitted road snaked away into the distance to where blue-grey mountains loomed, never seeming to get any closer. Still, he drove on, the hours slipping away behind him like the endless evolving scenery. His shirt was damp and uncomfortable as the heat grew but he hardly noticed it.

Playing over the conversations that he would have conducted with Meiring had he but been prepared, the miles and hours slipped away. But, like all fantastical conversations, they went on and on without changing, like the road, and he knew that it was all fantasy. The road, although seemingly unchanging, would eventually come to an end and he would arrive at his destination and none of his lacerated feelings would have changed.

He came to himself in a little nameless *dorp* with one dusty high street and a tiny dingy convenience store. It was an exact copy of so many little towns that he'd already passed through, and he would later be wholly unable to recall its name.

He stopped the car, its screechy brakes loud in the punchy mid-afternoon sun. There was one other vehicle parked outside the shop — a beaten dejected vehicle that once was white but was now a jaded dirty-cream, pockmarked with rust and dented as if regularly driven into solid immovable objects. The number plate was bent, and insect encrusted. The air reeked of burnt sand and the heat rushed upwards exploding from the orange, brown soil that puffed around his feet in little orgiastic clouds.

The shop was dark, in contrast to the bright afternoon light, and at first Kobus could see very little except dancing sunspots. The interior was shrouded in a murky, musty darkness that felt furtive and unnatural. The floor beneath his feet was alive with dancing mites and his legs below the bottom of his tan shorts immediately began to itch.

A tiny movement to his left showed a small, cowed figure perched at a till. The wizened man indicated that the drinks were at the back of the store in a tall fridge that had long ago lost the fight against the intense heat. Kobus ducked against the fly paper hanging dangerously low from the ceiling. From the look of them, they had not been replaced for many years and Kobus wondered idly how many thousands of flies had been caught in the old mangled gluey traps. A small buzzing sound emitted from the fly paper with the last dying sounds of trapped and defeated insects. Rows of melted and strangely deformed chocolate bars lay disconsolately on the overheated shelves.

A quick check showed him that he was three hours away from Uitenhage. The hazy road stretched away into the unknown as lonely as a dust cloud. The radio played a few popular songs before turning to unrelenting static. He had reached the outer edges of human civilisation, it seemed. Now that he was alone and had played out his fantasies of confronting Meiring, Kobus began to feel the first edges of fear. Or was it fear? Fear of something. Something unknown. What lay ahead in Uitenhage he could not begin to imagine. Not so young any more and, if he was honest, feeling his age, he wondered how he would find the energy to start again. The energy to withstand Marta's disapprobation.

Then the road began to narrow, and Kobus began to feel closed in as stubby dense bushes of dark green impenetrable vegetation crowded the vehicle. For the first time on the journey Kobus began to feel claustrophobic. Suddenly, about one hundred yards ahead through a small almost invisible gap in the vegetation a dishevelled woman burst onto the narrow side of the road. Kobus automatically slowed.

The woman, small with ripped clothes and black tearstained face, clearly distressed, waved her arms at him, urging him, as if with every fibre of her being, to stop. He slowed but did not stop and turned his head to watch the woman as he moved past as if in a slow-motion scene of a movie. She fell to her knees with her hands up to her throat and her face raised to the skies. Big tears — so big that he could see them sliding down her face — fell to the dry ground. Still, he kept driving — he'd heard about these sorts of things. Ambushed people he'd read about in the papers. Usually, white women but sometimes white men found days later in the bush with their throats slit and all their possessions gone.

Still the woman haunted him — she had looked real, like someone truly in trouble. He was amazed at the details that came to him still. The ripped bodice of her dress, the dark discoloured marks on her face. Those huge tears. Had he glimpsed someone else in the gap? He couldn't say for sure, but he imagined that he had seen something.

As the miles dwindled his mind was now occupied by thoughts of the woman and Meiring was temporarily forgotten. He felt a sense of irrational irritation — why could he not just dismiss the woman? She was, after all, only a *kaffir*. A *kaffir* alone in the middle of nowhere. It was nothing to him. But still she came back to him, a kneeling figure in the road with her hands praying. Praying to a pitiless god that seemed to have abandoned her in that harsh, unforgiving place.

But even this journey must end and finally, creased and slick with sweat he clawed his way out of the sweltering car. He was stiff and heavy from eighteen straight hours of driving. He stretched into an aching arc pressing his hands into the small of his complaining back. When he was younger, journeys like this one never bothered him. Perhaps it was just old age. He didn't know any more, he didn't feel old. He felt just the way he'd always felt, but he supposed that no man could evade time. With a shrug he began to walk up the small concrete path to the house.

It was an unprepossessing, low squat bungalow and just for a moment he faltered, almost got straight back into his car and returned to Pretoria. He could picture himself, for a moment even at this late date, demanding a meeting with Meiring with a proper response prepared and pouring slickly from his lips.

He sighed. Even if it were possible, he doubted he could face another day in the car on the return journey.

Kobus, in his bewildered panic after leaving Meiring, carefully surveying his map, had gone to his collection of encyclopaedias, a by-product of a brief friendship with a salesman who had joined a weekend barbecue and sold copies of the Britannica Encyclopaedias. "Uitenhage (he read), a small insignificant town, lies in the dust bowl of the Little Karoo." Then he had to go to the 'K' section to read about the Karoo.

The Little Karoo — a semi-arid piece of land, a couple of million hectares of nothing. There was a big Karoo — a proper sub-Saharan desert that presided over a large eastern section of Southern Africa. The little Karoo, therefore, was the little fractious brother of the wider area which had then been divided out and renamed because of its geographical separation from the Big Karoo. This defeated and dreary piece of land had not even the dubious honour of being part of the proper Karoo.

Uitenhage nestled alongside the black, surly waters of the Swartkops River. Although he had to be fair — he couldn't know that the waters were black and surly, only they looked that way in the monochrome photograph which could have been a photograph of any river anywhere in the world.

Furthermore, the Uitenhage entry stated: the 1820 settlers in Algoa Bay — a good forty-five-minute drive by fast car — had hardly glanced at this tiny spot on the Swartkops River, preferring to stay at the Port named for a long-forgotten governor's wife — Port Elizabeth. When the new settlers eventually did branch out into the hinterland, they hardly paused at the small *dorp* of Uitenhage as they forged inland and westward to the richer, more beautiful lands of Cape Town and the staggering sights of what was to become the famous garden route. Uitenhage had nothing similar to offer, so with no great sights and riches, it became the forgotten place. Nothing. It was merely Uitenhage where all the flotsam and jetsam of life came to settle when they had nowhere else to go. Kobus was now part of that flotsam and jetsam.

He noticed an entry for another little town called Despatch. This place warranted only a sentence. Despatch, a town situated on rich clay soil and the site of a flourishing brick industry. Also, a few words at the end of the entry caught his eyes. Despatch, the entry stated, had a glass library, a dubious claim to fame if ever there was one.

It took Dutch settlers', homesick and displaced amongst the British settlers in Port Elizabeth, to strike inland and develop small towns on their dogged route for independence. Along their way the Dutch named hamlets and villages for their homeland. Graaff Reinet, Middlesburg, Patensie and Uitenhage. The last was named for Den Haag in the Netherlands — a small reminder of home out in the desert, thousands of miles from home. It was only then that Uitenhage began to shrug off its hopeless air of lost souls and offer something a little more promising.

The English ignored their Dutch counterparts and were content to plunder on the coast and invested in gold and diamonds in the north of the country. The Port Elizabeth harbour became vital for importing and setting up factories for production.

The Dutch worked the hard intractable land away from the lucrative gold and coastline. They forged small, hard little farms that bore little in the way of food and took much more of the hope and courage of their farmers. But out of this breed of settlers there rose a stubborn, hard core of white men and women who refused to give up their claim on the land and through sheer will and determination, a promising settlement began to grow.

Kobus read that there were many opportunities for advancement away from the gold mines of the north. A kind of South African dream for any poor person down on their luck who was willing to work hard there was a reward.

For many years Uitenhage provided slim pickings. With hardly a discernible rainfall and annual droughts taking regular hold of the land, farming animals and crops was almost impossible. However, the indomitable Dutch and then their Afrikaans inheritors continued to carve out precarious livings in the dry *veld*, refusing in the face of the devil to give in. After a while there emerged a small elite group who proved successful, and they became enormous land holders and drew envy from their landless English counterparts in Port Elizabeth.

Then, because of the deep black river, the huge conglomerate companies, seeing an opportunity, came to Uitenhage in the early twentieth century. And along with the river, there was a huge workforce as yet unplundered. This workforce lived in Langa and was black and was just as valuable as the river.

Uitenhage, by now staggering into adulthood and seeing an opportunity to attract business, gifted land to two of the biggest conglomerates: Goodyear and Volkswagen. The Americans, British and Germans, once so uninterested in this hellish place, now brought their famous names and invested in the area. The Americans brought their tyres and the British and Germans their cars. Goodyear and Volkswagen became a byword for success in Uitenhage and finally put the little *dorp* on the map.

They were there in the encyclopaedia, those enormous hulking factories, built as temples to profit and enterprise and not to please the landscape, which was in any case always barren and unappealing. They dominated the little town and soon Uitenhage became an unlikely success. And so, the people came. Labourers, entrepreneurs, smallholders, investors, chancers, crooks, and others of dubious history and intent. Like a Wild West boom city, a tiny gold rush town emerged with all the riches and poverty, morals and immorality to be expected from such unpromising beginnings.

Disgusted, some of the original South Africans began to move away and left it to the ignorant foreigners.

The capitalist colossus did not come alone. Myriads of tiny and medium-sized businesses came to worship at the temple of capitalism. Little satellites that provided hundreds of jobs and poured countless dollars into the poor and deprived community. Uitenhage, despite first impressions and all predictions, began to thrive.

Not that Uitenhage, the aspiring city ever looked prosperous. Despite all the money, it still looked like an unfinished gold mining boomtown. That is what Kobus saw on the day he arrived in Uitenhage. None of the pictures he'd seen showed the poverty, dealing as they did with the white newness of it all.

Alongside the managers, business owners, entrepreneurs, American and German supervisors, Afrikaner workers arrived to live in the Promised Land. The Afrikaners gravitated to the smaller houses in Fairbridge Heights, but they were no less precious than the grand houses of the German and American elite. Pushed out onto the cheaper, less attractive side of the golf course, these suburbs were carved into the inhospitable country through sheer tenacity and need. In the Heights, although not all houses sported pools and double garages, the white people believed that they were living the dream. They were joined by white workers hungry for a stake in the new land, desperate people from European slums suddenly promoted to landowners and high positions. They became a new subset of South Africans in this most unpromising of paradises.

Some even started businesses of their own and quickly grew rich and prosperous. These people were soon joined by policemen and teachers. Soon a mosaic of Europeans speaking a riot of languages caused a small rainbow community to thrive. It was true that some Europeans stayed apart and hardly ever assimilated but others mixed and some soon identified more with their new land than their old homes. They forgot their birth places and became newly invested in this land and had no interest in the claims of the people who had already been living there for centuries. All the new immigrants had one thing in common — they were — every one of them — white.

And along with all the industry, infrastructure came, a spanking new motorway carved mercilessly through the hard dry landscape. The road came as a surprise to Kobus as this had not been in the encyclopaedia.

The newly laid road, big and stark with the ground laid bare, like a war wound. The lanes of the motorway ran over Uitenhage and through Despatch, its forgotten, depressed neighbour. Neatly on one side the suburbs lay a green oasis where the people thrived in their white mansions, and on the other side of the great wound of a road lay the township of Langa.

This part of Uitenhage was not described in the encyclopaedia. A great roaring township with tin houses leaning haphazardly up against one another as if thrown there by a giant recalcitrant child. Here the vast unskilled workforce of Uitenhage lived. Thousands of young men and women in pursuit of a dream too. The orange dust and darkness were always upon Langa. No electric wires bore the gift of light. No sewerage bore away the human effluence. No green manicured lawns awaited the residents here. Only patches of dry scrubland inhabited the streets and byways, the signature of the Little Karoo. In between the houses and small patches of iron-like grass, goats and cattle grazed disconsolately.

Donkeys, the preferred transport of little business holders in the township, tied to ropes hammered into the ground, ate circles of grass around their feet before being moved on to the next piece of brittle grey grass. The bells on goats and cattle mixed like background music with the bustle and noise of the township.

No servants awaited the workers' homecoming. No dip in a cool sparkling pool. No fresh drinking water unless it was carried across the wound of a road on the head of a woman returning to her family for the evening.

But despite this, the residents of white Uitenhage would often hear laughter drifting across the wounded road. Little lights in the dark would twinkle like small fireworks where open fires glowed. Sirens would often break through the dark of the night, alarms from cars or houses set off accidentally by night birds or even winds. Alarms that shouted out vainly in the night air and were ignored. Langa rested in deep dark night while the white lights of Uitenhage never went out and exposed the great raw scar of the road. Sometimes angry voices rose into the dark night and white people huddled together and ignored the suffering on their very doorstep.

None of this was in his encyclopaedia — this Kobus had to see for himself.

This was the place that Kobus Jonker came to in 1984 when the summer was gearing up to bake the land into a heated seething mass of resentment and longing. Kobus brought his prize possessions, the weapons of his trade, on the front seat of the Land Rover Jeep. The R1 rifle and handguns (two) carefully placed and fully loaded with the extra boxes of ammunition on the floor of the passenger seat.

The house had already been picked for him. At the end of Pretorius Lane, Vanes Estate, it offered a view of the huge road and Langa as well as the golf course. These two opposing views did not interest Kobus. Nor did they seem in any way incongruous. The care of the house would fall to his wife. He would hire a 'boy' to mow the lawn — there was sure to be such a creature lurking in the shadows.

Kobus was a man of habits. This was how it had always been.

Kobus could see that any money that was spent in the town went into the pristine whites-only suburbs. Suburbs with names like Vanes Estate and Fairbridge Heights. American and German business bigshots came to live in ten-bedroom houses with double garages, acres of lush patches of emerging green lawn against the blue-black Bloukrans Mountains, an ever-present glowering backdrop.

The encyclopaedia described these mountains as a place of unique habitats for plants and animals that only thrived in the Eastern Cape. Kobus sneered as he slammed the book down. Surely all entries for every single part of the country described their area as unique. It certainly didn't look unique as he cast his eyes up at the mountains and then back at the houses surrounding his own. Through weary eyes, all he could see was the unpromising shape of hard hills.

Kobus hardly noticed the great sprawling township at his back when he opened the house, which was hollow and empty without any of the furniture which was due to arrive later the next afternoon. Kobus brought the guns safely in from the car. It was heavy and unwieldy and raised a clammy sweat on his brow. He had to bend his tall body and slide sideways through the door with the great safe pressing against his protruding stomach. Kobus already felt like an alien. The long drive still hung around him like an echo of stale tobacco. Voices drifted towards him, and the township twinkled like blinking eyes. Although it was the start of a new life, it felt only like the end.

Chapter 7 — Goodyear

'You know there is no point in hanging on to the old days any more. It's time to move on,' Looksmart said, one of those Saturday mornings when they all gravitated towards Cleva's presence. They were sitting around a small fire, and someone was already playing a monotonous tune on the guitar. Winston liked these weekend meetings. These moments of feeling connected to her as if the yearning had brought her to him.

Today Cleva, in her faded tight jeans and clean white shirt, seemed more than usually gleeful as if overexcited by something. Her eyes gleamed and at first Winston was happy, too. Then he noticed her eyes filling with moisture and he wondered with surprise if she might cry. A number of times she had started to talk but had then broken off and turned away. Winston longed to go to her and make her sit down with him, but he knew from experience that she would not like this. That she would pull away and start another conversation. He sat on the edge of his seat and could not take his eyes off her.

His sense of unease steadily increased, especially as this behaviour contrasted with her usual carefree style. Usually, she would sing and dance as she had on that first day but today, she did neither. He doubted that the others noticed because she spoke as she normally did. It made him jumpy, and her sudden outbursts jarred in the mid-morning softness.

Then she went into the house after spitting out something he didn't quite hear and all Winston could see was laughing, mocking Sydney. Then she reappeared with a letter scrunched up in her hand as if it were a piece of rubbish that she'd taken out of a bin. 'Here,' she spat, 'look what they want now,' and thrust the paper into Sydney's hands. He looked at her as he smoothed the paper out on his knee and then looked down at it.

He stopped smiling and everyone else went silent. Cleva folded her arms over her chest and glared at them all.

'What is it?' Looksmart asked, the only one bold enough to do so.

'It is a letter…' Sydney began but then Cleva turned her full glare on Looksmart, and he shifted uncomfortably on his stool.

'A letter,' she enunciated as if each word were a painful jab at her throat. 'A letter telling me, I mean *gogo* and me, that we are being moved.'

'Being moved?' they all chorused like parrots hardly able to understand.

'Yes, moved to another township, KwaNobuhle,' she pointed upwards and vaguely away to her left. 'Moved because Langa is no longer our home. It no longer exists. All of you will get a letter like this soon.'

They all broke out into spontaneous chatter like angry sparrows and Winston found, to his surprise, that he was one of them. Babbling, angry, futile words that soon petered into confusion.

A voice broke through, one of the men that Winston did not know said, '*Hayi,* comrade, you are wrong. This is our home, no one will take it away. This is a mistake. This is our location, our township!'

Another voice said, high and panicked, 'What is this KwaNobuhle?' No one answered.

'Yes, it's true. We don't have a letter.' Looksmart looked at Winston in confirmation.

Cleva threw back her head and laughed — more like a bark than a sound of joy. 'It does not come in the post; they stick it on to your door.' She hesitated and then her voice was as hard as flint. 'They nail it to the door. Some of the young men saw them doing it and pulled down the notices from all the doors. I found this one in the gutter.' She pointed to the paper as if it were about to leap up and attack them.

There was silence now — a cold hard silence that, despite the heat, sent a shiver down Winston's spine.

'What does it mean?' he whispered, afraid of the answer.

'It means,' answered Cleva, 'that the white man doesn't want us to live here any more.'

'But why?'

'Because the white man takes everything that he wants. Even if he doesn't want it, he takes it anyway. You see how they come. The white man brings all of his things from his own country. He brings his own people and then he looks around and takes everything he wants.

'He never asks us if we want anything. He never asks…' she stopped, and they all looked at the ground. This was not the answer they were looking for. Cleva covered her face and turned from them.

'Look at those white people,' she said without turning back. She waved her arms and started stalking up and down behind them. As if what she had to say could not be said by someone sitting down or standing still. She did not look at them.

'They come to our markets and lift their lips up and say it's disgusting. They say we are pigs and that we live in mud. Then they go back to their own houses and try to grow daffodils and tulips to remind themselves of their own homeland. They don't want to be part of this land, but they will take it away anyway.' Despite her obvious distress her voice was strong now, almost strident and it rang clearly slicing through the hot air like a knife.

Now some of the men were nodding their heads sadly and the morning was no longer bright and exciting.

Looksmart jumped to his feet, his customary charm and good nature evident on his face. '*Hayi*, comrade, this is true, but we don't have to care. Look at me. I have a job. A good job and Winston too. And I am smart and soon I will have money. They can't stop me; nobody can stop me.' He smiled at the group, but nobody smiled back.

'Come on, you can't be negative, comrades. We are strong, we are young.'

Cleva shook her head. 'Don't you think, comrade, that many of our old broken relatives thought the same thing? We have been fighting for forty years now and every year we lose more. Now we will lose Langa. We will cry for our country, comrade, but no one will hear us. We are suffering and no one cares. Wake up.' At last, she turned to face him.

It seemed to Winston in that moment that Langa was a great pit of want, but even so it had begun to feel like home.

Looksmart thought only of his money and how it came every week in a little brown envelope on a Friday at five o'clock handed out by a bored foreman, his great bulk squeezed inside the yellow kiosk.

The envelope was stuffed with Rands — glossy notes — and some coins. After paying his rent and sending some to his mother, the rest of the money went on clothes. He wasn't like the other young men who spent their money on drink and oblivion. Clothes were his pride and joy. And he didn't care that people mocked him, none of that mattered. Once, on a whim, he'd bought a multi-colour peacock scarf for Cleva. She never wore it, but he noticed one Sunday that her grandmother wore a very similar scarf to church on Sundays.

The only time he ever bought anything for somebody else was a shirt for Winston, who he sensed would cherish the garment. Langa was not a place where generosity flourished.

The silence settled over them all and it was hard to break it. Winston took the battered letter from Sydney and read the words. They made no sense, being in Afrikaans — a language that he did speak but could not read. The black words were stark and mysterious, and he could not see any danger in them at all.

It seemed so cruel. Only a few weeks had passed since his arrival and already this home was going to be denied to him. Winston remembered that first Sunday in Langa when he tried to fit into his new life as he watched Looksmart caressing his clothes. Winston tried to broach the subject of the search for his auntie a few times. It was hard when Looksmart seemed only to be interested in his clothes and their preservation.

Winston tried for what felt like the tenth time that day. 'Looksmart, what am I going to do? Tomorrow I must try to find...' he petered out. Looksmart turned, his eyes glazed as if returning from another place.

'You must call me comrade. We all call each other comrade. It is what we are, you know. All together.'

Winston nodded and wondered how he was going to be able to do that. It felt strangely pretentious and unnatural.

Suddenly, Looksmart spoke as if it were the most obvious thing in the world. 'You must come with me in the morning; they are always looking for men in the factory.' And that was it. Winston could get nothing more from him that night.

Looksmart's place of work, Goodyear, a gleaming hulk of a factory, spread over several acres of land, was a place which both filled him with pride and disgust... a disgusting pride. It was here that he had been able to walk tall and become a proper man. A proper man, one who helped to support his mother and one who could buy his own clothes.

The factory was lanky and lowered darkly over the landscape. Management had made an effort to landscape the gardens in front of the office block and the plants valiantly tried to hide the looming working factory in the background. All of this was only visible through a chain-link fence that darted around the entire acreage of the factory. The gardens and office block were visible only in diamond shaped blocks from the outside of the chain link fence. The company did not need the general public to see the blackened walls of the factory; they did not need the public to see the wearied, blackened workers trudging out at the end of their shifts. The finished product was, after all, a huge quantity of blackened tyres and the shareholders cared not for any of it but the money that it generated. Still, it didn't hurt to project a clean image to the public.

Winston felt a small quailing as he walked beside Looksmart. This looked like a place that only white people went into. His heart hammered uncomfortably, and he wondered why Looksmart had brought him to this place.

A low hum, like a large group of giant bees, swarmed through the area, creating a hive of the building. The hum never stopped. Next to a huge, oversized tyre with the name Goodyear emblazoned on its side stood a sign bearing the words 'LAST ACCIDENT AND FATALITY — 36 DAYS.' Parallel to this on the other side of the fence stood another sign. This sign read 'Volkswagen' at the top of a huge billboard bearing the picture of a yellow Golf Jetta with a half-naked white woman on the bonnet. Volkswagen had no accidents or fatalities to report.

Then behind the sign, running away to the distant office block and factory, stood an enormous car park. Miles and miles of matted tarmac. Behind it the building looked small and squat over the roofs of hundreds and hundreds of glistening newly minted Volkswagen cars that looked like ants stranded on the blackened, glistening tarmac.

Winston had never seen so many cars in one place. The fence here was finely meshed and impossibly tall. It had no holes, kinks or flaws. It was clear that Volkswagen was anxious to avoid any threat of theft or damage to their precious product. They took no chances with security and huge warning signs in three languages warned passers-by that the fence was electrified and extremely hazardous. Just in case the signs had not been enough, warning pictures of electrocuted and charred trespassers were clearly displayed on every side of the fence, framed by huge red lightning bolts.

Looksmart worked at Goodyear on the workshop floor. Hard, unforgiving manual labour. Most of the men that worked on the workshop floor were young and strong. Looksmart man-handled hundreds of tyres every day and this had given his frame a hard muscled look. Looksmart explained that he had been given an orange overall and learnt very quickly to wear only rough old clothing to work.

'Remember, comrade, only wear your old clothes,' Looksmart had warned, and Winston wondered how he could not have seen that all his clothes were old. Not that he had, that many clothes. But then Looksmart had only eyes for his own beautiful collection.

Although Looksmart was obviously pleased that he had good work that paid well, Winston saw the shadows in his eyes. What it had cost him and how much he longed for the day that he could take his place in the clothing warehouse and wear beautiful clothes all the time.

After only a week Winston became aware of how his hands and skin became infected with a fine black carbon. That carbon was everywhere now that he was aware of it. There was no escaping it. Shaking his head after work produced a black mist that settled in between every tiny crease on his body. The orange overall soon became dark and stained with tyre carbon. Since there was no place to wash, the overall became stiff and cracked with dirt.

Looksmart explained that after a period of time — he was vague about the details — they could qualify for a pair of new overalls. In the meantime, the overalls became stiff and uncomfortable and chaffed badly. It seemed to Winston that new overalls were not a priority for the workers on the factory floor. All of this he figured out in his first week.

And the factory was hot. Hot like hell, the men said. The heat was a tangible, violent thing. It battered and relentlessly punched every living thing into submission. The men often worked stripped to the waist and some of them even stripped to their underwear. Women were warned to stay away and as a result it became a male environment where no softness ever entered. Looksmart had only worked at the factory for eight months and had yet to go through a summer. He told Winston that he could not imagine what it would be like. No one tried to explain, and he did not bother to ask.

The thermometer rose dramatically to over 50 degrees Celsius, but the men never looked at it. There would be absolutely no point as there was no temperature too hot to work.

Looksmart, confident and sleek, sauntered up to the foreman. The foreman was white, but his skin was so pitted with black carbon that it had permanently stained his face. His brown floppy hair was the only indication of his race. He was thin and wore a pair of blue overalls. He hardly acknowledged the black man and continued to shout incomprehensible commands to the small army of glistening black people swarming the shop floor. Looksmart continued to talk but Winston, hovering near the door, could not hear what he was saying. That they were talking about him he knew, as Looksmart waved his arm at him, and the foreman did eventually look over at Winston and shrug. Looksmart broke into a wide, white grin and walked back to Winston. 'You can start today, comrade.'

And that was it. Just like that Winston had a job.

'You are lucky because you are a farm boy,' Looksmart said when they dressed in the shapeless overalls. Winston looked hard at Looksmart. 'Farm boys are strong.' Looksmart laughed.

Later that day on a short break from the noise and the heat from the shop floor, Winston made a point that had been troubling him for most of the day. 'I thought it was hard to find work.' He was surprised at how normal his voice sounded after the noise and bustle of the shop floor.

'*Hayi,*' Looksmart smiled, 'not jobs like these.' He waved at the others all huddled over their tea. 'Comrades don't work here for long. Maybe one year or a little more. Mostly they go somewhere else after a while.'

Winston shook his head. Some of the men were old and from the looks of their skin and hair they had been working in this place for a long time. He left it, there was no point in antagonising his new friend. Besides he had more important things to worry about. The overall was itchy and sticky. It rubbed his skin so that he could not settle, and it felt like a thousand ants were crawling slowly over his body. He abandoned the idea of getting comfortable.

Winston had not known homesickness before and although the township felt unreal and strange, his new friends had made him feel welcome and safe. In the factory, a real home-longing nausea now enveloped him, welling over him in a pressing heat-filled wave.

In the factory there were no windows, only artificial light and a lively antagonistic heat. He'd known heat in the valley but nothing like this. It pressed onto him, into him and stopped up his lungs so that he felt like a swimmer struggling to get ashore. The air was filled with black carbon and although not visible, when he coughed or sneezed it would leave a black, snotty slug on his sleeve.

And still he had to work, dragging huge unwieldy tyres up onto a machine that stood waist high. When a friendly older worker, small and wiry, had shown Winston what to do it was done so quickly that Winston had to ask him three times to repeat his instructions. The man was not offended but was impossibly patient and seemingly unaffected by the heat. Somehow his friendly patience made Winston feel worse and perversely he would have felt better if the man had been angry and short-tempered.

'You'll get used to it,' he promised. Winston did not respond and doubted this hostile hell would ever be something that he became used to. He also felt a small frisson of fear that he too would one day be like this small wiry man.

For the fourth time he shoved the tyre onto the machine and levered in the inner tube that was squishy and unresponsive. It was like a spiteful unwieldy grenade that could explode at any moment. Winston's hands began to bleed. His back burned and his feet blistered.

Everywhere he looked, men with shiny black bodies toiled in the chaotic heat without stopping. The noise was loud and clanging and people only spoke by shouting otherwise they would not be heard. He wanted to scream. He wasn't even sure that he would be heard.

He broke two nails on his right hand and opened a deep cut on his left hand. The cut immediately filled with an evil-looking black dust. It mingled with his deep red blood to make a dirty crimson line down his left arm.

His shoulders ached in tune with his blistered feet. He started to walk with a limp. Later that evening he found the money he'd forgotten in his shoe. It was soaked crimson with blood. He fell into his bed and knew nothing until he was shaken unwillingly awake the next morning by Looksmart.

Hunger now became a constant companion for they only ate once a day. Stopping at a small, fantastically filthy café in the morning, they bought half a loaf of bread each which they hollowed out. Looksmart did it for Winston whose hands at the end of his tired arms did not feel like they belonged to him. For twenty cents they bought a tin of pilchards and emptied this into the hollowed-out loaf. To Winston it tasted like nectar. Money was low so it was the only food of the day, but all the men were the same and they carefully saved their little coppers for the rest of the week. There was talk that the factory, knowing that workers needed food, were planning on building a workers' canteen. This would come but it would be too late to sate the hunger of Winston's generation.

The shopkeeper, a large Mediterranean man with a torn vest, turned the bloody Rand note around and looked carefully at it through the grimy light from the window as if he'd never seen one before. In the end he must have decided, blood encrusted as it was, it was real money. Winston tried to save the middle of the loaf, in a hard ball in his pocket for later in the day. But somehow, he ate it before he even got to work. Hunger now became a regular gnawing part of his life.

In the factory, hot sugared tea was served out of a huge black filth-encrusted cauldron. Tin mugs were hung around the cauldron on crooked nails. The tea was a point to look forward to: once in the morning, once at lunch, and once in the afternoons. These little breaks became a welcome distraction for the bewildered and homesick Winston. He wondered how Looksmart could be so happy, laugh so much. Winston felt as if he might never laugh again.

Somehow as time moved sluggishly and reluctantly forward, as many had told him, things did begin to improve and towards the end of the second week this new world began to make more sense and the heat, and the noise seemed to retreat into the background. His legs and hands throbbed less and then he noticed that he was able to think of Cleva again. The work and heat had dimmed his memory so that he could not quite picture her properly. He heard her laugh and saw her hands moving in time to music but couldn't quite see her when surrounded by the tangible heat in that place. The windowless, soulless place made it impossible to imagine anything beautiful had ever existed.

At six in the evening, a loud piercing siren indicated the end of the shift and the men left in single file. A hose at the back of the factory provided a shower. There were no bathing or shower facilities for black men in the factory. There were no bathing or shower facilities in Langa either, only stinking communal toilets. Patiently waiting their turn in the queue for the hose the men would start to chatter and pretty soon the laughter would ring out loud and uninhibited.

Winston's ears would adjust to the quiet and the ringing would gradually stop. Some men left, too tired to wash, their small, shuffling black shapes getting smaller and smaller as they retreated.

'See that,' Looksmart pointed, 'don't get like that — they have given up — soon they will stop coming and then they will starve. Always wash, always keep clean, comrade.'

One of the men in the queue for the hose told stories of his time in the mines. The deep diamond mines in the Transvaal. He told them that they should count their lucky stars that they weren't working in the dirt and dark underground, picking up diamonds like thieves in the night. Diamonds that would make millions for the rich white *baas* but nothing for the miner himself.

One of the others joined in. Wasn't it one of the best paid jobs in the land? The man thought for a few moments and then agreed. It was a good job, but it was hard and unforgiving. It made you sick every morning when they dropped you in a cage to the bottom of the mine shaft, a sickness that would take all day to disappear. And he remembered that once you were underground without the sun on your back, you were stuck all day, with no way out.

'No,' he said, 'I much prefer this. Here I am not an animal in a cage and an animal underground. At least here I am a human.'

Looksmart took the longest with the hose and only regretted that he couldn't change immediately into clean, smart clothes. Winston welcomed the cool water and green grass under his feet. Almost before he got home, he was sleeping on his feet.

Chapter 8 — Settling In

Despite the desperate manner of his leaving Pretoria and the changes that had taken place, Kobus felt relief that it was all finally over, as if taking a huge breath and then being able to continue breathing normally again. His life in Pretoria had pressed down onto him until it felt that the pressure had been there all his life, squeezing every ounce of joy out of him. In those last few years, his life had consisted of long sweaty nights and waking from gruesome nightmares to find that reality was just as bad as the crushing nightmares.

At the end, Kobus had suddenly found that Danie was absent. Even though he saw him every day at work, it had been impossible to approach him. He became even more isolated in the secrets that consumed his nights.

Marta was no help at all; she would keep house and tend to the children as if that were the extent of her business and Kobus knew he could not look to her for comfort.

Within a matter of days Kobus was cut adrift in a sea of uncertainty and then most unexpected of all he found a new beginning. It felt to him as if the contract of his life had been torn asunder and now there was only Uitenhage. As new beginnings went, Uitenhage was not the finest start, but it was something.

Now, even through his feelings of isolation and despair, he recognised the move to Uitenhage for what it was. A new, imperfect beginning. The move to Uitenhage meant that the past had been obliterated. No more cover-ups, the throwing of a blanket over the past.

Not for him to concern himself over the increasingly silent wife. Not for him to fret over a distraught Marta. Not for him to dress up his demotion to her and in the end, she said not a word and took her heartbreak away and kept it sealed in her private world.

That, these days, was his marriage. A scene avoided by explaining that they were moving and then leaving the room. Her silence reproached him, but it was better than a row. It was better than being battered by a barrage of words. Her silence allowed him to use fewer words himself. And he liked it better when he had less talking to do.

They moved further and further apart. Kobus was not looking forward to her arrival in Uitenhage at the end of the week. When he looked at the calendar, he realised that the weekend was the very next day.

He had always freely admitted that he found the emotional world of women exhausting, as if clearly drawing the lines between women and men. When his son arrived, then he would have someone to talk to, someone who would understand. It frightened him sometimes at the amount of anticipation and excitement he built around his son. He tried to quell his joy and push it away, but he could not.

Kobus found himself pathetically pleased with the Uitenhage house, squat and plain as it was. Of course, it did not compare to their palatial residence in Pretoria. That house had been situated in one of the most prestigious suburbs of the city. Tall, cooling trees lined the streets, and the trees were large and well established, giving the suburb a feeling of permanence and graceful old age. The houses were partially and tantalisingly hidden by green and luscious vegetation. Huge double-storey houses, no common bungalows here, behind shrubs and walls that housed pools and even tennis courts. Round-the-clock security firms discreetly advertised their services with small colourful wall notices. His Pretoria residence, for twelve glorious years, had been a sign of his illustrious success.

The Uitenhage house by contrast was a bungalow, a single-storey, plain residence with no pretence to glorious ostentation. There were hardly any trees in Vanes Estate and those that did grace the streets were small and stunted like all the vegetation in the area. There were no walls surrounding the house, which sat on the side of the road with an expanse of plain and unappealing lawn running down to the stark road.

Kobus wandered from room to room, his own footsteps his only company. A small transistor radio had been left in the kitchen. He pushed the red button on top and an anonymous voice suddenly boomed into the silent echoing room. A voice full of Friday night joy, a heaving, invading voice too powerful for the lonely room. Weirdly the loud messy voice made Kobus feel even lonelier. He switched it off, preferring the void of silence. The kitchen seemed roomy — open and airy. It looked out onto a sparkling pool. Even in the rapidly darkening evening it still glittered with warm captured sunlight. Just about the only appealing thing about the house.

Kobus had been told by an Englishman once that the African dusk was too quick, that there was no twilight or gentle easing into the night. Africa, he'd said, did everything suddenly. Kobus preferred this change to full darkness hiding as it did the tiny imperfection of this new house. This was his favourite time of day. He secretly admitted that the rapid descent into total darkness was his favourite time of day.

Marta would hate the house. He could already imagine her anger, white-hot, hidden behind a pale face and tight lips. An anger that would be tinged with sorrow and accusation. He would have to prepare for that and put on his cloak of indifference so that her anger could not touch him. He tried to think of this new house with her presence and that of his daughter Sissy. But he couldn't quite grasp hold of it, trying as he did so to remember a time when they were happy.

The memory seemed like a film of somebody else's life. In the past, he had envied Danie with his obedient wife and perfect sons and their willingness to live in his special version of perfection. When he thought like this, his anger built again and that made it better. Better the anger than to let the creeping sorrow and regret take hold.

He shrugged as if to shake off his thoughts and opened the sliding door and walked out to the pool. The water was cool; he could still feel the heat of the day lingering in the air, but it had already left the water. This wasn't so bad. Marta would come to like it. It wasn't so very different to Pretoria. At least here he could put the nightmares to rest. He was already forgotten, his old friends now friends with others as he and Marta would find new friends.

He had to admit the last few weeks in Pretoria had been hard; he was like a ghost in his own life. Now, at last he felt a little relief and for the first time in a very long time he was looking forward, with a small frisson of excitement at summoning his son to Uitenhage.

He had to admit that it was true that Uitenhage was a place of insignificance, but it was somewhere that he could get lost and start again, stop being a ghost in his own life. That is what the *Kolonel* had said, 'For

God's sake go, go to Uitenhage, Jonker. Take charge and get them in shape and who knows?' He must have seen the disappointment on Kobus' face because he added, 'Who knows? After a couple of years, maybe you can come back. You'll be a hero again. We've got to let it all die down.' He referred to the incident with distaste, his mouth curling at the edges.

Kobus unreasonably held on to that slender hope and after he'd thought about it, he became convinced that he would be back in Pretoria after a few years. Maybe, if he was lucky, he'd come back after a few months. But then his unruly thoughts would stray back to that ill-fated raid. He saw Danie, out of control and raging, and then he knew that he was banished to Uitenhage forever. The hurt and anger burned until it became a hard knot of resentment, and he could taste the blood in his mouth. Most of the time Kobus couldn't even name the feelings that raged within. He felt a great overwhelming anger build until he thought he would burst. These great switches from contentment to despair made him feel nauseous and he took three deep breaths and made himself take note of the garden and forced his thoughts into order.

This new garden was not big. The pool dominated the whole area so there was hardly any space for pacing and thinking. Kobus was pleased to see that someone had kept the pool clean and the Kreepy Krauly machine bubbled, eating the bacteria that would turn the pool green.

Kobus sat wearily in a garden chair that had been newly painted and smelled like creosote. After a while he became aware that it was completely dark. A slight breeze sprang up, playful and warm. He shook himself.

The kitchen was new at least. Surely it must have everything a wife would want? Marta could always add her own touches, but he knew she was used to a much larger and better-equipped kitchen. His heart sank. Anyway, Pinkie would be the one to use it the most. Why should he concern himself with what a black maid wanted?

Slowly moving back into the dark, lonely house, he closed the sliding door and went into the living room which was dark now that the sun was gone. The furniture was pushed against the walls as if waiting for a dance to commence. The TV in the corner was opposite the patio doors; there were no ornaments or little knickknacks that Marta was so good at. If it were left to him, the room would stay this way.

He reached for the patio doors, unsettled and reluctant to stay in the stifling, silent house. His reflection stared back at him. A grey-haired old man stared back. His stomach looked huge in the reflection as if he were viewing himself through a magnifying glass. When had he got so old? And fat? Marta was always trying to tell him about eating healthy food and cutting down on drinking. She did it in that snivelling submissive way that was calculated to bring out the sneering, mocking Kobus. Anyway, she was one to talk. Where had that lovely young girl gone? Never one to wear revealing clothes, she had still been an attractive slim figure. In fact, her hiding herself away behind prints and long skirts had been the main attraction for Kobus. These days she wore big floral twin sets — exactly like her own mother before her.

Sighing, he went out of the door into the night again and was greeted by the sound of a thousand crickets serenading the night. From somewhere over to his left a red glow marked the township of Langa — a place he would have to get to know. A low murmur of many voices reached him. Someone was playing a monotonous tune on a guitar that ebbed and flowed with the wind. Sometimes a shriek or loud cry would reach out of the noise and jar the night awake. A dog barked further down the street immediately to be answered by a chorus of dogs.

He closed his eyes. Marta would be here in the morning. Then things could finally get back to normal.

Chapter 9 — Elands River Valley

Elands River Valley outside Uitenhage, early 1980s

The strikes brought hunger. It surprised Winston to think that he had been hungry before when now he really began to know real, debilitating hunger. His stomach felt as if it cleaved to his backbone and his head was swimming and he felt as if he would fall down. This disjointed feeling was not helped by the people swarming in and out of his vision as he traversed the township with his friend Looksmart. Hungry as they were, they went out. There was a forlorn hope that scraps of food could be found and sometimes this happened, but they hovered on the border of starvation.

With no work, they passed listlessly from one group of men to the other. The days were long and dusty and over it all lay an unidentifiable sense of unease. The malaise was strong, and the days were long. Knots of young men and women congregated in groups where they did nothing and let the hot sun beat on their heads. Underneath it all lay a menacing layer of discontent.

Looksmart, Winston and Cleva were regulars at her grandmother's house, but the legendary ginger beer had long ago dried up. So, they sat and grumbled, but there was very little heat in their talk any more. A listlessness and lethargy replaced their lively chatter. The others came but there was no music and no singing. Cleva no longer danced.

Now when he returned to Looksmart's little hut, he lay on the hard pallet of wood too hungry to sleep, too broken-hearted to think of anything else but his old home.

After all that had happened, he still felt the wrench of his leaving and the pull of that old life. Sometimes a smell would jolt him back, or a running, laughing child would transport him back to his own childhood. But mostly it was when he lay on that old hard bed that he would remember home.

Then he would think of his childhood which seemed to belong to someone else so very far removed from his life in Langa. Then the pain would flood his body like an unstoppable river, and it felt like his limbs were forcibly torn from him.

Now with the lethargy that the strike action brought, it became harder for Winston to keep the thoughts of his old life away. He would have done anything to stop the thoughts creeping up on him like ghosts. He was powerless to stop his unruly thoughts from returning to the valley.

When he did finally fall asleep, lurid dreams of the valley filled his nights. He felt a strange sense of divine happiness which fled when he awoke to the sounds of Langa creeping in with the dawn.

And even with Langa filled only with poverty and men dressed in rags, he noticed there were more young men and some women arriving and standing at the bus stop. They would soon, he knew, be absorbed into Langa. He did not have the energy — the overwhelming sense of homesickness engulfing him — to warn them and send them back to their old lives. As he had once done, these newcomers stood on the brink of the township looking dazed and confused. Like him they wandered off clutching small, insignificant belongings and disappeared into Langa. He felt a strange sense of pride that he could now spot the young men and even women sometimes, little more than girls, the danger hovering over them like a shroud. He marvelled at his own good fortune.

In all his memories of home he did not allow his mind to drift to Doda lying on the ground and Mama crying with her head in her hands. He thought instead of his mother, his sisters and brother in the beginning when they were all young and Mama still laughed. Doda, too, laughed and swung him onto his strong shoulders in the evening when he came home from the fields.

If his thoughts did return to the end, he remembered the bus, shabby and dilapidated and how it rocked to a stop, empty save for the bored fat driver and the conductor. The driver did not look at Winston as he gingerly climbed on, holding on to the unfamiliar railings as if they would infuse him with badly needed courage.

The overweight and profusely sweating conductor barely glanced at the coins in his pale hands and inserted them into the right slots on his money belt with unnecessary precision. Winston's mother, small and painfully thin like a starvation victim, stood in the dust framed in the filthy window looking not at Winston but at the ground as if looking at him was too difficult. She'd been fading away ever since it had happened, and Winston could sense he was losing her but did not know what to do to reclaim her and bring her back. For months she had been getting thinner and thinner until she was merely bones. Her clothes, inherited from the white madam, were many sizes too big, making her look like a child dressed for fun in adult clothes.

The clothes seemed out of place, so bright and colourful, as if they mocked his small grey mother. But she hadn't always been this way, hadn't always been grey and shrinking.

Winston tried hard to remember the tiny dynamic woman who had skipped through his childhood like a busy bird. Nothing seemed, in those days, to overwhelm or defeat her. His mother had seemed indomitable — undefeatable. That was all a long time ago — before that catastrophic day, before... his mind shied and shrivelled away like a small, frightened animal. The contrast between the tiny waif of a woman to the one before only served to highlight how very wrong everything had gone.

He thought of his sisters and tried to push aside the sadness of not being there to say the final farewell, the sisters who had encapsulated the essence of his laughing, teasing childhood. Pumla, the daring, bold child who seemed to have a strange unnameable affinity with nature. Two years younger than him but braver by far. Her voice, always with a laugh in it, teasing him into something that would earn his father's rebuke.

Then there was Tendisa, small and wiry like their mother. Pumla and Winston were always teasing her into some indiscretion which made her brave in her way. Like the time Pumla and Winston built a small floating craft out of diseased wooden logs and launched the craft onto the lake. Tendisa was eventually teased into accompanying her two elder siblings onto the raft.

'Come on, Tendi.' Pumla's voice was impatient as Tendisa stood first on one foot and then on the other, her toes lapped by the gentle waters.

Winston added his voice. 'It will be fun. Come, Tendi, let's go!' He smiled at her, and she shrugged and clambered on to the rickety raft falling to her knees and squealing. Pumla used her hands to move the raft deeper into the water. It was slow as they had no oars. After a while Pumla sighed and stopped and they drifted quietly into the honey-warm day.

Then Pumla looked at Winston, that little mischievous smile on her lips and in her eyes. She started to rock the raft. Tendisa screamed and clutched at the raft, her little fingers seeking a hold on the old logs. Winston rocked his side and the raft tilted. He was bigger and stronger than the two girls.

Tendisa screamed again and begged them to stop but they did not. Then the raft gave up the unequal struggle and came apart and they fell into the lake laughing and screaming. Tendisa held on to one of the bigger branches and kicked towards the shore.

'I hate you both,' she screamed and stalked away, her shorts baggy and dripping water as she walked, looking accusingly back at her brother and sister swimming in the lake, laughing so hard that they could hardly climb out.

Tendisa never told their parents, preferring to keep their misdemeanours to herself. She was a child of many secrets and an expert at hiding and never getting the blame for any of their pranks.

Monica, too, Winston's eldest sister, had not been around very much but he remembered her. She crept lightly into his thoughts. She'd been the caring, doting sister who had already been buried alive in responsibilities at twelve. But because she was so much older than the other children, she'd been a shadow, a child herself with responsibilities. This was one of the sad realities of their lives. He had never really thought about it until he'd come to Langa himself and felt Monica's burden at last.

Although he could not remember her clearly, he knew of his mother's reluctance at letting her go. Monica, with shining, bright eyes had heard about a school in Port Elizabeth — a whole planet away for people like them with no means of transport other than walking. But in the end Monica's enthusiasm for the idea and her yearning to attend a proper school had won. She had left. She was sixteen years old. Mama said that they'd lost her to the city, and she would never allow any of her children to follow her to the city, never. Until the thing with Doda happened.

Winston remembered his parents talking about Monica, snatching pieces of conversation but then out he had gone into the *veld* with Pumla and Tendisa. Tendisa had slipped her hand into Winston's as if sensing the unease of her parents and they followed the rampaging Pumla. This time they were on a search for African dragons that everybody knew were the best and wildest dragons in the world. And soon Tendisa let go of his hand and they were engulfed in Pumla's game.

Then, later, Monica was gone, and it was just Pumla, Tendisa and himself. Three wild, happy children playing in the *veld*. They believed that they were luckier than all other children. They heard stories of the way that children lived in the townships, mysterious places where people lived in tin houses all on top of each other.

Even though they spent their time playing the children knew that responsibilities would come soon enough. So, they made the most of their time for playing.

Then there was Melikhaya, the youngest of them all. Melikhaya could never play with his brother and sisters and so was left behind, which felt unkind and cruel but never stopped Winston and his sisters from running away and leaving Melikhaya behind.

Melikhaya had been born in a hospital, which was unheard of out there in the valley. Hospital births were for white women only — the Africans got on with and ministered to themselves. But there were problems with Melikhaya and so his mother had been rushed in a huge white ambulance to the hospital in Uitenhage, the first time his mother had ever been to the town. The first and only time his mother had ever left the valley.

She was not taken to the hospital on the hill where the white people were treated, but the hospital at the bottom of the hill, a much smaller place which was cramped, and grim and black people waited patiently in corridors all day. Waited while men groaned and were reduced to the sum of their pains while harried doctors did the best they could.

Winston was too young to understand what had happened to cause Melikhaya to be born in the hospital. At only nine years old, it had seemed to be that his mother was gone for a long time, and they were lost without her. There was a huge hole where his mother had always been.

Two aunts cooked and cleaned as best they could, and they spoke mysteriously of his new brother and his mother in whispering voices. Visiting his mother was never considered and after ten days his mother returned on the back of a pickup truck with their new brother naked and wrapped in a blanket. Winston found the fact of his naked brother embarrassing and wished that Mama would put him in proper clothes.

His mother seemed shrunken and pale and brittle. He had not run to her to look at the new baby as his sisters had done. She seemed to be a different person and he was afraid to touch her. He did not look at the baby with its scrunched-up eyes and moué of a mouth.

Melikhaya, their mother explained, was different. Winston sensed that his mother carried the burden of his brother's differentness and that up at the white house they spoke only of this new child in hushed whispers. The white children he saw never commented on the new black babies, but they did about this one.

The new baby was quiet as if aware of the shame around him and was wrapped closely against his mother's back as she cleaned in the white house. It was as if Melikhaya was still attached to his mother and that invisible bond would never be severed.

Melikhaya could, as soon as he was able, sing beautiful, bright songs that would only have to be sung to him once for him to capture their essence. He learnt to crawl and walk a little but the dangers that he faced daily ensured that he stayed in one place rocking from foot to foot as if tethered on a short lead.

Mama lived in continual fear that the boy would step on the fire and instilled her fear so strongly into the little boy that he moved only by rocking and never going anywhere at all.

He was chubby and compliant and never complained even when he heard the delighted screams and shouts of his brother and sisters playing in the tiny woods at the back of the house. He would call out, 'Car, car,' and clap his chubby hands when no one else had even heard a car. Then the car would come by on the road and Mama would pat his head and he would smile.

He could hear the smallest bird and the tiniest croak. His brother and sister could never creep up on him and this was a game that they would sometimes play, until they lost interest and drifted away and left him to his tiny life.

In Melikhaya's small space in front of the house, his whole life played out. Here the ground was hard, orange clay, beaten down by the constant traffic of people.

Melikhaya swayed back and forth quietly to his own music while his mama or other adults sat talking through their days making plans that did not include him. Melikhaya was just there, a small shadow in the background and the only person who really saw him was Mama. His little white useless eyes rolled back into his head as he stared at the sky in a world of his own. The flies settled into the corners of his eyes and snot ran freely under his nose. Sometimes he was gathered up into the arms of an adult and then he laughed and squealed with delight.

Sometimes, Mama would call out, 'Pumla, watch Melikhaya,' or 'Tendisa, sit with Meli for me,' and they would groan and complain. Pumla would say, 'Why do you never ask him?' pointing an accusing finger at Winston who was never asked to do any of the work around the house.

Winston smirked. 'I am a man, I work in the fields like Doda,' and walked away. Pumla called, 'Mama, he never looks after Melikhaya.' Her voice was loud, and Mama looked at Winston speculatively.

'Yes, you can watch Melikhaya. It will do you good. He is your brother.' That day was seared on his memory when his mother, in a hurry for a task that had been thrust on her at the last moment, had thrown instructions over her shoulder as she hurried away to her white madam.

Winston, then twelve, remembered with shame his feelings of indignation. He was a boy, and it was not a boy's job — babysitting!

Melikhaya, sensing that something was not right, had moved closer to where he thought Winston to be. Winston, brimming with twelve-year-old indignation, moved away slowly at first but Melikhaya kept coming more quickly. He noticed that Melikhaya, who never ventured from the front door space, had now gone further than ever before. This amused him and made him think of a game. The little blind boy made little clucking noises as if to test the area with sound, like a bat. Winston was as silent as a grave. How long this would have gone on Winston did not know but just then the little blind boy stumbled forward straight into the embers of the breakfast cooking fire.

The boy did not cry out loud although tears ran down his cheeks to join the increasing snot. The tears fell onto his charred and blackened feet. He held his right arm to his chest as Winston lifted him clear of the fire. It was evident that it was bad, and Winston ran towards the big house.

At first his mother was too concerned with the injuries on her helpless boy to question Winston. Winston stood in the kitchen petrified and the only thought in his mind was that his little brother might die — his imagination running wild now that he could see the real extent of the burns.

He watched the white madam bandage Melikhaya's injuries, as if watching could help his brother who could not see for himself. Madam said nothing, her lips pursed into a thin line. All the time his brother was silent too and the never-ending tears ran down his face and pooled on the floor in a little forlorn puddle.

'*Ja*, now you must change these bandages as much as you can. At least once a day you hear? Clean it thoroughly with clean water. Come and fetch the water here from the kitchen every day.' Madam spoke Afrikaans and Mama had to concentrate on the words to understand fully. It was a language that had not come easy to Mama.

'*Ja*, madam,' his mother replied quietly, her head down. Winston thought about the dirt patch and the hut that smelt of wood smoke. The hose that brought water ended in the white *baas*' orchard. He thought of the old bucket grimed with green algae that they used for the water He shifted uncomfortably on his toes. He put his hand on his mother's arm.

'I will fetch the water, Mama,' he said, his voice soft. She smiled at him, and he shrank back, feeling his unworthiness.

The white madam wiped Melikhaya's face with a cloth and grimaced when she saw the cloth and threw it in the bin. She handed the silent, weeping child to Mama where he buried his temporarily clean face in her neck. He wore only an old pair of shorts and Winston looked away from his shabby mother and the near-naked toddler and felt their poverty. The white woman wore a beautiful dress of sunshine and rubbed her hands as she waited for them to leave, and Winston felt an overwhelming sense of shame.

As they were leaving the white woman spoke again. 'Here, take this.' She handed Winston a bottle of purple liquid. 'It will hurt when you put it on, but you must do it. Every day, mind, you don't want his burns to get infected. If he cries don't let that stop you, you must put it on.'

A small girl dressed in a pristine white dress appeared in the kitchen doorway. Her mother waved her away. 'Not now, Christine.'

Winston's mother was very strong for a small woman, and she hit him so hard before he got away that his arm and leg ached for hours after his beating. He hid in the little woodland until it was almost dark and Pumla came to fetch him.

For what seemed like weeks and weeks, Winston went to the white woman's kitchen and fetched clear fresh water for his brother. The buckets were heavy, and he staggered under the unfamiliar weight. It felt good to do this, like a penance for his part in his brother's injuries.

One day as he waited for the buckets — new buckets given to them by the *baas* — to fill in the kitchen, he heard the white woman talking to someone. He could not see or hear the other person, but he heard the Madam clearly.

'Well, you know he probably should have gone to the hospital.' She waited and then said again, 'Well, if it had been one of mine, I would have gone straight to hospital but then this child…' She was silent and then she said, 'Well, I can't say for sure, but he's blind,' and Winston knew that she was talking about Melikhaya.

'He's not right you know,' she continued. 'He's got hardly any life at all.' Again, there was a pause. 'I don't know, probably because of syphilis, you know how these people are. Anyway, it would be a blessing if he didn't make it.' She said all of this clearly and her voice came to Winston in a solid block like a punch to the solar plexus. Then suddenly she was there in the kitchen and Winston quickly turned his attention to the buckets and kept his head down. As he pushed his way out of the kitchen, he looked back at the white woman and noticed that a pink colour had moved up into her face. His mind was filled with knowledge, for the first time, that this woman thought that his brother would die and that she thought it was a good thing. In fact, he thought about that so much he forgot about the other thing. The strange word, syphilis. He didn't ask anyone what the word meant. Later, when he found out what it meant, he burnt with shame and anger.

Worst of all was his father's coolness. He did not beat him — he almost wished he had. That at least would have been an end to it. But the months of coolness made him feel as if he had been banished. It was the first time he had been separated from his family and only Pumla would speak to him during those months of punishment.

Astonishingly, Melikhaya still loved his brother and rocked and sang for him and was delighted when Winston sat on the hard ground in front of the house and tickled him and teased him with feathers.

Winston was once again shamed. It was Pumla who had discovered that the boy liked feathers to be gently wiped over his face and arms. Melikhaya's pleasures, like everything else about the boy, were small and few and all the big stuff went on around him while he was left behind.

His mother had grown instantly older after the birth of Melikhaya, as if the burden of this small child had taken something from her. She constantly spoke of snakes, as she never had before and how they would come for her little helpless boy. Winston now felt his mother's fears and helplessness. It was taken for granted that all children knew how to recognise the dangers of snakes and could run away and take sticks and beat them away or even kill them.

Melikhaya was not like other children and took all of his mother's love and concern and there seemed to be very little left for anyone else. Winston did not resent this — it was life and there was plenty of life for him and his sisters, until the thing that changed everything.

Chapter 10 — The son

Uitenhage 1984

It was not often that Kobus allowed himself to think about his boy. Kobus Junior. To the everlasting chagrin of his father, Kobus Junior wanted to be known as Peter. An English name that he had adapted from his maternal grandfather Pieter. Kobus could not understand — this was an English name and part of his son's overriding and complete rejection of his Afrikaans heritage. Kobus, of course, refused to use it. But Marta, ever doting on her son and daughter, allowed her children all their whims. Marta had tried to explain, as if speaking to an imbecile, that their boy lived in a different world to the one that they'd experienced, and it made Kobus' anger rise in waves of disgust.

He had noticed his boy's ever-increasing steps to disassociate himself from his family and his Afrikaansness. The only answer Kobus had was to sink himself into his work and try to forget that he ever had a son. Now it was not only distance that separated them but an ever-increasing chasm of indifference.

On good days he felt sure his boy would return to the world that Kobus had made, and he would be able to think again of his boy in the proper way. On bad days he banished his boy completely from his mind.

And now in Uitenhage there was nobody who knew them as a family so perhaps he could reinvent the history of his family and completely reinvent his wayward boy and turn him into the son that he'd always wanted.

The inactivity that Uitenhage brought upon Kobus forced him to think about his boy in a way that he never had in Pretoria. With a sinking nausea, Kobus realised that while he'd been so busy with the A-team, he had allowed himself to create a fiction around his boy. A fiction that was unconsciously added to whenever he spoke to Danie and the others. A fiction that included a dutiful doting son studying at university and who would return wiser and miraculously prepared to follow his doting father into the police force.

If asked, Kobus would never have been able to explain this deep, long-held yearning. It had no name, but it was centred around his boy. Perhaps a need to pass on himself to his boy. Now he had a horrible realisation that when he looked at his son, he could see nothing of himself. A sense of *déjà vu*.

But now with all the time on his hands, Kobus, with a sinking realisation, saw that his boy, his *seun*, was not coming home like the prodigal son. At Marta's insistence, there had been a few fleeting visits where the name Peter had stuck in Kobus' throat, and he'd not been able to utter the name. These awkward silent visits had driven Kobus, with relief, back to work before the boy had left.

Kobus had been married at his son's age, married with a child on the way. Looking for promotion and getting on. Although the meetings with his boy were brief, as far as Kobus could see he didn't even have a serious girlfriend and absolutely no intention of settling down. When he got the boy home next, he was going to lay the law down. He didn't even fully understand what the boy was doing in Cape Town nor was he particularly interested.

The university course was a shrouded in mystery. Besides, it was all pretentious crap and he, Kobus Senior, would see to it that his boy, who he now decided he would call *Seun*, to avoid the calamity of the new name, made some commitments to the life that Kobus had so carefully planned. He frowned as he remembered the word *Seun*, so sweet on his tongue, had been corrected to the English word 'Son.' His son was in for a few surprises.

Then a thought, like a bolt out of the blue, occurred to him — there was national service — and that Kobus knew from bitter experience would come as a nasty surprise to his ungrateful soft boy. It could not be ignored; it was the law and Kobus would see to it that his boy understood. It was time the boy became a man.

When the boy had been little, Kobus had allowed himself to fantasise about working in the police together, an unbeatable father-and-son team. Just like other father-and-son teams he had met during his own service in the police force. He was not a man to make close friendships but there had been a few in the A-team and they all in turn had close and enduring relationships with their sons. These were the men he wished to emulate and now that he was separated from them, Kobus would need to forge a closeness to his son in order to fill the gap left by those who now lived hundreds of kilometres away in Pretoria.

When Kobus thought about it, if he thought about it at all, he remembered that Marta had many friends. Kobus often wondered what they talked about, twittering in the kitchen like birds in a comforting kind of friendship that brought a pang of surprising jealousy in him. With a shrug, he remembered that her friendships were not serious and of no interest to Kobus. With a son by his side, he would have someone close, someone to confide in, and someone to share the pressure — father and son united.

What hurt Kobus the most was that he was prepared to be so much better than his own father. His own distant, cold, and demanding father, an army man and someone that expected his sons to follow in his footsteps with no questions asked. An unapproachable man who would brook no argument. All through his boyhood years, Kobus had yearned to be in the army. But his own father had been distant, difficult and overbearing. Kobus had drifted further and further away on an ocean of doubt. When Kobus finally joined the army, his father had unexpectedly made no comment at all. Kobus could never tell if his tall grey father felt pride or disapproval but worst of all he felt that perhaps he felt nothing at all.

Kobus had made a pact with himself and was determined not to be like his own father, but his boy had never given him the chance.

And then the army had not gone as expected and his father had withdrawn even further, and Kobus was suddenly and unexpectedly an outcast in his own family. Luckily an uncle from his mother's side had managed to introduce Kobus to the police force. It had been a relief to get away from his father's overbearing interference and be his own man. But Kobus was not like his own father. He had tried so hard not to be, and he knew that he had nothing with which to reproach himself.

Even before he joined the police he was married. When he first moved into his own police house, that his father had never deigned to visit, he'd sworn that he would never be overbearing towards his own boy. He had tried in the only way he knew to make his son into a good man. But almost from the moment he was born, the boy was puny, a little mommy's boy. From the day of his birth, it had been a battle between Marta and Kobus over their boy's soul.

Kobus blamed himself for not realising soon enough how damaging the mother-son relationship was. In the end, Kobus had resorted to inflicting a few timely blows on his wife and it helped a little, but she would never fully understand. Nothing changed and still the boy preferred to read and even played chess at school, and he could only attribute these unmanly pursuits to his soft wife. The boy wouldn't even consider rugby and Kobus stopped taking him to matches in order to avoid the humiliation of a son so clearly unsuited to the physical challenge that rugby presented. The school, like Marta, was delighted with the boy and spoke of academic success. They even printed a volume of his poetry. Kobus didn't even look at it. What kind of man wrote poetry?

Marta and her friends spoke of a sensitive boy, words that further drove Kobus into despair as they in no way described a man. Or in any sense that he understood what was expected of men.

In the end, he'd lost those battles but was still not prepared to admit defeat. Somehow the boy would realise that being a man was more than playing chess and writing poetry. If pressed, Kobus would not have been able to explain what it meant to be a man. Kobus, bewildered and out of date, floundered around on the periphery of his boy's life until he grew old enough to go away. Kobus told one of his friends one day at a drunken party, 'If I could have picked my son, I wouldn't have picked him. That's for sure.' There had been a horrible, shocked silence and he'd staggered away to see if he could find someone who did not know about Kobus Junior. It was so much easier to talk about other subjects.

Marta insisted that they did something as a family and Kobus remembered one particular day when he'd been persuaded to drive to the beach. Pretoria being inland meant a long and tiring drive. The journey had started with very little enthusiasm from Kobus, and he'd delayed the start of the journey with a long unnecessary phone call to Danie but in the end Marta would not be thwarted and had packed the car herself. He could sense the excitement emanating from his son and wife when he climbed reluctantly into the car. He was overdressed with long socks and a heavy shirt and shorts, but it was too late to change. The car was hot, but it was a beautiful day, warm and sharp and clean from the rain that had fallen overnight.

Kobus, argumentative and annoyed, had elected to drive all the way through to the coast, but was persuaded to stop at a lonely dingy café where Kobus Junior had eaten an ice cream with the delight of a child who rarely received treats. This had the effect of relaxing Kobus, and he began to look forward to the mini holiday.

The place, somewhere Marta had visited as a young girl was, miraculously, not crowded. Too rocky for sunbathers but perfect for little children to ferret and play amongst the rocks. Kobus bought a net for the boy, and he spent a few hours dipping in and out of the rocks trying to catch fish. The boy daintily carried a piece of colourful seaweed to his mother, and she kept it beside her on the rock with the shells and pebbles that he'd found earlier. During the journey Marta had sat on in stony silence with the baby on her lap and the small boy in the back. Kobus never concerned himself with babies; especially if they were girls. He itched to do something interesting, but the boy stuck close to his mother.

Marta seemed happy to simply sit and watch her two children and Kobus wandered off on a small walk around the beach head into the warm salty breeze. He was surprised at how breathless he was after such little work and patted his stomach. He needed to get back into shape, get into the police gym and get some weight off. To his surprise, the pathway led through some sharp and evil-looking rocks out suddenly into a wide golden beach. There were people in the distance swimming in an area that had been roped off. Two bright yellow vehicles parked on the beach belonging to the lifeguards he assumed marked where swimmers could safely enter the sea.

Charmed and delighted by the beach he returned to fetch the boy, Marta and the baby too, and urge them to move to this friendlier part of the beach. It was obvious that the boy was disappointed, and he sat next to his pile of delightful treasures averting his face from his father. But at his mother's urging he agreed to move. It took a while as the treasures had to be packed into a small pink bucket and carried with them to this new section of beach.

Here the waves, unhindered by the rocks, crashed onto the shore in relentless continuity and there was no place for the boy to fish. The big crashing waves seemed to frighten the boy and he cowered behind his mother's legs. However, she was able to help him to empty the contents of the bucket onto the sand. Then he was content to build little sandcastles and complicated childish creations, muttering and chattering all the time to himself.

The boy seemed uninterested in the other children who bravely ventured out to sea on surfboards. Kobus established from the lifeguards that the shark nets were in place and holding. There was absolutely no danger.

After a while, he too joined the swimmers and surfers by discarding his shirt. He noticed that many of the other fathers were accompanied by sons that were smaller and younger than his own son and returned to Marta who was dozing on her towel.

Eyeing the boy, who was still filling and emptying the little bucket while humming, he smiled. 'Come *seun*, let's go into the sea.' He held out his hand, but the boy did not stop his filling and emptying of the bucket.

'It's warm here. This is the Indian Ocean.' He laughed and felt slightly foolish. How would the boy know about oceans? Why would he even care? It was obvious that he was not even listening to his father.

Just then two men with a horde of children came running up the beach. They were laughing and some of the children were grabbed and swirled around over their father's heads. Kobus felt a sudden jolt of longing. He switched his gaze to the small, undersized boy who had not for one instant stopped his game. A strange little secretive smile played on his thin lips. Kobus felt a return of the old anger.

Suddenly Marta spoke. 'Leave him alone, Kobus. He's happy playing in the sand. Can't you see?'

It was as if the boy was deaf to both his parents, and he continued to pour sand.

Driven by his wife's support of the boy and by the boy's clear lack of interest, he jumped up and clumsily grabbed the boy under the arms and ran towards the sea. He could hear Marta screaming at him, and Sissie, only a baby, was awakened and added her screams to her mother's.

Kobus ignored them both and then they were drowned out by the boy's wails of distress and the crashing pounding of the waves. Soon Kobus was knee deep in the sea and a huge wave crashed towards them and he threw the struggling boy into the heart of the wave which grabbed the child and flung him in turn towards the shore.

The boy landed on the beach, his arms and legs entangled like a stranded jellyfish. Marta, her face red and streaked with tears, was suddenly by the boy's side. She said not a word but picked him up tenderly like a baby and carried him back to the thin wail of his sister abandoned on the dry sand of the beach.

When Kobus came to them Marta was still fussing over the boy whose face was covered in snot and sand and the baby had stopped screaming but hiccupped and fussed in distress. Kobus could hardly think, with chagrin and anger warring inside him all the way home on that terrible drive. No one spoke as if words could not cut through the atmosphere of accusation. For that he blamed Marta. If only she could have let the boy alone.

The boy was six years old on that terrible trip and Kobus could not remember a time after that when he had ever been alone with the boy. So now was the time to set the record straight and get the boy to see sense. At twenty-two, his boy should finally be able to let go of the past and see that he needed to step up and be a man.

Marta was triumphant to have the boy to herself. It broke her heart when he went away, and Kobus derived more than a little satisfaction from that. But the boy was determined, and without actually leaving the country, he got as far away as possible. Cape Town. Like another planet. Kobus had never been to Cape Town. For all the hype about it being beautiful, he couldn't see it. After all, it was just another mountain. There were plenty of mountains in and around Pretoria. Even though he hated himself for it, he exulted in Marta's loss, felt glad that she too now felt the same sense of loss as he had done for many years.

His daughter, too, disappeared into her small life, and at last Marta, like Kobus felt what it was to be alone. Marta and Kobus now lived as if they had no children at all.

So, he found that Uitenhage had one small advantage in that it allowed him to give his boy one more try. A clean slate to begin again. Even though it choked him, he thought he could use the hated Peter and meet his boy halfway. Then they could talk man to man, his own flesh and blood. Surely now when he needed his boy more than ever, it could be like Kobus had always dreamed it would be.

Chapter 11 — Relatives

The days became increasingly muddled and slipped through Winston's fingers like water until he could not remember which day it was. Even more strange, the past now seemed more real to him than Langa. His dreams were populated with relatives that he had not seen in years. They ran through his mind like a film reel.

Suddenly, one day his older brother stood before him, a warm smiling lad who looked as if he were about to burst into laughter. And even though he had only ever seen him a handful of times, he could see him clearly now. Themba was tall, especially when Winston himself had been young, small and wiry. In contrast, Themba had been broad with thick shoulders and very white teeth. Themba had grabbed his suddenly giggling, silly mother into a hug and twirled her around. Winston could only stare in amazement; he had never seen his mother like that.

Mama often spoke of her mysterious son. 'My first born' — she never called him by name and her voice took on a joyous tone that Winston had never heard before. 'My first born has gone to my parents,' she told the white madam who nodded and then turned away and gave her an instruction about cleaning the wooden furniture.

'I don't want you to polish the furniture and leave a smear on it. Here, like this. Can you see? You use too much polish, Regina.' For a moment Winston had wondered who Regina was and when his mother answered, he realised that it was his mother's name. Different to what his father called her, but then the white people always changed the names. Doda said they did this to help them remember names. They could not get their tongues around the Xhosa language. For a time, this had made Winston proud, that their language could be so difficult that not even white people could use it.

'This is my second born. His name is Xolile,' and his mother had pointed to him. She pulled him closer so that his head met her sharp hip with a shrill bump. The white woman hardly glanced at him.

'Remember Regina, polish all of these tables and the cabinet over there by the window again. I don't want smears.' She turned to go.

'By the way, why have you brought him to work today?' Her voice was hard and her eyes harder as she looked, really looked at Winston so he shifted a little behind his mother.

'He was sick this morning, Madam, so I brought him with me.'

'Well just make sure that he isn't sick here. Make sure that Aneka and Johannes don't come in here. I don't want them getting sick too.'

'Yes, Madam,' his mother said meekly. Winston had never heard her so meek before.

Then as she was leaving, she turned back, half in and half out of the door. 'Oh, by the way. What did you say his name was?' She shook her head. 'Never mind. Let's call him Winston. That's easier. And that name is a good one. After Winston Churchill.' His mother nodded and so Winston, at seven years old, had his name changed and was not known as Xolile any more. The memories reminded him of those old times, and he had almost forgotten it himself.

All of these memories, like little anecdotes belonging to somebody else in another world, returned again and again. His sadness and regret were tinged with a sense of grief that Winston had lost himself and he knew with real regret that he could never ever get back to that carefree boy he had once been.

Even in the midst of all the memories about his family he began to merge the place and the people of the valley so he could hardly tell where the place ended, and the people began. He began to understand that the valley was in his soul and that his life had been the best that it ever would be. That was what caused the grief. That letting go of something joyful and beautiful knowing that it would never return.

Those tall blue gum trees, like an invading army, lined the Elands River as it meandered its way to the Indian Ocean where it crashed onto the shores of the huge city in Algoa Bay. It sucked the clean river water out into the sea while fresh rainfall replaced its loss further up the valley that Winston had never visited.

The blue gums that looked like they had been there for centuries had actually been introduced by white settlers desperate for wood and fuel. Those indigenous trees, like the yellowwoods and acacias, were no good for the industrialization of the new world. So it was that these new trees in an environment very similar to that of Australia grew to be giants in their adopted world. They dwarfed the natural melkhout and gardenia bushes and Winston was not aware that already these foreign invaders were destroying the world that he loved so very much.

Although the blue gum trees were invaders, they were beautiful along the river. To Winston they felt like Africa, and they provided much-needed shade. They found very quickly as children that it was refreshing to suck their pungent leaves. Their wood provided fuel for badly needed home cooking fires and so Winston and his ancestors never saw the danger they presented until it was too late to do anything about it.

Winston's uncle, Mukeseli, lived in the remotest part of the valley on the river banks. The invader blue gums and the shorter but fast-growing black wattle were the backbone of his firewood business. His part of the river was a place too isolated for the white man to intrude.

It brought a smile to Winston's face when he thought of his uncle. Strong and independent and unusually a servant to no white man. There was, after all, nothing for them this deep in the valley.

As a small boy, he'd followed his father over the ancient beaten track to visit his uncle and cousins once a month. Mukeseli, his father's only brother, had stayed in the area.

Mukeseli treated the land as if it was his own, settling into a way of life that was separate and thriving and all his own. It was so very different from how most other black people lived. He built an empire on the banks of the river hidden deep in the valley. No white man would take the land from him, he'd made certain of that. No white man came this far into the unwelcoming, hostile valley. Here he built a settlement of quickly assembled huts of grass and mud and sometimes even reclaimed tin. Here the beautiful Elands River meandered a path through the impenetrable vegetation that grew almost from the river bed up onto the mountain side like a green blanket.

Wild game roamed freely in the undergrowth and provided a rich source of fresh meat for the families that lived there. Baboons and monkeys lived in the tree tops and knew no fear of man and their chattering. There were people who lived in this settlement who had never been to the white cities and would never leave the valley. There were people in that tiny settlement who had never heard of apartheid.

Long-extinct hippopotami had hollowed the river in places so that several bull elephants could stand end on end and still not reach the surface. Great lazy fish inhabited the river without ever being disturbed except by annual storms and flooding. Sometimes white farms and white towns further up the river caused flooding but his uncle would avoid this by moving and waiting for the river to settle again.

These floods would bring interesting and useful objects. That is why one of the houses had a perfect picket fence and another an empty hanging basket.

Winston loved the visits to his uncle and sometimes, sitting on a wooden crate amongst the bustle and noise of Langa, it was almost too much to bear to think that he might never see that magical world again. When he was with his uncle, he could never even imagine that there was bad in the world; he could never have imagined a world like Langa.

And even though the walk was long and took a great deal of the morning, when they reached his uncle, the welcome was generous and noisy in a way that soon banished memories of the trek. And it was true that no walk went to waste. His father carried his long-hooked staff to pick prickly pears along the way. Rolling the small pears in the sand to dislodge the deadly feather thorns, his father would take his pocket knife, a long-time prize possession, and cut the thick skin away to reveal the cool sweet fruit inside.

The prickly pear bushes were hard to find but they were another import and the danger they posed to the veld was not obvious in that faraway valley. But years later from the bus, Winston would look at the huge fleshy cacti leaves with their deadly thorns lined up alongside the road as if they were about to invade and conquer the town. To his dismay, there were no other trees or bushes, only miles and miles of the thorny hostile prickly invaders, as far as the eye could see.

But when walking with his father, the hot sun on their backs, the prickly pear was a rarity — a rare jewel in a hard country where wag-'n-bietjie thorn bushes were ready to shove their white bladed thorns into unprotected skin. These bushes were easy to spot and easier to avoid. Their flowers were covered with millions of African insects and little spritely birds darted in and out of the bushes' protective cover, gathering insects and berries.

Some white men had travelled into the valley but soon found that they could not bring their electricity and telephones with them. Their vehicles foundered on the hard rocky ground and keeping the hard bushes and even harder insects at bay was a pointless battle. Then there were countless dangerous spiders and snakes, deadly and invisible to those who were not familiar with the area. In the end, those white men built their grand houses on the high ground away from the river. Isolated above, they attempted to mould the land into crops and grazing land for sheep and cows. These dirt farmers stayed away from most of the river.

Although there were some farmsteads on the most accessible parts of the river, most of the land remained inaccessible except to all but the most determined. And Mukeseli was determined, had no objection to living in a mud hut, knew how to live without electricity and other white men's necessities, and so he thrived.

Mukeseli had mules, donkeys and carts where other people had trucks and cars. The mules and donkeys had a knack for living in harsh inhospitable conditions where horses would have withered and died away. The people who lived in the camp were like the mules and donkeys. Tough and hardy and they knew things about the valley that many would never even have guessed. Winston loved listening to his cousins and their stories about adventures. He fancied he could still taste the doughy bread and sharp ginger beer that his aunt would press into his hands. He would shuffle the bread from hand to hand until it cooled, not taking his eyes off his cousins.

Mukeseli was an entrepreneur who knew how to work with the tools that he had been given. And so, he worked that magical place and carved out a life that had been more than a mere existence.

Once a week he loaded the wagon with chopped firewood and the mules and donkeys, strong and stubborn, hauled the wood out of the valley to the market and even sometimes went as far as Uitenhage itself. No motor vehicle could have achieved this result as the ever-changing road was narrow and stony with sharp, crazy bends that required dexterity and a nimbleness that only those hardy creatures possessed. In fact, sometimes the road moved and where it had been one day it was no longer the next.

This caused no dismay for Mukeseli. Winston could see him scratching his head under his hat and clicking his tongue until he found another way, and on they went.

Twelve stubborn, burly mules and donkeys, their coats shining black coal beneath their rippling muscles, straining, born to work hard like no mechanised vehicle ever could. Winston would hitch a ride perched precariously on the back of the wagon feeling like no weight at all.

Mukeseli was the most successful business man in the valley, black or white. Once a month the wood was taken to Uitenhage, sold and then for the return journey the wagon was filled with supplies. This was a vital service to people who had no transport of their own. Many said that Mukeseli was a millionaire. Winston believed it. Often, he saw his uncle with money — the only real cash he ever saw. He never saw his own father with any money at all.

The journey to Uitenhage took all morning and some of the afternoon. And after getting out of the valley there was a further, slow mule-paced journey over dusty roads that Winston found out later took a car half an hour to negotiate. Winston loved those journeys. His uncle and his two cousins laughing and talking and sharing the hard baked bread made by his aunt that morning. Then resting in the shade under the wagon while his uncle made deals and offloaded the wood.

His uncle and cousins lifted the bags of wood as if they were little bags of sticks. They laughed when Winston could hardly shift the bags from the ground. 'Come on, puny, put your back into it. I was lifting two of those when I was your age,' they teased. Overnight they stayed next to the Swartkops River on the other side from the town.

'No need to get too close to the white man,' his uncle had said before sitting in the shade and closing his eyes. They would often camp close to the Chinese wholesalers, Kin Yat and Son. Kin Yat was a rude, ancient man who played cards fiercely. It was the only time that Winston ever saw his uncle give someone else money.

But the Swartkops River was not blue and slow like the Elands River, but dark and sinister and fast and slick. The town was noisy, and Winston could not hear the night birds and mysterious little animals like he did out in the valley. He was always glad to get going the next morning.

Ornery and bad tempered, the mules too seemed to relish the journey home, their coats shining blue black in the morning sun. They were his uncle's pride and joy. It was a life of industry filled with work that brought reward and the rest was needed and relished and deserved. Sometimes Winston wished that he too could live in the valley with his uncle.

He would never mention this deeply held wish to his father, knowing as he did how very proud his father was of being the 'head boy' on the farm.

The life they had was good too and also filled with hard honest work and pride in jobs well done. Besides, his father joked, however unlikely, there was a chance that Mukeseli could be dispossessed of the property; he didn't own it after all. Much better to be in a house that was theirs and work on a farm where everyone knew where they belonged. How wrong he had been, but then Winston was not to know that nothing was secure and never would be.

Chapter 12 — Kobus Junior

The boy (Kobus just could not think of the skinny boy he knew as a young man) had easily agreed to visit the new Uitenhage home, stopping Kobus's list of inducements before they emerged.

With stalling trepidation Kobus picked up the phone, gripping it as if he could send his yearning down the line without words. He was aware of taking several fortifying breaths before dialling the number, feeling foolish and childish. After all the things he'd done in his life, difficult life-changing tasks, this simple call should not have made his heart beat and his breath come short.

At least, he thought with relief, he would not have to reveal the humiliating reasons for the move to Uitenhage and there was no cause to tell his son. Marta would never reveal the truth.

The phone was answered in English by a girl who'd called out the name Peter loudly as if she had not held the receiver away from her face before calling. The name stung Kobus's ear.

The boy, his son, had been surprisingly agreeable, something that Kobus had never had before, and it sent a warm feeling to his chest.

Tentatively he said, 'Dad, do you mind if I bring someone?' Kobus made rapid readjustments to his plan. This had never happened before. He wondered if it were the girl that had answered the phone. It was a shame as she sounded very English, but he could suffer the girl if it meant that his boy was finally coming back to him. He would put up with just about anything.

They arranged themselves like old-fashioned servants on the driveway. The lawn, he was satisfied to see, was looking a little greener — a testament to his work over the last few weeks.

Marta had manoeuvred herself so that she stood at the head of the queue and Kobus found himself pushed slightly to one side like an outsider in his own life. Then little Sissy and finally Pinkie at the back like an inadequate shadow to the family.

Marta had complained bitterly to Kobus that Pinkie was as excited by the boy's arrival as if she were his mother. Kobus had listened with half an ear, but his mind was so full of his boy that he only heard one word in every three. What cared he for women's troubles?

A few times as they waited, Marta had shooed the girl using her hands as if the maid were a dog. But Pinkie only retreated as far as the front door and then slowly edged back as if pulled by an invisible string. It became a macabre game as if Marta and the girl were putting on entertainments to pass the time.

The car port — a wooden pergola — sported a rampant purple bougainvillea which had burst into purple flower only the day before as if it too wished to be part of the celebration. A small struggling hibiscus at the end of the drive, marking the beginning of Kobus' property, bloomed with one large, magnificent orange flower. Behind them, the now almost green lawn ran up to the front door that stood ajar as if the house too welcomed the errant son.

Kobus was the first to notice the battered brown Kombi turning into the street and warned the others in a voice hoarse with anticipation. He hated that his voice did that. He turned away. His heart leapt and he would have done almost anything to banish the others into the house to savour this moment alone. It felt as if it had been a millennium since anything good had happened to him.

Marta had been sitting in the *voorkamer* all morning, hardly daring to breathe as if she thought oxygen might mysteriously drive their son away. Pinkie, installed in the kitchen, was uncharacteristically quiet as if she too was afraid of breathing. Kobus imagined her standing at the sink, still as a statue. He wished Marta would set her to work.

Earlier, when the phone had exploded into ringing, Kobus had been propelled out of his seat before Marta could move to answer it. He snatched the phone up and barked a greeting. His son's voice came tinny and echoing. 'Hey, Dad, we'll be there in two hours.' Then the line went dead. There had been no farewell, just those eight words.

The phone's dial tone made a long buzzing and Kobus slowly lowered the phone. Kobus held the phone to his ear for another minute or so as if in real conversation and he said, 'Yes, son, I will see you then.' Slowly he lowered the phone and felt childish for pretending but then he noticed that

Marta watched him like a snake, and he turned with a smile, the first smile he had given her in days.

'They will be here in two hours.' He left the room.

Now here came the battered van and his heart hammered as if he had been running all morning.

The boy, grown taller than Kobus, climbed out of the muddy van and in that act went from a boy to a man. Gangly and tall, he loped towards his mother, not sparing a glance for Kobus who noted how thin he was. Because he had nothing else to do, Kobus noticed that the boy had climbed out of the passenger side. Frowning, he realised then that the girlfriend must have been driving. He knew he was old-fashioned, had been told so often enough, but who would let a mere girl drive?

Marta was making crooning noises like a hen clucking around her chicks. The man, and Kobus could see nothing of the boy in this lanky man, bent down, kissing his mother on the cheek and was enveloped in his mother's fat hug. Marta was both crying and laughing like women did and it made Kobus unaccountably angry. He impatiently shifted, waiting to be noticed, and cleared his throat.

Kobus Junior emerged from Marta's embrace and shook his father's hand, the smile gone. '*Seun.*' To Kobus's embarrassment, his voice broke and he looked down at his own feet, hoping for a hole to open up and swallow him whole.

'Where's your friend?' Marta broke in. His smile back in place Kobus Junior embraced Pinkie who had her arms wrapped around his neck. 'Come on, Ariel, come meet the family.' That infernal English clattered like an unwanted guest. But there was real laughter in his voice as he lifted Pinkie from her feet and twirled her all around. All eyes turned to the muddy van. Ariel?

Kobus, unable to bear the sight of his son and Pinkie, the bloody maid, concentrated hard on the van as if by doing so he could eliminate the unsettling evidence of his son's affection for a mere black woman. In all his imaginings, he had not thought that it would go like this.

The first twinges of disaster hovered around Kobus and do what he might he could not change it.

A short dark curly-haired man emerged smiling into the gaps between the family.

'Ruben Ariel, sir, I've heard a lot about you.' He advanced with his hand outstretched towards Kobus. Dreaded English. Kobus, forcing a smile to his rigid face, shook hands.

Kobus would dearly have liked to ignore this new interloper but there was Kobus Junior smiling and happy and he felt — felt stuck to the tarred pathway. Marta pointedly looked back at the van but no one else emerged and even though, she still smiled at her son, a small frown had appeared.

Then there was a whirl and it emanated from Ruben, a moving, noisy force that moved from person to person.

His voice was soft and high pitched almost like a woman's, but his body was thick and solid, and all his movements were confident as if he were used to being the centre of attention. 'Where can I park the Kombi? Bearing in mind that we will be sleeping in it. The closer to the house the better.' He grinned looking from Kobus to Marta and rubbed his chin. 'I could also use a shower and a shave,' he said, ruefully, smiling now at Marta. Then he nudged Kobus Junior saying, 'You too, Pete, you look like a wild man.'

In the silence that followed he looked from face to face, Kobus did not take his eyes off his son's reddening face.

Then Marta, who had managed to translate his words, her lips moving slowly over the words, looked dismayed. Visibly drooping she spoke to her son with her back to Ruben. *'Seun, ons het kamers vir julle. Ek het die bed reg gemaak. Alles is reg.'*

Ruben laughed. 'Come on, give an Englishman a break.' He raised his hands and let them fall.

Kobus Junior frowned. 'My mother has prepared rooms in the house,' he said, and his voice was curiously flat. Like Kobus, he had always hated that whiny note in her voice when things did not go her way.

Ruben answered for them both, 'That's really lovely, Mrs J., but Pete and I have been all over in this Kombi. It's really comfortable and suits us.' He paused as if thinking and then continued. 'We've been to... oh, let me see. Namaqualand to see the daisies. We also went to Outeniqua. What a week that was! Then the Tsitsikamma. Let me tell you, I have been hugging a lot of trees.' He ticked the places off with his fingers.

'As you can see, the Kombi is very important to us. We are making unforgettable memories.' Then he smiled at Kobus Junior. A small secret smile that, had Kobus been looking away, he would not have noticed. But he had seen it and struggled to understand what it might mean.

Marta jabbed him in the ribs and Kobus hurriedly interrupted the inexhaustible flow and pointed to a place on the drive. He had learnt to pick his arguments carefully. Later, he would fix this. Later, when he would have time to think of a solid irrefutable argument to throw into the face of this loud rude man. Then Ruben could move on to his next 'memory' and leave his son with the family that had waited so long for him to return.

With Ruben carefully reversing the old muddy van into the driveway, Marta took the opportunity to usher her son into the house. But he could not be so easily borne away as he had been when little. Smilingly, he hugged Pinkie again before following his mother and clasping her hand and dragging Pinkie with him. Kobus frowned.

Kobus found himself alone in the *voorkamer* hearing voices in the kitchen. He remembered Danie once telling him that men need to let the women make a fuss, then afterwards it was easier for the men to take over and organise. That, he decided, was good advice and he settled into his favourite chair. Later he would finally get the boy to himself and that would be the time to outline some of the plans that he had so carefully made. For a brief moment, the early confidence returned. He waited.

But the stagnant hours of waiting, staring into the back garden, weighed on him like a heavy invisible hand. Then, and he couldn't help it, he began to fume and boil. He could hear the women in the kitchen fussing and the two men, their voices also high and excited. The kitchen, he fumed, was no place for a man. Why couldn't Kobus Junior just come into the *voorkamer*? Kobus poured himself a drink. That was his first mistake.

He drank quickly and noisily, not caring about the trickle of hot brandy on his chin and with a grim satisfaction eyed the stain the spilt brandy left on the counter top. Above all the chatter, one voice rose laughing and spinning stories. That voice came from the unwanted guest and by the others' silence he knew that they were all listening to him. Kobus strained, listening, and hating himself for wanting to but unable to go to them now, not after his tacit disapproval. He realised grimly that he'd put himself in the *voorkamer* on purpose and the others (certainly Marta and Kobus Junior) would know that he did it to show his opprobrium. Now he could never go to them — they must come to him, and a hollow feeling shook him into the realisation that they would not come.

His plans started to unravel around him like unpicked knitting and fell to his ankles in ruin.

At long last they did stream into the *voorkamer,* but Kobus felt no victory now that they came of their own volition. Suddenly and perversely the room felt small, and Kobus felt foolish with his empty glass and hollow thoughts.

And now that they had moved from the kitchen into Kobus's domain, it became clear to him that they had not even noticed his absence. Ruben moved to the middle of the room holding court. Several times Kobus took a breath and began to speak but Ruben spoke louder and the opportunity to interject was lost. Kobus poured another brandy and drank it neat in one swallow.

After a long rambling story about one of the places that Ruben and Kobus Junior had visited in Stellenbosch, Kobus noticed Pinkie standing in the doorway. She was openly listening and drinking in the atmosphere, her eyes gleaming and her mouth twisted into a joyful smile. Kobus frowned and wanted to reprimand and scold her but could not do so without interrupting Ruben and he felt, in an odd discomforting way, that the maid might well disobey him. He poured another brandy. Pinkie would only ever enter this room to clean, and he made a silent vow that she would understand that for the future.

Ruben had moved on to another story about university which was vaguely upsetting as it described an uninteresting and unrecognisable world. Sissie now moved closer to her brother, turning her face, like a flower to the sun, to watch his reaction. That was the moment that Kobus began to feel like an outsider in his own family.

Try as he might, Kobus could find no natural place to interrupt the garrulous Ruben and wrest back control.

Marta began to fuss and shift uncomfortably on the *rusbank.* Surely her son's shirt was dirty, she fingered the collar, and the boy gently shrugged her off. Kobus recognised what she was doing. She was, and more successfully than him, imposing herself into the conversation. Making it about her and her son.

She was not deterred by the rebuff. Surely, he could change into a clean shirt, she urged. She had a pile of new shirts, in all colours and shades, shorts, socks and underpants. Kobus pictured the pile of clothes in the room allocated to his son. They lay on the bed in neat piles that Marta lovingly stroked as if they were pets. But Kobus Junior could not be moved. His eyes were settled on Ruben with that odd little private smile fixed to his face. Even Marta could not get between the two.

Ruben's supply of stories seemed inexhaustible. He was well travelled and had seen places that Kobus had never before even given a thought to and now the brandy had started its work. He felt a little dizzy and a small ringing intruded on his mind so he could hardly hear what Ruben was saying.

Ruben spoke confidently of Europe and Israel and his wish that Pete would one day join him in these travels. Kobus had an odd, disjointed feeling and wondered briefly who Pete was until remembering that this was of course his son, his son, his precious son, but it felt as if he had stumbled into the wrong house and was now stuck and could not leave without giving offence.

He was reduced to pretending to be part of the family by being as still and silent as possible in case an unruly movement caused them to notice and throw him out into the street.

'My uncle has a kibbutz. Somewhere in Israel. I am not really sure where.' Ruben waved his arm towards the ceiling as if the kibbutz was situated in the attics.

'It's the original community living. A bit like communism or better still socialism.' Kobus winced but no one noticed. He tried to nurse his brandy. Was it his third? Or fifth? He couldn't remember, better not have another. Meanwhile the voice droned on, and Kobus finished the drink without realising.

'Everyone works for everyone else. They grow olives. My old man says that olives are the way forward. The new gold.' Ruben rubbed his hands together as if he could feel himself getting rich.

'But it's not about wealth. It's about living together and helping one another. Everything they eat on the kibbutz they grow themselves. Nothing goes to waste. It's the ultimate in living really. Pete will love it.'

He turned to Kobus. 'You would love it Mr J. It's all about…' He stopped at a loss for words, but then just as quickly began again.

'Then it's off to America. The land of opportunity.' He laughed a genuine, rich laugh and in it lay all the joy in the world.

Finally, Kobus Junior interrupted, seemingly the only one who could. 'Come on, Ruben, we've only just arrived. We can wait for more, surely. If you are not careful, you'll tell them all your stories at once and then where will we be?' Kobus marvelled at his English, so smooth and natural and hardly any Afrikaans inflection at all. Where had that boy he knew gone?

Into the silence Marta said, '*Ag* man, you boys must stay in the house. *Seun,* I've got the rooms ready for you.' She held on to her son's arm as if that way she could force her will. He said nothing.

Kobus noticed Pinkie standing inside the room, away from the door and he turned on her, his voice unnecessarily loud and harsh, the brandy driving him. '*Voetsek you*, get out of here. Go back to the kitchen where you belong.'

Then his son's voice was gentle with steel. 'No, pops.' He had not called Kobus that in years. Not since that ill-fated trip to Durban. 'Pinkie is my second mother.' He turned to his mother, her face pale now and strangely empty. 'You remember, Mom. All those times I would sit in the kitchen with Pinkie, learning how to make cookies.'

He turned to his father and then back to his mother, her face now a dark red as the blush rushed into her face. He laughed a little, but his face was serious and pale too.

'Remember that Pinkie was the one to fetch me from school. Sorry, Pinkie.' He smiled a warm smile full of apology at the woman, the only real genuine emotion that he showed. 'I made her carry my books and she never complained.' Pinkie waved her arm to refute the apology and she never took her eyes off him.

'She was always there in that kitchen, always there. Pinkie, soon you and I must catch up and you must tell me about your son and that husband of yours. I have been thinking about you, you know. Did you leave them behind in Pretoria?' He stopped himself and looked down. 'But that is for another time. Come, Ruben, let us show Pinkie the van. It is bigger than her room that she used to have in Pretoria.' And the three of them left the room and thick, slobbery silence descended on those who remained.

Kobus heard Pinkie asking if they would like her to clean the van. Kobus could not meet Marta's eyes and by the clock he could see that it was early afternoon. Soon he would have a hangover. He needed to take some aspirin.

Later, when Kobus knew that nothing he had planned for his son's visit had gone or would go according to plan, he watched the pool in glum silence. Ruben had insisted that he and Pete would *braai* so that Pinkie did not have to cook. As if Pinkie, like them, was a guest. The smell of barbecue meat began to fill the air as Marta bustled, arranging salads and plates.

As the sun set and plunged them into darkness, Kobus found that Pinkie had been invited onto the *stoep* and he began to seethe again.

Finally at midnight the two young men retired. Kobus and Marta said not one word to each other as they watched the boys out into the African night. Pinkie slipped silently away so there was nothing to do but go to sleep and hope that the morning would bring some respite.

Chapter 13 — Uitkyk

It was accepted that farming the veld would be Winston's future. He'd never questioned and never imagined another future, had never wanted anything else. Now he found it hard to imagine what that life would have been like when he looked around at brown, dusty Langa.

He would follow his father and Doda's father before that. And Winston had loved the land, the feel of it as it ran through his fingers like silk. He could not imagine any other life away from his birth right. In his wonder, Winston never thought of such concrete things as ownership and rights of possession. He'd never understood that it could all change in the blink of an eye.

It had never been explained that the land would never belong to him but that had never mattered. After all, it had never belonged to his own father or his father before him. They had lived in and around the valley for generations. It had been enough that he was on the land.

Every day, there was a new wonder in the very grasses that he stepped around, new wonders in the plants and bushes that he scoured for fruit. Doda spoke of the land in words of lilting Xhosa poetry, telling stories that all his children knew by heart. The land had been in their hearts.

Doda had not grown into a young man in the Elands River Valley, but ten miles away on the Van Staden's Reserve where delicate indigenous wild flowers grew on a peculiar swathe of land that lay in the way of annual rains. The rains that never strayed into any of the other local parts ensured that luscious vegetation grew to a brilliant green in an otherwise brown land.

Many parts of the reserve lay completely untouched by man for thousands of years. The reserve boasted the biggest collection of indigenous succulents in the world. Doda's father was not book-learned, nor did he know the botanical names, but he did love those strangely delicate plants and handled them with a sense of ownership that betrayed his deep and abiding love.

The reserve boasted a few thousand visitors every year and they counted themselves lucky to be part of the best-kept secret in Africa. In the end, most tourists chose to visit the game farms and safari parks, so looking at a flower reserve hardly featured on their to-do list. Through one of those strange quirks of government that go unnoticed for generations, the reserve received government grants and funding that allowed it to operate despite its lack of profitability.

Doda called that place home and all that lived there knew how fortunate they were.

Doda's father, who was perennially old even when Doda himself was a young man, knew about the rare flowers and cycads that grew on the reserve. He knew about the tiny insects that thrived in the loamy earth and how the brilliantined sun birds pollinated the aloes with their curved, unique beaks. He knew about the ground-cover succulents that looked so sturdy yet hid many vulnerabilities.

And it was not only the vegetation. There were many birds too. Small darting birds who built intricate nests, then reared broods of chicks in precarious yet glorious circumstances. Large birds that strode, camouflaged, through the grasses and were only visible to those who knew where to look. Angry African bees made their homes in spekboom and acacia trees and made their thick yellow honey by harvesting the veld. Doda and his brothers knew exactly where to look for them.

This tiny piece of heaven was teeming with life, most of it unseen. Doda and his brothers hardly noticed the snakes, spiders and small rodents that lived, bred and died in the landscape of their childhood.

A man of few words, he told his children stories of the *veld* by letting them handle the plants, small animals and the orange ground that bore the story of the veld. He knew where to find the fat, colourful *vygies* that the children struggled to locate. Doda never forgot that feeling of joy transmitted somehow from his father's fingers into his own via the small treasures of the reserve. And as soon as he was able, he brought his children to those plants so that they too could feel the magic of the *veld*.

The old man knew how to look for and find the succulents that could be eaten and help slake thirst when there was no water. He knew how to find leaves that could soothe burns from bites and plant burn. He always had an answer; Doda had never seen him at a loss.

Doda had eight brothers and sisters and they had only a one-roomed shack. Life was hard and there never seemed to be enough food. His mother did the best she could with the little resources that they had. She made pap in a black pot that was not big enough and shared it among her children, fairly and without argument.

There always seemed to be another baby on the way and two daughters shared the childcare, as was expected by all girls when they reached twelve. Doda grew to work hard and expect very little in return. For a long time that was good enough.

In time, Doda's sisters started families of their own and while one of them stayed in the one-roomed hut, adding another baby to the mix, most of Doda's siblings moved away.

The reserve, thousands of acres of natural wonder, needed only one man to work it and that man was Doda's father.

Doda was the last son, the fifth child and fourth surviving boy. Many little graves at the back of the hut testified to the children who had not survived. Doda felt grateful to be alive.

Doda's choices were limited, and he was a boy that had loved the land, so he looked for work as a farm labourer. In the end there was nothing else and although he dreamt of the reserve he could never go back. All his adult life, his heart ached for the reserve.

He would have liked most of all to show it to Winston, his son, who was so very like his grandfather even though they had never met. At these times of reminiscence, he would shrug and pick up his axe and walk out into the veld and use the physical farm work to beat out the pain. He understood that it was no use hankering after a life that could never be. But there was some good in life to be found on the farm and Doda got used to this other way of life and taught his son as best he could and tried not to let the sadness show through.

What Doda had inherited was the soft knowledge of the *veld*, the world of his father and that would have to be enough. The stories would continue through his bloodline, and it was the boy's only inheritance.

Mama also added her stories to the fireside narrative until they had a family legacy worth more than gold. Mama's stories were not the same as Doda's, they were the stories of great baobab trees and animal legends. They were stories of a different, wilder Africa but no less entertaining.

Doda spoke with quiet pride of his family. In those long summer evenings when the sky dropped into warm darkness, they gathered around the fire. It was a delight when Mama joined them, as she rarely did. They clamoured quietly to sit at her feet as if noise would scare her away. She told her stories only at night where all their faces were rubbed out in the dark. Mama never spoke loudly, and the children drew nearer, and they soaked it up like a rain-starved field.

She told stories about how vanity, greed and immorality were punished, and her stories involved all the plants and animals that crept in the darkness all around them.

When the biting flies got too much, Doda would light his pipe, worn through with age, and smoke some of his precious tobacco and the flies would flee before the pungent smoke. The tobacco was rolled into the ancient yellow packet and safely stowed in the pocket of his best jacket which he always wore regardless of the weather.

Lying on his back on a sweat-stained blanket, thinking of the farm and his father, Winston smiled. A little smile that faded away when he got to the memory that was stamped into his mind with a branding iron. He could not go there. He could not.

It was never his father's farm and could never be. In fact, when all was said and done, they owned nothing, not even the small mud hut. So, it was inevitable that it would all fall down like a pack of cards.

When Winston was sixteen, the farm had changed ownership. Gone was the Afrikaaner family. In came a new order, a new family. And that was when it all changed.

Chapter 14 -The Law

Uitenhage 1984

The narrowing of Kobus' world drove him, like a merciless apocalypse, back to his work. Search as he would, his recent short-lived jubilation had gone, imploded, and now his hopes and dreams lay at his feet along with the rest of his life.

At night, the face that rose and smote him was Ruben's. When he closed his eyes, he could not see the face of his son any more — the lines were blurry and faded as if his son was like the print on an old decaying newspaper. And his son only spoke to him in that voice as if everything was his fault. Sometimes the voice came with a look that made Kobus feel that it was, in fact, all his fault. That every sorry, shameful thing was his fault. And after a while he believed that they all thought that it was his fault. He could see it every day when he turned in desperation to Marta and then after that he went back to work. It shamed him, that fault, as if it were another being in the house. He wanted to shrug it off and smile and laugh and pretend that nothing had changed. But he couldn't.

The dream started at about that time as well. A dream where he would see his son fading away before his eyes. He was walking in the dream, and he was wearing a very white shirt that was the only colour in a dark tunnel. In fact, his son's head and body were blurred and faded into the darkness but he knew it was Kobus Junior. In the dream he was beset with an overriding sense of doom.

The dream started the same way every time. A feeling of dread first and then that old, familiar feeling of doom like a huge anchor pulling him down. Kobus called and although he knew that his son had heard him, the figure continued to walk. Then he got further and further away until finally he disappeared. And when he disappeared Kobus fell as if from a great height and realised, achingly, that it was he who needed his son to turn and catch him. But the man never did stop.

At the end of the dream, he would wake — every time just before he reached the ground — and it would take many long minutes before he could properly fill his lungs. Marta said, 'Go back to sleep,' and irritably turned away, drawing the blankets around her cold shoulders.

Slowly the sweat would dry in the dark early hours and his galloping heart would slow. Then his heart felt as if it were broken. On those nights when the dream came, he could never return to sleep, and he would toss and turn. In the morning he rose wearily, more tired than when he went to bed. On those mornings it was a relief to get into his *bakkie* and take the short drive to his new police station.

It was a relief to throw himself into his daily routine of inane petty law cases. In those clinic offices he could finally clear his mind and stop thinking about the problem of Ruben. Stop his mind from whirling round and round.

Strangely it helped to see the old mundane laws, the ones he'd forgotten about for so long. The same stupid robberies and pointless muggings. It helped that his new colleagues knew nothing about that interloper Ruben. Here at work, the loud and compelling Ruben could be banished. When he was at home there was nothing, he could do to shut out Ruben. The name echoed around his head on an endless loop. Ruben. Ruben. Ruben.

To his everlasting frustration, though, when it was time to return home Kobus would feel all the old hopeless enthusiasm returned. A kind of hopeless yearning that this time it would be different. This time he would miraculously find some time alone with his son. That he would somehow find the words and even say them. Articulate that, until now, hopeless ambition of the son and father working together. It would take the nightmare to dash all those dreams to smithereens.

Sometimes on the journey home, anger would burst through like machine gun fire, and it was all he could do to hold on to the steering wheel and not break out in a flame.

He could even indulge his impotent rage in wild imaginings. Seizing and yanking a sleepy Ruben out of the van and doing what? And then the crushing blow of the truth. His boy was not the kind of man that he had imagined. His boy was not the kind of man who would happily live alongside his father in a place like Uitenhage.

There, the naked truth. That should have been the end of it, but it wasn't.

Even as these truths seeped into his mind and the crushing defeat beat him low, he clung to a small irrational hope. After all, if he did not, then he would have to admit that he was finally all alone and that he could not do. There was the army, he thought, clinging to this as if in a fast-moving river with only a rock to cling to. His son could not avoid that. The army that had so spectacularly failed him would not do so with his son. His mind, a quivering cowed animal did not think, would not think, of his own days in the army. It would think instead of Kobus Junior and in the early hours of the morning with his heart knocking violently against his ribs he used thoughts of the army to quell and subdue his growing panic.

This was not a new thing, this clinging to his son who represented, he realised, a second chance. A chance for Kobus to start all over again. And this time it would work. He was older now, wiser and his son would benefit from that wisdom. Did he not have a right as a father?

Kobus had no idea that on the mornings after the nightmare when he entered the police station, a small grubby affair in downtown Uitenhage, his face registered a grim, grey look. An unapproachable look that frightened his new subordinates. There were not many of them, but he would have been surprised and somewhat pleased to learn that they were afraid of him. They took it in turns to draw straws; the loser had to go into his office with the warrants from the day before and the police business of the present day.

There were no large briefings in this tiny, police station. In fact, it was nothing like the dubbed American police dramas that they all watched on TV. *Kojak*, a new popular drama that Kobus and his friends in Pretoria had sneered at, did not translate well into Afrikaans. A policeman with a lollipop seemed ludicrous to Kobus.

This was a place that dealt with small crimes, small nothings that could be shuffled like a deck of cards and dealt out among duty officers who could quickly disappear onto the stuffy streets of Uitenhage.

Kobus became used to the small pettiness of it all and surrounded himself with files and paperwork which allowed him to push, with grim determination, thoughts of Kobus Junior, Ruben and his own crippling disappointment out of his mind.

There was one morning which stuck in his mind because it had rained the night before, a rare occurrence, and the dampness, fast fading in the heat, had given the streets a temporary fresh feel. He suddenly realised his son had been avoiding him. This realisation caused him to see all the little ruses that his son used. He caught the flash of a leg leaving the room as he entered. Then of course the boy was never awake in the morning when he went to work and he found excuses to be out at night, often only returning to the house very late.

And in that moment, sitting at his desk, he realised that he needed a confrontation. He, Kobus Senior, was good at confrontation. That confrontation would be called duty and Kobus Junior could no longer evade his duty. All at once his head cleared and he knew what to do.

He would reclaim his son and the boy would take his rightful place in the family and Kobus would be restored. Ruben could go hang. It was all so simple really and he was surprised at his own timidity.

It was, after all, the law that all young white men in South Africa were conscripted to the army. No excuses.

That was the morning he smiled and finally relaxed. He would not allow his mind to dwell on details. He would not think about how it would work in practise. He only knew that he was desperate to begin, and he would begin with the army and once he had a starting point all of those stupid doubts could be cast aside.

He forgot his own horror because the past was jammed deep down into a place that he never went, misgivings he never gave a thought to. He could never return to those horrible truths. At times, Kobus even imagined that he could feel the lifting of all the hurt that had built and accumulated through years of bitter disappointment. At last, he would be able to go back into the fold of his own family and the arms of those old expectations. Such was his daydreaming that he could almost feel the old tensions dripping away and his step felt light once again.

So it was that the police station, uninviting and sterile, became a place of solace for Kobus. His silent wife could not reach him with her reproaches and her eyes could not tell of her lost son. In the police station, all of his irritation at his wife was lifted and put down somewhere out of sight like dirty linen.

Many times, in their worst arguments about Kobus Junior, he had sensed an unkind triumph in her looks, quickly turned away. But he knew his wife was pleased that there was a rift between him and their son. That look spoke of victory and he hated her for it.

He felt her hand in all the memories of Kobus Junior's school days. Those days were clouded by the shock of reading a school report left on the *voorkamer* dining table. Reading the report, he was struck that this was the first time he'd ever seen a report. This feeling was followed by a sense of foreboding. What had been hidden from him? He slit open the envelope using his nail.

There it was — Literature, Art and even Music and right at the bottom with the lowest marks in Mathematics. Just above Mathematics was Physical Education and the teacher had written: *Kobus Junior should try to join in more. He will take himself out of sporting events, especially team games.* He threw the report down on the table as if it were infected and went in search of his wife.

He could hardly trust his own voice and stood in the doorway of the kitchen and watched her while she spoke to Pinkie, and they prepared food at the sink. He spat the words, 'So how long have you been hiding those school reports from me? I see it's all the girlie subjects that he's good at.' His voice shook slightly but it was hard, and brittle and he was pleased at the threatening note.

Pinkie scurried from the kitchen, quickly drying her hands on a kitchen towel, her head down, her feet soundless.

Marta too dried her hands and turned slowly to face him. No contrition, no shame, nothing in her face.

'You should be proud of your son. He is the number one student at that school.'

'I'm not surprised he's the best student — he is the only student who is doing these… what is Literature anyway?'

She looked away — out of the window but her eyes were filmy as if she were in a dream. He thrust his hands, clenched fists, into his pockets to prevent himself from strangling her.

'They want him to go to university in Cape Town.'

'Like hell they do. He has to stop. What do they want? To turn him into a *sissie*?' Then he sputtered and stopped because he did not know what else to say. That made him angry because suddenly he was unsure, and nothing made any sense. Marta was miles away from him and she was so far away that even though he stretched and stretched his memory he could not remember how it had ended that day.

From then on, Marta and Kobus only ever argued about their son. One memorable argument had been on a windy Saturday morning. The air was crisp, bitter and brittle from the rain the night before. Kobus had wanted to join his work colleagues for a rugby match. He often did this; it was not unusual. It was also one of the few times that he had ever been close to his own father. The rough justice of the battle for the ball which meant that almost anything was possible and the brief approval that he felt emanating from his father had felt like a strange mixture of magic and heaven. In amongst those memories, he would like to have dropped his own son and after that wretched report, here seemed a perfect opportunity.

After a few enquiries, he found a small rugby club on the outskirts of Pretoria and enrolled the boy for the season. He phoned Marta from the station. It felt good to be doing something and it was good too to present Marta with a *fait accompli*.

The boy had already gone to his room when he returned from work and because he could no longer contain his excitement he ran up to the boy's room. Marta frowned and followed him slowly up the stairs, but he stopped her and said, 'Let me, for once, talk to the boy without you mothering him.'

Marta shook her head and defied him with words that she'd never used before. Words that made him stop and frown and shake his head in disbelief.

'I forbid it. He is not a hard boy; he can't be expected to play rugby with those boys. I've seen them and he will be hurt. I forbid it,' she repeated. Kobus, not accustomed to being forbidden anything, let alone in his own home, could hardly spit out the words.

'Nonsense, woman, I will not have this boy growing up to be a *moffie!*' And when she looked at him blankly like a huge cow. 'Like one of those men who act like women and then go with other men. A *moffie!*' He shouted sure his face was red. But shouting was all he knew as if the loud words would help her to a greater understanding. He was fighting now for his supremacy over the boy.

127

The shock ran up her neck and into her face in a rising tide of scarlet.

'Our boy is not like that,' she spluttered, and her voice was dangerously quiet. 'You think that a man is made through fighting, killing things and being a thug. Kobus is a sweet boy and just because he's not rough like other boys you can't leave him alone.' She took a breath and stared at him, right in the eye. 'He's not a…' She hesitated over the word but then in a rush, spat, '*Moffie!*' She stamped her foot. 'He's not a *moffie*. He's not!' Her face was all red now and shiny. Then she turned her back on him. He knew that she hated it when her face turned red. He would very much have liked to take the boiling pot of goo that bubbled on the stove and pour it over her head but instead he turned and stalked up the remaining stairs to this son's bedroom.

The boy had been reading quietly and appeared not to have heard the altercation on the stairs. This was one of his powers — the ability to eliminate his parents from his small world. But Marta had spoken through gritted teeth so that it was Kobus who shouted and therefore Kobus who engaged in arguments and it was Kobus the boy was afraid of.

The boy had not seemed unhappy to see him and Kobus sat on the bed and the room smelled a little stale and unpleasant. He tried a careless shrug, but the boy did not look up from his book even though his father never came into his room. A strange unidentifiable feeling overcame him which was something that always happened to him when he got close to the boy.

Kobus cleared his throat and the boy looked up from the book but kept his finger on the page where he'd been reading. He did not ask the boy what he was reading, although he could have and later wished that he had. He did not ask the boy anything at all and the silence grew until it filled the room like a great oppressive cloud. He was awkward and clumsy with his own son as if the boy would somehow crack down the middle and he would be hollow inside.

All of Kobus' plans had been for nought because in the end the boy had been ill on the next day. Not something that Marta had cooked up to help but Kobus had felt the sting of rejection, nevertheless. Honest to goodness sickness did nothing to dull his utter loneliness as he sat on the stands and watched the other boys play rugby, his dreams of a relationship with his son in tatters around his feet like the autumn leaves blown into the spectator stands. The laughter of other families mocked him and made him feel even lonelier. Somehow too, the childhood ailment had meant that the boy had never got to play rugby and Kobus let the ambition slip quietly away.

After the rugby there had been other attempts by Kobus to insert himself into the boy's life, but these had been half-hearted, and in the end, it was better to give up.

Kobus had been ready to forgive all of that when his son had returned, but nothing had worked out the way that he thought it would. Instead, Ruben had come, and this had thrown everything into the air and his son was further away than ever.

Chapter 15 — Farming

Barend Daniels had finally found his true love. The Elands River Valley farm answered to something deep inside, something that he hadn't realised that he wanted or even needed. He soon grew to love the farm almost as much as Doda and Winston. It did not seem in the least bit odd that the place, arid and hopeless, had wriggled into his soul and he could now never imagine living anywhere else.

Doda, silent and grave, listened to the white man and heard the unmistakable devotion to the farm. And Doda was such a patient, non-intrusive teacher that soon Daniels was looking at the land with the same deference that Doda and his father before had done.

First, he showed Daniels the surprisingly rich, loamy soil that lived deep under the hard, dry crust of clay. After that they moved on to the surrounding brush *veld*, a never-ending grey, green smudge running away to the blue, black hills. Doda stooped and picked up a handful of gravel and slowly picked out the seeds and insects and Daniels was captivated. Then, they moved on to the deep cleft that ran between the two mountains that stood like sentinels at the back of the house. In that *kloof* lived cycads and ferns that Daniels remembered seeing in biblical drawings as a small boy.

Finally, they climbed the mountains rising to look down on the farm and then over the entire valley with the Elands River meandering in the distance. The wind was hot and warm and to Daniels' surprise there rose further mountains without end on the other side. Here at the top grew stunning protea bushes. Large, majestic blooms on plain bushes turned boldly to the sun, their black velvet tips impervious to the hot wind. Then groups of bushes with yellow pincushion flowers, bright and ecstatic. Further still, glistening in the distant haze, a purple and pink patch of flowers called watsonia. The boys picked handfuls of the lily-like flowers for their mother and Daniels knew then that he had indeed found paradise in the most unlikely of places.

Doda and Winston dug a vegetable garden and although at first it appeared unpromising, yellow and grey as it was, it soon yielded beans and carrots and tomatoes and puny lettuce soon wilting in the heat. Then they added beetroot and spinach, bold orange pumpkin and big creamy potatoes. For the first time Doda and Winston knew their land to be plentiful and generous. Doda had only to ask for the seed and they would appear beside his tin mug where he drank his morning coffee outside the kitchen. For a while life was good, better than it had ever been. Daniels was not the only one living in a paradise.

Daniels found that the house was small but neatly presented in a bright white that contrasted with the thick brown thatch that never quite reached a dark black. The hot African sun bleached everything and even the thatch gave up its dark lustre. Doda joked that the only thing that the sun did not rob of its colour was them. The thatch grew in the surrounding veld, dominating the natural grasses that peaked out like small, frightened children through the thick stems of straw.

At the back door which Mama used for entry was a small, paved area that was accessed through a little wrought iron gate and down two misshapen concrete steps that had set before they could be moulded into the right shape.

The kitchen led on to a small bathroom and toilet to the left and then on into a *voorkamer* on the right. Doda had never penetrated as far as the *voorkamer* and had only even been in the kitchen on one memorable day.

That was the day that a Cape Cobra, menacing and hissing in hateful terror, had slipped through the open kitchen door and become bewildered and lost in the unfamiliarity of the spitting kitchen.

Mama had edged around the small kitchen clinging to the walls and cupboards, not taking her eyes from the creature. Of all her terrors, she feared the cobra the most. Everything she did was concentrated on the effort it took to close the door to the *voorkamer* and then leave the kitchen without making a noise.

Slowly and with a trembling arm she closed the *voorkamer* door where the four white boys played most mornings. She put her back to the door. The boys were immediately attracted by the unusual occurrence of the kitchen being denied to them. Mama, unaware that she was doing so, had begun to make a high keening noise. The small, white boys were inquisitive and fearless, not yet at an age where they understood the real danger posed by the cobra in the kitchen.

Mama later said that she had been standing thus for hours until Doda, alarmed by his wife's wailing, arrived. Doda had armed himself with a spade. Only once before had he heard his wife make such a noise and that had been when a snake was about to strike at their blind son. Winston, a strong, wiry eleven-year-old, warned to stay back, nevertheless came too.

The snake, now driven mad with fear and in a foreign environment, slithered with dangerous power on the unfamiliar linoleum. It blindly licked at the air and then, to Mama's horror, stood as tall as it could, its brilliantined hood open, swaying as if in a breeze.

The cobra, perhaps sensing its own perilous position, came forward to attack. Doda calmly opened the bottom half of the stable door that led to the kitchen — the top half was only ever closed at night — and tiptoed into the kitchen. Winston, his eyes huge, held his breath even while he admired his father's bravery. While talking to his friends and siblings, he would often brag of disposing snakes such as this but suddenly faced with the deadliest of them all his bowels turned to water, and he could hardly move.

The snake was quick like water running through hands, but Doda was sure and bold and in moments he struck with the spade and the snake was disabled, its head under the blade and its elastic body winding up the shaft of the spade in its death throes. Mama and Winston stood in appalled silence while Doda applied all of his weight to the spade, and they waited for the snake to go slack.

Finally, the snake capitulated, and its once glorious hood turned limp and the bright hot colours faded. There was a clattering at the living room door and the four white boys spilled into the kitchen. Their cries of glee and clamour made Winston turn away. Doda and Mama had no answering smiles for the boys.

The boys wanted to keep the snake and they probably would have but for the intervention of their mother on her return that evening.

Daniels was less sanguine about the death of the snake. He showed Doda an anti-venom kit — ancient in a battered tin. Opening it, he revealed a large syringe besides which lay tiny phials. He explained that the serum could be injected should anyone be bitten by a snake. Only Winston knew that his father was not listening.

Then came the only time that Doda and Daniels disagreed. Daniels on first seeing the snake and listening to his boys' pleadings to be allowed to keep the snake and their requests to be photographed holding it, turned to Doda.

'I want you to understand that I do not want snakes killed on this property.'

'*Ja, baas.*' Doda nodded, not understanding. Something in the black man's demeanour seemed to irk Daniels. Something that Doda had never been seen before, not in this white man.

'I mean it. If you see a snake you should try to get it away from everyone and let it go into the mountain.' He waved vaguely at the mountain. Doda said nothing.

'We can't just go around willy-nilly killing these creatures. They are our natural heritage.' His voice had risen and Doda's head got lower.

Winston felt the first stirrings of anger. Why did his father not explain how dangerous snakes were? Why did he not tell of his cousin Thabo who had died at six when he unwittingly stood on a snake? Why did he not explain about the snake standing in the kitchen ready to strike? Why did he not speak of the boys in the *voorkamer*? But Doda said none of those things and neither did Winston. Then Mrs Daniels took her husband by the arm, and they went with the boys to bury the snake.

Doda and Winston never spoke of the incident again.

The house had an added attachment in the form of a garage. Daniels did not often park his car in the garage and like a lot of these spaces it was filled with random tools and other antique treasures that had not seen the light of day for many years. Some mornings Doda would be asked to go through the garage with his rusty knobkerrie, the stout fighting stick he always carried, and rustle out tarantulas and mountain adders. A small shed opened out of the garage and also onto the side of the house and that was where Doda kept a few ancient hand tools. There was an old spade that had seen many hours of toil and an old shovel plus a selection of rusty crowbars for the excavation jobs of clearing the hard red clay which acted as the top layer guarding the loamy rich undersoil. More sophisticated tools had never been made available to Doda.

Daniels was the first white man who understood more tools were needed. He was the first to understand that the African *veld* would not be tamed unless he could procure the right tools. Daniels, with a background in engineering, had found exactly the right challenge that appealed to his talents. He began to haunt the local farm sales and auctions. He searched and found all of the things that Doda so badly needed to turn the farm into something that resembled a success.

Daniels found a local auction called Fitches Corner Sales, a piece of farmland given over to the monthly business of selling cattle, sheep and sometimes even horses and smaller farm livestock. Once the animals had been sold the real business that interested Daniels would begin. The viewing and purchasing of farm equipment — some of which was almost brand new. So, Daniels' big vanity project began.

Sometimes, if he were lucky, Daniels would be able to bid for machinery that he had always coveted with hardly any competition.

The auction site boasted an open-sided van that sold teas, coffees and *koeksisters* dripping with fat and sugar. The boys loved the auction where they could roam amongst the animals and poke around in boxes of miscellaneous tools without rebuke.

Stronger drinks were available at the bar housed in an old outbuilding with little tables and uncomfortable chairs and this was where lonely, isolated farmers would sit and talk. This was not a place that Daniels frequented. The old farmers, many of them with broken, fractured English, looked on the *rooinek* with distrust and even sometimes with hatred. In this place, Daniels was almost as much of an outsider as Doda was.

Most of all Daniels liked the unexpected surprise of finding something that was not listed on the auctioneer's list. Boxes of useless nuts and bolts that seemed to be recycled month after month with a new farmer buying them every week only to return the box the next month. But these boxes could sometimes yield up an important treasure. Something that the farm desperately needed.

The many hours of trolling through boxes were a place where Daniels could escape from his city life and dream of becoming a full-time farmer.

Doda had hesitantly explained, after the shock of finding himself being asked, that the area was very good for growing *mealies*. A crop that needed many hectares and little water. Without any expectations he was surprised when Daniels gave him a copy of *The Farmers Weekly* and exclaimed, 'You are right. It's in there,' leaning down to the smaller man and touching the cover of the magazine. '*Mealies*, it is. See it's at the beginning. It says corn is the way forward.' He laughed and added, 'Corn is the new gold.' Doda stared woodenly at the magazine dangling from his hand. Daniels frowned and it never occurred to him that Doda could not read. Winston in the shadows felt a deep and abiding shame and later that night he threw the magazine on the fire.

Daniels was soon to redeem himself by buying a tractor. A big red tractor that looked like it breathed fire. It was so shiny and new that Doda could hardly bring himself to climb into it when invited. Doda wondered how he would ever be able to use this toy on the farm. But the tractor's attraction soon became too much to resist and after a while Doda became as delighted with the tractor as Daniels himself.

Doda recognised that he would need to master the new machine and as soon as he did, for a man who had never driven a car and could count his journeys in a car on one hand, it became a source of great pride, immediately elevating him to God-like status once again in Winston's eyes. Even his uncle Mukeseli only drove donkeys and mules.

The tractor, lovingly cleaned by Winston and, not without protest, sometimes even by his sisters, brought with it various mysterious attachments to plough and cut and dig and plant. The ploughs were huge and looked like excavated monsters, their teeth bloody orange from the clay soil.

The ploughs, with their sharp teeth, bit into the recalcitrant earth and soon Doda had hectares of *mealies* strong and tall growing towards the bright sun, willingly yielding up their shiny yellow fruits. Daniels was on his way to being a real farmer.

The tractor also brought unwanted visitors. Neighbours ostensibly eager to see the new equipment and then realising that they too would like such useful machines themselves and beginning to covet Daniels' possessions. Particularly popular was the new John Deere Rotavator, an expensive machine that was the envy of all the farmers in the valley.

Thienus van der Merwe, the biggest and most successful farmer who had never invested in machinery felt personally affronted that this *rooinek Engelsman* could have such a machine. Thienus considered himself a real farmer. Unlike Daniels, he did not work in the city. He farmed and his old broken-down tractors that had to be cajoled by a canny old hand were now an embarrassment. Not because they were old but because they were exposed by a *rooinek* with too much money. Thienus could envisage the clumsy *Engelsman*, his neck and arms going bright red in the sun, standing amongst his tall crops. He felt an unreasonable sense of rage that such a novice could be so successful.

Whenever he saw his own farm hand — an ancient, coloured man who was rumoured to have served in the Second World War in Alamein — he wanted to kick something. And he usually did. Thienus surprised himself at being in a position to covet anything at all from the hopeless *rooinek.*

Not being a man for introspection and furthermore, being bitter and scornful, Thienus thought only of ways that he could deprive Daniels of the rotavator.

His own father, a gruff white-haired man, was a successful CEO of a large, international company in Port Elizabeth. He had for many years denigrated his son, and Thienus was now determined that he too would show both his father and the *rooinek* what a proper farmer looked like. It never once occurred to him that he might buy his own machine. Not even when he'd had the foresight to marry well — a daughter of a minor minister in government. The minister might have been minor, but he was important. He was, after all, the minister for rural affairs and farming.

When Thienus stood on his own *stoep* while the servants *braaied* on the lawn and scurried around the dinner table, he was pleased with his life. With his family connections he did not have to prove himself. He need never think of all the vast land holdings and sheep that he owned. He need never think of the fact that even with all these trappings of what looked like a successful farming venture, his father still supported him. A fact that his father never neglected to mention whenever he came to visit.

But then Daniels had arrived in the valley. A minor *Engelsman* a *Rooinek* to boot. Thienus had done the only thing he could. He ignored him. But then his hectares of *mealies* became a constant reproach to Thienus. He, after all, had never in all his life ever grown a thing. He decided that he too would use the rotavator. After all, he reasoned, Daniels was finished with it. He had his *mielies* and he, Thienus van der Merwe, could surely borrow the machine for a few days.

That Daniels would not be happy with that arrangement never occurred to Thienus. Surely a part-time farmer such as Daniels could not begrudge his white neighbour, his superior white neighbour, an essential tool. Thienus could trace his family all the way back to the *voortrekkers* when the original van der Merwe's had negotiated with the heathen Xhosa for land. He supposed that negotiation was a generous word. Most kaffirs did not understand the art of negotiation and besides the land was never owned by any of them and never had been.

Borrowing the rotavator had two strands. It allowed Thienus' labourers to finally cultivate his land properly and it punished Daniels for allowing his kaffir so much liberty. Getting the boy a new tractor, and then taking orders from him was too much. Besides, if he let a kaffir use the equipment, he could hardly refuse a white neighbour, could he?

Chapter 16 — The Police Station

Uitenhage 1984

It could only have been the isolation and intense feeling of being overwhelmed that made Kobus return to the past. A past that seemed devoid of anything worth remembering. His other bewildering feelings of loss drove him deeper and deeper into himself. The loss was wrapped in unfettered and unnamed rejection. It was all so unfamiliar, and he knew no way to seek help. He felt trapped in a labyrinth of despair with no way out.

While preserving a robotic exterior that mimicked the life of a real policeman, he yearned desperately to be freed from it all. In the day-to-day minutiae of the Uitenhage Police Station, his tumultuous mind churned over with confused feelings that he hardly recognised. Yet he knew that there were things he had done, terrible, bad things and that there could never be any relief. He could never cauterise his mind of those bad things which surely would be called much worse by the victims. From those thoughts, his mind, like a timid night creature, hid in the shadows and refused to come out into the light.

The police station, low and squat like a particularly unattractive tramp, was painted a fading blue that had been jaded even at its first painting. The building emitted an air of despair that melded exactly with Kobus's feelings of loss and confusion.

In an effort to preserve his superiority, he had reserved a parking space for himself in front of the building, his name and rank neatly displayed on a small sturdy sign. Soon, far too soon, he had drifted into a familiar routine of arriving early to face a day with little to occupy himself and even less to do.

The crimes that the police force in this tiny town had to process every day were of little concern to Kobus. He struggled with the petty robberies and assaults, looking for a bigger mission that he had so long embraced and now craved. He followed the same path to work every day, traversing the narrow neglected concrete paving with fading hopeless agapanthus, blue and spindly on either side. They filled him with an inexplicable hopeless despair. He supposed someone cared for them and mowed the brown, listless lawn. Their very sparseness and spindly growth seemed to Kobus to indicate that they too had little desire to be there.

Opening the door revealed a dim, grim interior with a high counter that separated the receptionist, Yvonne, from the stream of bewildered populace reporting crimes. Also, by a strange quirk this was the reception desk for those appointed to take their driving tests. No attempt had been made to adorn the small space and no attempt had been made to separate people reporting crimes and driving test applicants.

The walls dripped institutional grey and were bare except for a very old notice board that displayed long out-of-date posters warning all visitors of the dangers of pickpockets, night-time walking and stranger danger. One of the notices with large red letters capitalised to emphasise the imperative *GEVAAR!* was so old that the danger it wished to warn of was now faded and unreadable. Someone had written below in black biro *SWART* with a picture of a black man.

There were small, disinterested posters advertising the need to be on the lookout for named dangerous criminals including artist impressions of the wanted men and women. They all looked the same to Kobus and he could not be certain that these flotsam and jetsam were in fact still wanted or apprehended and no longer posed a danger. The notice board was always the first thing that Kobus saw when entering the room so that he made yet another mental note to do something about it. He could, he'd been assured, enter through the back way but he preferred this way, bleak as it was.

The back entrance was through an area that was utterly depressing to Kobus. Bleak and flooded with the dark effluence of waste, it reminded him of how far he'd fallen. The air was pungent with the smell of bins and urine and something else unidentifiable but decidedly vile. Once in the building he would have to pass through the corridor with the holding cell and the occupants. They were best avoided.

The front way at least offered him the possibility of meeting the night staff, if they had not already left, and often the friendly face of Yvonne, a small yet welcome comfort.

Sometimes too there were young men and women, pale and shifting in their seats, testament to their nervous apprehension about their driving tests. At least it meant that there were people present to stay the feeling of loneliness that threatened to overwhelm him. With these strangers he could cloak himself with the delusion that there were people around that saw him even though many of them looked right through him. He felt often that he was a ghost in his own life.

There was a small innocuous door behind the high counter, and it was the entrance to the rest of the station. The door was protected by a code to imply a security that was absent from the rest of the building. Through the door was another small office where the intractable Ursula waged war on paperwork. Ursula was as unfriendly as Yvonne was friendly.

Through that door there was a large room that was referred to as the precinct where the police officers gathered. There were three large desks and each desk held two police officers. There were phones and folders and on one of the desks a new computer — big and bulky and neglected. All the desks sported wire baskets, and all were spilling over with papers. There were pen holders filled with blunt pencils and pens and the phones rang apologetically and only occasionally. It was surprisingly subdued, and Kobus began to feel the new feeling of lethargy as it spread up his legs invading his body.

Posters and cabinets vied for space against the dull grey walls and haphazard wheeled swivel chairs scattered around the floor space. Some of the chairs looked as if a police officer had dashed away on an emergency leaving the chair swivelling in his wake. The room was not carpeted so his shoes squeaked shrilly as he tracked his way to his small office.

At the back of the room, another corridor led to the holding cells and if the door was not closed the occupants of the office could clearly hear the prisoner's complaints. The door was usually kept tightly shut to avoid prisoners and officers hearing one another. Next to this corridor was Kobus' office.

His office was no different from the rest of the station. He had made no attempt to make it his own. The previous occupant had left no evidence of his tenure. A bald desk, old enough to bear witness to etchings of doodling boredom, and a chair were left as if by mistake for Kobus to make of what he would. Two battered filing cabinets, tall and inscrutable, occupied the space next to the window which opened onto a tiny section of lost brown grass.

Lately a strange inertia had settled over him and although he intended to empty the drawers and the filing cabinets he had yet to start on those tasks. He knew without looking that there would be paperwork dating back to the 70s and it filled him with a sense of futility. Those papers were so meaningless and irrelevant that often he caught himself imagining driving into the *veld* and blowing them up with Semtex.

Most mornings there were some mundane papers to be signed and even discussed with the team, but they were so inane that Kobus suspected that a baboon could have done it. There had, of course, been police business and he conducted those tasks himself with competence. He suspected that the officers, except for *klein* Jannie, poked fun at him. He'd caught the tail end of some jeering talk about his manner of staying in his office. It was true he hardly ever left his office. And he didn't care enough to rebuke the officers.

There was once a time when he would have riled at such talk. Officers beneath him would quail. Not any more. He found that the condemnation of his own force no longer had the power to hurt him or even force him into action. He found that the position that most suited him was to slump in his chair and put his feet on the desk. He found a perverse kind of pleasure in the childish act. Also, he was not the first person to do that as there were definite marks where feet had been before. When he first noticed it, he had thought that it was his own feet that had made the marks but then he saw that they were different and that somehow gave him permission to indulge himself.

In this position, many hours would mysteriously leak away. On looking at his watch, he would be surprised to find that it was time to go home. Whole days would pass in this way. He did not sleep because his mind went away, and he was reluctant to bring it back. That this was not a dignified way to spend the day troubled him not at all. What troubled him more was that his mind went to the past and no matter what he did he could not stop it. He remembered his old grandfather — a formidable shambles of a man — who spent his days glumly in the past so that his children and grandchildren stopped visiting him. Kobus wondered if he was becoming like that old man.

Lately Kobus' thoughts were returning to his own parents. It still rankled that he had never recovered his parents' esteem. He examined these thoughts closely, like running his tongue over a sore tooth — gingerly and carefully.

His father had been scornful of the police, a view he had held all his life, and he had never accepted that it was a career equal to that of joining the army. No matter how much Kobus tried to persuade, and he was enthusiastic then, with youth on his side and a zeal for approval. The old man shook his head and refused to be persuaded.

Then when he had actually joined the police, the old man had remarked on one unkind day that his youngest son was indeed a failure. Nothing and no one could ever change his mind. Kobus never stopped yearning for parental approval with a hopeless, childish kind of desperation that left him with a corroded sense of despair. Not even the halcyon days of the A-team had been enough to convert his father.

He felt the loss of his parents' support more than he should have, and his success in the police force felt hollow and was never as great as that of his brothers in the army. Of course, it went without saying that he failed to eclipse the careers of his own father and his grandfather before that.

Now, sitting in his little grey office he faced the truth; he would never achieve the regard that he ached for.

When he could, he skipped away from these morose thoughts and returned to his own son. Never once did he recognise those old family inherited pressures now directed towards his own son. How could he think of himself as a copy of his own father, wrapped up as he was in his own grief?

Now all he wanted was for his own son to rise up and to fill the void. All of Kobus's thoughts and energies now turned in that direction.

Kobus shifted in his chair, feeling the blue shirt peeling from his back where it had become damp in the heat, and tried to contemplate the past without regret. For the first time in his life, he longed for someone who could share the burden. Something to replace the loss of the A-team. Someone to replace Danie, who with all of his shortcomings, had a one-track determination that had supported Kobus's frail inner world and filled it with confidence. A confidence that had fled as soon as he was removed from Pretoria.

All of these feelings became a great deal worse because, in the way of women, Marta failed to understand his deep-seated hurt. She had held on to the injustice of being made to move from her home, her friends and ultimately her family and children. It had never occurred to Kobus in all his long years of marriage that the feelings that he could hardly articulate himself were not apparent to Marta.

It had appeared as a sign from heaven, made all the more poignant because he was not sure of the existence of heaven, that his son had responded so positively to the request to visit. It seemed divine and preordained that his son would sweep away all of the past. His son, in becoming a man, had restored Kobus, for a short while at least, to a place of success and happiness.

Sitting in his office and pondering as he was, Kobus came up with an idea. He would bring his son to the precinct and show him around and although the place was not glorious like he wanted it to be, the boy would come with new eyes and a new soul. The more he thought of the idea, the more he liked it.

Gradually his thoughts took on a more active pattern and he began to devise ways of separating his son from Ruben and bringing him into the station. He would enlist Yvonne and *klein* Jannie. That made him think of the new man with more interest. Perhaps the young man could befriend his son. This, like no other task, imbued him with a new energy. Finally, he was able to get out of his office and the Uitenhage police force was injected with a new energy.

The old lethargy fell away before his great masterplan and Kobus began once again to hope.

Chapter 17 — A Clash

All the local farmers were envious of the Daniels. Uitkyk, they said, had an endless water source running down the *kloof* and, despite almost perpetual droughts, it never dried up. It bubbled up from deep under the ground, clean and bright like the sweetest nectar. Emerald coloured water creating an emerald, green paradise in a sea of brown.

The old brown Uitkyk lawn sprang to life running from the sloping front right up to the plain white house and playfully disappeared around the side and out to the back.

Doda worked long and hard in this strange master's garden even though there seemed to be no earthly use for it. Doda liked the vegetable garden and set all of his children to work in it. But the garden was strangely captivating and despite himself he liked the new style of gardening.

Only he and Mrs Daniels worked in the garden. He loved the huge red hibiscus flowers that bowed their heads to the ground in the heat but stood up at dawn and dusk like revived dancers. Never had he seen anything so preciously exotic and when Mrs Daniels told him that they came from India he thought that India must indeed be the most beautiful place on earth.

He tended carefully and softly to the golden heads of the creeper that grew up onto the *stoep* and crawled under the eaves. The creeper shone brighter than the sun and little birds with curved intricate beaks came to feed and flit between the flowers, hardly bigger than the bees.

Mrs Daniels produced many more plants until the garden was vibrant with scented glory. Bold roses that Doda learnt were greedy for water and manure and hid their beauty in delicate flowers armed with thorns. Then there was the bush with three different-coloured flowers that smelled so sweet that it made Doda sneeze.

Doda loved the unorganised symmetry of the plants. And then he discovered his own country in the strelitzia with its magnificent bird-like flower in orange and blue like wax. The cannas with their yellows and oranges and reds that Mrs Daniels did not like. Doda reluctantly dug them up, but they always returned like determined relatives refusing to be repulsed. Doda felt a sense of triumph whenever they came, and he chuckled to himself and his delight in the garden grew and more and more time was spent under the palm tree planning Mrs Daniel's new beds.

The only plant that Doda did not like was the huge, rampant bougainvillea showering purple blossom over the car port, another import from India that had Doda revising his opinions. The creeper with its dark green leaves was the perfect hiding place for *boomslang*. A tree-climbing snake that Mr Daniels said was not to be killed. Before any garden work Doda would take his *knobkerrie* and bang the tree, making much noise to frighten off any snakes. If he had his way, the bougainvillea would go.

Then more visitors came to the garden. A mountain tortoise and his mate arrived one morning, dusty and solid, disappearing into the undergrowth. Chameleons and lizards lived in the rockery and slithered into the cacti, making the garden come alive with a movement all of its own.

And Doda was busier than he had ever been before. Many hours were divided between the *mealie fields*, the garden and his favourite, the vegetables.

His evening pleasure was to bake the cream potatoes in their skins on the open fire and taste the victory of his toils. His children came to treasure the small hot potatoes straight from the fire. Winston always associated the taste of baked potatoes with long summer evenings by the fire that wonderful year of his father's success.

And there were strawberries that Mrs Daniels said had been a favourite of hers in England. Doda, with only a vague idea of England, imagined that if the whole of England tasted like strawberries it must indeed be a wonderful place. Doda would fold his shirt from the bottom holding strawberries for his children who would clamour and dance around him as if he were offering armfuls of sweets.

Suddenly the long-forgotten orchard was revived and produced juicy oranges and sweet *naartjies* even though most of the trees were ancient and covered with lichen. Plums abounded amongst sweet yellow loquats and figs and guavas.

Fruit was now plentiful, and laughter was everywhere as if the two were interchangeable. Winston was permitted to run in the orchard through the soft grasses and help their father fill the round wells at the feet of the trees with clear water.

The avocado tree, not to be outdone, sprouted and grew so tall that only Winston was brave enough to climb to the top and pick the best fruit. His mother knew just how much pepper and salt to mix into the rich green flesh and they ate it right under the tree. The hard stones were kept for the white children to grow in jars on the kitchen ledge.

Around the side of the house, protected from the punishing warm wind and the sun, bananas, untidy *pawpaw* and mango trees grew but only yielded fruit rarely, like deep-mined diamonds.

In those days, laughter became the background noise to their play and work. The two families lived side by side. Daniels was the only white man Winston's uncle Mukeseli spoke to, long into the dark night.

Doda grew more confident and more outspoken. The shy, soft man had become a man of opinions and knowledge beyond that any of his family had ever guessed. He consulted his brother Mukeseli and together they taught Daniels how to respect the strange reluctant land that would, if correctly coaxed, offer up its riches.

And on those soft summer evenings Mama cooked the ripe golden corn over the fire and made the floury bread that tasted like cake. They ate like kings and imagined that it would last forever.

They had reckoned without Thienus van der Merwe, who was fuming. He passed his life in the valley giving very little thought to anyone else. Suddenly there was an *Engelsman* called Daniels and he, Thienus, had been forced into unacceptable insignificance. Daniels, a complete *rooinek* who would usually have been beneath Thienus' notice, was suddenly almost as important as Thienus himself.

Daniels had made his black staff important like no other white man had ever done before. Thienus and everyone knew that you never gave an ignorant *kaffir* command over machinery. So went Thienus' thinking. The truth was that *kaffirs* were too stupid to operate machinery. Fact. That is why so few of them drove cars. This is what drove Thienus to his English neighbours with a hard knot of anger tightening around his throat like a fist.

The last time Thienus had seen Daniels was when the man had been digging through the useless boxes of rubbish at the farm sales. From his vantage point at the bar, he watched the *rooinek's* red hair as it flopped over his brow. Thienus' friends, people he'd known all his life, talked of sheep and the failure of the rains. The same talk they had every month. Then suddenly new words began to penetrate the conversation. Alien, strange words that jarred against the comfortable world that Thienus understood so well.

'That *rooinek* lets his *kaffir* drive the tractor. A brand new one too. Also, he lets the kaffir make decisions about what is planted on the farm.' Thienus sat up. Old du Plessis, dressed in trousers held up with bailer twine, spat in the dust.

They were talking about Daniels, and he felt an unfounded sliver of shame. After all, the man lived in his valley and unreasonable as it was, Thienus felt responsible for what happened in the valley. Then came the words he dreaded.

'You should watch it, Thienus. He's close to you in the valley. He will spoil the *kaffirs* and then there will be a revolution.' Then morose Marius Kemp who hardly ever spoke got to his feet.

'You need to sort it out, Thienus. Get this stupid Engelse *rooinek* sorted out. Go and have a chat.' After that they returned to their usual conversations and Thienus knew what he needed to do.

Then there was the thing that made Thienus angrier than anything else. That old farm that had never been anything and suddenly it blossomed under Daniels's guidance. In fact, it thrived and while Thienus could never admit to actual envy, there was something very like it festering in his gut. He told himself the anger was because he wanted to do what he had always done, ignore the smaller farm. The anger came from being forced to recognise that someone other than himself had made the valley prosper. Not only that, but Daniels had also committed the ultimate sin by allowing his *kaffirs* a share in that success.

Arriving home, he hardly noticed Charleen hovering in the door but as he brushed past her, she cleared her throat.

'The girl in the kitchen has left and taken some clothes with her,' she said, her voice clipped and short as if keeping her words to the minimum. Thienus continued walking but she followed him.

'So?' he struggled to keep the irritation out of his voice.

'She has gone to work for the Daniels. She says that they pay more.' That's when he knew he had the perfect excuse to tackle Daniels, face to face. He dressed in his favourite safari suit; it made him look big and strong.

Almost from the moment he stepped from his *bakkie* it began to go wrong. Daniels, it was obvious, was not there. A small dark-haired woman came from the house wiping her hands on a drying cloth and smiled at him.

He stood at the driver's door of his *bakkie,* and he was conscious of the smell coming from the bed of the vehicle — the last time he'd used it was to transport chicken manure. Also, he was suddenly aware of the orange dust that lay in a thick layer all over the cab except for the space on the windshield that had been cleared by the windscreen wipers. Why these things should so embarrass him he could not say. The woman by contrast was neat with nothing out of place — her dark hair pulled back severely in a bun. She seemed so self-contained that all the while he stood in giant, dumb silence.

She smiled but it did not reach her eyes. 'Mr van der Merwe, can I help you?'

'Er, I was hoping to see your husband. Is he here?' he asked without hope. The English felt false and high on his tongue.

She shrugged, 'Well he is away and won't be back until much later. I could get him to phone you if you like.' Thienus shook his head. He hated the phone, the tedious party line where nothing was safe with Mrs Swanepoel listening to all the conversations. He swallowed and she turned and gestured to the lawn.

'Why don't you come and have some tea and we'll see what we can do?'

Blast the *rooinek's* and their impeccable manners. It had an underlying kindness that was foreign to him.

There were white wrought iron chairs under the huge pineapple-shaped palm tree, cool and unflustered in the shade. The garden was bustling with blooms ranged in a rainbow of colour and it was unlike any of the other gardens in the valley.

Mrs Daniels called into the house and a small shrinking maid brought a tray with a teapot and cups. He hated tea.

Seeing him eyeing the tray with distaste she said, 'Um, bring some lemonade, or would you prefer coffee?' He shook his head.

'Lemonade will be fine, Evelyn.' The maid scurried away.

'So, Mr van der Merwe, what is it you want?' Gone was the famous politeness and now she seemed to him insolent and despite her smallness she was unafraid. There even lurked small crinkles of laughter at the corner of her eyes and mouth.

'Lady, I have to talk to you about your *kaffirs*. Actually, it's about one of the new girls that you employed recently. He sat back and was pleased to see annoyance on her face and the smile lines disappear. He continued, 'You know we have to make sure that we are all on the same page when it comes to the *kaffirs*.' She flinched. He waited.

'I'm sorry Mr van der Merwe but we don't use that word in this house.'

For a moment he was truly bewildered. What word? Then it struck him.

'The word *kaffir*? But…' He stumbled on the words and then lamely said, 'They don't mind.'

She swelled and pursed her lips. 'It doesn't matter. It is highly derogatory, and I don't like it. And I'm sure if you asked any of them, they would tell you that they hate it.' He felt his face growing hot and angry words rising in his throat.

She held up a hand and smiled, 'But don't let's argue about that now. Why do you want to talk about this *woman*?' She emphasised the word 'woman' and he glanced away from her. The conversation was slipping away from him, and he took a firm hold of his temper.

He tried to remember that he was the one who was in the right. He found words rushing again to the surface and this time he let them out.

'You have a *ka*… maid here that stole from us.' Now the words were lining up and falling over themselves. He was hardly aware of what he was saying. It didn't matter as long as he could wipe that stupid smile from her face.

'She stole from us, and my wife had to fire her,' he said. She stopped smiling and looked concerned.

On second thoughts he began to think that it might have been better to discuss this with Daniels himself. This woman, it was clear, was too soft-hearted — something that Thienus deplored in women. He could see that even now when she was feeling anger, she did not frown so much as lose her smile. Her eyes too became serious.

'Now tell me, what did *Margaret...*' she said, putting emphasis on the name, 'steal from you that has caused you to come over here all *bedonnered* and upset?' He shifted uncomfortably.

His face, already a deep brown became reddened, and he stiffened, a great clumsy contrast to the relaxed woman across from him. It was foolish to feel insulted by the Afrikaans word, but it was used so obviously and sounded strange coming from her, an insult.

He was conscious of the swelling sweat patches under the arms of his khaki suit. He wished he could stand and move a little. Sitting with the woman, he began to feel like an insect that had been pinned to a board. And she continued so calmly and unperturbed and casually gestured for him to continue.

For a while he said nothing as he searched for the familiar anger. His mother had often teased him about being a man of action, not words.

His head, a jumble of order-less words, hurt him and he wished for a strong drink like brandy.

Even more annoying was the woman's ability to sit in silence while he yearned to fill the void with something pithy and clever, something to make her sit up and take notice of him.

The foreign sounding words tripped him and tied his tongue in knots. He wished for the simple clean sounds of Afrikaans but here in the *rooinek's* den he had to indulge the woman. And he seethed to think that the woman, he had heard, was learning to speak Xhosa. And finally, when he thought of that, his anger returned with a reassuring burst like gunfire.

'Call the *ka...* girl and I will show you what a liar she is.'

Mrs Daniels had stilled but she only said, 'By girl, I assume you are referring to Margaret, a fully grown woman? I will do no such thing. Do you expect to harangue and berate this poor woman under my roof?' She would have said more but Thienus stopped her.

'She stole a pair of *takkies* from my wife.' His voice was drained of emotion.

'That's what this is about, a pair of trainers?' She stopped, obviously at a loss.

'*Ja*, that's right…' He would have said more but the infuriating woman lifted up her hand.

'I'm not going to sit here discussing a perfectly ridiculous subject. Mr van der Merwe, I am sure that you have better things to do than come here over something so trivial.'

Trivial, she thought it was trivial! He opened his mouth, but nothing emerged. He let out a long breath and then noticed that her face had changed. She too seemed to be struggling. He had a sudden flash — maybe she couldn't say everything she wanted to. For him it sounded as if she had said everything but the demeanour of the woman sitting opposite him suggested otherwise. Good.

Strangely this made him soften a little and he settled back in his chair. He knew that an unlikely victory may even lay within his grasp now.

'We've had a lot of thefts over the last few years. You wouldn't know because you are new to the valley. Hansie, you know he lives over there,' he waved his arm towards the rolling *veld* as if this person would emerge from behind a bush. 'Hansie had his whole house burgled while he was in Uitenhage. They just came and took his truck and loaded all the things from the house. His whole house. All his clothes, his food, the television. Even the safe with his guns. They just took it all and the police know it was his own staff, but they can't do a thing about it. They all just acted deaf, dumb and blind.' Here she made a gesture as if to talk but Thienus blundered on.

'I warned Hansie, I told him that his head-boy was bad news, but he wouldn't listen. Now he has proper security. I helped him build it.' He could not keep the conceit from his voice. Still, she said nothing.

'We whites must stick together you know. I could do the same for you. It did not take long to build the fence around his house you know. Now no one can get in.' She shook her head but did not say anything.

Again, the silence rose like a massive void between them. He felt a familiar compulsion to continue.

'And Hansie is quite hard on his *ka*… Bantu people. So, you see if you don't come down hard on them, they will rob you blind. It starts with small stuff but soon it becomes…' He stopped considering his words.

'Much bigger.' Still the woman sat as if turned to stone and it seemed as if a huge impassable gulf had opened between them. How he would love to get her to understand properly. He would love her to see some of the films that he'd seen in the army. Some of those scenes where black people showed their true nature. Then she'd change her tune for sure.

At last, she spoke, her voice thin like hair, 'Well, trainers, Mr van der Merwe, hardly the crime of the century, is it?' The laughter was back in her voice. He felt himself stiffen and all his resolve fluttered away like glitter. They just didn't know what they were dealing with these people; they had forgotten which side they were on.

He cursed — it had been so long since he'd been in a position like this, and he didn't like it. It was easy not to have to question himself. He had never had any doubts.

'*Ja*, and then she came here to you, and you even paid her more money! It's outrageous. The next thing you know you will have...'

He didn't finish and she stood.

'Mr van der Merwe,' she said, her voice cold and colourless. 'I only had Margaret work here temporarily because I wanted a little extra help. I can hardly say where she is now. And I might add that what I pay my servants is of no concern to you.' There, he had heard it, a slight tremor. She was not as cool as she pretended!

That was how he found himself standing on the *stoep* glaring at the little *Engels vrou* trying his best to wrest back control. She folded her arms and straightened her back — this was indeed the end of the conversation. Even though she was small and slight there was something regal in this; something that made him — as big as he was — feel small and somehow shamefully dismissed.

She too, though, had been affected and in the end, she used the only way she could to relieve herself of his presence. 'I will certainly bring this up with my husband, Mr van der Merwe,' she said. 'As soon as he comes home.' Her voice implied that her husband had bigger things to worry about. 'In the meantime, I suggest that you forget about those *takkies*, they are hardly worth worrying about for a man of your sense.' She couldn't help the last dig.

Her dismissal, while feeble and small, angered him the most. The thing that he could not forgive her. All of the people who knew Thienus knew that his anger would lead to something catastrophic and that he did not care if the wrong people paid. Thienus would have his revenge.

Later he would recall turning and walking slowly to his truck, not fast because that would suggest he was running away. Also, he wanted to suggest that he was leaving on his own accord, leisurely, and not because she had ordered it. He was almost at the car when she spoke again, leaning over the parapet that was covered in a golden creeper. Strangely, that was the only thing he remembered seeing, all that gold.

'Oh, and Mr van der Merwe?' He remembered turning slowly and that was when his eye rested on the golden shower of flowers — he could not look at her. 'The other day my husband and Doda were looking for the rotavator and I think you have it. What we'd really like is for you to return it as soon as possible. My husband bought it for a specific job, you see, and that job is still not done. Doda desperately needs it. Shall I send him to fetch it?' Her smile of triumph made him slam into his truck and he sped out of the yard, the tyres spraying gravel in a brown shower.

Next time he visited he would meet with the husband even if he had to wait all day. Never again would he talk to that bloody *Engels vrou*. Never in all his life had he ever been bested by someone like her.

In spite of their biggest neighbour's ill-will, Uitkyk began to thrive. A beautiful lush green garden grew miraculously out of the hard dull clay and turned it into a magical rainbow of colour. It was as if the ground had only been waiting to be brought to life in an explosion of colour.

But it was a success that rested precariously on the whim of Thienus' uncontrollable anger.

Chapter 18 — Danie Swanepoel

Pretoria 1970s

Kobus had a problem. How to impose his authority on the station at Uitenhage. Despite Meiring's assurances of waiting out for his retirement, he wanted something big. Something that would have everyone change their minds about him. All the doubters to doubt no more.

Only he knew not how. Where was he to find the dynamism? The fire? It had all but gone out.

Those were the days that he started to think about Danie Swanepoel again. Dreamt of him until he could clearly hear his voice, see him and when he awoke in the mornings, a little piece of Danie clung to him like a tiny shred of cotton.

The days waiting to sweep his son into the police station dragged on and on, and while he waited, he imagined what Danie would do. Kobus had been here before. The slinking away from the army, his father's grim disapproval and an opening of a void that meant rejection and exile from his family.

It was only when Danie burst into his life that he suddenly realised that the void of rejection had gone. Danie had an innate understanding that went beyond words. It was an unexpected and unlooked for release.

Danie arrived at the Pretoria *Polisie Sentraal* station one day as if he'd been working there for years. He was casual and dressed as a civilian. He carried an assumption that everyone knew who he was, and it worked because before long his name was falling from everyone's lips. Before long, most of them that worked at the headquarters would swear some old connection that had only just come to light. Or they would tell an anecdote copied from Danie, word for word.

Danie's special talent was stories. He was fond of saying that everyone likes stories. These stories did not start at the beginning but somewhere in the middle and this assumed a shared intimacy. It made the listener feel as if they were already friends with Danie. Danie managed also to infuse a sense of great privilege to those with whom he connected and his favoured few would hold that intimacy close and never give it up.

Kobus used a forensic study of the case to understand how Danie gained such loyalty and control. He knew that Danie always told stories, long, elaborate stories that did not always appear to be relevant. Sometimes, Danie's rude interruption took everyone by surprise but after a while most of the talk began to revolve entirely around Danie. No one ever chastised Danie and in fact the only thing that did happen was that Danie acquired complete loyalty and control.

What had seemed like an amusing little distraction was a masterful assumption of power. Kobus idly wondered how he might be able to emulate Danie now that he had his own team. Strange unfamiliar stirrings began to make him feel that he might do it. He, the perpetual second-in-command, Kobus Jonker, might mimic what Danie had done. Then Meiring and all the others who had doubted him would see their big mistake. It had always felt like a sop to his intelligence when those high-ranking officers had patted him on the back and assured him that he was essential as second-in-command. Second best. It still rankled. Well not any more; he would show them.

After many months Danie had assumed an innate authority and no one questioned him — not openly at least. This authority was not like any that Kobus had encountered before. It was not brittle and hard — it was a much softer, slithery thing but no less bullish for it. Very few people, although there had been some and they were swiftly dismissed, doubted that Danie had a good reason for being there.

To capture something of Danie, Kobus had to go back almost to the beginning. He would not, could not go back to the army days, they were too painful. He could expunge the memories of the army by imposing the more successful days of the A-team over them.

Kobus smiled at the memory of his younger self. A younger man, and although a little shaken after his army experience, he had begun to regain confidence and had some success in the police force. Yes, he had done it himself and in fact had hardly noticed Danie at first. Danie was friendly and amusing but Kobus thought of him, when he thought of him at all, as aimless. So, it came as a surprise to find out that Danie had a very serious role. That role was to form a counter-insurgence agency with powers that exceeded that of the government itself.

And Danie had done this despite the fact that he was not a clever man, Kobus had found that out quickly.

Had anyone taken the trouble to see his school reports they would have noticed that Danie was average, but he did have something that school or college could not teach, and that was cunning. And he knew people, he knew people very well. He was able to make judgements and assessments about people and he was hardly ever wrong.

Kobus wished now that he had paid more attention. He began to watch his new Uitenhage team and assess the members, but it seemed very slim pickings indeed.

Danie understood two great truths. Those truths were that while he had to recruit from the *polisie mag,* he knew that a counter-insurgence agency operated outside the rule of law. He also had one other thing that Kobus knew he lacked himself. Danie was free of any moral code. This double standard was something that Kobus had only ever half-adopted, and he knew now that he had to act without compunction if he wished to make his mark in Uitenhage.

Danie appeared to drift from day to day, filling rooms with words and noise. His voice became louder and louder as if he could command by sheer volume alone. It worked and nobody questioned him even when he took over other people's words and shaped them around his own. Danie was an all-consuming dominant presence.

Those were the times that Kobus had the most doubts. His model was Danie and deep inside a small part of himself knew that he was not Danie.

Even Danie's clothes were not like those of the other *polisie*. He wore civilian dress as if it were a uniform, a uniform peculiar to him. Beige safari suits with long socks that covered his lower legs up to the shorts that exposed only a small part of his ruddy legs and knees. He was big and gruff. His hair flopped over his forehead, and he shook it back in an irritated way that became an intrinsic part of him like his accent or the way that he walked sloppily so that his shoes made a slipping sound. He wore his hair long as if in perpetual need of a cut. He smoked continually, leaving a trail of smoke and ash behind him like an afterthought. He smoked Camel cigarettes, pungent and lively like the adventurous picture on the front of the packet. Two rugged men in a four-by-four off road vehicle in a deserted desert embodied Danie's own vision of how he saw himself.

In his most honest moments, Kobus could not see himself in that role. He longed for the loyalty that Danie inspired. Those were the times when he felt most lost. Kobus longed for the type of confidence that Danie had.

Danie knew who to approach and who to avoid. Those who he avoided found themselves surrounded by strange dangerous stories that they found hard to curb. Often, they found that they were discredited in some mysterious way; they were forever marked. Such was his power that the members of the precinct began to dread that they would not be approached to join the A-team. That somehow, they were not good enough for his mysterious task force. The stories Danie concocted were often wild and preposterous and yet even though Kobus found them laughable the others were entranced. He had never considered how powerful stories might be.

But the more unbelievable the stories the more they were circulated and in the circulation they became true. Within a very short time, Danie became the real leader within the Pretoria *Polisie Sentraal* and soon everyone played by his rules.

Danie's stories were cruel and usually involved the degradation of someone weaker than himself. These stories drew people to Danie so that they did not become the centre of one of those tales. Danie's stories were peppered with the weak, especially women, and he never lost an opportunity to gather the faithful at his side and denigrate an unfortunate outsider. The truth was that Danie admired people who broke the rules, adopting a mantra that the men would soon come to know: 'You snooze, you lose pal.' Kobus imagined he had picked it up from one of the cheap shows he watched on television. 'Always have a saying, something that people remember you by,' he said to Kobus.

This happened one day where Kobus was witness to a trivial incident of a parking violation. That was, Kobus supposed, the power of Danie's stories. Another day, the incident would be completely ignored. The unpredictability meant that all of his subordinates were kept in suspense, too afraid to act out of their own volition because they never knew when they might incur Danie's wrath.

On the receiving end of Danie's spite one day was Barbara, an expert in her field of fraud detection, parked right outside the precinct in one of those bays that had been cordoned off especially for her. She was obese and found it extremely difficult to walk great distances. She blamed a hormone problem which earned a loud rude snort from Danie that relegated her to ignominy. This would have been the end of it, but it gnawed at Danie because of the parking. This he saw as something that undermined his power.

When Kobus and the others had forgotten about Barbara and her parking Danie saw his chance. Danie, arriving early, parked his car in her spot and then disappeared from the office and could not be contacted to move his car. Barbara arrived eventually, wilting in the heat and leaning heavily on her walking stick, demanding to know who the culprit was. Barbara was not popular and after much sniggering she was informed that it was Danie, and he was not available. Defeated, Barbara retreated to her office and when Danie was informed, he had used his much-vaunted phrase, 'You snooze, you lose, pal,' and high-fived a fellow officer with glee.

He was, of course as he intended, greeted with gales of laughter and from that time on parked in front of the precinct. Where Barbara parked nobody knew and she became the butt of many of his most lascivious stories and she never came into their part of the precinct again.

Kobus knew it was petty and had felt a small stab of sympathy for the woman but for Danie it was just another way that he cemented his leadership and drew the others around him.

Another time Danie was telling a story, Marius beckoned Kobus over. 'Listen to this,' he urged. Kobus liked Marius, a diligent worker and someone Kobus trusted.

Danie was talking, 'So there was an excellent *sersant* working his way up the ranks. He was working in Bloemfontein, but he could never catch a break. Everybody was after this guy. The wife, the taxman, the bloody neighbours. Everybody. The poor guy could never catch a break.'

Kobus recognised the story, he heard something similar before, it was meant to resonate with the men. A rally cry.

Many of the men sitting around drinking coffee and listening intently felt a connection with the victim in the story. That was often the allure of

Danie's stories. The personal touch. These ordinary *polisie* too could not get a break. They too were tied down by rules that seemed heavy and clumsy. They too had wives and families that did not understand them.

'So, he's going to work one day, it's the night shift and he is driving along minding his own business. He's not on duty yet but then he sees a *kaffir* steal a bag. Snatched it right off the shoulder of a white woman. Even though it was getting dark there was still enough light. Then the *kaffir* starts running, you know how they run right? This *sersant* thinks to himself — I'm not running after this *kaffir,* no way.' Laughter came from the others — they had experience of this. It was a mug's game.

'But the woman, she's good-looking so he starts to rev the engine of the squad car and chases that *kaffir* right up the pavement. He just doesn't care any more. So, people are jumping into shops and down alleyways and the kaffir keeps running and the *koper* keeps coming.' More general laughter and now the atmosphere was almost festive. Danie even adopted a terrible American accent as if he were in a television series.

'Then the stupid *kaffir* runs down a dead end and there's nowhere to go so the *koper* just eases the car right up to him so that he's pinning him against the wall. The *kaffir*, scared now, drops the bag and the cop quietly picks it up and saunters back to the woman. It takes him a long time because the *kaffir* has run for miles. And he just leaves the *kaffir* there pinned up against the wall.

'The woman is so grateful that she will do anything for the cop. She's got R1000.00 in the bag. Her husband's rich, she says and she's sure that he'd like to reward the *koper*. He's just thinking of that arse and those...' Here he cups his upper chest and makes grinding movements with his hips. The precinct is bathed in laughter.

Then Kobus notices that Marius is not laughing quite as loudly as the others. He remembered it because that was what he would worry about the most. What if he were telling a story and the men did not laugh? He worried about men like Marius. Good men Danie never even noticed. Even if people did disapprove, that was their problem and what's more, they were not team players. They would all find out that Danie was ruthless with people who were not team players. Kobus wondered if he would be able to have that same ruthless streak.

Danie ended that story as he always did, 'You snooze, you lose, pal,' to screams of laughter and even some cheering. Slowly everyone drifted back to work, some shaking their heads at the audacity of Danie. No one noticed that Marius was not laughing.

This is what troubled Kobus the most. The casual way that Danie put together his A-team belied the thought and care that had been poured carefully into each of his choices. He recruited entirely at the *Sentraal Polisiestasie* Pretoria which was where he was based himself. It became clear that Danie had been invested to act by a higher authority but because he never revealed who that was. Many believed that he was not under any orders other than his own.

Kobus liked this about Danie — the air of a free agent — and he was easy to be around. In the beginning, Kobus had always harboured dark secret hopes that he would be chosen for the A-team even before he fully realised what it was.

In many ways Danie was everything that Kobus had wanted himself. After the disaster of his national service, Kobus' concepts of himself were blurred and indistinct, but Danie provided a sharp, distinct outline. Kobus could be stronger, more respected and most of all, the best law enforcement officer in the force. Once again, he'd been given a change. Uitenhage was not ideal, but he had a chance and that was all he needed.

But after a while, the rumours started and many of the others in the precinct drifted away from Danie, but Kobus held his nerve and stayed loyal. They were jealous, he reasoned. That was what happened to people in leadership. Others became jealous and that led to them being toppled. Kobus' own experiences made him peculiarly sensitive to the value of loyalty. That was the crux of the matter. How to inspire loyalty? The men in the Uitenhage *Polisiestasie* and his own wayward son. How to do it?

When one of the rejected colleagues in Pretoria approached Kobus with a snivelling revelation of the falsity of Danie's stories, Kobus gave him short shift. Never did he once realise that was how myths and loyalty were created. They worked hand in hand and people like Kobus kept them going.

Kobus felt the biggest betrayal on Danie's behalf because it came from Marius. Someone who Kobus liked and admired, and Kobus had confided in him.

A tall decent man who had visited Kobus outside of work and even spent time with Kobus Junior. An infinitely patient man prepared to invest time in the awkward, girlish boy. No words of judgement passed Marius' lips.

The only time the boy had seen a gun was when Danie had produced it from the holster under his arm. They were at one of Danie's *braais* and the boy had shrunk into his mother's skirts and Kobus had shrunk into his drink.

Marius did not seem to think it strange that the boy was uninterested in fighting and guns and had spoken to the boy about the big, illustrated book that was his favourite possession, with Shakespearean figures drawn across the enormous book with bubbles for speech. The boy read the book over and over again. Marius had patiently listened to the little boy's pleasure and said to Kobus, 'You have a little genius here, Kobus.' This unlooked-for generosity had caused Marius to be universally popular with Marta as well.

Unfortunately, the man displayed a sad lack of loyalty to Danie and even tried to dissuade Kobus from joining the A-team. This betrayal severed their friendship and Kobus wondered if it had been jealousy that had caused this breach. Marius had not been chosen for the team.

Danie, it seemed, could smell out trouble and that was something that Kobus had to learn. He had already made many colossal misjudgements, placed his trust in the wrong place.

Marius was able to make clear judgements, but he was not as wily as Danie.

Marius tried to warn his friend. 'You know that Danie is on the edge of criminality himself. Sometimes, *boet* I am not even sure how very different he is from the criminals that we arrest every day.' Then he said something surprising which seemed to have nothing to do with anything at all. 'Just ask him about his National Service. Ask him what the *weermag* was like.' Then he was gone, and it was easy to shrug it all off and put it down to the ravings of a jealous man.

In those days, Kobus saw all his future waiting like a golden rainbow, and he could see nothing else.

Gradually, like a seeping leak, those words would flash into his head. In the early hours of the morning when he first awoke or when their work at the A-team moved sluggishly, his thoughts would drift back to those words. Was Danie a criminal himself? Then he would viciously dampen down those words. It would not do to let them in.

Kobus had been made second-in-command — even given a title, *comandante*, and he supposed now that was one way of securing loyalty.

The only time he had actually met their superiors, a bluff uniformed Kolonel had warned Kobus after Danie had left the room. 'Watch him, Jonker, just watch him. He's a loose cannon. You are here because you have your feet firmly on the ground.'

Those words and Marius' came back again and again until one day, a slow crisp day, he boldly challenged Danie, as if the answer did not matter.

It happened after the terrible days of the incident. The time he could not think of. Another time to shelve away and ignore.

'So where were you stationed in the *weermag*?' At first Danie did not reply, and Kobus was not even sure that he'd heard. But then slowly as if considering his words, Danie began to speak. Quietly and measured as if the words had great importance. The words sounded detached as if Danie were speaking of someone else.

'*Ja*, I was stationed at Noupoort for a while. *Ja*, Noupoort, the arse end of the world. Basic training was okay, but you know it was the real fighting that I wanted. We all wanted it.' He flicked Kobus a glance like a lightning flash. There was something small and dangerous in that look and it took a great effort for Kobus to keep his face neutral.

'They didn't want me to go to the front where the fighting was. You know because of my karate. I was the area champion and could have gone to the Olympic Games.' He paused for a long time as if examining each word carefully. 'Only we're banned, aren't we? No Olympics after all. So there didn't seem much point in carrying on so I said, no, send me to the Caprivi Stip.' He puffed his chest out and looked again at Kobus, and again there was a light in his eyes and again Kobus schooled his face to remain impassive.

Did Danie know? There was something in the way that Danie was looking at him, and for the first time in his presence Kobus was a little afraid. What if Danie did know? Would that make a difference? After all, he'd worked very hard for the A-team, surely that should count for something? The only person who was more committed to those ideals was Danie himself.

But after a while, Danie and the A-team were garnering praise and Kobus cursed himself for listening to Marius and he cursed himself for asking Danie that question. He vowed never to talk to Marius again.

There was only one disappointing episode during his tenure with Danie and that was his own family's reaction to meeting Danie. Every year, the Jonker family held a family *braai* at the beginning of the summer holidays in December. The time was exciting and always had the ability to make Kobus that frisson of excitement that he had as a child. The long holidays stretched before them with Christmas and New Year sandwiched in between. Only family and close friends were ever invited. Kobus burned to introduce his new friend and colleague.

He felt sure that Danie would melt his father's stiffness and quell his boisterous, teasing brothers. He was even confident that his cold, aloof mother would find something in Danie that would bring back the childhood family that he knew.

Almost from the very beginning of the day when Danie arrived, slightly worse for wear and reeking of tobacco smoke, it began to go wrong. Danie was too loud, talking in the voice of a heedless drunk man. The stories were a little too involved and convoluted. Stories that he'd once laughed at seemed crude and unbelievable here in the family setting. Marta and his sisters-in-law exchanged glances and his mother and father became stiffer and stiffer as the day wore on. Some of the stories even embarrassed him and were far too lewd for a family party. He tried to catch Danie's eye but every time he moved, Danie would move away like the end of a rope just out of reach.

Kobus doubted that his family, who hardly knew Danie, noticed that his speech was slurred, but he began to wish for the day to end. The louder Danie became, the quieter his family were, as if watching a show unfold before them, afraid to interrupt. A grinding concern pushed the embarrassment to one side when he noticed that Danie was drinking more and more. Kobus began to feel like a raw teenager, desperate that his family would soften and like his new friend who had seemed such a short time ago an engaging rogue with his heart in the right place.

Sometimes his brothers would engage with Danie, dropping words into the rare silences. But Kobus caught the looks of contempt that passed between them.

Towards the end of the day when the crickets were calling loudly into the night sky, competing with the frogs, his father finally spoke into the gap when Danie had disappeared inside. It was not until he heard him speak that Kobus realised that he had not heard his father speak all day.

'You say this Danie character is the boss of your crack unit?' His voice dripped with scorn. His mother, an ever-ready source of support, made a sharp sniffing sound. Boetie, Kobus' older brother by three years, laughed scornfully and put his arm around Kobus. Kobus hated it when he did that. Kobus was not a small man but when Boetie did that it always made him feel small, inadequate.

'*Ja*, what a wanker. Really, I can't believe that he's in charge of something so important. The man's a complete, doos, a first class *doos*.'

His mother slapped him on the arm. 'Don't use language like that, Boetie.'

'*Jammer* ma, but Kobus, seriously if this guy is in charge of homeland security, we are all doomed.' Kobus knew that if his mother had not been there, he would have used a great many more forceful words.

When Danie left, Kobus gathered his wife, who would not look him in the eye, and ushered her out to the car, carrying their sleeping boy in his arms. In the hallway his mother had hissed into his ear, 'Don't bring that man again, Kobus.' The words followed him to the car attached to all his other failures.

After that, an even bigger rift opened between Kobus and his family. He did not blame Danie. Of course, Danie could have been more sober, but his family could have made an effort. They had never cared for him, and he felt like a small boy all over again. So it was that he drew closer and closer to the A-team.

That is why it had been an ever-greater shock when he'd lost the A-team and Danie all in one go. All of it wiped from the earth as if it had never been. The concrete certainty of the Danie and his A-team had been tossed like confetti into the wind.

It was hard to start again, especially at his age and in a place like Uitenhage. Kobus had never been good with new faces, and it took him a long time to make friends. Sometimes when Marta had gone to bed, and he looked out over the valley at Langa he wondered what had happened to Danie. Where he had gone. How he could have vanished so completely. People always said that Danie would land on his feet and Kobus supposed this was what happened. When he thought about Danie, he knew that he should really worry about himself.

Well, he would do that.

He slammed his feet onto the floor. Enough! His son was finally home. He would ignore Ruben. After all, what was he? Danie would have known how to deal with Ruben. He would take a leaf out of Danie's book and be strong. Make unpalatable decisions and his son would thank him for it later.

Chapter 19 — The Incident

For a while Daniels and Doda believed in their dream and one of them lived it. Winston grew from a young boy into a man, and for the first time harboured an expectation that he would have a place on the land of his birth. He felt the swelling in his chest like a palpable thing, lodged there and it felt good. He had a place of purpose, and most of all, opportunity.

For the first time in his life, Doda felt what it was to be valued and in turn passed that on to Winston. Their lives, for so long ignored and one of unforgiving and unrewarded labour, changed and became one of praise and consultation.

Sometimes Winston had to stop his treacherous heart from asking if it was too good to be true. Mama scolded him and said that he was too young to be such a cynic. In those times he would look to his father, and he would shake his head and laugh. Just before he turned his head away there would be a fleeting glimpse of dubiety.

When Winston was away from the censure of his family, walking in the lonely *veld*, he would ask the question: how long can this last? Until the old orchard trees stopped bearing fruit. Until the farm was no longer a farm but just a hollowed-out piece of *veld* with nothing left to give. But the *veld* never answered him; it lay there silent as a grave.

Mrs Daniels did speak to her husband about the strange visit from their neighbour and she was angry with him but even angrier with herself. He had towered over her, and she'd felt small and insignificant, not a feeling that she was familiar with. She was also in a strange inexplicable way angry with her husband although she had never told him. Angry that she was alone when the Afrikaner had come, a bitter unreasonable anger that she pushed deep into herself.

After Mr van der Merwe left, she returned to sit under the palm tree, her mind roiling with indignation and humiliation. For once the garden lost its power over her. She could not say how long she sat there, but eventually she was called away by one of the boys and it was a merciful release from the teasing anxiety that Mr van der Merwe had dropped so suddenly into her life. Lingering at the back of her mind was a small but potent dread. She would not have been able to explain it, but she could not get rid of it. It was a relief to submerge herself once more into the life of small children and household chores.

Later, when her husband returned, weary with the factory still clinging to his work clothes, the dread and humiliation was once more resurrected.

He still had the smile that always came when he was home. He'd once explained that coming through the bright yellow and orange blossom of the golden shower was like entering through a shaft of sunlight. Then he was embarrassed by the unexpected poetry and they both laughed together. On this evening, his wife would not answer his smile and turned away as he greeted the boys.

Thienus van der Merwe's accusations and racism had caused a rift like an ugly scar. A weapon that had beaten the *Engelsman se vrou*.

It was rare that his wife greeted him with hard angry words, but she did on that day leaping at him with distress in her voice. Her husband, surprised to be so accosted, was angry and she, feeling a further injustice, flew into a rare rage. They argued, such a rare occurrence that their boys fled out into the *veld*.

Daniels, finally left to his evening solace, felt all the injustice of working hard and thanklessly in a place that no longer held anything for him. Longing to focus entirely on his farm, he often indulged in the sport of daydreaming about working full time on his farm. He knew that it was not yet possible; that it might never be possible. But after a tiring day, he allowed himself the fantasy and resented being denied that solace. So, he sat on the *stoep* and did not come for his supper knowing, with grim satisfaction, this would niggle his wife like a sharp pointed knife.

The crickets were already loud in the black night by the time he returned to the *voorkamer* where they usually ate. His food congealed hideously on the table, a rebuke for his churlishness.

Mrs Daniels, contrite now and having the luxury of time, thought kindlier of her husband. He was a good man and perhaps her reaction to Mr van der Merwe was overblown. Also, when she was tucking in her youngest son, he had blurted out, 'Mommy, are you going to get a divorce?' She rocked back and stared at the little face so serious and so young. She could not answer as her tears clogged up her throat and threatened to choke her. She kissed him on the forehead, and he closed his eyes.

When she saw Barend standing in the doorway as if unsure that he would be welcome, she put her hand on his shoulder. This gesture was all it took, and she related the incident to her husband as if telling an amusing story. She could see that he was tired. Commuting for hours every day was taking its toll. She was aware of his dream, and she too wished that they could farm full time and then he could give up his job. She knew he hated his job without him having to tell her. It was in his stance and drooping shoulders, and she saw it every morning. She wished with all her heart that it could be so.

After she told the story of Mr van der Merwe's visit, sounded out the words as if hearing them for the first time, it seemed that it was of no importance. She quelled the small feeling of dread, mentally stomping it down until it was there no more.

After that, their conversation filled with everyday particulars of the boys and the garden. She knew without witnessing the grinding hardship that boredom made of his days. She loved the farm herself. Her little shade house with myriads of ferns and cycads. Her cuttings and seeds that she too left most days to work and work somewhere else where she did not want to be. She also knew that farming was still a faraway dream especially while the boys were so young. She, like her husband, cherished the hope that one day… One day, maybe.

Often of late, when faced with her tired drooping husband, it felt hard to be the cheerleader when she too felt the weight of a dream so very close.

When it actually came time to tell her husband about Mr van der Merwe's accusations, she surprised herself by laughing.

Never did she, for one minute, think that it was not an amusing story, and it would be one with such tragic consequences. As she told the story, Mr van der Merwe was a clumsy clown of a man standing under the palm tree with his accusations of bloody trainers like he was about to crack the crime of the century. And finally, it happened; her husband laughed and the tired lines around his mouth and eyes disappeared, and she knew she was forgiven.

Daniels relaxing into the night ready for sleep was shocked into wakefulness when his wife said that she'd demanded the return of the rotavator. This shock was as nothing compared to the fact the rotavator had been returned that very afternoon.

When at last the longed-for clouds, arrived the whole valley sagged in relief. Longing for rain was expected in the region, dry and arid as it was.

Only they were not rainclouds bringing the promise of the end to the drought but something else altogether.

Thienus, still smarting from his treatment at the hands of the *Engels vrou,* wanted his own back. On his return that fateful day, smarting and mixing his anger with several whiskies drunk one after another, he wrestled with a new sensation. A sensation that told him that he had somehow been bested by a woman. A *vroumens.* A *rooinek.* The sensations almost overwhelmed him and so unfamiliar that he almost got back into his *bakkie* to return to place a gun against her head. His hand was shaking as he raised the glass to his lips, and he knew it would be many drinks before the shaking got under control again.

Also, he was sure that before long the whole valley would know of his humiliation. He could see the men at Fitches Corner sitting in judgement. He could hear them. 'You let an *Engels vrou* best you? What kind of man are you, Thienus?'

This could not happen. He would make sure that everyone knew him to be the most powerful man in the valley. It was all he had.

In his family, he was God, and he was not used to such treatment. He could almost accept the wicked story about the *takkies*, the *Engels vrou* wanted to preserve her dignity at the expense of his. She couldn't admit that her servants stole from her but the rotavator, that was the final straw. What could a part-time farmer like Daniels want with it? Out here in the *bundu,* all white people were his, Thienus van der Merwe's, family, dammit, and they needed to understand that he was only doing it for their own good. Every white person suffered if one family let their *kaffirs* run wild. So, fortified and restored to the right he would again tackle that *Engels* family, only this time he would be ready and no tiny *vrou mens* would stand in his way.

Not a man for careful internal reflection. Thienus brooded only for a short while and then took action. On his arrival he barked for Paulus, his head boy, and spat out the command for the rotavator to be returned. His staff, afraid of his wrath, had obeyed his command. Almost immediately he regretted the decision. Was that not an admission of defeat? Had he cut off his nose to spite his face? Didn't he need the machine? Wasn't he the real farmer here in this godforsaken valley?

Stewing over the dilemma, Thienus reasoned that the only solution was for him to speak directly with Daniels, man to man. Daniels was not a proper farmer and Daniels therefore could not need the machine as much as he did. Besides, he wanted to send a message of his own. He could take the damn machine whenever he wanted.

For a second time in two days, Thienus set off for the Daniels' property determined to speak to the Mr Daniels himself. He would not make the mistake of becoming embroiled with the woman again. She was nothing to him.

Thienus prepared his words carefully — he only needed a few after all. He would make this white man understand that they were in it together and anything left to chance was putting the whole community at risk. He would make this silly *Engelsman* see that this was more than just a rotavator.

In his inner deliberations, which were short, he felt certain that his strong words and stronger presence would definitely cow the man. It had to. Suddenly, what had been a little irritant had now become a matter of life and death. He would clearly establish his superiority by taking the rotavator away with him. He needed it and he needed it more than this part-time *Engelse* farmer did.

Thienus, in the interests of being rightly understood, brought his three sons — versions of himself, big and clumpy.

The *bakkie*, resembling an army tank, more suited to the dusty terrain of the *veld,* drew up in front of the garage at Uitkyk. Thienus ignored the ominous sign that there were no other cars in the driveway, choosing to assume that a vehicle was concealed in the garage. It was after all a Saturday and the Daniels should have been at home. Without a word, all four men climbed from the vehicle into the silent farmyard. Without a word Thienus took the shotgun that he kept bolted in the back and carried it with the muzzle harmlessly pointing to the ground. There was nothing unusual in that; he liked to carry the weapon.

His sons forming a vanguard behind him, Thienus sauntered on to the *stoep*, brushing aside the rampant golden creeper with an irritated arm. Mama was sweeping the cool flagstone. Sensing something, she looked up and was immediately dismayed to see the glowering white men. She felt a cold trickle down her spine.

She could barely speak, her eyes on the shotgun. No, she didn't know when the *baas*, was coming back. She shuffled to the door, her eyes shifting from side to side, glancing to the lawn as if the answer lay there, and then back again to the gun.

A bird cage hung on a black metal stand and blocked her exit. She would have to go around and if she did this it would bring her closer to the four silent men. She stayed where she was, and the unsuspecting red songbird sang for freedom in his cage.

For a big man, Thienus moved quickly and positioned himself in the doorway. Let her sweat, the cheeky *kaffir*. He had not forgotten the shoes and his humiliation. Thienus smirked at the small dark woman through the bars of the birdcage and bared his teeth in a smirk. Let her sweat.

No, Mama stuttered; she didn't know when the madam was coming back either. Thienus knew that despite her fear she could not be pressed for any other information. No, she didn't know anything about the rotavator or the red tractor or any of the ploughs. Her voice shook as she pronounced the words as if she were testing a new, unfamiliar language.

Her face cleared as she caught a quick flash of Doda's coat in the garden. She called rapidly, her voice shaking and her hands forming a cup around her lips, shaking violently. Her eyes darted between Thienus and his sons and then briefly on the gun. At first the shout was frail and feeble, too small for Doda to hear. A small wavering sound that could not pass the tall thickset white men who caged her. But her desperation made her voice bolder, and she called again, this time louder; this time loud enough to be heard at the back of the garden. Thienus smiled. This would be fun with only these *kaffirs* here. His sons, sensing their father relaxing, also eased their own bodies to the side and put their hands on the wall that ran around the *stoep* and looked over the valley. It was a good view here. Such a shame that it was wasted on a part-time farmer like the *rooinek*.

171

Doda appeared from the shrubs, his *knobkerrie* in one hand and a question on his face. It was unusual for his wife to call at this time of the day. If she called like this it was something urgent and unpleasant. Also, there was a note in her voice, one he recognised as alarm like the day he'd killed the cobra in the kitchen. Danger was quick to rise in this place; it could appear from nowhere in the most unexpected places.

Thienus, from where he was standing in the doorway, lifted the shotgun, not pointing it but as an extension of his arm to point directly at Doda's chest. '*Kaffir*, I want the plough. The new one.' The white *baas* spoke loudly, too loudly, and his insults felt like daggers. Doda glanced quickly behind but there was no one there, just the long green lawn and dots of colour where the Hibiscus bled into the garden.

Then he saw Thienus standing in the doorway blocking his wife's entry into the sanctity of the house. Doda reeled. The red blob of a canary singing, oblivious to the turmoil of the humans. It had been so long since a white man had spoken to him in Afrikaans. It had been a long time since a white man had called him *kaffir*. The words were hard and unforgiving like little bullets, and Doda could not make out what they meant. He frowned and stood immobile, and the late morning went very still.

Even the birds paused and finally the bird in the cage grew quiet. For an age, Doda stood still and indecisive, unsure what to do next and how to respond to the angry white man with a gun, the silence bursting all around him. He thought then of Winston kneeling in the rose bushes and told him to stay there. He thought of his wife trapped on the *stoep* with the four men and he did not look at the gun.

Then slowly the noises returned. The day crickets began to buzz in the tall grass. Thienus too waited with barely concealed anger and something else. A menace that Doda, used to consultation and discussion, had long since forgotten. Thienus leaned forward and brought the shotgun closer and Doda finally looked right into the muzzle. So many of the white farmers carried arms that they had become part of the man — something that was hardly noticed but Doda could only focus now on the gleaming silver maw, glinting in the bright, bright sun.

Doda's mouth moved but it was a few moments before any sound came out. He couldn't connect with the words from Thienus. He heard instead the voice of Daniels. 'You know the farmers around here like to take this plough. Last time it was months before we could plant the seed and I want to get the meadow planted this weekend. I have a new idea for the kikuyu grass that might just work.' Doda remembered when the plough had finally been returned and how it had to be moved. The frayed temper of his usually calm boss, as they tried to manoeuvre the rotavator out of the driveway where it had clumsily lain. He remembered the relief and frustration, both in equal measure. So, even though the white *baas* on the steps of the *stoep* was talking loudly he could only sense what was being said. The only words that he could hear were those of the man who had been so very kind. A man who had consulted and generously spread the success.

Finally, Doda looked up into the face of the white *baas* Thienus and it was hardly less fearful than looking into the barrel of the gun. He raised the knobkerrie that was almost an extension of his own arm. The *knobkerrie* that he used to clear the garage and bushes of snakes and beat back branches and replied with something that Thienus had never heard from a black man. '*Nee, baas.*'

'*Nee!*' the white *baas* exploded and then 'No!' in English just to make sure and it was as if the man had been engulfed in a sea of red, a sea of red rage. The scarlet, rich and vivid ran up his neck and into his face.

Then his face contorted as if something inside had taken control. He would later say that he was unaware of the rifle being raised to his shoulder. Unaware of the shot ringing out. Unaware of the huge hole opening in the black man's chest. Unaware of the wild feral screaming of the frantic little black woman. Unaware of the little black boy darting from the shrubbery and flinging himself on his father's body.

And when the ringing slowly dimmed was when he became aware of his own sons pulling on his arms and shouting into his ears. It was only then that he was able to witness what he had done. Then he did not look at the corpse but only saw the *knobkerrie* lying harmlessly a few feet away to his left where it had fallen.

After a while, it felt like an age but could only have been a few seconds, the smoke from the powerful shotgun cleared and the screaming had turned to a desperate sobbing. He became aware of the wretched rag of a woman bent over the lifeless form of the black man lying in a spreading pool of red ink.

Chapter 20 — The Visit

Uitenhage 1984

Kobus stopped at the front entrance to the *polisiestasie* and hitched his trousers up over his stomach. He sucked in a breath and opened the door. Yvonne was at the front desk, and he drew in his breath even further.

He was aware that he desperately needed to get into shape, had let himself go over the last few months, but for now he held his breath in a little more and smiled at Yvonne.

He had made small gestures to fitness, but a dreadful inexplicable inertia had settled into his bones setting hard like concrete. Nothing, except his son, mattered any more.

Things would be easier now. Now that the boy was coming back into the family. Perhaps when it was all settled, he could do something, walk, maybe even run.

Yvonne was as usual welcoming, her clothes falling haphazardly around her large frame, but she smiled, and Kobus relaxed a little.

He was prickingly aware of his son's presence and stepped aside so that she could see him properly. He felt a little stab of pride; the boy was good looking, if a little thinner than Kobus liked. He was also very tall and almost blocked out Ruben behind him.

Kobus was still reeling from the realisation that Ruben was to be present during the visit. It was to have been only him and his son.

During the arrangements, which he had explained in pointed detail to his son on the previous day, he had been aware of Ruben. He had carefully positioned himself so that Ruben was not in his eye-line and talked only to his son. He deliberately omitted any mention of Ruben from the planning and gritted his teeth waiting for his son's reaction.

When it had become obvious that Ruben was coming (something in the way that his son would keep bringing Ruben back into the conversations as if attached to the other man by a string), Kobus ploughed roughly over his plans for the day again. He was aware that he was repeating himself, but he could do nothing about it. He had ignored this unwanted intrusion, but in the end had to concede defeat. His son had been strangely quiet but unmoved.

Kobus saw in Ruben something surprisingly steely, an unexpected trait from a young man that Kobus had dismissed as fluffy and superficial. Also, Ruben appeared impervious to the telling comments of rejection that Kobus hurled at him like small hot stones.

Ruben, feigning ignorance, remained terminally cheerful and filled all silences with relentless conversation until Kobus' ears hummed and he had to leave the room. Simply had to put distance between himself and his unwanted guest. If his son noticed any by-play between his father and his friend, he made no sign. Kobus was heartened by the fact that his son appeared to look forward to the outing. The fly in the ointment; the closer they got to the day, the louder Ruben became, as if sound alone would dismiss Kobus' misgivings.

Even Marta commented that she had not seen her son smile as much for a very long time. Neither of them noticed the small lines around the boy's lips and the rigid tension in his shoulders. Kobus did the only thing he could. He reluctantly conceded defeat and began to talk of the visit to the *polisiestasie* always including Ruben.

Despite Kobus setting a strong unrelenting pace from the car to the *polisiestasie,* Ruben arrived in the reception less out of breath than Kobus himself. So, it was him that said the first words, stepping forward and around his much taller friend. 'Hello, I'm Ruben.' He smiled, showing his teeth and turned towards Kobus Junior with his hand on his hip. 'And this long string bean is Peter.' Kobus scethed.

Ruben held out his hand to Yvonne, lurching forward, and in his eagerness grasped her arm instead and shook it and almost before she could thrust a visitor's badge at him, he sailed into the inner sanctum and could be heard talking to the coarse and surly Ursula.

Kobus left feeling disjointed, waved his son to follow Ruben while he frowned at Yvonne who shrugged. But he'd seen it, before she looked away, written all over her face, disgust as if she were looking at something extremely disgusting.

Kobus' stumbling words to introduce his son to Ursula were drowned out by the loud voice of Ruben who had managed to get the ever-surly

Ursula to laugh, loudly. It grated on Kobus who could hardly think with the noise of a thousand buzzing angry bees in his head.

However, an unexpected advantage of Ruben's occupation of Ursula, who hardly spared Kobus a glance, was that he was able to usher his son into the main precinct where *klein* Jannie and the others were assembled ostensibly awaiting instructions for the day.

This had been Kobus' grand plan. He wanted his son to see him at work and to advantage. *Klein* Jannie rushed forward like an eager puppy, his arm fully outstretched, smiling widely as if meeting a celebrity. Kobus noticed the little hesitation before his own boy stretched out his hand, his face strangely impassive and unsmiling. *Klein* Jannie was gushing, his voice high and thin. For a moment only, this was enough to create an illusion of clamour and the boy seemed to be swept up into the precinct and Kobus' plans were almost about to become a success. With the two young men side by side, *klein* Jannie small and slight and Kobus Junior tall and lanky, Kobus wished that his boy could be more like his new recruit. He quickly quelled the thought as if being caught out in some kind of heresy.

At first Kobus did not notice that the others had not come forward. He was satisfied to stand and watch the awkward exchanges between *klein* Jannie and his son. *Klein* Jannie did most of the talking and it was clear to everybody that the two men were awkward and stiff with each other.

Then he noticed that Old Retief, two years away from retirement, and now starting to look older than his years, remained seated at his desk twirling a pen around and around his eyes on Kobus. Yes, he had been disappointed to stay a desk sergeant but then Kobus could not be blamed for that.

Retief did at least manage a smile, unlike the bitter hard Stephaan — a man who radiated resentment and bitterness like a night searchlight. Stephaan, Kobus knew and had not considered with any compassion, had also felt the bitter pain of being passed over for promotion and wore that disappointment like a cloak. Being much younger than Retief, he had many years yet to nurse his disappointments. Stephaan did not smile, nor did he offer any greeting and when he looked at *Klein* Jannie and Kobus Junior, his face wore a sneer of contempt. There were others but they had faded into the back office like retreating soldiers avoiding a war. Kobus began to feel a slow burning anger as his glorious day started to slip unheeded from his grasp.

Then Ruben, in a volcano of noise, entered the precinct, still laughing from something Ursula had said and carrying, to Kobus' amazement, a mug of coffee. The mug proclaimed; 'World's Best Son' emblazoned on the side. The words were like knives to Kobus' chest.

'Hey, Kobus, at least your coffee is half decent,' Ruben exclaimed and walked into the centre of the room as if he owned it. He surveyed the space as if inspecting a house on the market, again his hand on his hip, and taking a casual sip of the coffee. He grimaced, 'Maybe I spoke too soon.' He put the mug down on Stephaan's desk and turned slowly to *klein* Jannie.

Klein Jannie, looking stricken, his pale face reddening, slunk back to his desk and sat down looking at the floor.

Ruben, knocking the desk with his hip and sloshing the coffee over the side of the mug, began poking at some papers on the desk and then looking at the bare walls with evident distaste.

'Where's the big white board with details of a gruesome crime, hey?' He asked in a mocking voice designed to grate on Kobus until he felt that he might explode.

Surprisingly it was Stephaan who stepped forward and gripped Ruben by the arm and explained through gritted teeth something Kobus could not hear. He felt a brief sense of gratitude towards Stephaan until he noticed his expression reflected in the inner office window. A slow sneer stained his dark face.

Then all the others, even those that had fled to the outer office, came back and they were all openly laughing. His son, abandoned on the far wall, was staring at Ruben who had escaped Stephaan's arm and was opening and closing the cabinet and firing questions at Stephaan who remained silent. *Klein* Jannie was unhappily staring at his desk as if willing himself anywhere but there. The only noise came from Ruben who seemed determined to fill the void. He remained cheerful as if it were all a joke.

Gone were Kobus' carefully laid plans. The tour of the jail cells. The ride in *polisie kar* with sirens blaring and full speeding emergency. Gone were his demonstration on how to brief a team; blown into a million little

177

useless pieces. Now his only aim was one of extricating himself and his son. He gave the interloper, Ruben, not one thought.

Kobus Junior seemed strangely impassive and lethargic and content to watch Ruben as if he were viewing a play. Kobus grabbed his arm, bony and compliant, and led the boy away while the voice of Ruben, loud and false, continued to fill the room drowning the awful silence of the others.

Ursula, who it was obvious had hurriedly gone back to her seat, having viewed the precinct through the small window in the door, said in a falsely cheerful voice, 'Going so soon? I thought that you were…' Kobus cut her off. Here at least he was on safe ground. She was nothing, a fly, a speck of dirt easily ignored and brushed away. In any case his full concentration was bent on quelling the broiling, dangerous anger that now was beginning to erupt inside his chest.

At that moment he was dragging his son who made little resistance towards his car. Why did he have to park so far from the building? All of a sudden, he felt the idiocy of trying to impress his son, even though in the *polisiestasie* he was king. He was king of nothing, and Ruben had ruined it all.

Finally, at the car he noticed that his shirt was damp, and his hand had made a dark wet mark on his son's sleeve.

Ruben was suddenly there, smiling and laughing as if the visit had been a great success. Kobus said not one word, could not trust himself and kept the bubbling words deep in his throat afraid to let them go. To free them would cause a destructive implosion. Besides he couldn't. Not here. Not now.

Ruben, with a satisfied grin, laid his arm on Kobus Junior's chest, his fingers wide and caressing in an unconscious soothing motion. Kobus felt an overwhelming urge to rip that arm away but got into the driver's seat and started the car, gritting his jaw until his teeth ached.

Ursula, panting, was suddenly at the driver window indicating for him to open it. She smiled and there was bright red lipstick on her teeth. This gave Kobus a momentary feeling of superiority as if the lipstick represented a failure in her. He opened the window and she handed him an envelope, white and pristine. He reached out and took it from her and her over red lips curled into a vicious smile.

He revved the engine and thrust the envelope onto the dashboard.

'It's important that you read it now,' she said, the cruel little smile growing even wider. She folded her arms and looked him straight in the eye. She had never done that before, and her eyes were glinting with something unfamiliar and dangerous.

Kobus unfolded the envelope — it was not stuck down — and read the bright red words written in lipstick across the page.

It was nice to meet your son and his *moffie* boyfriend.

Chapter 21 — Trouble

Langa, outside Uitenhage, February 1985

Winston had tumbled into the strike action as if inside a hurricane. The strike was at once exciting and worrying in equal measure. Winston was getting accustomed to holding two opposing emotions at any one time. Especially here in Langa where everything was so unpredictable.

Worry was also an ever-present companion which now became a crippling, overwhelming obsession. Men and women who had been friends now became contestants for small scraps of food. Fights broke out over money and property. Desperation tainted Langa and Winston, with hundreds of others, began haunting the streets in the daily search for scraps, for anything to eat. Through the desperation, anger boiled and bubbled and with darkness, Langa turned into a boiling cauldron of murderous danger and no one but a fool would venture out alone.

Activity became impossible and men could only fret and gnaw at themselves in the place of food. The anxiety pulled at their stomachs and knotted them into inaction. It brought grown men and women to a worried wakefulness in the early hours of the morning, drenched into a sheen of sweat and hopeless agitation. There was no glory in their starvation. There was no glory in the inhuman daily scrabble for food where the weakest faded into the dust and were instantly forgotten.

Men who were usually gone in the early hours and absent for the whole day were now underfoot and taking space which had once been the busy realm of women. Even the children were not exempt and avoided the angry outbursts of men on a knife-thin edge.

The township, an ever noisy, bustling place, fell into a brooding sullen silence where the children no longer played, and the men had nowhere to go. Children instead learned to scrap for food and space like the adults and they were children no longer.

It seemed that every man, woman and child was reduced to something like a speck, a tiny speck of dust. A speck that existed only to find food and water. People who had already been thin began to look like skeletons and they rattled in the slightest breeze. There were now children with bloated bellies who had only ever known starvation and strife. They sat in doorways with no energy to brush the flies from their faces. Their eyes were empty and devoid of hope.

Men lined up for food at the makeshift church and if they couldn't get food, they bargained for cigarettes like hungry dogs. Everyone smoked if they could — it dulled the sense of hunger, driving it to bay like a wolf at the pit of the stomach. But the pain did not go away; it inhabited their bodies each day and night in a never-ending cycle of pain.

Winston, no stranger to hardship and hard work, suddenly felt a new sensation: that of hunger and despair. Sometimes the despair even overtook the sadness of Doda that lived in his heart.

Now when the people of Langa were so close to making a political statement, their rancour felt like a faltering, stifling heartbeat under the compelling selfish need for food. Even though their anger and struggle were ever present, their conversations were stilted and brief. Who could argue about the rights of man when man needed food to live?

Anonymous, threatening men loitered and fumed on street corners and the conversation was muffled by hunger — the worm that ate at their insides and caused their stomachs to writhe in pain, everything else fading to nothing.

COSATU union reps called the starving workers to meetings, where they went willingly, following the small hope flickering like a candle in the wind. It helped to get away from the hateful poverty and hunger that surrounded them at home. Not one man thought of refusing the call to action. Even those who were not political, although they were rare. Most of the strikers bore the gleam of righteousness in their eyes and deep in their hearts the marks of suffering like the wounds of war. The suffering of those anonymous men spread across the land in a huge fist of pain that made them call *amandla* to each other and receive in reply the word of power — *awethu*. They believed in the midst of their hunger and angst that power would finally come to the people.

Winston was drawn into the new political dawn and a close comradeship with many others who were beginning to feel an outlct for their anger and grief that for so long had lain dormant, as if hibernating like a small winter animal.

The men, some no more than boys, felt the first stirrings of a liberating excitement and dawning change. This imagined freedom felt as if it was closer than ever before, and it ran like wildfire through the township from mouth to mouth. That fire now took the place of food and fed the men and women of Langa.

The boys, used as they were to near starvation, could list any number of reasons for complaint, but they all knew why they were striking. Having no political voice and feeling the despair of being rebuffed every day of their young lives, they turned to the one small power they had. That power was called labour and they took their power and held it above their heads in a fist and shook it in the face of the white man. Then, and only then, they began to see fear and they tasted the sweet taste of liberty.

One day, a new small urbane man joined Cleva, Winston and the others where they still met most days. They did not sing and play music any more and there were no ingredients for ginger beer, but they used hard words to help nourish themselves. It was all they had left.

The small man wore glasses and was dressed smartly. He spoke slowly and with a voice that belonged to a much bigger man and there hung about him a strange electricity.

'Comrades, we are now near the time where we throw off the shackles of colonisation. At last, we will be free. We have many supporters across the world.' He spoke without raising his voice, but they could all hear him. His voice held a musical note like a song, and they wanted to hear more.

'Now we must start to see that we are good, and we are free. We are black and we are...' Here he paused, looking around at the pinched faces and they held their breath. 'We are beautiful. We must be beautiful. We are not like our parents. No more for us the servitude of the oppressor. We will not listen to the language of the regime. A regime that has taken all of our young men and women and made slaves of them.'

There was silence and even the night crickets were still. The words were like a rising tide of warm water. Winston felt a sense of swelling as if he would burst. Those faint words that had always lived inside were now finally able to escape.

Winston recognised the sensations that he was experiencing as they ran across Cleva's face like small ants. She smiled as she had not done in a long time, and he heard her tell someone nearby that the speaker's name was Gwala and that he was her cousin. The pride made her seem bigger, taller and her voice was stronger and clearer. Her eyes gleamed into the night like stars.

Winston started to feel another sensation — the sharp pricks of envy.

Gwala spoke throughout the township and became a kind of saviour and suddenly rumours abounded. Men and women looked into the sky and thanked their lord that a saviour would come.

And Gwala was everywhere like a preacher. He travelled up and down the township speaking to informal groups, and as word spread the groups grew.

Cleva went too and the two made a team and the people of Langa, with very little else to do, fed on their words and flocked to their talks as if their words were food.

Winston, unable to stay away and hating himself, trailed after them, hearing the words and feeling them stop up his own mouth. The township grew harder and rough, and the streets were paved with despair. Small irritable fights broke out and ran through the streets like unruly drunks.

One day Winston and Looksmart were walking on the east side of the township in silent hopelessness. So far, the east side, being closer to the white suburbs, had remained as it always had been as if to present the township's best side to its white neighbours.

But it was possible to see the signs of hunger and despair. It too had started to slip. Even Looksmart had caught Gwala's words and was looking forward to the day's speeches. Winston was listening to Looksmart as he put his own words to the struggle, but his thoughts had wandered to Gwala and Cleva.

Out of the corner of his eye, he caught a streak like a blur running along the gravel road and down an alley. Then a sound came, a dull shouting and a high, long scream. They stopped and Looksmart was silent, and Winston sensed that Looksmart had also seen it.

'Come, comrade, we must go,' he said, grabbing Winston's arm.

'What is it?' Winston stopped and felt Looksmart's hand, stiff and strong, pulling him away. He resisted and the blur evolved into a man, naked except for a blanket clutched to his chest, but as it was hindering his running, he dropped it and ran. The reasons that he had done this became obvious when Winston saw that the five or six men chasing had stout sticks that they waved in the air. Their faces were angry and blank with venom. The man became cornered and like a rat his eyes darted from side to side as the pursuers approached. Winston could not recognise these people any more. He had always known that the people of Langa were tough, but this? What had happened to the people? What had they become?

Looksmart pulled him and he allowed himself to be led away and Looksmart's soft words followed them down the street. 'Leave it, comrade, there is nothing you can do.' Behind them the sound of screaming hysteria swelled, and Winston put his hand over his ears and followed Looksmart.

Listening to Gwala, the smooth politician, all Winston could see was the naked, cowering man and the mindless gang following him.

'What do you suppose he has done?' Looksmart just shook his head. For the first time Winston felt the true danger of a starving Langa.

Looking at Gwala on a makeshift stage, Winston could not see what it was that allowed Gwala to be so different to them all. He could never imagine Gwala running through the township. Could never imagine Gwala standing before a white *baas* with his father's blood staining the ground at his feet.

Gwala, although not much older than Winston, seemed to know exactly what to say and how to act. He was so confident it felt like he was decades older. Once when he and Winston had been talking, he told Winston, 'I am a political animal, comrade. It is no good being a warrior. The white man knows that the black man brings a spear to fight when he has guns. But in politics the white man brings those same guns, and the black man brings logic. Even guns have to bow to logic.' Winston was not sure that he agreed, remembering the gleaming gun that had ended his father's life. He knew that no amount of logic would deliver justice.

But he said nothing because Cleva had returned and when she looked at Gwala, Winston could not kill the gleam of hope that she held in her eye.

That day of the chased man he had listened to Gwala like all the others, and they were all silent. The man spoke with steel running through his words.

'We stand here now with no right to own land comrades. Land that we were born into. Why? Because we are black, that is why. The white man wants us only for our labour and then they want us to disappear. Well, the only thing we have is labour and that we will take away. We are suffering, this is true, but we have always suffered.'

Winston thought of the man and wondered if he were still alive.

'Comrades, we must stay strong, and we will win. Victory will be ours. *Amandla*!' He screamed and the crowd raising their fists answered him, '*Awethu!*'

'White suppression will not prevail,' another man shouted, his voice loud and hard like nails, and he joined Gwala on the platform. Gwala stepped to one side and Cleva was there smiling and glowing at him. Even though Winston was standing at the back of the crowd he could feel her energy and excitement.

Another time, on the street over a blazing fire, Gwala began to speak of white men who had struggled. White Russians who had overthrown their regimes. This history was new to the men who listened. This was something that they had never known before.

'Karl Marx wrote a book called *The Rights of Man*. He said that every man has the right to live freely.' Murmurings broke out and they tested the word freely and tried to imagine a world where they were free.

'The white man brought capitalism to us here. They make us work all day and then others must work all night. Why should we do this? If I work this week and I have enough money, then I won't work next week. Why should I? But the white man does not like this. He says we must work all the time. The factories where you work must stay open all day and all night. The white man is a slave to money.' He paused and the men nodded to each other.

Soon everyone was saying it, 'Black is beautiful,' chanting it in the streets so that it chimed with their steps. Gwala even had a book which he often held aloft. The book was called *Black Beauty* and it was only when Gwala accidentally left it on his seat one night that Winston could awkwardly trace the words on the blurb. He found the book referred to a horse and when Gwala returned, he slipped the book back and he never asked Gwala about it.

It was easy to chant the words and push the suffering to one side. It was easier than confronting Gwala, especially when everything he said was so good. If it had not been for his annexation of Cleva, Winston would have liked very much to be his friend.

Winston remembered one day when a tall thin man with yellow teeth had shouted out, 'I have heard others say these words. These are not your ideas.' Winston had seen him before, a cruel man who liked to ridicule.

But Gwala had only laughed, a truly happy laugh and he turned to the tall man. 'Comrade, you do not own words, they are things in their own right. Words are better than bullets and they will help us. You will see now we have been fighting with bullets and now is the time for words.' The tall thin man spat in the dust and turned and melted into the crowd.

Suddenly their grief and their struggle had words and a language and a logic that not even the cruel white regime could deny.

Gwala came from Soweto and sometimes he spoke not of the struggle but of the city where he grew up.

'The streets are small, like here,' he said pointing at the streets all around them. 'But in Soweto it is always busy. Doesn't matter if you go out in the middle of the day or in the middle of the night. There are always people.' He sighed and smiled. 'Here it is so quiet.' Winston wondered what he would have thought of the valley, but he didn't ask. When Gwala spoke in that contained way, so clear and so quiet, everyone listened.

The person most affected by Gwala's presence was Cleva. She drank his words and shaped them in her own beautiful mouth. Where everyone else was dull through lack of food, she became shiny, as if Gwala had polished her with his words, as if he fed her and Gwala had taken a match to the tinder of her ideas. Where Gwala spoke softly, she shouted angrily, battering her listeners with the barrage of her words.

Soon she gathered a new following of her own — a knot of angry youths — youths who clamoured to add to her outraged cries with shouts of her own. Cleva was the rallying cry for the young and disaffected.

Suddenly she was not the young angry girl that Winston knew; she had become something that frightened Winston. Her hunger was also not like the others — yes, she had as little food as all of them, but her hunger was for something that was just as elusive as food. Cleva wanted liberty above anything else and it drove her on and on. She could not wait for her liberty and if anger could get her closer then she would use it. Winston hardly recognised this new energised girl.

Although starvation settled and gripped them in the thrall of apathy, something began to awake as if words really did replace food. Now with the arrival of this man and his words, there was a buzz and something to wake for every day.

One day before the dusty heat had settled, Winston and Cleva found themselves together in a smoky yard. This was rare and Winston watched her, his eyes darting sideways. Cleva was no longer the easy laughing girl that he had known when he first moved to Langa. She made him quiver and shrink.

Even though there was little to eat, and meals had long ago become extinct, many people still drifted to this central place that Winston had stumbled on so many months before.

Cleva had aged but she appeared even more attractive to Winston. He supposed they had all aged. Lack of food and worry had made them all into old men and women.

He was no longer shy of her, but now the electricity that he felt was strangely dangerous and she was even more of an impossibility. Cleva seemed oblivious to him and drew away into her new political narrative and Winston was further away from her than ever.

But Winston loved to listen to her anger and now she had a new mesmerising energy. He loved the exciting hitch to her voice tinged with something that made her different and made her... He couldn't identify it, so he asked her what had changed. 'Hope,' she said. 'It is hope that things will finally change.'

She looked into the fire and then up at the sky. 'Soon I am going to get me a house. Like those ones over there.' She pointed to Vanes Estates. 'Then I'm going to get a car, a BMW and I'm going to ride on the roads and I'm going to drive through Africa.' She laughed at the possibility of it all and Winston laughed too. It had been so long since they'd sat like this.

'What is your dream, comrade?' Winston started and then looked at her. She looked down and mumbled an apology.

He shrugged and tried to speak but suddenly the words would not come. He could not tell her that he wanted to go back when she was always saying they had to move forward. How could he tell her that his dream was to go back to the valley and live by the river as he had done as a child? How could he tell her when he knew that it no longer existed?

After that conversation, Winston didn't know if he could identify hope any more. His dream now lay in tatters at his feet, and it was hard to catch any of the excitement. And he did try, tried to focus on Cleva's hope, but all he could see was Doda lying in the dust leaking his life away.

They needed hope, she said, and now in this terrible darkness of struggle, she had found her hope. Many others joined her, and they knew that change came after a time of great suffering.

Cleva drifted further away, pulled closer to Gwala.

Gwala spoke the words that the people of Langa wanted to hear. Gwala had a confidence that spoke of big cities and a street life that was a million miles away from Langa. Winston felt strangely inadequate, like a country bumpkin, clumsy and tongue tied, unable to articulate his hopes and dreams and set adrift in a sea of struggle.

He knew it was a betrayal, but he did not like Gwala. He tried and would often move closer to the man when others had drifted away. Tried to listen and then one day a coloured man was speaking Afrikaans and Gwala, who never raised his voice, jumped up and shouted.

'No, comrade, we only speak Xhosa here. Only African languages.' And for once the smooth talker was jittery and disjointed. 'No, no,' he repeated. Winston, feeling sorry for the other man, tried to intervene.

'Comrade,' the word still felt clumsy on his tongue, 'Comrade, he is coloured, his language is Afrikaans.'

'No,' Gwala repeated and then swallowed hard. 'No, we must only speak our languages. Afrikaans is the language of the oppressor. English is the language of the colonialists. We must speak our own language.'

He walked in the small spaces between the seats, and he was breathing heavily.

'You must speak your own language. That is the only way that you will be able to say your ideas. If you try another language, you can't think properly.' Here he turned to the coloured man.

'I am sorry, my friend, but my ideas form in my head in Xhosa. If I have to translate it into another language and I don't have the words, then some of my ideas are lost. Do you understand?'

The coloured man nodded and Gwala sighed. 'One of the ways that the regime keeps its foot on our necks is by taking our language away. They already take our names, don't let them take your words, comrades.'

And even though this was the least prepared speech that Gwala had ever made, Winston felt his words as if they were a physical blow. In that moment his antipathy for the man evaporated and he fully understood what he was saying.

Now Cleva was lost to him and drawing further away in her anger. Winston was pulled closer to Gwala, and it was Gwala who spoke openly of his own family and tragedy. Gwala said that all African families had some sort of tragedy. It was what the white man brought.

A few days, after Gwala announced that he was organising a demonstration, Winston asked him why he did it.

'It is because of my Auntie Gcina,' he said. Then, with smiling sadness, he said, 'She is so tiny. Only about this big.' He held his hand about four feet from the ground. 'But even though she is so small she had four sons. All of them huge.' And here he held his arm up as far as it would go.

'But we are all afraid of her. She had a shoe that she hit us with when we were children.' He smiled, lost in his memories.

'Auntie Gcina and Uncle Xolile were both involved with the struggle. Uncle Xolile went away to fight somewhere in Africa. I don't know where because I didn't really know him well. Soon all my cousins were working in the struggle. They did not go to their father but stayed in Soweto, but everybody knew the Gcina family. Shortly after that they arrested my Auntie Gcina and sent her to jail.' He shook his head. No one made a sound.

'One day news came that Uncle Xolile was killed in Angola. It was in a letter that came from his friend. My auntie can't read, and she had to ask one of the other prisoners. She knew it must be bad news because no one in her family would write to her.

'Then one day there was more news. Two of her sons had been killed by the regime.' His voice was cold, and Winston shivered. Gwala continued with tears clogging his voice.

'In her dark and soulless cell, the guards told her and then left her in that tiny cell. She stayed in that cell and the first words she said when she came out was "I want to see my boys." They laughed at her and told her that the funerals had already been held. Those white men allowed the funerals to go ahead when they knew that their mother was sitting in a cell all on her own.'

Then a strange thing happened. That terrible tragedy became entwined in Winston's story, and he supposed that all of Africa's tragedies became one in the end.

He let himself drop out of the circle surrounding Gwala and allowed himself to drown in the memories of Doda. A man who loved the land; a man who understood the land and wanted nothing more than to live on that land for the whole of his days. A man who had not been allowed to become an old man surrounded by his grandchildren. A man with modest dreams brutally snuffed out.

These memories made his eyes water which he dashed away with his arm, carelessly and gruffly.

These memories would mean the end of him, so he thought instead of the old lady in her lonely cell while her sons were laid in the ground with no one to mourn them. He imagined Gwala's Auntie Gcina, prematurely aged by the tragedy of her life.

Suddenly his own feelings of loss and isolation, long ignored, rose to the surface with a force that almost knocked him over. Now the deep sense of suffering bubbled to the surface, and he was swamped with images of his father, lifeless on the ground that had callously sucked up his precious blood, his tiny shrinking mother keening and kneeling over the body. Numbed with shock, he could hardly remember the funeral — a strange ceremony that was the first that Winston had experienced, not having gone to his grandfather's funeral.

Then the final blow. A pale and dishevelled Daniels, apologetic and subdued. The news like persistent body blows; the property would sell. Daniels would go back to the bustling city and the farming dream was over. And as he walked away Winston stood on the dry hard clay and felt his own dream melt away like retreating mist.

That one single shot took his Doda, his home and his livelihood.

Chapter 22 — The Army

Somewhere in the Transvaal Province, South Africa

After the disastrous exchange at the police station, Kobus avoided his son. The son he had thought so close, now a chasm had opened up between them. What had seemed so simple, what was easier than loving your son? Now he felt not only love but feelings of envy, scorn and even hate. That was certain, the love, but he had never bargained for those other feelings, and they pummelled him into confusion.

And all the time all around him he saw fathers and sons talking and laughing as if it were the most natural thing in the world.

As he grappled with the crippling antipathy towards his son, he developed a headache and he longed to go to sleep and never think of any of it ever again. Over the years he had become good at this sort of cauterisation. He put it alongside the other memories that he wished to forget, and it lay there like a festering sore.

Sometimes he would put a loathsome memory away only for another to surface as if dislodged in the overflow.

Reminiscing about his son brought back memories of his own father, who was forever linked to the army. In fact, Kobus had grown up in the army, he would sometimes joke, and for as long as he could remember he'd been a soldier, as if his father ran a regiment rather than a family.

In those early days when his father had still commanded respect and awe, he and his brothers had been proud of their father. A tall, commanding man who others respected, admired and obeyed without question. Those days his hair was dark and short cropped, and the deep lines had not yet settled into his face. That was before old age and the army life had bent him a little, made a mockery of his knees and peppered his hair with grey.

They'd laughed then at his eccentricities, at his pathological hatred of everything that was not the army; even the navy and the air force could not escape his scorn.

But it was for civilians that the old man saved his most poisonous scorn and ridicule. Kobus could still hear his voice, brash and challenging, condemning those that would not fight. Could still see the gleam in his eyes that had retained the old fire even while the rest of his body bowed to old age.

As a young boy Kobus and his brothers had waited each night for inspection, standing by their beds with a barely suppressed craving for approval. A riot of conflicting emotions inhabited his mind. Wanting to be noticed yet dreading that he would be. It was then that he'd first felt that yearning desire for approval.

Those days were filled with a trembling desire to do things but instead a crippling inaction would often grip him. This was because the old man was so exacting, and Kobus was destined to do wrong. Once when camping, his father made him prepare the *braai* where they were to cook the evening meal. Over and over again his father found fault. Nothing was clean enough; nothing was ready and the more he felt his father's scrutiny, the more he froze as if turned to marble. This only caused the old man to shout and become even angrier until at last one of his brothers had taken over.

That night he made Kobus sleep on his own in the woods as a punishment. He tried to laugh it off and turned away from the pitying looks in his brothers' eyes. But still, after all these years, he could remember the fear and his limbs shaking throughout the night and jumping at every fearsome sound. He must have slept because he awoke the next morning with red-rimmed eyes. His father barely looked at him as they hiked their way through the woods and up into the mountains. That day was the longest, most gruelling that Kobus had ever experienced in his young life. He swore to himself that he would never subject his own son to such treatment.

Despite this, Kobus worked even harder to earn his father's approval. He, like his brothers, would make a life in the army, of that he was certain. This was as set as the sun coming up every day.

Then at eighteen he was called up to do his duty through conscription and it was understood that he would then make the army his career. He hadn't given it much thought because, after all, it had been decided almost before he was born that his life would follow that of his own father and his grandfather before that.

And like all the other boys his age he was glad to do it, proud even. He'd fantasised about the day that he would become a soldier, leaving behind boyhood inadequacies. And he so wanted to be a man that he was glad to say goodbye to his cool, aloof mother and hoped to be admitted to his father's grown-up world of soldiering.

He even dreamed about the uniform, could feel it in his sleep, rough and coarse like the one he remembered his dad wearing. He recalled stealing into his father's room and then setting the uniforms on the bed as if they were the soldiers. In that time alone while the others could not see him, he would lay on the uniforms and imagine a life as a brave, famous soldier, like those soldiers he read about in the comic books.

He always took care when returning the uniforms to their neat hangers, stroking them as if they were pets.

Sometimes, taking them carefully from their hangers, he put them on without undoing any of the buttons. Then he would stand in front of the mirror and let his imagination take flight. Even though they were too big, and he was a small boy with long sleeves and huge trousers trailing behind him, there in the mirror he only saw glory. Never in all that time did it ever occur to him that the army would be anything other than a triumph.

In that forbidden room that belonged to his parents, it felt exciting and thrilling. He liked the stiff parade uniform the best. Shining blue with the South African *Vierkleur* stitched proudly above the right breast pocket, over the heart. Over his heart that beat strong with pride and would one day have his own flag, his own uniform.

He too would have rows of glinting medals just as his father had. He stroked those medals and made his own stories of bravery and honour.

His battles would be bloodier and much more daring than even those of his brothers. He never questioned this because it never occurred to him that it might not happen, and he thought of his heroic actions as if they had already been achieved.

But when the day came and he finally joined up, almost immediately it began to go wrong. The base camp, a place so banal and ordinary that Kobus had no memory of the journey, was hard and sterile like a two-dimensional drawing that a child had painted.

Strangely, among the other recruits he was clumsy and uncoordinated. He'd never noticed before. School athletics and rugby had not prepared him for the climbing, running, crawling and physicality of the army.

Shouting, nameless commanders resurrected memories of those ill-fated camping trips. He began to freeze and became stilted and afraid. It was easy to fake athletics at school. Now there was no place to hide.

In the Transvaal bush veld miles from any sort of civilisation amongst all the other recruits, thousands from across the country, it was obvious that he was out of his depth. Three months of initiation — they all said that it would pass quickly — suddenly seemed like a lifetime.

'You are too busy getting fit and working. You won't believe it when the three months are up,' his father told him and smiled for the first time in a very long time. But time stood still. Days and nights soon merged until it felt like one long never-ending nightmare.

Worst still were the endless stream of practical jokes. Initiations that were the mysterious and unspoken lore of joining the army. He had been prepared for it, but in reality, he'd never given it any real thought.

Now the initiation rites rushed at him with a boundless infinite cruelty. Who were the people that started it? Did they sit around all night preparing their tricks? He didn't know because he was too tired and too dejected and besides, he was by now tightly locked into his own misery.

Small factions were formed. There were those who joined with the leaders of the bullying and those who were the recipients. The recruits had to be quick and if they were too slow like Kobus, they became victims.

The perpetrators grew less imaginative and returned again and again with monotonous regularity to upturned beds in the early morning hours or water tricks also involving beds by saturation and reducing the sleeper to a cold, huddle, dreading the morning when the officers would add their own weight to the humiliation.

So, the mindless initiations continued. And in the interminable and arcane rules of the army, everyone was punished in the morning for wet beds. Even the offenders were punished, but it did nothing to dampen them.

Worst of all was that the leaders of the squad did nothing. It would, Kobus was assured by one of the men, make real men of them and most importantly, it would lead to them becoming soldiers. It was something that had to be endured.

Platoon Five was made up of eighteen men, boys really, just released from school. Boys who had been given permission to act like men.

His father's only piece of advice had been to never divulge any of the family history to his superiors and fellow recruits. For some strange inexplicable reason, the army did not like its new recruits bragging — bewildering army logic.

Jannie, the big burly redhead who naturally assumed leadership and was the principal instigator of the initiations, led the charge against bragging. Kobus never did find out why Jannie was so vengeful, but he saw how Jannie, through a combination of brutal and unsubtle force, had submerged everybody else with his ideas.

One day, a small wiry-looking boy with no facial hair mentioned an uncle who was a general. The boy had returned from exercises one day with a swollen face and two black eyes. One of his front teeth was missing and his whistling breath that night kept the platoon awake. Kobus vowed never to reveal his own connections.

Jannie, colossal and with dumb strength, assumed control of the platoon and no one challenged him. And Jannie was spoiling for a fight.

He was fanatically followed by Hendrik and Justin. These boys were so similar that many assumed they were brothers although they had never met before joining the army. Both blond and nearly as tall as Jannie. Like two bookends.

In Jannie there was to be found the schoolyard bully now promoted to manhood.

Jannie and his followers soon homed in on the weak, scenting them out like a bloodhound. As if they could smell the uncertain, the lost and homesick.

It was the first time that Kobus had been in contact with the sons of English, French and Dutch families, having only ever met people like himself before. Soon a small, lonely recruit emerged as the perfect target. Alain.

Alain was proud of his French heritage. Proud of his winemaking Huguenot relatives. Proud of his ability to speak French as well as English. Kobus quite liked the little man, and one day in the canteen he was talking of his home near Cape Town, a place that Kobus imagined he might visit one day.

'I am going to make wine. Wine is the new gold. South African wine is amongst the best in the world.' There was a pleased note in his voice like a chorus of joy, a note that had been missing from Kobus' voice for a long time.

'You know the Australians are becoming very well known for their wine and there is no reason why we shouldn't have the same success.' His voice was low and something in his tone spoke of reading and education. He stopped and considered something over Kobus' shoulder and although the canteen was a noisy place, on their table no one interrupted the Frenchman.

'We can't expect to be as good as the French,' he said putting his fork down. 'They have after all got centuries on us. But one day my vineyard — it's in Stellenbosch you know, well, my father's vineyard — one day it will be one of the best in the world. You mark my words.'

Alain was smiling and picked up his fork and resumed eating and suddenly a shadow appeared at the table. Jannie.

He wore a scowling smile. Without a word he hauled Alain to his feet and shoved his own red face into his. Alain's feet dangled and he let the fork drop but did not say a word. Jannie shook him, like a rat, and then pushed him so that he staggered back into the hard chest of Hendrik.

'Hey, watch it you *doos*!' Hendrik's voice shook with menace. Alain turned and fled, and Kobus found it hard to swallow and he stared hard at the table, the same thing that everyone else was doing.

It was after that when the torture of the Frenchman began. No longer was he to hear his name.

Jannie said, 'That's a *sissie* name. The French they are a bunch of *sissies* as well. No, we are going to call you the Frenchie. That's your new nickname!' Kobus saw in that instant that the name hurt Alain and he wished that the boy could hide his feelings because at that moment Jannie saw it, too. Jannie turned to the others, and he wore his frowning smile and Kobus knew that Alain was finished.

'Isn't your name a girl's name?' Jannie sneered, cutting off Alain's denial. Then in a high pitch voice, he taunted, 'I'm making wine and I like to drink a girl's drink.' He turned to Alain. 'What's wrong with you, man,

did you not get enough food when you were a boy? You are so small.'
Here the others laughed. 'Maybe wine stunts you. Come on, Frenchie, why
are you small like a girl? Hey.' Here he was prodding Alain, his huge
finger punching into Alain's chest.

From that time on, Alain started to become invisible. The others, good
boys from good homes, followed the rules determined by Jannie. The good
boys, like Kobus, ignored Alain. Even when he returned to the barracks at
night missing teeth and his face showing where fists had landed and his
body where boots had landed, they turned away.

In the night when he turned to the wall the others put their pillows
over their ears so that they could not hear his sadness.

When they were called on by Jannie, they laughed and sniggered and
Jannie was satisfied. Then the officers too began to pick on Alain. Like a
pack of dogs, everyone was drawn towards the poor French boy who knew
no peace. He was too slow, not upright enough, not loud enough, not brave
enough. Not Afrikaans enough. Then another day he was too quick, too
stiff and too loud, and he could do with being a little less reckless. The
officers called him the Frenchie, too.

Frenchie, if it was possible, became even smaller, even thinner,
slower and shabbier. And now he brought punishment onto them all and
natural justice became another reason to hate him.

The hatred was piled on deeper and deeper until Alain was far out of
his depth and barely treading water. The men could not now help him by
encouraging him or giving him advice because they had made him
invisible and to talk to him would mean their own demise.

One day after finishing watch duty Kobus was returning to the
barracks along a cold lengthy corridor; he heard a sound. A small furtive
sound. He slowly crept forward wondering if some trick was about to be
played on him. It paid to never relax; Jannie was an ever-present danger.

Phone privileges were only earned after the first month. They had
only been on the base for three weeks and as the time drew closer, it was
all the men spoke of. Kobus began to feel anger, like a boiling tide rising
up from his legs all the up to his neck. There in the telephone booth was
the Frenchie talking into the phone.

Kobus was surprised to find that in amongst the anger, he felt a begrudging sense of admiration and he quickly trampled on it. It would never do to admire the Frenchie.

They all knew about where the phones were on the base. Many of them in the offices at the back of the barracks and one in the corridor where Frenchie was now speaking rapidly in nonsensical French. This phone was fixed to the wall, and it was the phone they would all be using when the time came.

He stopped and listened for Frenchie's words. Even though he couldn't understand them, he recognised the whining, plaintive note and sneered and felt the hot, rising anger again.

Not only was he not speaking Afrikaans, but he was also using the phone. The phone that Kobus himself itched to use but could not.

Kobus began again to boil. He would love to unburden himself, if only there had been someone to listen. He tried to imagine his tall, cold mother on the phone and almost laughed aloud. Then all the injustices came crowding in like wild beasts and he wanted to smash the Frenchie into little pieces. The anger surprised him, and he found that he'd curled his hands into tight fists.

Then, to his astonishment, Frenchie began to cry and was silent for a long time. Kobus shifted uncomfortably and again the rage of injustice, frustration came, and he knew he would have to get even.

He would let Jannie know about the phone, and he felt the burning spite rising to overwhelm the anger. Jannie would make the Frenchie pay.

But Jannie was a difficult person to approach. Not someone who was quick to grasp ideas or allow someone to dictate to him. Nobody would risk approaching him for fear of accidentally becoming the target themselves. Kobus most definitely did not want to be noticed. He had managed to avoid the worst of the initiations. It was true that he'd had his fair share of cold showers in the middle of the night, but it had been no worse than what anyone else had suffered.

Yes, there had been the time when he had been dragged out of bed by his ankles; that night everyone had suffered that. Others had been thrown in the small slimy pond at the bottom of the training ground still wrapped in their own bed linen. That had earned them even more trouble in the morning when the sergeant had inspected the beds. Days of punishments had been the result. Only Frenchie had been subjected to every single humiliation. Frenchie's soaking and beating continued night after night. Kobus, remembering the torture, had no wish to unwittingly become part of it.

Kobus hated this life in a frightening passionate way, and he could almost taste it. Hated the ridiculous and unnecessary early mornings, standing around on parade for hours of tedious uncomfortable hours. Hated the pettiness of it all. That after standing on the parade ground for hours, a corporal would send them all back to the barracks because they were not wearing the same belt as him. Then the parade would begin again at the whim of a corporal.

He hated the fact that there was never even the slightest piece of praise and had never known before that he wanted it. Hated himself for wanting a hint of a smile or some sort of encouragement. Sometimes he thought he would die of the bleakness or never knowing. Never knowing if he'd done it right, done anything right.

There were times he felt that his whole life led up to this point. The point where he was finally exposed for the fraud he really was.

Most of all, Kobus feared Jannie, as if the man could look deep into his soul and see the small cringing animal that he had become. Kobus had never been in this position before. Never had reason to fear one man above all others. Jannie was the success that Kobus always assumed he would be. The army loved Jannie as it did not love him.

Kobus kept the phone call close to his chest as if it were a rare jewel. He kept it next to the pain and hurt and disappointment that were his constant companions. After the compulsory service was over, he promised himself he would never join the army. Never.

The phone call sat in his memory like a dangerous beast. Nothing he did gave him as much pleasure as merely sitting and mulling over what to do with his knowledge. Even when he was issued with his R1 rifle, it gave him hardly any pleasure at all. This longed-for treasure was unwieldy in his grip, clumsy and rigid, unbending and unyielding. He even struggled, to his surprise, with the stripping and reassembling. He, who had been stripping guns from the age of seven.

His father would not recognise the clumsy fat fingers as they dropped and mishandled the small parts, with bored officers frustrated and despairing as they oversaw his shame.

He returned again and again to the phone call. To the forbidden audacity of the Frenchie.

Every time he heard laughter that he was not part of and every time he heard the joy in others, he raged and raged.

That rage made him, for the first time, feel a little better, a little more like he might survive this somehow.

One day with his head down, walking into the searing wind, Kobus bumped into one of Jannie's henchmen. The block-like shape of Hendrik. Shocked, Hendrik dropped a piece of paper that immediately scurried away on the wind. 'Hey, watch it, *doos*,' he sneered, the insult like poison dripping from his lips. Kobus' heart beat a little faster. Kobus breathed fast and tried to sidle round the man. 'I said, watch it.'

'*Jammer*,' Kobus stammered out, hating the way his voice trembled and came out high like a girl. He moved away quickly following the now distant paper fluttering playfully in the hot wind. Hendrik put a cold hand onto his shoulder. It was suddenly quiet. Very quiet. Even the wind was still for a moment. The paper had stopped on the edge of the parade ground. No one stirred. The squat barracks were like dark smears against the blue early morning sky. Kobus began to be afraid. 'I… I was just thinking, thinking about the Frenchie,' he blurted out. Hendrik removed his hand, although his face was still dark. 'So what?'

'Well, I noticed the other day that he was using the phone in the office. You know the office at the end of the barracks near the canteen. I saw him. He was crying.' Then, he said, 'I didn't know we could use the phone,' the last coming out in a rush like a flood.

The sneer grew and encompassed Kobus. 'Don't talk *kak,* man. No one is allowed to use the phone.'

'Fine, if you don't believe…'

'How could he be on the phone?' Hendriks' voice wavered. Kobus sensing his advantage began to walk away.

'Why don't you ask him yourself? I know what I saw, and he was talking on the damn phone.'

Jannie broke the Frenchie's nose with the first punch. The Frenchie didn't even make a sound. Just held his face in both hands as if holding the bones together as he crouched against his bedside locker. Bright satin red blood streamed in a river through his fingers. Jannie made a pretence of being held back by Hendrik and Justin while screaming obscenities.

Kobus wondered why the officers did not come and began to feel the edges of fear in this too close room with the bleeding Frenchie. Jannie's mouth was foaming, full of spit and his face blotchy red.

Alain said nothing and now Kobus could hardly bear to watch; both repelled and fascinated by the blood that seeped unchecked onto the Frenchie's arms and chest. Kobus sank down behind his bed not wanting to leave but too afraid to stay. All the while the Frenchie's eyes through his fingers locked onto Kobus with an accusation that told he knew the source of Jannie's knowledge.

Unexpectedly and suddenly the shrill whistle summoned them to parade. A surprise that even Jannie could not ignore. Ten minutes only were available to prepare for a parade. Automatically the recruits started to prepare but assembling without the Frenchie would mean certain punishment for the entire platoon. A wall of tangible hatred borne out of panic was directed towards the Frenchie. No one dared blame Jannie.

The two stooges dragged Frenchie into the shower and splashed his face with freezing water and then he began to scream. They screamed louder and Justin aimed a kick at the Frenchie's backside.

In the end the platoon was not found wanting. Frenchie, a pale facsimile of a soldier, did not draw any attention although Kobus noticed Commandant Viljoen eyeing him and then with a shrug passed on.

Later that evening the Frenchie, on the way to the showers, stopped at Kobus' bed. Kobus did not look up. He noticed a dark bruise on his leg, blue and purple in the shape of a shoe just below the knee. The Frenchie spoke to Kobus' unlistening shoulder.

'I just wanted to say that phone doesn't even work. It's just good sometimes to pretend that someone is actually listening.' Kobus said nothing.

The next morning the Frenchie was gone.

Jannie said that if they caught him, the Frenchie would go to jail. The army would not forgive an AWOL.

Someone said that the Frenchie had been sent out of the country by his commie parents. He'd been sent to France where he was living in the terrible ghettos of Paris. Everyone knew that Europe was a mess and no proper South African would want a life like that. Trust the Frenchie to choose a life like that and all Kobus could think of was the sound of his voice as he described the vineyard in Stellenbosch.

There was another wilder theory that he had joined the ANC. That the ANC had spirited him out of the country, and he was training with *Umkhonto we Sizwe*. Jannie, forgetting what a lamentable soldier the Frenchie was, hoped that this last story was true. Because one day he'd find that little commie bastard and make him pay.

After the Frenchie went, the three months dragged on, and the entire platoon passed out and they were posted to the border. They were going to war and all Kobus could think of was the end of the two years and finally being free of them all.

There were times when he envied the Frenchman his way out. He longed to leave each day himself, but he could not. He had two years of compulsory service and only then was he out. He had no parents who would rush to his defence. His parents, hearing of his ignominious performance in the army, had already turned their backs. In his decision not to join the army his family turned their backs, and he was adrift in the world on his own.

Chapter 23 — The Court Case

Port Elizabeth, Winter 1983

On that morning, Winston had woken to his first day as his father's assistant. For months Doda and Daniels had been speaking of this day and Winston had felt as if it would never come.

Rolling from the thin mattress and joining his father for a breakfast of hot thick coffee, his heart swelled with pride. It was early and even the birds were not yet busy. The sun, weak at this hour, peeked coyly over the mountains. Winston sat next to his father and waited.

Doda silently handed him a pair of boots, shiny and new. Winston had never had a new pair of shoes and could only stare at them. Doda laughed and gestured for Winston to put them on. He supposed that Daniels had bought them for him and fumbled with the laces. His feet felt heavy and clumsy as if they belonged to someone else.

As he ran to catch up with Doda he marvelled at how quickly life was changing and he felt as if he could hold out his hand and touch his dream. That floundering in the strange twilight zone between adult and child worlds had come to an end. At seventeen, manhood now beckoned, and Winston was ready.

The morning that had started in such a promising way gave no hint of the harrowing events to come. On that golden morning, Winston only thought of the future, and it looked like a bright gleaming star. But before the end of that day, he found that dreams could be short and fleeting and over in the blink of an eye.

During the walk to the lands and stepping to the tune of his father's hum, he told himself that he must remember it all. But that hideous day became seared forever into Winston's mind for something else entirely. And no matter how much he shook his head and closed his eyes, the picture of his father's broken body would not fade. After that shot rang out into the clear day and his father crumpled to the ground like a rag doll, he knew in that instant that everything had changed. Even before he reached his father's prone form, he knew that he would never again see his father return to their small hut and share his smile and sit by the fire.

The funeral had fittingly dawned a dank and rare rainy day. The minister's voice had been soft and could hardly be heard over the sobbing of his mother and aunts. Then suddenly it was all over, and the body was in the ground and there was no more to do but look for justice that would never come.

Mrs Mbele was called twice into Court Number Two in the Port Elizabeth Supreme Court, a strange, bewildering place where white men called black women by their surnames. Where black men and women could sit in the same places with white people. A benched, clean sterile world so alien that it took Winston a long time before he understood that the court official was calling for his mother.

As Mrs Mbele did not step forward, the court official, holding his clipboard like a shield in front of his face, went back through the imposing doors into the courtroom. But he came back almost immediately, his light blue court-issue shirt pulled tightly over his protruding stomach and called the name again in staccato tones. A few people at the end of the corridor, standing in the light of a grimy window, turned but they were all white.

"Mrs Mbele. Mrs Mbele!" His voice was rough and hard like stones.

Winston, perched uncomfortably on the wooden bench next to his mother, nudged her with his elbow and spoke in a quiet voice as if to a small nervous animal.

"Mama, come, it is time." Her hand, bird-like, trembled and quivered in his. For a moment Winston doubted that she'd have the strength to rise. He wanted to tell the man, impatiently sweating and tapping the clipboard against his disapproving leg, that it was impossible, and they were in the wrong place. He wanted to close his eyes and wake up again in his beloved valley.

When he closed his eyes, he could only see the sheet covering Doda, could only hear the cries of his mother. Then later the hole in the ground that had been carved into the hard clay next to the old church and the minister singing his words of sorrow.

Somehow his mother found the strength to rise shakily, like a very old woman dwarfed by the grand high ceiling and moved towards the peevish door. The white man, using the clipboard, gestured towards the silent waiting room. She passed, almost under his arm no more than a small child next to his bulking height. Rows of silent faces followed them as they tiptoed to the front of the room Winston peeling off into the front row as he'd been instructed.

Doda would have hated this place and Winston, stealing a glance around the room, recognised no one and swallowed as the bile rose in his throat. He prayed that he would not be sick. There was no one here who would have known Doda, seen his body lying in the dust.

Even with the arrival of a nonchalant ambulance and the removal of his father's corpse, the horrible images remained like a stain. His mother could not be consoled, nor could her heart-breaking sobs be silenced. His aunts and uncles, hearing the worst news borne through the *veld* on a cry of despair, had arrived in a flood of grief. His mother, with her broken heart, could not be reached and in the end the aunts abandoned her to her seat with her rocking son, Melikhaya, between her feet. The aunts made food that would not be eaten, and the uncles spoke in hushed voices but did not disguise their ugly words from the children. They spoke of the dead but did not mention the future and time stood still.

He could not say how long he knelt beside his mother in the blood of his father before he felt a hand on his shoulder. Looking down he was surprised to see it was a white hand. He looked up then into the pale, ashen face of Daniels with new deeply ingrained lines making him look older and far away.

Mrs Daniels emerged from the house, as if in slow motion, holding a sheet that had begun to unravel from her hands and placed it over the corpse. After the white cloth the body looked like a ghost. Mrs Daniels bent and raised his mother with the blood now staining her dress. Mama moved with small robotic movements as if she'd forgotten how her legs worked. Daniels tightened his grip on Winston's shoulder, and he rose older and stained, like his mother, by the death of his father.

Then an ambulance and the police, white, all of them, and talking only to Mr and Mrs Daniels while his mother wept, dry heaving sobs, hunched on the abandoned *stoep*.

Daniels was like a man who had lost something. His answers to the careless police were vague as if he had only part of his mind on the question. None of them spoke to Winston and he hovered on the edges while the ambulance staff wheeled the body into the ambulance. The body was small and shrunken.

A policeman, a hefty, red-faced man, was sitting on the *stoep* and although he tried to speak English, switched to Afrikaans almost immediately. The babble that flowed from him brought frowns to Mr and Mrs Daniels. Mr Daniels stopped speaking altogether. Still the police asked nothing of Mama or Winston.

Winston only heard the strange words rising and falling like cold water. And he watched as the ambulance rocked down the driveway taking Doda away.

Now at last his mama would be heard and Winston hoped that she could speak, would speak. Winston, the lawyer had said, had been too far away and could not bear witness in this trial. Those words, 'could not bear witness,' seemed to Winston in that instance to banish any memories of his father forever.

The judge, a portly white man with a ruddy, rubbery face, sported a ridiculous white wig over a blood-red cloak that almost matched his fiery face. He tapped impatiently on the desk with a pencil. He was high up and seemed larger than all the others in the room.

The rows of white faces turned to watch the little child-like figure of Mama walk painstakingly to the witness chair. A white man helped her into the seat which seemed to have been designed for a much bigger witness than Mrs Mbele. The man shoved a Bible towards her, the gold cross glinting in the hazy light.

Although she was sitting across the room with a wide empty space between herself and the hearty robust Thienus van der Merwe, she shrank into the chair as if to make herself invisible. Winston, seated behind the prosecution, turned his head to the right and looked at the farmer, the first time he'd seen him since the shooting.

He stared for as long as he dared but then he saw the immense sons in a row of shiny suits, and he looked down quickly so as not to catch their eyes. He looked at his own shirt — it had belonged to his father, and he had not wanted to wear it. His loudest aunt had insisted; she of all the family knew about the courts. She knew that he needed to be formal; it was hard enough for black people in the white man's court. His trousers, which had once been dark blue, were almost grey and they were too small.

His sisters had put the trousers under a rock to flatten them, but they still looked creased and old. He wore his father's old work boots encrusted with the dirt of his toil. The new boots lay somewhere in the garden where Winston had shed them that day as he raced to his falling father.

The long bus ride to the city had started in the dark and gradually they had rattled into the daylight and the dust on the shaking floor rose in little puffs to choke and stifle the passengers. His mother wore her work overalls, a stained pinafore over an old, faded dress. His tiny mother had wailed her grief into the tin bath as she'd tried to wash out the many stains which would not move. His aunts had tried to reassure her that she looked presentable. She looked, Winston now saw in the light of the courtroom, old and as if she had been wrung by huge unforgiving hands.

Never before had Winston felt so alone surrounded by white faces in the big formal courthouse. The grey walls firmly shut out the natural world so completely that bright artificial lights were needed to shine a light on this, the white man's justice. He longed for the valley, the air spilling over him like a caress. He wanted to get up and run and never stop until he reached the valley. He wondered how to find the way back and knew that if he were left here in this hard place, he would not know where to walk. He was lost in grief and lost in space.

In the midst of his despair, he felt a pressure on his elbow and looking down saw a small white hand. He turned slowly, afraid of what he might see, but saw the sad smiling face of Mrs Daniels. Her lips were pressed together as if to stifle the smile and her hair neatly tied into a bun. Her hair had lately started to run with streaks of grey.

'I can't stay long, just nipped out of work,' she whispered and applied a surprisingly strong pressure to his elbow but said nothing. It was more than he had expected but it was enough, and he looked back at the table where the murderous white *baas* sat with his sons. They leaned into each other, smiling, almost jovial as if on a family outing.

In front of Winston sat a clean white man, thin with a moustache that was fashioned into two fine points on either side of his mouth and next to him a lone shabby black man. Winston recognised the white man as the bored lawyer that his mother had spoken to in the morning.

The lawyer had said that he represented justice and the law would seek out the truth for Mr Mbele and Winston had felt a stab of elation. A keen hard awareness that quickly faded in the face of the white institution of justice.

In that moment, he realised that since Doda's death even the act of breathing had seemed so hard. When the letter came and there had been that brief hope, his breathing came strong once more like it always had. But now in this room filled with white people, his throat closed and try as he might, he couldn't catch his breath. He remembered then his aunts and uncles erupting into a chorus of approval. At last, they cried, this man will pay for his crime. Even Winston was excited, felt a new stirring of what might be and all of that came crashing to earth in that hard courtroom.

Having no experience of the legal system and no expectations of what might be expected, Winston and his mother had travelled to Port Elizabeth on the appointed day filled with questions that no one could answer. Winston had hardly slept the night before and had awoken irritable and filled with dread.

His uncles had returned to work and only one aunt remained. There was only enough money for two tickets so it had been agreed that Winston would go with his mama. The aunt had thrust the unfathomable papers into Winston's hands, and he clutched them, afraid that his sweating palms would destroy them. He laid them on the seat next to him but immediately picked them up again. It seemed to him that moment if the papers were destroyed, they would be denied entry to the court. He added the worry to those already lodged in his chest and prayed for the day to be over.

The courthouse in Port Elizabeth, Main Street huddled next to the glorious Victorian library that drew the eye and drove all other buildings into insignificance. The courthouse was low and squat and reeked of 1960s industry and squalor. Side by side with office buildings and a few retail businesses, it was marked out by the large statue of a woman holding the scales of justice. Unused to the rush of cars, buses, vans and trucks, Winston and his mother were buffeted through the front door on a wave of alarm. Winston presented his papers to a white woman at a desk, and she did not touch the papers and hardly glanced at them. She pointed to a small, stuffy room and told them to wait.

The room was stifling and smelled strongly of sweat. There was a white man with a well-manicured moustache already sitting in the room. A quick flash of irritation passed over his face and he stacked the papers in front of him into a neat pile. In a clipped bored tone, they were informed that a man would shortly be arriving to help as a translator. The trial would be held in English mostly, although some of the case would be heard in Afrikaans for the convenience of Mr Thienus van der Merwe. The man's mouth turned into a sneer. 'None of the trial will be in Bantu so...' He shrugged.

The minutes ticked by, and the man sat leaning back in his chair with his right leg crossed over his thigh. He whistled and then stopped.

'Look, I can't wait much longer. Do you speak English?' He looked at Mama and then Winston. Winston nodded.

'I need to know what happened. I have some stuff in here,' he waved at the papers, 'but you need to tell me.'

Haltingly Winston began, 'That man, the white *baas*.' Here the white man held up a hand.

'I need names, there are millions of white men. You need to be specific.' Winston took a breath and tried again. Again after a few words he was stopped.

'What time is this? You need to be specific.'

Winston did not know and looked at his mother. She looked at her hands.

'Were you there?' The man asked, biting the top of his pen and leaning even further back in his chair.

'I came when they shot my father.'

'So, you didn't actually see it?'

'No, I was in the garden, but I was there when he fell to the ground.'

The man sighed. 'So, who saw it then?' Winston looked at his mother and his heart sank. She looked only at her hands not looking at the white man and not looking at Winston.

Tentatively he asked her, and she shook her head.

The hard voice of the man broke in. 'So, she didn't see it either?'

'She did see it... but she can't talk about it.'

The man said nothing, but he pressed his lips together and frowned.

Mama began speaking again so softly that Winston had to lean forward to hear her words. The man abruptly uncrossed his legs and sat forward, and Mama stopped speaking.

He turned to the white man and pointed at the papers. 'It is there. I think the policeman wrote it down. You can see what happened.'

The white man waved him away, his golden hand glinting and he shook his head. 'We don't have time and I hear what you have said but you weren't there, and your mother says that she didn't see if her husband had a weapon. It's almost as good as saying she wasn't there either.' He sighed and sat back.

'No, he had no weapon, *baas*,' Winston broke in, but the man flipped through his papers.

'It says here that he had a stick... a sort of... ah, here it is a *knobkerrie*, he had a *knobkerrie*.'

'Yes, *baas,* it is only a stick.'

'No, it's a fighting weapon.' His voice was hard now, and Winston could only shake his head and his mother trembled next to him and twisted her hands tightly.

'A fighting stick that the Zulus use to almost kill one another from time to time. So, you see it is a weapon.' Winston shook his head, but no words could come out through the lump in his throat. Drowning now in helpless frustration he tried to speak, work his throat as if to conjure the words that would tell of his peaceful, gentle father who'd never ever raised his hand to another.

The man sighed. 'Okay, what's the story? Ask your mother and then tell me what she says.' He leaned over the desk but did not write anything down.

Once again Winston haltingly told the story adding to his mother's sparse and painful words as if one more time would make the careless white man understand. He listened, bored now, without interruption and then he straightened as if coming to a decision and stopped Winston with the rest of the words still in his mouth.

Winston longed for the promised interpreter, clutching at the hope that the white man could be made to understand. But the white man was stacking his papers, they were little enough, and yawning without covering his mouth.

'You heard that knock on the door? We are now being called into the courtroom. You and your mother will wait outside and then you will be asked to come in. Okay, do you understand?' Winston felt himself nodding.

Then there were more words, but Winston wanted to go back to the story, explain the words, tell him what really happened, make him understand but it was too late.

They were shown to a bench in the hallway. The bench was a little too low and too hard for comfort. The white lawyer disappeared into the courtroom and suddenly there was a black man. The only other black man that Winston had seen in this place, and he was the translator. It was too late in any case to tell him the story and he was born away with the white lawyer after a brief nod to Winston. So, they waited; they were used to waiting. He patted Mama's hand, small and cold, and hoped that she could tell them what really happened the day Doda died.

Another man shuffled forward and asked his mother to raise her right hand and as there was no response, he lifted her right hand himself and put it on the Bible where it lay like a stricken bird. He made her promise to tell the truth in front of almighty God and she moved her lips without sound and that was good enough. The translator stayed seated with the bored white lawyer and finally Mrs Mbele was ready for questioning.

Then the droning voice of another man, the man sitting next to Thienus, spoke and he did not stand, the defence lawyer. His voice was muffled and strangulated as if the words had to be wrestled from his throat. His mother's white lawyer leaned back so far that Winston was certain that he would fall out of his chair. His head almost made contact with Winston's chest, and he tented his fingers, closing his eyes as if savouring a particularly fine piece of music.

The defence lawyer stopped briefly and lifted a bottle of water and drank deeply before continuing to speak. Winston became aware of his own thirst and slumped into his chair feeling at once hopeless and tired. He wanted to close his eyes, curl up in a small ball and never open them again.

But no matter how much he closed his eyes and how much he wanted to sleep he continued to return to the wretched courtroom, not able to escape the unfolding macabre show.

The words rolled out, expressionless and floating away almost as soon as they arrived. For a long time, it seemed as if Mama would not be asked any questions at all. 'On such and such a date you were cleaning in Mr Daniel's house. The house is situated at such and such a place. At some time in the morning this man' — here a little movement as he pointed towards Thienus, no longer laughing with his sons — and his mother nodded.

But now in the courtroom, faced with the sea of white faces, her throat closed tight into a fist, and it was finally too difficult to tell her story.

At last, the black translator cleared his throat and stood but stayed behind the desk. He spoke gently, reading from a well-worn piece of paper. He read, as if from a story book, and when he was finished, he looked at her with a tiny question. She nodded and the judge said irritably, 'You have to say the words Mrs Mbele.' She said a tiny yes and then the black man sat down fading into his chair like a stain.

The judge, in English asked, 'Is there anything else you would like to add, Mrs Mbele?' Faltering, she began to speak her voice hardly more than a whisper. She held her hands over her heart. Reluctantly, the black man stood again and took her words and changed them into something else, something that the court could understand.

Almost before she had finished speaking, the man beside Thienus van der Merwe leapt to his feet and began in a badgering, belligerent tone, an assault of words that bowed her down.

The translator spoke again trying to soften the white man's words. But this time questions were fired at her like bullets. Question after question with no answer. Her voice already soft and tremulous, almost disappeared.

"What could you see on the day in question?" Looking at the translator with a shrug, she said nothing.

"When did you go on to the veranda?" Inaudible reply.

Not waiting for a reply, "Can you indicate on this drawing here where *Meneer* van der Merwe was standing?" After some more inaudible comments, the witness could not be sure where he had been standing.

She wanted to explain about the white *haas*' gun. A big gleaming weapon that had a glowering life of its own. And when the gun finally spoke with a great resounding roar, she had no eyes for anything else but the crumpled broken body of her husband. So, she could not look at the

213

huge drawing on the mounted flip chart and show the white man where the white *baas* was standing. That was impossible.

The white questioner became more aggressive as he sensed his advantage. "Mrs Mbele, can you show me on the chart where your common-law husband was standing at the time just before *Meneer* van der Merwe defended himself from this unprovoked attack?" No, she could not do that either. Then the lawyer spoke again.

"Mrs Mbele, did you see your husband lunge at the defendant with the *knobkerrie*?" Now her voice tiny and shamed could not be heard and the lawyer bludgeoned on, laying waste to her testimony. "Could it be, Mrs Mbele, that your vision was obscured by the huge posts that are part of the veranda here and here?' He pointed to the diagram. 'Could it be that you did not see anything that day?"

She tried to speak, her throat bobbing up and down, but her words were so low that the translator could only look at the judge and shake his head.

Winston could sense the moment that the room turned against his mother. The translator, with pity in his voice, tried to translate but it was too late. Mrs Mbele might be able to clearly see the body of her blameless husband lying in the hot sun with his blood seeping away into the orange soil, but the court wanted more. She had no words to make the white men understand.

And as she sat opposite *baas* van der Merwe, surrounded by a sea of white faces, she had no words. The white men were smiling now, a gloating smile of triumph.

"Isn't it true that your vision was totally obscured by the veranda pillars and that there is no way that you can say that your husband did not attack *Meneer* van der Merwe?' The lawyer began to pace, confident, his words no longer strangled but strong like victory.

'Therefore, Mrs Mbele, I put it to you that you were unable to see Mr Mbele, your common-law husband, lunge at *Meneer* van der Merwe brandishing the *knobkerrie*.' She shook her head and Winston half rose from his seat finally understanding what his mother did not. Mrs Daniels behind him let out a loud breath and shouted the words, 'Shame on you.' For a while there was a shifting and ripple of shallow sound, but the judge banged his gavel loudly and ordered the court into silence.

Never in all their talks and discussions had they ever considered that *he* might be blamed for his own death.

The judge, his voice equal parts boredom and irritation, told her to speak up and she squeaked her dismay as the lawyer went over the events.

How could she explain when all she saw was Doda crumpled and destroyed? How could she explain when the white *baas* glowered only feet away?

Winston bowed his head and tried to shut out the images. The images of a man who would never again lie in the sun in his favourite place, a man who would never again laugh with his children; a man who would never again put out his hand and stop his child from walking into danger.

The white lawyer finished with his questioning and sat back into his disinterested seat, and it was over.

The simple truth was that his father was dead, and he was dead because a white man had shot him. This had been clear in the flickering light of the fire, as he discussed it with his aunts and uncles, but now the truth was like those flames, fleeting and short-lived.

By the time Winston could focus again the judge was talking and none of it made any sense for a long time.

"Let the records show that Mrs Mbele was not able to see her husband brandishing a weapon." Then there was silence and one of the sons grabbed his father's arm in a congratulatory grip and the white judge was talking again. "Would the prosecution like to redress the court?"

"Nothing further, M'Lord."

Then, just like that, it was over, and the judge announced that he would be ready to deliver his verdict later that week. In the meantime, let the defendant continue a free man.

Winston and his mother emerged from the court into a bright burning winter day. A cold spiteful wind tugged at their clothes. Cars sped unfeelingly away, and Winston wondered how the world could have changed so much and yet so little. His mother, if it was possible, had shrunk even further. She moved like a broken toy, and he longed for home and oblivion.

The court loomed behind him, and he did not look back. Knew he would never return. The white farmer and his sons were gone. Even the reporters, few in number, were gone. The place had quickly become deserted; it held no interest for anybody any more. This was already an old story and a useless part of history that would hardly be worthy of a footnote. Their white lawyer had explained that the verdict would only be delivered later in the following week. There was no way of knowing when. He said that he would let Winston know but didn't say how.

He tried to steer his mother across the street to the taxi rank that he knew was under the mess of bridges and roads that made up the motorway bypass. There were no gaps in the traffic and his mother was slow, not understanding the need for haste. Lanes of cars sped uncaringly and there seemed to be no way of getting across this road; his world suddenly narrowed to tiny insurmountable difficulties. An old black man with a young boy came towards them. He nodded and proceeded down the pavement away from the red-bricked courthouse.

"Ai Doda, how do I get across to the taxi?" The man stopped and considered Winston and his mother, withered and beaten by his side.

"Come, *impi* and bring your grandmother, it is this way. You have to go down this way by the big baking house and then you can cross at the lights. It is the only safe way." Winston didn't tell him that the fading, shrinking woman beside him was not his grandmother.

Chapter 24 — The A-Team

Alexandra Township, near Johannesburg and Pretoria, 1980

Danie had a short attention span. Everybody on the team knew that. There was only ever one exception. And that exception had happened nearly a year before the team was disbanded when an important mission had gone wrong, horribly wrong.

At first it had seemed as if the mission had been a huge success. The team had celebrated the arrest of a well-known terrorist working with the ANC. The terrorist, who they'd called *Kaffir* X, had been on the most wanted list for many years.

Kaffir X had not only evaded capture for years but had taunted the police from hiding places deep within the townships. His laughing face smiled out from hastily erected overnight posters covering the hoardings of derelict buildings.

Even when the police tore down the posters, they would appear somewhere else within hours. The posters helped *Kaffir X* attain a heroic reputation and soon right throughout South Africa he was an icon. A man of hope and vision and his followers adored and worshipped him. Even the newspapers were printing articles about his exploits and using the language that was usually associated with heroes in fairy tales. He was the tireless hero of the townships. He was a knight deprived of his horse but still willing to fight. He was a man of dreams, someone to rally around.

Kaffir X was responsible for the great chagrin that the police now felt, and it had become a matter of great urgency that the man be taken into custody. They needed to obliterate this man and wipe clean the hope that surged through so many breasts. That's when they called the A-team and the folder for *Kaffir X* hit Danie's desk.

But even then, when the A-team had been called to halt the menace, still *Kaffir* X roamed free, and newspapers clamoured for interviews. Not only South African press, a few liberal papers that could easily be ridiculed, but international press with inquisitive and clever journalists. Not all could be detained at airports or in hotels. Some of them got through and some even interviewed *Kaffir X*. Of course, they called him by his real name.

These foreign reporters did not call him by his rightful name and title or name his crimes as terrorism. Then they started quoting him and the final straw came when Reuters ran an article with the headline screaming: A NEW ERA IN SOUTH AFRICA — A FREEDOM FIGHTER OF SUBSTANCE. Next to the headline, a smiling familiar picture of a *Kaffir X*.

The article detailed a day in the life of a freedom fighter and then, insults of insults, a quote from *Kaffir X*. Not just any quote but a quote from Shakespeare: 'O heaven! that one might read the book of fate and see the revolution of the times.'

That's when Danie's wandering attention was really captured.

It mattered not to him that *Kaffir X* was a qualified lawyer and an educated man, although *he* doubted it. The man was a terrorist, not a freedom fighter. And everyone knew that terrorists had to be eliminated. Danie remembered the *kaffir* they had captured only last week who had insisted on being called doctor. 'Doctor,' he scoffed, 'You are no more a doctor than I am.' And laughed as they bundled the man away to be processed and then sent to Robben Island. What good did an education do when all they were good for was breaking rocks in prison?

Then when Danie's team had surprised *Kaffir X* at a football match it had been, he claimed later, one of the greatest days of his life.

Plotting the capture of *Kaffir X* had been the one time, Danie had been meticulous. Everything had been rehearsed and prepared over and over again. And this was unusual because his normal work was haphazard and chaotic and there was evidence of his inefficiency everywhere in his office. Suddenly, Danie had been particularly careful planning the raid and showing in the process a flexibility of mind that Kobus had never suspected. This time, in a strange and inexplicable way, it had become personal. As if by taking his story to the world and quoting Shakespeare, Danie had been personally insulted.

When they finally found *Kaffir X*, Danie was wired like a too-tight fishing line. He was rougher than usual and had shoved the man to the ground and gloated over his captive despite the jeering crowds of men who had surrounded them. *Kaffir X*, although on the ground, had raised his hand and urged his followers to quietness and they had immediately obeyed. He rose to his feet, dignified as if he had himself tripped and fallen to the ground.

He was tall and able to look Danie straight in the eye which made Danie shift uneasily. The man spoke calmly and quietly, which made Danie turn away and grind his teeth. The man did not respond to taunts and walked slowly and majestically to the unmarked police vehicle accompanied by many whistles and boos and hisses from the huge crowd no longer watching the football.

Kobus, looking around, felt, for the first time, fear when he saw a never-ending sea of black faces. Hundreds, no maybe thousands of people were moving with them towards the vehicle and every one of them with anger radiating from them, oozing purple-black hatred which fell on him and Danie.

Danie seemed oblivious but he did rest his hand on his gun in the holster and the men waiting at the vehicle straightened and shifted their rifles, ready for action. The crowd moved no closer and only those at the back now booed and hissed.

The capture of a prominent terrorist had been a victory for the A-team. A coup. No amount of hissing black disapproval could alter that. And Danie had been the recipient of high prestige. Accolades from high in the regime had rained down on Danie, turning him into a new *wunderkind*. 'The saviour of South Africa had defeated the terrorist,' he grimly announced, and there were no headlines about that from the liberal, ridiculous press.

Danie, never a modest man, had basked in the glory and some of this had rubbed off on to the entire team. Kobus too felt the honour of this new-found fame. It was good to finally be recognised. He looked to his family and although not effusive with their praise there was a promising softening.

The glory lasted for many months while *Kaffir X* languished in prison awaiting trial. Danie had not given the trial much thought. He had completed his job and when the time came, he would be called to bear witness to the arrest and nothing else. It was not his job to prove the man's guilt — that, after all, was easy for everyone to see. It was all over the newspapers.

The trial, Danie had assured all of his colleagues, would be secretive and a foregone conclusion. Nothing but a show trial and he for one couldn't wait until they put that *kaffir* away for the rest of his life.

He couldn't have been more wrong. It seemed that Danie had underestimated *Kaffir X* and on every single front Danie was outmanoeuvred. The black man, who Danie could not speak about without the spit rising to his mouth like poison, was clever and smart. Much smarter than Danie, much smarter than the lawyers that the white regime threw at him.

Danie was, of course, called to give evidence at the trial, although it took several months of legal bargaining so as not to break his cover.

The black man's lawyer had for a long time portrayed Danie as arrogant, but this was not received as the insult the lawyer intended. Danie rated his own charms as great, and arrogance was something that only a fool would think was a bad thing. Danie could not see the danger lurking, ready to pounce in the courtroom. After all, he'd been at many trials and each one had been a foregone conclusion. Danie had the most powerful men in the country on his side. He had nothing to worry about.

Danie appeared in disguise behind a screen. He even went to the extra precaution of distorting his voice and wearing a cap low over his forehead.

Everyone in the A-team knew that he'd been called to the trial; no one had spoken of anything else for weeks, in low hushed voices. The trial was followed closely in all the newspapers and television station reporters camped outside. Commentators from around the world spoke at length about *Kaffir* X. By necessity, very little was known about the A-team and hardly anything at all about Danie. As a result, there was very little said about Danie, but he was confident that after the trial they would be singing another tune.

Danie had been humiliated. It had proved too easy for the defence lawyer. Danie had no answers to simple, reasonable questions that he'd never had to answer before. He'd been surprised and ambushed on the stand. He'd never had to answer questions before. His bumbling replies had been evasive and surly. The lawyer had ended by laughing and dismissing Danie with a wave of his hand as if Danie were no more than a child. The judge had seethed. Danie could see it in his ice blue eyes and shivering moustache.

The result: the black man walked free from the court into the arms of his enormous following. He was embraced by his people and draped in their adoration. Danie left the courtroom through the filthy back corridors of the Pretoria High Supreme Court and was bundled into an unmarked car which sped through the dingy forgotten streets of Pretoria.

After that, Danie went on a four-day bender and when he next appeared in the A-team offices, he looked like death. He looked like what he was, a defeated man.

From that day forward, his one and only mission was to recapture *Kaffir X* and this time he would not be walking away from court. This time he wouldn't even make it to court.

There was now only one mission for the A-team and that was the recapture of their quarry. This time Danie planned and schemed as he had never done before. This time there was a grim determination that none of the team had ever witnessed before.

They were all to have dark clothing, a true uniformity, full face protection and head coverings. Weapons, assault rifles and handguns were checked and unnecessarily checked again. As the inspections and instructions wore on, barked from a raspy Danie — he'd contracted a filthy wheezing cold the week before — the men became edgy and nervous. As if the fever of revenge could be caught.

The vehicles, a bulky *buffel* and a white pickup truck, were already running inside the warehouse when Kobus arrived. The filthy noise was low and was a grating irritation to Kobus and he longed to request that they be silenced. One glance at Danie kept him quiet. Danie was wired and volatile emotions ran across his face in waves. He jiggled and trembled and could not stand still. The rest of the team watched him as if they were keeping an eye on an unpredictable dog.

The instructions were simple enough and each man was provided with a copy of a picture — there were four faces — all black. These were the men they were seeking. The sole reason for this mission was to find them and then immobilise them no matter what it took. It was no longer enough just to capture *Kaffir X*. All of his accomplices would fall with him.

They all knew these faces — had been looking at them since the trial. The men in the picture were very similar and in the dim light of the barn it was hard to tell them apart. But they'd all studied the faces and Danie settled a little and became less agitated. One of the men in the pictures had a scar running across his right shoulder blade. A scar that had been inflicted by the team the last time they'd met in the football stadium.

Danie had an axe to grind. Nobody ever escaped the justice of the A-team — this was payback time.

At last, just as Kobus thought he would be driven mad by the grinding engines and toxic exhaust smoke, Danie gave the order to begin. The driver, an anonymous man who dressed in army fatigues, sat at the front of the *buffel* with Danie and Kobus. The others, eight young men jittering with nervous tension they had caught from Danie, were in the back. The white pickup, which Danie called a *bakkie,* would follow. The *bakkie* had been fitted out with wire fencing so that the rear resembled a cage. A cage for the prisoners.

So, Kobus thought, *it is beginning*. Danie had worked doggedly and methodically on this mission, investing everything. Kobus could almost see the fervour, the zealot in Danie and he perfectly understood. Finally, after these months and months of humiliation he would get his restoration and that day was now. Danie was ready and his team with him.

Everything started well as they raced through the abandoned Sunday morning streets. They'd met no impediment. They had planned well. Once sleepy Pretoria was left behind, they were approaching the township before Kobus had expected it. They waited for their orders so close to their targets who slept unaware of the menace that stalked them. Kobus, despite his own tension, wanted to laugh.

The orders had been clear and short. Danie's team would head directly towards the place where he knew *Kaffir X* was staying. Kobus would cover the escape routes and round up those that worked for *Kaffir X*. They studied the photographs one more time. They were ready.

In the dark retreating morning, they walked as carefully and silently as ten well-armed, heavy-footed men could towards their goal. Danie, different now, calm and humming very quietly under his breath seemed happy. More like the careless commander that Kobus recognised.

Danie's team broke away through a small pungent alley, disappearing like shadows. Kobus and his men walked down what looked like a well-trodden thoroughfare. No need to hide at this hour of the morning — there were no people as yet.

A piercing, unruly bark was quickly stifled in the direction that Danie had taken. Kobus and his men flattened themselves against the wall of a tin hut — the tin cool against their hands. Kobus traced the map through his head running over the ground that they'd covered in the office. This was the right place. This is where those men would run, and Kobus would be waiting if that happened.

He waited. That was all there was to do. Then he heard the shouting and knew it had begun.

'*Kaffir, hande op, kop*!' Clearly and then again. '*Kaffir, hande op, kop*!' Then the screaming started, and the filled air began to drum with disaster. Kobus signalled his team and began to move slowly towards the sound — ready for escaping shadows. They rounded the corner into a small square where the screaming and shouting rose together with the day into a cacophony of terror.

A small skinny dog with huge teats almost dragging on the ground ran blindly past his team and one of the men aimed a kick at her. She yelped and fell to one side and then crawled away on her belly. The noise, a crescendo now like a wall, rose and rose and all around them the township was erupting into life.

Danie strode amongst the kneeling men who, despite the noise around them, were silent and shrinking, isolated on the hard orange hellish clay. The area quickly filled with ever more shaking trembling people. Like ghosts, they moved to witness from the shadows, making no sound now, afraid to attract attention to themselves.

These raids were not uncommon. The people knew to stay out of it and some even slunk away saving themselves. This was no place for heroes.

A woman came out of one of the houses screaming and lunging at one of the armed men who she caught by surprise. He, suddenly afraid, raised his rifle slowly and pulled the trigger. A short lethal string of shots from his automatic weapon rose harmlessly into the air. She fell to the ground clutching her ears, tears making furrows of grief on her face. Deafened and immobilised, she lay on the ground howling into the earth.

Even though adult hands grabbed at them, some little children, confused and naked, emerged into the square, drawn like magnets to the carnage. Unlike the adults, the children were strangely silent and grave. Shaken and shocked into silence and unable to pry their eyes away from the horror. They were immobilised, only able to watch, as if in a nightmare, their beloved parents became dust in the ruin of the white man's rage.

'*Kaffir, wat is jou naam*?' Danie, imposing and taller than the rest, asked the black man at his feet. The black man did not answer but Danie had seen the scar on the right shoulder. A cruel smile curling the corner of his mouth Danie lowered the shotgun and carefully and deliberately forced the end into the black man's mouth. A woman whimpered and finally the children found their voices and began to wail.

'*Kaffir, wat is jou naam*?' Still no reply, the silence lengthened. Shuffling his feet, Kobus raked his eyes over the scene. It was late, it was time to move. They had already been here too long. They were supposed to be on the way out with the men already.

Then in the morning air the shot rang out like a shout of the devil. The black man kneeling at Danie's feet slumped over carefully, almost in apology with his hands held in prayer and then lay in the dirt with the back of his head missing. The deep dark jagged scar on his right shoulder raised and dark against his skin.

'Fuck, that's going to be one hell of a mess to clean up,' Danie said casually as if someone had spilled the morning milk. Kobus noticed the laughing lilt was back in his voice, the lilt that had been missing since the trial.

Slowly, as if coming back from a long way off, Danie turned away from the scene at his feet and barked some orders. His men, galvanised into action, hauled the three others to their feet and herded them, terrified and trembling, the short distance to the prison vehicle. Here they were shoved into the cage. Nobody else in the square moved, the women and children, frozen figures of alarm and grief. Kobus walked backwards, never taking his eyes from the wide-eyed children. It was awkward walking backwards while two of his men carried the body. One had grabbed the arms and another the legs and the man's head hung down dripping blood and brains.

A woman rushed forward, and Kobus slapped her away. He could smell her fear, a small animal fear, and she knelt keening on the ground. It was the last thing he saw before turning to the prison vehicle. The two men, cursing, threw the swinging body up onto the back of the truck and roughly shoved it further in and the three live prisoners shrank into the back moaning quietly.

And then they were gone. Some children, Kobus noticed, must have run after them because they stood in the small dirt road and stared, while the woman he'd slapped, knelt on the ground all alone and uncomforted.

But they were gone and the only evidence that they had been there was the palpable grief and sticky blood congealing on the pathway. Kobus swore he could hear it. It began as a tiny forlorn cry but was soon taken up by other stronger voices and the song of grief swelled and followed the A-team out of Alexander, a useless woeful noise.

'Hey Danie, I can't believe you actually shot that *kaffir.*' Young Kenny was feverishly overexcited and very talkative. In the *buffel* on the drive out into the broken *veld,* he'd talked non-stop and the others began to wish he'd shut up. Now he hovered around Danie like a small boy looking for approval.

'*Ja,* well, the *donnerse kaffir* was ignoring me.' Danie was already on his third can of beer, his voice was gruff and hard and slightly slurred. That was all he would say and none of the others spoke. He was no longer laughing.

The terrified prisoners still huddled in the van as far away as they could from the body and the policeman. The body lay stiffening on the bed of the truck in exactly the place that it was originally flung.

Soon they were speeding into the low, flat *veld.* The day was rapidly filling with light and there was now an urgency that they all felt. Every one of Danie's men understood the importance of concealment. The raid, well planned as it was, had not made contingencies for this yet Danie seemed calm and careless.

Now they were surrounded by veld, brown and featureless, and the only sound was Danie's comments to the driver to continue. It was hours before Danie found a place that was secluded enough. An anonymous piece of land that could have been anywhere, anywhere at all. They would all have been hard pressed to find this place again. Danie knew how to get lost.

Although Danie was calm again, the next steps of the mission were unclear, and no one wanted to ask him what was next. They huddled together outside the *buffel*, avoiding eye contact with Danie, and wondering what they were going to do with the body.

Like a devil's cauldron, the *veld* began to heat up. It was the middle of summer. Soon it would be too hot to think, and the suffering was only just beginning. A desperate urgency began to fester and Danie sipped on his drink and said nothing.

Kobus knew that he had to speak to Danie. The only command that Danie had given was for the men to make a bonfire and it burned bright and blistering while Danie remained impassive and unapproachable. He opened yet another can of beer and Kobus wondered if it was his fourth or fifth. Still Danie said nothing.

Kobus began to fret. They had three prisoners — he was sure, as Danie said, that they were terrorists and that made their mission successful. The blot was the one dead body. What were they going to do?

Suddenly Danie broke into speech — a rambling damning of the court systems and how justice did not work led to his decision about what he would do with the remaining prisoners. He wanted to kill them. He rattled the thick chicken mesh, and the prisoners shrank even further back like shadows retreating from the sun. They rolled their eyes like trapped wild animals.

Kobus, who until this moment had not considered killing the prisoners, felt all of the dangers of his own position. The cowering prisoners irritated him, and he did not wish to linger on them. Floundering for words he watched Danie open another beer. He accepted one and, not finding the right words, remained silent.

Kenny, always a favourite of Danie's, recovered from his earlier outburst, knew now to remain silent and the others followed his example. They said nothing and Kobus could sense a shift. They could smell blood and were eager to prove themselves. This was an opportunity for them, and they might even supplant the favourite Kenny.

Kobus remained silent and waited, hardly daring to breathe. Danie was the leader after all and had reiterated many times that the decisions were his. They all had evidence from the past where his authority had been questioned and like a juggernaut, he'd squashed any dissent. He was the commandant. He would speak when he was ready.

The A team would follow Danie's orders — they worshipped him like a god. The small black shadows in the cage would not touch them.

Danie also had clout. He knew people, important people. He could make or break a career and there were plenty of legends circulating the police headquarters to support this. Kobus knew that in the end his friend would make this better — he'd bet his career on it. He had to admit that lately the missions had become more and more unpredictable, especially after the disastrous court case. But now that Danie had finally got the man responsible, perhaps it would all be over. It was hard to tell. In the meantime, he opened another drink and passed it to Danie.

"What are we going to do with the body?" Kobus asked, driven by a boldness that had increased as the sun rose to its high point and the day ran on. He could feel the sweat trickling down the back of his shirt. Danie's face was red — heart-attack red — and his shirt had huge dark patches under the arms. Kobus could hardly recognise himself from the morning. He was definitely getting too old for this shit.

Danie shrugged — looked at the prisoners briefly as if he'd forgotten about them. He was still drinking, but this was usual — he always drank after a mission, it was he claimed, the only way he could get the paperwork done. One of his standard jokes: "Pass me a *dop* and don't bother with the paperwork."

And as the sun began to turn and the nightmare looked set to continue, Danie suddenly burst into action. "We should burn the body — we can say it never happened. Who's going to believe these *kaffirs* anyway?"

Two of the men dragged the body out of the van. The rest of the men made the flames tall and fetched more wood. When the flames were so big that it was almost impossible to stand next to the fire, Danie and Kenny swung the bloody carcass onto the flames. Another crate of Castle beer appeared, and everyone drank. It was like being at a *braai*, Danie said.

Very soon the smell of cooking flesh reached them all. A horrible, singed odour of flesh and hair. The terrified prisoners crouched in the back of the van and cried into their knees. Kobus heard them offering up prayers but ignored them.

As if triggered by the smell, some of the men went away in the *buffel* to fetch meat and more beer. Even after three hours, the shape of a human was still visible in the flames. Some of them thought that it should have been over by now and small rumblings of dissatisfaction wafted in the softening air.

A small team went half-heartedly to fetch more wood that by now was badly needed to keep the fire going, but wood was hard to find. The *veld* was sparse and spindly and most of the wood had been gathered in the first foraging. Besides, these young men were tired. Alcohol and time had curbed their enthusiasm.

There were eight of them, so similar that Kobus often had trouble telling them apart, and although they had started the day as men, as the day had worn on, they had dwindled into callow boys. They broke off into little groups and some of them were now openly appealing to Danie to let them go.

The prisoners were not offered anything to drink or eat. Kobus realised that the heat in the van must have been unbearable, but he could do nothing for them. Danie was still to make his decision.

The sun began to set and still a human form was visible in the struggling flames. The day had run its cycle and they were still not done. The clumsy *buffel*, the only vehicle they could use, was sent to fetch petrol. It left on the small track like a lumbering beast. None of them were laughing any more.

A smell of putrid shit came from the prison van.

It was almost dark when the *buffel* returned with the petrol. The driver reeked of alcohol. Kobus threw the petrol on the fire, and it blazed in quickened anger. There was no more wood, and Kobus remembered reading somewhere that crematoriums burn at thousands of degrees Celsius, but he said nothing to Danie.

At around midnight, Danie made the decision to kill the other prisoners. Although sleepy, the team were immediately awake as Danie discussed the details. He didn't keep his voice down even though the prisoners could clearly hear every word he spoke.

The prisoners now numb and beyond terror meekly emerged from the van under the trained revolvers of the A-team. They were lined up as before with their hands behind their heads. Danie wanted them to dig their own graves but clearly, they were too weak and terrified.

Then there was no need for words or shouting. No touches or even insults as one by one they were shot in the back of the head. Danie insisted on doing it himself, no doubt thinking of it as a strange kind of honour. The bodies fell with no fuss, kneeling corpses fallen sideways, then shoved into shallow graves.

By morning it was all done. Twenty-four hours after the mission had begun, it was brought to a close. Years later when Kobus returned to this scene in his mind, it began to feel as if it were not quite real — like something out of a story about someone else. Danie would see to the details, he'd said, by which he meant the explanation back at headquarters. Any stories coming out of the townships would not be believed. No one believed *kaffirs,* he assured his men. All they had to do was stick together and keep their stories the same. He even gave them the rest of the week off and sent them home to the heart of their families. They deserved, after all, a holiday after the great work they'd all done. Kobus could not quite meet his eye.

On their return to the A-team office, a small office inside the huge building amongst even bigger skyscrapers in downtown Pretoria, Kobus at once felt his intense weariness. A dull sensation and an unusual awareness of having to force his legs into movement. There was a slight buzzing in his ears as if he'd just left a noisy nightclub. He needed a shave — badly. Some of the younger lads had slept in turns in the cab of the *buffel* and one had even gone into a deep sleep like a child. Kobus envied him and had been unable to shut his eyes. Every time he thought about sleep, he saw the flickering outline of the body in the fire. He knew now that sleep would evade him for a very long time.

A sign on the office door said 'A-team' in white letters on a black background. Inside there were four desks piled high with haphazard folders. Each stack towered with papers, dishevelled and disorganised. A pile of files was stacked on a swivel chair, and some had fallen to the floor. It looked as if the place had been recently ransacked. Judging by the dust on the surfaces, the office had not been cared for in a very long time.

Danie had claimed that the A-team would generate no paperwork, but this had proved to be another of his wild claims like 'no pain, no gain,' whatever that meant.

A whiteboard on one wall was festooned with photographs. Four prominent photographs in the middle sported the heading 'known terrorists.' Kobus did not look at the board; one of the faces would never leave his vision and the pulsating scars seemed to beat in time with his stuttering heart. The board stood sentinel as a horrible reminder of the terrible fiasco.

Danie walked to the board and wrote in a thick red pen 'exterminated' across the top, some of the red ink dripping onto the photographs like blood. 'No longer a threat, hey!' he said, his voice high and false in the lingering emptiness of the room. Those still remaining laughed, but they were starting to look gaunt and uneasy.

The truth of what had happened had begun to penetrate the wall of alcohol that had temporarily hidden the truth. Kobus knew from experience that this was just the start. One day they too would treat this like just another day as Danie did. Never had he felt so out of step with his team, never had he felt so alone.

Danie, staggering, weaved towards his desk and sat. Behind him were two posters that had come with the office. One of Madonna — someone had written the word 'slut' on the bottom in bold black pen. Next to that a picture of Michael Jackson. Someone had written 'slut' on this poster too but then crossed it out and written 'wannabe white boy' with the same bold black pen. The posters had been on the wall for so long they were yellowing, and they hardly noticed them any more. Possibly they had been put up to maintain an image that the office was an ordinary place where people did ordinary things. Or perhaps the people who'd occupied the office before them wanted to appear young and fashionable. One of the lads lit a cigarette and threw the used match on the floor. Kobus was too tired to protest. The room filled with a grey haze and the sour smell of cigarette smoke.

Danie half-heartedly fiddled with some paperwork. 'Jeez, it stinks in here — someone open the window." He laughed to soften his words, but it was true. They all stank with the lingering stale odours of the past twenty-four hours.

Kobus shifted from the edge of the desk where he was perching. He wanted to suggest that everyone go home but he hesitated. He knew that Danie did not like anyone else taking control or giving orders. Kobus continually trod the line between Danie's temper and his unpredictability which seemed to have worsened lately. Kobus felt a great weariness that threatened to overwhelm him. He sighed. A bored, bewildered Danie was very dangerous. Kobus could not predict what would happen next.

After making several attempts to sort out the bewildering array of paperwork, Danie threw down a sheet of paper. He brooded at the desk. Kobus took down the four photographs and fed them through the shredder. Whatever else happened, the men would not be traced through the A-team offices.

Danie, as if hearing Kobus' thoughts, finally ordered the young men home but put up a hand as Kobus started to leave. Kobus knew what was coming next. The obligatory talk. When Danie got drunk, the talk became more and more emotional. Danie was drunk a lot. He was also emotional a lot these days.

Kobus thought of the drive home via Danie's house. A good forty minutes out of his way. But there was nothing he could do; Danie was in no fit state to drive. He contemplated taking the keys away from Danie now, but they were placed next to his right hand on the desk and Danie would not appreciate the implication that he was too drunk to drive. Kobus, a veteran of many unpleasant arguments with a drunk Danie, knew to bide his time and it would work around to Danie accepting a lift from Kobus. It would be a favour dressed up to look like a privilege. Kobus wondered how much longer he could keep up the terrible pretence.

Chapter 25 — Ruben Ariel

For two days since their arrival in Uitenhage, Ruben had been gently mocking Pieter. Meaning nothing by it, he had found out, from a careless Sissie, that Pieter's real name was Kobus Junior. Ruben could not explain why this was funny except that Piet (his special abbreviation of the name) had always seemed so complete, so calm to Ruben's continual bustle and chaos. So self-assured.

It was amusing to suddenly see Piet's calm exterior ruffled. To see Piet in this new light was a revelation and Ruben, not meaning to hurt Piet, played the fool and joked in an attempt to amuse Piet out of this state of confusion. Ruben, who'd known that Piet was Afrikaans, had never fully understood how completely steeped in the Afrikaner tradition until this visit.

Ruben had never before been exposed to any Afrikaners, attending as he did the very elite school in Cape Town where the children all mocked each other as being the last colonial outpost of English South Africa. The Ariels had mixed in an exclusive set of people who cherished and maintained very English traditions while maintaining strong Jewish ties with their Lithuanian relatives.

Strange to say that, in a country that had leaders and a government who were almost exclusively Afrikaans, the Ariel family and their friends had been separate from this part of South Africa.

Ruben found Piet's strange, repressed household totally bemusing. Kobus Senior was a gruff man who exuded confidence yet was strangely and mysteriously undermined in his own house. He was separate from his family, but this seemed to be by his own design. Ruben, a congenial, gregarious man who had never been rebuffed or made to feel uncomfortable around people suddenly found himself on ground that continually shifted, and he did not like the feeling at all.

Whenever the two men had spoken of their respective families, Ruben had been aware of a reticence on Piet's side and out of an unusual feeling of respect and generosity, he never pressed for more information. He liked the tall uncertain Piet and didn't want to drive him away with too many probing questions. Besides, there were many young people at university trying to reinvent themselves. Ruben, a social animal, reinvented himself regularly and had many and varied friends on campus and in Cape Town. None of them asked too many questions; they were all ready to accept that a person was who they said they were. Why not? This was a new age, and the country was changing and would change even more. In this mood of hopefulness, Ruben and his friends adopted new manners and ways every day and boldly went into a future that would be better than the past.

Ruben did not think too deeply about himself or press his friends into seriousness. More than one of his friends had accused him of being shallow. He did not care. He knew who he was, and he was comfortable.

Ruben was amazed that his friendship with Piet survived and blossomed into a real kinship. Besides, or maybe because of their differences, they grew tighter and tighter until Ruben could not imagine his life without Piet.

Piet was quiet and considered, his words very carefully chosen, and Ruben was the polar opposite, loud and blurting out the very first thing that came into his head without regard for the consequences. Physically too they were different. Piet was tall and rangy and under different circumstances could have been an athlete. Ruben was short and dumpy and already a little overweight.

While Piet was thoughtful and listened to others, Ruben was talkative and rarely actually listened to anyone.

As a child, Ruben had figured out that it wasn't the actual words that mattered, it was the way they were said. Therefore, he had only to read the expression and listen for the tone and he'd know exactly what people were trying to say. That is, except for Piet. Piet was different and Ruben for the first time in his life was forced to listen.

Ruben was liked because his mockery was more often directed at himself than others. His mockery too lacked the spite of actually being true but mostly focused on the foibles of society generally rather than on particular aspects of a person. His was a general caricature of the time and place.

While Ruben was liked, Piet was adored. He truly listened and while self-effacing did not drain a friendship of every last drop. His peers came to him for solace or companionship and while they marvelled at the unusual friendship between Ruben and Piet, no one questioned why Ruben would have picked Piet as his best friend.

Ruben's own parents were open-minded liberals and Ruben had never felt the usual childhood pangs of embarrassment or shame about them. He spoke of them, regularly and openly. He could never even begin to imagine Piet's childhood and the effort, he realised, was not in him — he preferred to make the most of this welcome companionship.

The necessity that Piet felt in changing his name and moving so far out of his own world had not struck Ruben fully until he went to Uitenhage. Here in Uitenhage, though, he caught small glimpses of what had driven Piet so far out of his own world, and he began to understand.

Piet's mother, while not overbearing, was a constant source of irritation. She treated Piet as if he were a child. Ruben's own mother had spoken to him as if he were an adult from as early as he could remember. When he had been perplexed about some of the words she used, she plonked a dictionary in front of him and, with a wry smile, told him to look it up. Ruben had obtained a reputation as a precocious child for butting in on adult conversations and having opinions that belonged to a much older person.

While at first Marta had been a source of some irritation to Ruben, he began to observe her more closely as if he were studying a particularly interesting insect. He observed that she never once asked her son about his degree except to congratulate him on the fact that he had graduated — this much she seemed to know.

Furthermore, she never seemed to be curious about the future. For a child that had been constantly grilled, mostly by his father, on his earning potential linked to the usefulness of his degree, this seemed very strange.

For that matter, Kobus seemed also to be uninterested in his son's future plans. He must surely be aware that they would be called up for military service. Ruben's own parents had for so long been planning ways for him to avoid military service that it had become certain that Ruben would more than likely be leaving the country.

All of his male friends both from school and university had similar plans and were supported by family. It seemed so very strange to be faced with these odd people who were so very far out of touch with their son.

Ruben thought about Cape Town and their student life and how Mr and Mrs Jonker would probably not even begin to understand anything at all about cosmopolitan, sophisticated Cape Town, as far removed as it could be from the rural backwater of Uitenhage. It was clear now to Ruben why Piet needed to change his name. What was less clear was why he'd come back to his parents at all. Piet was somehow diminished in his parents' company. He wavered more and seemed undecided about the future. This began to instil a sense of fear into Ruben, and it filled his chest like thick smoke until he felt as if he could hardly breathe.

It had been so much easier in Cape Town, and it became Ruben's sole mission to leave as soon as politely possible. If he could help things along, he would, he would do whatever it took to get out of the hellhole that was Uitenhage and get back to Cape Town where he could think.

Ruben, deliberately ignoring Kobus' hostility which had become more and more pronounced as the visit progressed, maintained his friendly banter. The never-ending banter that flowed over the Jonker family, that quelled the old man and beat his wife into submission.

Despite all Ruben's misgivings, Piet seemed to need something from his parents and even though Ruben could not say what it was, it appeared to be something important. Ruben also rationalised that if his plans for the future came to fruition, it would be a very long time before they met with his family again. And there were glimmers of hope; he could see how the old man's domineering manner would drive Piet away soon enough.

Ruben felt the narrowness of this life greatly. The tiny town of Uitenhage offered little in the way of entertainment and Port Elizabeth was at least a forty-five-minute drive away and he could not ascertain if the city had anything more to offer. No one in the family had ever been to Port Elizabeth and he didn't know if they ever intended to.

Ruben felt jaded and longed for the sophistication of Cape Town, the buzzing nightlife and the lively coast for the daytime. He was surprised at how much he missed the coast and the gentle seaside city air, so very different from the industrial bleakness of Uitenhage. He missed it so much that sometimes he could taste the bitterness on his tongue.

But Mrs Jonker — she hadn't asked him to call her by her first name — clung to Piet and every day her *seun* became younger and younger and more uncertain.

He couldn't help but contrast this with his own family. His easy-going, elegant mother with her 'call me Sheila' manners and innate good taste. He could picture her moving through her rooms at her regular parties and functions, ready to mingle and laugh with her friends. There were so many of them. He could see that endearing gesture of hers where she twirled the little heart necklace and before moving on, she would touch both ears where her clip-on earrings hung. He missed her, her easy chatter and languid movements that did not jar; her low melodious voice that sounded to him like a song — a song of his childhood. It was all he could do not to jump into the van and hurry back to Cape Town.

His mother had the gift of putting everyone at ease no matter their background, knew instinctively what to say and how to say it. A talent, she was proud to say, that she had passed on to her son. She was fond of telling people, in an amusing way, that her husband brought the money, and she brought the good looks. Everyone always laughed and there was never any of the Uitenhage vulgarity. That jarring, reeking hopelessness of Uitenhage.

Inevitability when in the company of Kobus, it brought comparisons to his father. Even though at first glance his father seemed to be a coarse little man who fitted every stereotype of the greedy Jew, he was in fact a perfect match for his tall, elegant wife. He'd needed a wife to make his home elegant and charming. She needed a husband to provide, and the deal worked very well, and the product of the union was Ruben.

Ruben worshipped his father for his Midas touch. None of those childhood references to Midas seemed so horrible to Ruben. In fact, his friends called him Midas and as a young child Ruben had believed that his father was the golden legend from the fairy tale. David Ariel was a well-connected man who knew when to sell and when to buy and he owned a chain of clothing stores that appeared on every high street from Johannesburg to Cape Town. Ruben had a real and enduring affection for both his parents.

Their well-appointed house in Hout Bay, with a view of Table Mountain in Cape Town, was elegantly furnished and tastefully decorated.

It was a place where Sheila could show off her own talents and discreetly show off her husband's money.

His mother had appeared in a number of fashion magazines, draped over various antique pieces of furniture, lovingly restored by her own hand. Her opinion was sought for celebrity articles and programmes. Despite this wealth, Ruben had been brought up to believe that all white people lived in this way. His small world had never admitted people like Piet and so it came as a surprise to understand that some parents appeared to not have the best interests of their children at heart.

Ruben's parents could not be described as racist, but they had never been described as activists or interested in politics either. They supported charities to help the betterment of the poor blacks, but Sheila could never be persuaded to join the ranks of Helen Suzman or other activists in the community. Not for her to stand on street corners handing out leaflets. Not for her touring the townships and witnessing the effects of the white regime. But it went without saying, as she told her friends, apartheid was bad and the sooner it was over the better.

Both David and Sheila sympathised and felt great sorrow at the way the country was going but neither felt it necessary to vote. Unlike his parents, Ruben had been seized with a brief fervour of political action when he first went to university. It was thrilling and he was able to easily assimilate into the activist groups. He had a photographic memory which enabled him to memorise political pamphlets and speeches, a great boon when attending political rallies at university.

Also, he found that he had a political pedigree by mere dint of the fact that he was Jewish. This often helped when activists, feeling themselves being superseded by this suave, smooth man, confronted him.

But he soon became bored with politics. He moved briefly on to drama clubs, writing groups and finally the poetry club where he met Piet. Piet, who, it turned out, had concealed a great deal.

It was surprising that only at university did Ruben come to the slow realisation that some of the young men and women in his circle of acquaintances were in fact a great deal poorer than he was. He was aware of the mountains of poverty in the black and coloured townships, but he'd never really encountered poverty amongst his white compatriots before.

He met Piet on a wet and windy day at a university writing day or some such thing. He could hardly remember the circumstances. Piet was tall and awkward and looked apologetic, like someone who had accidentally stumbled into the wrong venue.

His fine hands, out of place on such a tall man, were almost constantly in motion. These were hands that were more suited to a pen than any other tool. Piet was sitting next to a girl that Ruben knew from lectures. She was a messy-haired hippie type and Ruben could see that she was far more into Piet than he was into her. Just because Ruben was starting to feel bored again — something that he had been prepared for — he decided, impetuously, that this young man might be a panacea for his boredom.

And because Piet was someone Ruben would never have expected to befriend, he made a bigger effort than he would have done otherwise. There were many friendships that Ruben had not nurtured, sensing they would want more from him than he was prepared to give. It surprised him that he was prepared to shake off his usual apathy and work so much harder with Piet. There was something in Piet, something almost dangerous that appealed to Ruben on that wet windy Tuesday in the middle of a boring semester.

As the evening wore on and one boring poet was followed by another, Ruben began to fidget, all the while making snide amusing remarks as he'd done countless times before. He kept glancing out of the corner of his eyes hoping to make an impression on the withdrawn gentle Piet.

Still not looking directly at Piet, he played to the girl and the people in the row in front. This is how it usually worked — homing in on one person while ostensibly playing to everyone else. Ruben often thought of his life as a play, a huge pretence, but it worked and, in the past, it was how he had won countless friends and acquaintances.

He had a well-deserved reputation as a clown and raconteur and was as a result considered to be an excellent party companion. But when at last he turned to speak to Piet, he noticed that the solemn young man was not laughing, not laughing at all. He looked hurt, as if it was his own poetry that was being ridiculed.

Ruben, quick and adept at adjusting in company, realised his mistake and immediately turned serious, a little ashamed of his cynical abuse of the poets and performers. 'Oh God, don't tell me that you have some poetry here tonight?' He tried for a little laugh, but it felt forced and false. He stopped and briefly considered this strange new feeling of uncertainty.

'No, no, I can't write poetry,' was the simple reply. The accent was thick as if the user was not used to speaking English, but the voice was not unpleasant, being low and melodic. Piet had a quietness that was unusual in one so young and Ruben liked it and felt his uncertainty lift a little.

That was why it was so surprising when he did meet Piet's father. Not only did Piet not resemble his father, he seemed in every other way to be a changeling — a cuckoo dropped into the wrong nest. Ruben brooded on this and Piet's almost studied difference from his family. His mother was short and dumpy, his half-gothic sister dark and tiny while Piet was tall and fair. His blond hair was the only resemblance to his father.

Ruben had studied Mrs Jonker's face closely, her hand soft and limp in his. He leaned in for a kiss and smelt a soft hint of a perfume and something stale. His eyes traced her face for some lingering beauty but could only find a plain, careworn face.

Sissie was most like her mother but quiet like Ruben. Not quite a goth but one who teetered on the edge in her dark clothes and makeup. But the makeup was a little too subtle for a goth and her hair too manicured. It was almost as if in dressing in the morning she had suddenly abandoned her ambitions and left the real goth in her bedroom.

Ruben was at a loss to decide where these two children got their softness and serene quietness. Kobus was hard and a man of angles and lurking danger. His voice was strangely high for such a big man. His words, however, were gruff and cut off as if begrudging them the air.

The memories of taking Piet to his parents' house in Hout Bay brought an unexpected stab of joy to Ruben. Piet had seemed afraid to touch anything and had sat with a cooling cup of coffee by his side for the entire visit. Ruben was urbane and sophisticated, suddenly a young man and no more the messy, loud student.

But after a while and a few more visits Piet began to relax and even started to refer to Hout Bay as home. Piet seemed even more suited to his mother's sophisticated arrangements than Ruben himself. When he saw his tall, slender mother, still beautiful, next to the thin, stately Piet he thought how similar they were. They admired the same paintings and his mother had even quoted some of his opinions to her friends. It was almost as if Piet were her son.

The more time that Ruben spent with Piet, the more determined he became to prolong their friendship. So far it had been the longest that he'd ever maintained. It surprised him with a little jolt, like an electric shock, every time he looked at Piet. It surprised him how much he wanted to make Piet laugh. He sensed a void in Piet, and he wanted very much to pour some of his own happiness into Piet. It wasn't exactly that he saw Piet as a charity case, as his mother sometimes joked with him, but he did sense that there was something ultimately broken. And when he met Piet's family, he thought that he finally knew what that broken thing was.

When he looked at Kobus, he fervently hoped that he could do something, anything, to help his dear friend avoid the fate of becoming like his father. It was a strange feeling to consider the possibility that he would be friends with Piet for such a very long time. It had never happened before and he liked it, that sensation of permanency.

After that first night at the poetry reading the two men rapidly became firm friends and this for Ruben, used to a crowd of acquaintances, was a new and novel thing. Their other friends were struck too by the unlikely friendship. The girls would often mime heart shapes at them, but this gentle mockery did not disturb them. And so, they became inseparable and at the end of their university studies it seemed only natural that they would think of something they could do together when they left. What could be more natural than two varsity friends going out into the world together? But first they would have to tie up the loose end of Piet's family.

On leaving school Ruben had been given a flat in Cape Town by an uncle who wished to use the flat as an investment when Ruben was finished with it. Ruben, noticing Piet's everlasting search for reasonable accommodation, seized the opportunity to offer Piet lodgings. Ruben sensed rather than knew that he should not reveal that the flat was paid for. To Piet they were like any two other students in the city living together to reduce costs. It was a heady, wonderful time where the two young men found new and exciting places to visit and at least one of them studied hard and hoped for a good job after university.

The only clouds on the horizon were the call-up papers that came at the beginning of every year. The deferment notice acknowledged that the young man in question would not be starting the obligatory two years of conscripted service while studying for a degree but was a reminder that conscription was waiting for them, whether they liked it or not.

Each time the papers came, they were a horrible reminder of the real world. Ruben and Piet rarely spoke about the papers and in fact the only time they had spoken about it was the first and only row they'd had.

Ruben, recognising the envelope with its South African Defence Force logo, had mentioned to Piet that he too had his call-up papers. Piet never spoke of the future and Ruben, tired of keeping quiet said, 'What are you going to do?'

Piet seemed surprised by this. 'What do you mean? It's not like it's a choice. When varsity is over, I'll report for duty.'

Ruben was bewildered. 'You can't go, you should make another plan. Either study some more or...' he floundered around searching for something, anything to make Piet see sense. 'Or join one of the peace-loving churches. A church that prevents you from going to war. They can't force you to go if you say it's against your religion.'

'But it's my duty to go. I have to go.' It sounded so final and, coming from such a softly spoken voice, it was hard for Ruben to argue — he had no purchase, nothing to rage against. It felt like punching water.

'What about you, Ruben — you're Jewish so you can't say that you've joined a religious movement.'

'My parents will never let me go. I'll probably go to Israel. Hey, why don't you come with me?' Immediately he spoke he knew he'd made a mistake. He saw from the blank expression that Piet was scandalised.

Piet turned away and began to put books, papers and pens into his bag. Ruben held out his hand, but Piet swirled through the door, his face set and hard. Ruben ran after him, but Piet waved him away.

'Not now, Ruben,' he said, and he was gone.

After that for many weeks they hardly spoke, merely passing in the flat like two strangers. He should have known that a row with Piet would be like this. A slow burning resentment with no words and with no end in view. An unexpected stubborn Piet would not budge, would not consider avoiding the draft. It seemed so strange when he was so pliable on other issues. Ruben did not know what to do. His rows, although few, were always at full volume and over very quickly once the rage had burned cold.

With no end to the row and Piet and Ruben not speaking and avoiding each other, Ruben grew desperate. He approached his mother. She agreed to speak to her son's friend. Such a gentle loving boy would be eaten alive in the South African Army. She would fix this thing for her son.

Piet admitted to her that the issue of the conscript had been bothering him for a very long time. That was when he spoke about his father for the first time and Ruben, when told of this, felt a small niggle of annoyance that Piet had not spoken to him first.

This new information, a family history in the armed forces, was a shock to Ruben who had never been in contact with any kind of military family. It had always been clear that Piet was not close to his father. In fact, Ruben had got the impression that Piet did not even like his father, but Ruben assumed that this was just another young man who was not close to his father.

After all, most of his friends were the same. In fact, there were times when Ruben loathed his own father and at those times it was only because of his mother that he spoke to the old man at all. That and the fact that the old man held the purse strings, he added to himself as a footnote. He stored it away for later — it would draw in a few laughs.

When they were at last at home and reconciled, Ruben asked him. 'Do you know what they do to people like you in the army?' He knew that it was cruel, but he wanted so badly for his friend, his lovely, soft friend to understand the danger. He did not say 'people like us' because he had no intention of ever going. He would put it all off as long as he possibly could and then he'd go away. Israel was good; he'd been there many times before. No point in wasting your time here in South Africa when you might get your head blown off. It wasn't his fight — it had never been his fight. He was pretty damn sure that it wasn't Piet's fight either.

There was an unspoken belief that Ruben would inherit and run his father's business, but after all, there was no hurry as the old man was fit and totally in command. But Piet's parents were another matter altogether. It seemed in some strange and inexplicable way that Piet owed them some sort of explanation. His future, whatever it was, would repay his parents for the trouble of having raised a son. It seemed to Ruben that Piet had already made the choice and dropped away from his parents so why not continue to do so? Something troubling and inexplicable had drawn the young man back, something that even he could not explain, so Ruben in his new unaccustomed friendship fell into the bewildering role of reluctant supporter for his friend.

Ruben felt very sorry for Piet especially after he finally met his parents. It wasn't their very modest house, and it wasn't Uitenhage, although Uitenhage was by far the worst place he'd ever been in his entire life. It was the way that Piet's parents seemed to be at such odds with their son. Piet's mother, he had to admit, seemed very sweet but she insisted on treating Piet like he was a very little boy. And to make matters worse, Piet unexpectedly regressed when he was with her and started behaving like a small boy. When this happened, Ruben gravitated towards Kobus even though he knew Kobus did not like him at all. This was painful and very difficult. Ruben had never been anywhere in his life where someone had so arbitrarily hated him.

He wondered if this was what it was like to be black and because of this feeling he found himself talking more and more with the laughing, smiling Pinkie. In her little pink apron, white shirt and black skirt she looked like the very epitome of a house maid.

His mother's servants were almost invisible but when studied looked very like this timeless black lady who waited hand and foot on the Jonker's. For the first time in his life, he too was starting to feel invisible and the more that feeling grew, as if in counterweight, the louder he grew. He hated himself and wished that he could coolly rise above it all. Tried to think of how his mother would react or his father but couldn't. It was desolating, this feeling of animosity that seemed to seep out of Kobus and even to some extent Marta.

There was a bewildering resentment constantly swirling and seething below the surface of every conversation. For the first time in his life, Ruben felt a stirring, nudging fear. Although he joked and fooled around, he could sense that Piet was walking on careful tiptoe as if afraid of setting something off.

Ruben did not ask Piet about it because he knew instinctively that Piet would lie and deny that there was anything and he didn't want his friend to lie. Not now. It was possible that Piet no longer sensed the danger. It was possible that over the years this had become the natural way of things. This was a household of repressed and subdued dangers.

Ruben had rashly promised that, if necessary, he would break the news about Israel to Piet's parents. He'd even practised the speech, dropping in small pieces of relevant information about the kibbutz in Israel and then possibly travelling in Europe. But when he'd met them, he was secretly relieved that Piet had taken on the responsibility himself.

The feeling of repressed fear instilled in Ruben an urgent need to leave as soon as possible. Occasionally, he had an almost irrepressible urge to blurt out the truth. Get it out of the way, forcing something into the open, something that could be discussed. Something that might force Piet's hand and make their departure happen. Sometimes the compulsion was so urgent that he had to leave the room in case he said it out loud.

The only thing that stopped him was the hurt that he would see in Piet's face. He couldn't bear any more of Piet's hurt but he couldn't say how long he could hold on. And even worse a familiar feeling of boredom was starting to well up inside — an old feeling that he knew well. There were days now when he longed to return to the old carefree life that they'd had, would have again. He didn't know how long he could hold on.

When they were in Cape Town, it had been so easy to fantasise about the future. How they would build their lives and make a glittering life together. But in the face of Piet's family, it was suddenly much more complicated than he had ever imagined. It suddenly seemed as if they were suggesting that they fly to the moon.

Chapter 26 — Uprising

Langa and Uitenhage, March 1985

Trouble was everywhere. It seeped through the dirt on the road and down the walls of the huts.

Gwala saw the trouble clearly and recognised what it meant, preached that the end was finally here and that at last the white man would clearly hear the black man's voice. And his speeches were now delivered in a quiet determined voice that sometimes trembled with excitement was that of religion.

Some of the men had returned to work, scabs and hopeless men with small starving children, but many were still on strike. The men who were not working gathered daily and the streets and paths of Langa and were infected with anger and it rose up and filled the air and settled in the very pores of the multitudes.

The pressure was building and despite the banning of any meeting between more than three people, the residents of Langa began to feel less desperate. Tiny, almost invisible rays of hope could be found even here in the thirst and filth of Langa.

The men were ready for action but knew that in the white towns they could not gather in groups, not even to walk the streets looking for work. They added this injustice to the many they already harboured and Gwala called them together.

Let the white man come into the townships and stop them from meeting. Let the white man come. But the white man did not come into the townships. News spread of activists working right here in Langa. Men whose names were legend. Winston, Cleva and Gwala could walk the township and listen to the talk, and it was good. Things were changing. The message was clear.

Gwala wanted to organise a march. It was all he spoke of. But for a march to be effective, it would have to cross the line into the white man's world and that would not be allowed. It was his great dilemma and Winston, like Cleva, caught his excitement and waited for it to happen.

Gwala went away to the great townships of Port Elizabeth and returned rejuvenated. With his eyes sparkling and a spring in his step, he gathered his followers and spoke of ways to defeat the regime. His energy was infectious, and Winston was drawn closer to him.

When he spoke, his voice clear and fine, raising above the pettiness of poverty, his words lodged in Winston's heart like unexploded bombs.

'The black man has, after all, only one thing. That thing is precious.' He held his hands over his heart and waited. Winston waited and the crowd waited with expectation hanging in the air.

'The only thing that we have will help us to succeed. That thing is you, comrades. That is all we have.' Then he raised his fist and shouted. '*Amandla*,' and they answered him, their voices rising to the heavens. '*Awehtu*.' Finally, the language of power echoed through Langa, out onto the streets and into the towns to join all the other voices across the country.

And they would start, Gwala told them, by attending the funerals of all their fallen comrades. So it was that 1984 became the year of the funeral. This way the people could finally gather in groups of more than three and there was nothing that anyone could do about it.

Gwala said in a whisper so that men and women leaned forward to hear, 'The white man cannot stop us from mourning our dead. Our fallen comrades will help us to defeat this regime.'

Soon the men of God too were preaching insurrection at the funerals and no man could stop where the church led.

Now no one could stop them. Up and down the country, mourners jubilantly grieved for their comrades. The bodies of the dead were carrying the grief of a nation.

1984 saw a rise of activism and at the same time a wave of optimism streaked through the country as more and more black people began to vent their anger.

That new year, on a sweltering night as hot fireworks rose out of Uitenhage, overlooked Langa sat in the flickering light of wood fires. And the beginnings of revolution lurked in the twisted roads and byways.

Winston and Cleva, determined to be part of this new revolt, listened to the daily news and prayed for an opportunity to act. Even Looksmart joined with the hundreds now gathering on street corners and in the marketplace.

One day in late February when the year had descended into the hottest part of summer, Gwala came with his plans. He still wore his suit, the jacket buttoned up and his trousers carefully pressed despite the heat. His shoes shone and the white of his shirt stood out in contrast to the dark material of the suit.

Only close scrutiny would reveal that the suit was frayed and showing signs of wear. Everyone else wore ruined, stained clothes and they were thin, their bones sharp and their faces drawn.

Gwala said, 'There is to be a funeral. It is for two men. One was a man who worked all his life for the struggle. The other was an old man. We will all go and mourn at this funeral. We want five thousand at this funeral.' There was a hush as his listeners glanced at one another. 'In Soweto the other day nearly ten thousand people went to see the burial of five men. They had to close all the roads for the whole day.'

Then he smiled. 'You see what we can do when we talk to each other.' And for once he had to shout above the excited noise of the gathering crowd.

'All those white faces, up there,' he pointed to Uitenhage, 'must surely hear us now.' The roar was deafening. 'And comrades,' he held up his hands and it was five minutes before he could be heard. 'Not just Uitenhage and Port Elizabeth but the whole world will hear us now. At last.'

Then the cries rose again and again. '*Amandla, awethu.*' Over and over again into the smiling faces of friends and comrades. Winston never knew that hope could feel like this. Suddenly there was no need for food, no need for anything at all.

The day of the funeral broke hot and dry with a fierce, spiteful wind chasing dust through the narrow paths of Langa. Winston, Looksmart and Cleva had arranged to walk to the gathering place together. It had been so long since any of them had needed to be anywhere that it felt strange. Looksmart had taken extra care in dressing that morning. Much more care than he had taken in a long time.

When they got to the marketplace, there were hundreds already and it was still early. Winston had a feeling that this day would change everything. There were many faces that he did not know and some he never expected to see. Men and some women who had also caught the bug. Gwala had been very busy.

Someone began to speak through a tinny loud hailer, the words coming through a long tunnel of pain. 'Comrades, remember Fezile the man, the activist, friend and comrade.' Whistles broke out drowning the rest of the words and people began to sway and in the middle of the square they started the *toyi-toyi*. Their stomping feet raised the dust until it choked those in the middle.

This was no quiet, sedate funeral. No solemn dipped heads. This would be a sadness shouted up into the heavens that would shake the very foundations of the regime.

Winston looked for Gwala and at first could not see him. Many people wore old suits and there were so many people in the crowd that Winston thought that he would never find him. But then he saw him. Only glimpses through the moving crowd but then someone produced a box and Gwala was raised above the crowd.

At first, he said nothing, but stood looking at the crowd with a small smile hinted on his lips. Gwala had helped them mix their grief with anger and they now showed it through loud walls of noise and movement.

'Here at last the world will see,' Gwala shouted, and they cheered and sang.

The long snake of people wound through the dusty makeshift roads on a wall of sound that acted like wheels. No tiredness; no aching legs; no fading muscles. Teenagers and little children trailed on the outskirts of the chanting crowd. Winston paused in his progress, recognising two of them.

'You should be at school, comrades.'

'What school?' Julian, almost a man already, replied, unafraid. He had not learned yet to be afraid.

Then the buses arrived. Old crinkle-cut buses wobbling and smelling of stale diesel. Slowly the crowd came to a silence as they realised that there were only two buses. Some people stood on tiptoe to see if there would be more, but the road remained empty except for dust.

Winston tried to fight his way to the front but could not as bodies closed in around him and trapped him where he was. He looked around but could not see Cleva and suddenly here was no one that he knew.

Anyone could do the calculations — at the most sixty people would be going to this funeral. What of the others? Winston tried to count but couldn't. Probably there were hundreds.

At first the dismay of the crowd rose up in an awful din and then slowly individual voices could be heard. Hard brittle words, shouting. The mood had turned and had quickly become darker, and the smallest children began to drop back and fade away, turning down hot dusty streets in retreat to their small childish worlds.

Then the sound of the loud hailer. 'Comrades, comrades.' The crowd turned to the man standing on the steps of the first bus. Holding on to the railing he faced the crowd. 'Comrades, this is just a small obstacle in our struggle. Some of us will go in the buses and then we will wait for you. The rest must walk. What is a little walk in our long march to freedom? You must walk. We will wait all day. We must show solidarity, comrades, so we should all be at that funeral. We will wait.' As his words faded the crowd began to shout and sing and chant and dance once more. And just like that the feeling of hope returned.

Some of the men even laughed. 'First, they stopped us meeting, then they ban weekend funerals. But they can't stop us. We are too powerful.'

Others began to take up the cry. 'Let's go. Nothing can stop us, we are many. We will go to our brothers' funeral.' Raised fists and shouts.

'*Amandla*,' rose and was countered with '*Awethu*'. Power was in the voices of the people.

Some of the teenagers and children who had slunk away came back. The crowd swelled even more as if a silent message had gone out to the rest of the township and others joined in. 'What is happening?' they asked.

'Comrade, we are going to a funeral,' was the answer and the crowd swelled again.

A gangly boy on an old red bicycle cycled at the front, like a sentinel or guard shining a light on the way. Langa now at their backs they fanned out and faced the white town. The low squat houses of Vanes Estate lay in front of them, their green lawns like an oasis against the brown hard dirt of Langa.

The crowd beat their feet on the road making a tattoo of sound. They sang about the bugs of the earth rising up and taking over from the bigger beasts of the world. It made the pain of loss easier, the journey shorter. It showed the world that they would not be stopped.

Winston, carried along with this new urgency, found that he did not mind the separation from his friend. His new neighbours were comrades too and they were jostling for the front where they were sure that they would be able to see history rise up to meet them on the road. A man with a drum had also pushed to the front and now beat the sound of their steps. They felt like pioneers and leaders in the struggle, and everybody wanted to be at the front.

Gwala was there with Julien, the teenager who had not yet known the might of the white man. Cigarettes were offered in the absence of food. Real shop-bought cigarettes, not the roll-ups they usually smoked. The rich tobacco made Winston's head swim, but he did not mind. He smoked it quickly. It seemed so strange to be so happy, so carefree going to a funeral.

And suddenly the crowd opened, and he found to his delight that he was at the front. There were his friends, Gwala and Cleva linked arm in arm. He could not see Looksmart but knew that he was in the crowd.

He smiled at Looksmart's insistence that people not touch him and ruin his clothes. He was glad that all of his friends would be here on this day and when they were old men, they could all look back on this day and say, 'That's when it happened. That was the day we freed ourselves.'

Winston tried to think about the comrade who had died. Tried to remember that he had been in the struggle for liberation, the struggle against the regime. He rolled the words around in his head. Regime. Struggle. He'd heard that the man had hardly been older than himself but had been an activist all his life. He'd made it his special mission to be a thorn in the side of the white regime but, in the end, he had died because that was the only way of the whites. Death had accorded him honour and it was up to the living to deliver that honour. Death had taken them all away too soon and even though they were surrounded by death there were many more waiting to take up the struggle.

As they marched there arose, like an applause, a thin plume of dust and with it came their noise.

Some boys gathered at the front running alongside the bicycle, excited and happy as if it were all a game. They heard the words 'resistance' and 'struggle', but their lives had been nothing but hardship and poverty and this was a delightful diversion. The boys breathless and tired of pleading for a chance on the bike were the first to see them. They slowed and fell silent and the boy on the bicycle ground to a halt and climbed off leaning the bicycle against his hip. Then the first adults caught up and they saw it and slowed and then halted. Like a chain reaction of cards collapsing the whole crowd ground to a halt and fell silent; the red dust slowly settled on the ground once again.

A gleaming, shining line of police formed an impenetrable line. The sun at its height now, beat down on them all like a fist. Beyond the police the white gleaming houses squatted in the blazing uncaring day. Behind the silent crowd, gaunt Langa darkly brooded at their backs.

Like two armies they faced each other. Blue and khaki clad men backed by hulking armed vehicles and the tiny, puny, unprotected mass. The boy with the bicycle rang his bell. A tiny tinkle that was lost in the breathless expectant air.

A policeman stepped forward. Bulky, stomach straining against his shirt. Gun strapped to his thigh. He raised his hand as if to stop the advancing thousands. He spoke but they could not hear, would not hear, and an angry whistling came from the crowd. Small and insignificant at first and then louder and louder still. Years of oppression could not now bend these men — they outnumbered the white men. Gwala, nudged in the back, stepped forward and Winston's throat closed to see his friend so small against the line of police.

***

Kobus licked his lips with his dry, dry tongue and dried his clammy palms on his trousers. *Hemel, it's hot,* he thought. But there was no time now for God or heaven. He too stepped forward and strode towards the little black man, putting his hand on the comfortable weapon at his side. Gwala held his hands out to show he had no weapon and his hands trembled.

It did not matter that he had no armour, no gun, no vehicle to hide behind because he had right on his side. Gwala forgot everything. Could only see the long, long years of oppression and when he came up to Kobus, he spat out his demand. 'White man, we are going to a funeral, let us through.'

For a long time, the crowd waited but Kobus did not speak. Only the men behind him moved to spread out holding their rifles pointing to the sky.

The crowd held its breath. Gwala, from this distance, was threadbare, thin and small next to the huge white man with the stomach straining against his shirt. Gwala spoke again but they could not hear him.

Kobus answered and marvelled at the black man's nerve. But *klein* Jannie at the end of the line did not see a threadbare black man. He saw a black aggressor with thousands of supporters. An aggressor as he would later tell the inquiry. He heard the voice from his past. The voice from school and home; the voice that told him about the perils of the black man. He saw the threat that he'd been told about when he joined the police. His hand twitched on the trigger. His eyes flew to Kobus who remained resolute and silent. Gave no signal of distress. The sweat ran into his eyes, and he tasted blood on his tongue.

Gwala, shrugging, turned and began walking back to the others. '*Luister kaffir…*' Kobus blustered and would have followed but the crowd cast a large shadow and it was best not to get too far away from the comfort of his own kind. At first it appeared as if Gwala would stop. The crowd drew a breath like a sigh at the insult. But Gwala continued walking. Hadn't he and his comrades agreed a long time ago that they would not speak in Afrikaans? They would not use the language of the oppressor.

He continued to walk with his back to the white man. Let the white man understand that he would not respond to insults. No one here today would respond to insults. He fell into the people, and they cheered and clapped him on the back. They turned their bright faces to the white men barring their way. Some of them raised their clenched fists and shouted. The white policemen could see their derision, their might. For once the black men were not afraid.

Klein Jannie saw it all. He saw it clearly despite the sweat in his eyes and he began to know real fear. How could it be that this black man showed such disdain for authority? At the end of the line, he trembled and hoped fervently that none of the thousands could see it. And the more he trembled, the bigger the crowd looked, the darker and more foreboding it seemed. And the more he saw, the bigger the fear grew until it was all he could see.

It seemed to him that the black mass was now much closer. He did not see the fear in their eyes. He did not see the fifteen-year-old darting behind his older friend. He did not see the children and the red bike. He could not hear their pain.

Kobus, erupting with an anger that strangled his throat into silence, could only watch the black man become absorbed by the crowd. The crowd seemed to mock him with their smiling faces, and he swore he could hear jeering. In all his years as a policeman he had never had a black man so comprehensively beat him. The spit accumulated in his mouth and threatened to choke him. The blood rushed to his face in a tide of red shame. The words he so badly needed that would help him regain control now choked him. Besides, it was now beyond words.

Klein Jannie listened carefully, shaking and petrified. He was a boy with his head cut off. He listened desperately for instruction. The crowd, if possible, seemed even closer now. And still he waited for instructions — just like he'd been taught. Finally, the words to save him came — 'Open fire' — he heard them clearly, as if they'd been shouted straight into his ears. He would swear all the rest of his life that Kobus had uttered these words. In the end he was the only one to hear them.

Like the excellent recruit that he was, he knelt deliberately and calmly as he'd been instructed to do, positioned his rifle and opened fire right into the crowd that had swallowed Gwala.

The other recruits, nervous too, heard the gunfire and this was their signal to join the onslaught, just as they'd been taught. Kobus, still engulfed by rage, did nothing to stop them.

It was hard to tell in the chaos that followed but later evidence would prove that Gwala fell first from a round of automatic fire from an R1 rifle, his punishment meted out from a regime that would brook no insults. Hit in the back, he crumbled to the ground, nothing more than a bloody clump of clothing and at first Cleva thought that he had tripped. As she knelt to help him the noise of gunfire engulfed her and she became aware of the others, like fearful children, turning and fleeing as bullets remorselessly ripped into them. One by one her comrades fell as she curled in a ball and wept.

There were no trees for shelter; no holes to hide in; no shelter to run to; no place to hide. And there was no reprieve from the hail of bullets.

After a while, what seemed like a decade, the bullets stopped, and the exhausted gunmen paused for breath and reloading. Where there had been a mass of people there was almost nothing. Those on the ground, if they were still alive, pressed themselves into the earth as if it could swallow them up.

The gun smoke cleared to reveal the aftermath of a macabre battle scene. The musical cacophony of bullets stopped, to be replaced by an eerie silence.

Then the wailing started. The wailing of the dying. Kobus surveyed their handiwork, a small imperceptible smile at the corner of his thick lips.

Out on the ruined ground the bodies lay scattered like hopeless seed on the barren hard red clay. Patches of dark red clay surrounded the bodies. The sun, oblivious, shone hard and bright, illuminating the scene, showing no pity.

Kobus needed to think. He needed time when time was at a premium. Where he was red before he was now white. Where his mouth was full of hateful spit before it was now dry. This, he knew, was bad but despite it all he felt a sense of relief that it was all over. This, he knew, was worse than the A-team in Alexandra, worse than anything that he'd ever seen. He also knew that this was his greatest achievement. He needed to think. His men, his platoon, his pride and joy were still kneeling in line. Waiting faithfully for his instructions and he could not speak.

Finally, a movement came from his left. *Klein* Jannie, his rifle abandoned on the ground, was talking but Kobus, still deafened from the cacophony of firing could not hear. They were all deaf. *Klein* Jannie's eyes were different somehow, different from the usual adoration. Something had changed but Kobus had no time for that now.

Then his ears stopped ringing and he heard. '*Jy het gesê, jy het gesê.*' You told us. You told us.

Kobus turned away, feeling stronger now. *Klein* Jannie was a problem for later. In the distance, the sirens of ambulances wailed like miserable women. Kobus needed time. Time, he did not have. He sent Erasmus to stop the ambulances. Erasmus, solid and unquestioning, would do as he was told. The ambulances could wait. He needed time to think.

The other men gathered. Then suddenly he knew what to do. The old feeling of being in control returned. If he could be like Danie then he would know what to do. His men, veterans of lies and corruption would act as they were directed. They would follow instructions carefully and without question. *Klein* Jannie stood to the side like a wounded soldier, invisible and ignored.

The policemen were dispersed among the black mass of dead and dying. They passed Winston, just another black man who could no longer be helped. No one stopped. Then on, picking their way through the other bodies. Once a pleading arm reached out and held on to a leg and was shaken off.

The men, as instructed, found rocks and sticks and carefully placed them next to now helpless outstretched hands. One wailing boy with a reddened shirt was handed a large, gnarled stick. He clutched it with a puzzled bloodied hand and his head fell back onto the dirt. 'He's not long for this world,' one of the policemen commented.

In the background Kobus could hear Erasmus talking to the ambulance crew. Tobacco smoke wafted over to him. It was a welcome distraction from the rich metallic smell of blood and shit. *Klein* Jannie, not yet moved from his position, was close to tears and unattended. Annoyed, Kobus ignored him. His focus was on the men moving amongst the bodies as they assembled an alibi of rocks and sticks amongst the dying and defeated enemy.

Behind him Kobus knew that a number of the black protesters had managed to escape, helping one another to safety right into the white stronghold. *Let them go*, he thought. *What can they do now?*

They would storm the white provincial hospital, swarming over the attempts by the porter to stop them. Just as they had done in Soweto all those years ago. What did they care for the 'whites only' signs exhorting them to stay away? This did not concern Kobus. He needed to secure the scene.

After two hours Kobus was satisfied with the work of his men. He was ready and told Erasmus to wave the increasingly dissatisfied ambulance men through. It was too late anyway. Most of the bodies out there were beyond an ambulance now.

The police radio in the cars and *buffel* were now alive with noises, like dangerous animals. Kobus felt a strange sort of elation, and this gave him a surprising energy. Even as he watched his men and issued orders his brain had been at work and the great story of the Langa rebellion was ready. He was surprised at how breathless he sounded when he responded to the long demanding police radio that had been bubbling in the car for some time. He sounded as if he'd been fighting for his life.

Yes, he told them, there had been an incident. They knew of course because the hospital had been filling rapidly with wounded men, women and children; all of them black. White people had begun to line the street in Vanes Estate. They couldn't see it all, but they did have an excellent view of the police vehicles and had seen the ambulances. Clearly there had been a serious incident. No black faces had returned to witness the carnage. All was quiet, silent and grave-like where the little tin shanties glinted in the sun.

Yes, there had been shots fired because of an unprecedented attack by a mob of at least five thousand armed men. Let those bastards dispute that later, Kobus thought. Right now, he needed to cover his own back. Yes, there may well be casualties; this after glancing at the still muttering and strangely petrified *klein* Jannie. Yes, martial law would be a good idea. This to the commanding officer from Port Elizabeth. Let the army take over the situation. They would know what to do.

The commander from Port Elizabeth was a man that Kobus had never met but he was reassuringly supportive and unquestioning. 'Leave it to me' were the words that Kobus had wanted to hear the most and those were the words that came. Not to worry, the army were on the way. After all, the *kaffirs* were starting a revolution!

Kobus waited on site for someone more senior. He dispatched *Klein* Jannie in the first ambulance to hospital. He could not stand to look on the pale reproachful face any longer. Also, he would have to be punished for abandoning his weapon, perhaps even discharged from the police force.

Once they were released from their impoundment, the paramedics rushed to the scene. Overwhelmed at the devastation, they moved from body to body, shaking their heads and letting the stretchers fall to the ground.

They'd been laughing and joking with the policeman for two hours. They'd been led to believe that it was a minor incident. Erasmus had seemed so calm, so dismissive. He'd even made a joke about a black man slipping on a banana skin. They'd all heard it before, but they still laughed. It was a very funny joke.

There were only four of them and hundreds of wounded and dead. Now there was no joking and Erasmus had disappeared. They rushed from one body to the next. One of the paramedics tripped over a bicycle and the precious bell rang out. The paramedic rubbed his knee and continued on amongst the devastated bodies.

Hands reached out to them, pleading, begging hands. They tended those they could and begged for reinforcement. Many of the wounded lay face down on the clay, beyond the help of man, big bloody gaping holes in their backs.

The first ambulance was dispatched but that only contained a young policeman who had appeared perfectly well but there was no arguing with the commander who was forceful and strong.

Reinforcements finally arrived. More men in uniform. A colonel with a whole regiment adding new vehicles to those of the police. With martial law already enforced the blue of the police was replaced by helmeted soldiers in army camouflage; sunglasses making faces anonymous and unreadable. A sense of calm tension enveloped the scene and spread out into the town like a disease. The white people on the street with nothing more to see went home.

Langa remained silent like a grave.

After Kobus explained about the mob attack, taking care to exaggerate numbers and the black threat, the *Kolonel* asked about police casualties. Kobus shrugged and explained about pitiful *klein* Jannie on his way to hospital. A young man unsuitable for this kind of fight, he added.

The *Kolonel* nodded, already getting ready to take over. Kobus' men stood ready to be ordered home. Smoking near the *buffel*, they were veterans of scenes like this, now eager to return home and let others complete this dirty work. The *Kolonel* spared a brief glance for the scene, the scattered, battered bodies. He left, with a faint sense of disgust in his eyes and issued orders in a short staccato.

Later that evening the people of South Africa would be told by Botha's government that an incident had occurred. The white people of South Africa were assured that this rebellion had been quelled and stifled. A revolution had been stopped. Their brave police force had acted in the interests of all sensible people by stopping the evil that was brewing in their beautiful country.

The international community expressed its outrage and watched their television sets in horror and summoned blustering ineffectual diplomats demanding explanations but in Langa they silently mourned. That was all they could do.

Suddenly, Kobus was free to go home. For him it was over, but Langa would lie forever seared on the memories of a nation. Hope lay vanquished in the red clay of Langa.

Chapter 27 — Going Home

Uitenhage, the day after the Langa Massacre — March 1985

After that long terrible day was over and Kobus couldn't bear to think about those bodies lying in the reddening clay, with a weary glance at the commander, he left the offices. His car was hot and reeked of body odour. Soon the rhythmic rumble of the tyres lulled him into the past. And floundering as he was, tired, despondent and choked, Kobus latched on to the one thing that rose in his mind, clear and tangible.

He shook his head as if at an irritating fly and the words from the note that had been handed to him outside the police station returned. Big red letters scrawled across the page with lipstick, *It was nice to meet your son and his* moffie *boyfriend.*

Suddenly so much of the last few weeks made sense to him now. The boys arriving in the battered *kombi* together and refusing to stay in the house. The vivid memory of them sitting too close together. The odd touches and looks that had passed between them. The things that they had said with their eyes and little body movements. The body language of a couple. How could he have missed it? And now strangers that he hardly knew had seen it. Strangers. People who Kobus needed to lead and mould into a police force that he could control and dominate.

And as he drove Kobus was aware of a sensation of a drunken reeling as if he staggered through the many tiny betrayals from the people within his own castle; a place where he should have been safe. The betrayal had robbed him of words. And even in the midst of the Langa rebellion he could not focus on them — the black bodies — all he could see was Rueben smirking with his hand on Kobus Junior's shoulder.

The darkening drive did nothing to dispel the horrible events of the day and he saw them only as things that had happened to someone else. The police station, his police station no longer, was buzzing with menacing questions that he could not answer. He didn't want to answer them. He felt torn and broken as if he'd been the one fired upon.

Then the commandant spoke and there was a nameless accusation present in his voice, but Kobus hardly felt the censure. It ran off his back like water. The talk raged and fell around him, and he remained ice cold inside. He saw their lips moving and one time the commandant put a hand on his arm, and it seared him as if he had been in a fire.

The huge pinboard had been shoved against the wall and someone had drawn a timeline and they were arguing about it and the sounds made Kobus' head hurt. No one asked him and he remained mute.

Then the commandant wrote on the board in his cramped unintelligible writing, trying to shoehorn the details into the timeline. Kobus did not care, confusing the details about his son with those of this horrible day as he blundered through the night inquiry. The facts bled into one another until everything was red.

And it was strange that the day's shootings were not what he saw but the face of Rueben.

The picture of his face when they finally returned home on that disastrous day of the police station visit was more real to him than the lifeless bodies on red clay. Ruben, cocky and sure, sauntering to the *kombi*, laughing and telling another of his impossible stories.

Kobus stood in front of them and blocked their way, attempting to keep the fury from his voice but not quite succeeding. He could see the fear on his son's face and that was as it should be. Marta lingered in the doorway, and he spoke to her sharply, ordering her back into the house. She did not argue, disappearing into her woman's world.

His son, pale of face turned as if made of stone. 'Not you,' Kobus said rudely and shoved his son aside. 'You,' he said pointing at Ruben.

'You can get into that kombi, and you can *voetsek* as far as I'm concerned but before you do that, I want to speak to you alone.'

And even though the pavement was hot and uncomfortable, Rueben seemed happy to stand here in the street where everyone could see them.

Rueben's was voice rough and hard, 'What do you want?' And with what seemed am effort he smiled but Kobus. He knew that Ruben could sense that something had gone wrong. He did not know the lengths that Kobus would go to, but he was about to find out.

'I'm not speaking in front of you,' he spoke directly to Kobus Junior. 'Go into the house, my son.' Ruben laughed; the sound jarring on Kobus' nerves.

'Listen to you. *My* son,' Ruben said, with emphasis. 'You don't own him, you know, and he does have a name. His name is Pieter or Piet.' But Ruben was a little boy dabbling in a dangerous adult world that he did not understand. Kobus shrugged.

'*Luister jou domkop.*' Kobus erupted into Afrikaans, his words like little sharp daggers. Ruben, so cocksure and urbane, laughed again.

'Mr Jonker, you can insult me as much as you like. I don't know what your problem is, and I don't care. You don't have to worry any more. Piet and I'll be gone by this afternoon. I just think it's such a shame for Mrs Jonker that it has to be this way.' There was something courageous in the way he spoke. Something that despite Kobus' hatred made him admire the lad. He was not big, in fact Kobus towered over him. His glasses made him seem vulnerable, childlike. But he spoke in the words of an adult, in total control, and Kobus was suddenly reduced to an angry child.

'I want to speak to you. I have some information that you must listen to, and I want to speak to you alone. My boy should not be part of this.' Kobus was surprised at how reasonable he sounded.

Ruben looked at him as if gauging something. Piet, who had stood to one side, pale, attempted to step forward but Ruben laid a hand on his shoulder. 'Don't worry, Piet. I'll sort it out. Go and speak to your mom. Tell her we're going.' Piet nodded.

Kobus knew then that he would win. He knew how to deal with this upstart, this little boy who wanted to play big men games. After all, this was Kobus' special territory. Hadn't he dealt with many such boys all his life long?

Kobus led the way to his study. When he'd moved in, he'd never needed a study, had never had a study in any of the houses where he lived previously. This time Marta had insisted that he have a space to himself. He suspected that it was because she needed space for herself, and she liked having him out of the way.

At first, he had hardly used the space, preferring the *voorkamer* as it opened onto the swimming pool, and it had the added benefit of annoying

Marta. It was not a bad idea to remind her that she was not the one in control.

After a while, the study had grown on him in a way that was surprising. He started to store things from his police life in the study, forgotten papers and qualifications that he'd accumulated, photographs of colleagues from the A-team and articles from the newspapers.

The study had a desk that the previous owners had left behind. Kobus suspected that it was too heavy and cumbersome to move. An old, scratched piece of furniture with three drawers that could be locked. Kobus had nothing that he wanted to lock away except for his police issue weapons and those he locked in the safe.

He began to enjoy the solitary nature of the room. The peace and quiet that it offered. The door that closed out the rest of the house. No one came into the room; it was his alone. Not even Pinkie came in to clean — there was never any mess. It had a small window that opened onto the back garden, but the window was so small that Kobus would have to stand in order to see anything. This also Kobus liked because there was never anything going on in that garden and it meant that no one ever looked in.

At one time it must have sported a ceiling fan because there was a strange sturdy hook in the middle of the ceiling. Kobus noticed this on one of his days off and for a while had been intrigued. He could not identify it. He'd pulled up his chair and stood on it to examine the hook closely. Then on impulse he'd put both hands to the hook and it had taken all of his weight. When he'd discussed this hook with someone in the office, they explained that sometimes those old-fashioned ceiling fans were hung on those hooks and so the mystery had been solved.

This was the room that Kobus steered Ruben into, using his superior bulk to crowd the smaller man. Kobus had learnt to do this a long time ago when first interviewing suspects. Very few of his suspects were bigger than him. Ruben attempted to free his arm from the vice like grip but was rudely shoved into the chair and Kobus loomed over him.

He leant down into Ruben's face so that he could smell the sour, stale breath and it made Ruben want to gag. Kobus noticed that the boy was not smiling any more.

Ruben said softly, trying not to give away his fear, 'Mr Jonker, you cannot treat me like this. I have done nothing wrong. Please let me go.'

He tried to keep the fear from his voice, but it shook, nonetheless. He tried to rise but the big face was too close, and he sank back down again.

After a while Kobus moved away a little but remained standing, towering over the boy. 'Don't make the mistake of thinking that you can tell me what to do. You are breaking the law every single day that you walk on this earth. You are a suspect, and I am not going to let you get away with it any more. Do you understand?'

Ruben's head rocked back against the wall and his face paled. Kobus was huge and red and seemed to pulse with anger.

'Mr Jonker, I don't know what you mean. I've done nothing wrong, broken no laws.' Kobus could hear the tremble, could hear the doubt. He knew he had won.

'You are a *moffie* and that is illegal. I don't want to know about your relationship with my son and I don't care. I can lock you up and throw the keys away,' he said and clicked his fingers, 'just like that. I can have you in St Albans prison by this afternoon. Do you know what they will do to you there? Believe me, it's not pretty.'

So outrageous was this remark that Ruben almost laughed and shook his head. 'Are you saying that because I'm gay you will have me thrown in jail? That's ridiculous. What about your son? Will you have him thrown in jail as well?' Kobus was on him before he could even breathe. Those thick lumpy fingers were around his throat and Kobus used all of his weight to pin the boy against the wall, tipping the chair back as far as it would go. Little white specks of spit foamed in the corners of his mouth.

Ruben was reduced to making little choking sounds as he tried desperately to breathe. Kobus hissed into his ear. 'You'll be long gone, my son. I only need to pick up the phone and a van will take you. Like I said, by this afternoon you'll be in St Albans Prison. Your parents will get you lawyers, I'm sure.' Kobus sounded quite reasonable, almost kind as if pitying the young man whose hands clutched at his big beefy hands trying to relieve the pressure on his throat.

'By the time those lawyers get to you, it'll be too late. The damage will already have been done. They only have blacks in that jail, so they'll be pleased to see a little *moffie* white boy like you.' Kobus could see the boy's face working trying to beg. In a moment when the blue had worked its way over his face, he would let the boy go. Get him breathing properly again, but by then the boy would have got the message, loud and clear.

And Kobus knew it was time to let Ruben go. Without saying anything to Piet, Kobus, a veteran of these ultimatums, gave the boy twenty minutes to be gone. Then he would let the Cape Town police know — he knew people after all — he'd been in the police force for a very long time. Ruben was just another little Jewish boy with a problem.

With the bruises already starting to show around his throat Ruben had needed no more persuasion. Kobus could not have planned it better. His own son would have no idea and, besides, he was ensconced with his mother. No doubt she would keep him occupied for hours. In the end it had been easy, Ruben slipped out and was gone before anyone other than Kobus knew about it.

Kobus was proud of what he had done. He felt for the first time in a long time that he'd wrested back control, done something right. It was a shock when his pale son had confronted him in the study later that day.

'What have you done?' He asked with a level of hatred in his eyes that caught Kobus off guard.

'What I had to do,' he replied keeping his voice level.

'That is just nonsense. Don't imagine that I will stay here with you. I will go after Ruben, and we will be together.'

'Ruben doesn't want to be with you. You know how quickly he folded. I have never spoken to anyone who folded so quickly.' Kobus would have said more but the hurt in the boy reached out like a mist and engulfed Kobus so entirely that he felt as if he too would be swallowed by it. Relenting he stood and reached out to his son.

Piet stopped him. 'Don't touch me and don't talk to me.' He turned and left the room. Stunned, Kobus was left to the silent emptiness of his study.

Suddenly, a blue and battered *bakkie* swerved in front of him and cursing, he slammed on the brakes fully awake his memories fading like a nightmare. Kobus wondered if he'd fallen asleep.

And now fully in the present he realised the full extent of his weariness.

Home was dark, weary and as he levered his way out of the car he noticed how quiet it was. No laughter and singing drifting from Langa and it lay still in the darkness like a wounded beast.

There had been no sleep or rest for hours. Kobus could not remember when he had a break even for the most essential needs. His mind was hazy and sluggish, and he knew that he smelled bad, and it had been a relief to finally hand over command to someone else. But the hours spent in the police station had dragged unmercifully and now he was at last free. But try as he might he could not shrug off the day. His thoughts, like an untrained puppy, would keep returning to the station.

The new commander, fresh and disapproving from Port Elizabeth, was smart and ironed, his blue uniform sporting glinting medals reminding Kobus of his old commander, Meiring. His appearance only served to enhance Kobus' own dishevelled appearance.

Blurry-eyed and with ears buzzing, Kobus had become robotic, and he knew that he was irritating this new commander and the army bodies that seemed to suddenly fill the police station. They were everywhere and Kobus was faced with a bewildering array of people who he now suddenly answered to.

'You are not to talk to the press or television. You understand, Jonker?' The commander had boomed when Kobus had never had any intention of talking to anyone. He nodded, donkey like, and longed to go home more tired than he'd ever believed possible.

He did not allow himself to think about the bodies out on the Langa soil or the families now wailing in the township. His thoughts turned away from the event and inward as if like blotting paper the day's deeds were completely absorbed. It remained apart from him.

He wondered what had happened to his own men but in an abstract way and knew that he did not care. He knew that his own career was finally over, but it was as if something vital had been broken and he would never be whole again. He was strangely and utterly devoid of feeling, utterly numb.

This police station was now a scene of frantic bustle. Men that he did not recognise worked everywhere although what they could be doing, he could not imagine.

He'd seen Yvonne briefly, dark marks of mascara running down her plump face, no longer talkative. He'd witnessed a bulky drab man kindly usher her out of the building. The way his arm had lingered at her waist surprised Kobus who'd always thought of her as lonely and only ever at home in the police station.

And in that realisation, something in him broke. Yvonne had only been humouring him. Talking to him as if she cared when all along, she was like all the others. She didn't care at all. He knew that he was surrounded now by huge, more important matters, and he couldn't focus. A trivial unimportant thing obsessed him, and he was a ghostly presence in his own life. He managed to answer a barrage of questions and wrote pages of reports, but it was all like a pile of useless ash. He had no idea how he completed any of it, but he did.

Kobus had heard that the mind hides the worst thoughts from itself because that is how humans survive. Kobus could believe that. His mind, slug like, shied and skittered around the incident that they were now calling the Langa Massacre but would not focus on one single thing. In all of his reports he called it the Langa rebellion. He saw the images but out of context as if they were individual pictures made up to look like art, a dark macabre art.

They asked him questions. How many were there? And he could not think what they meant. Who they meant? For several minutes they waited in an awkward silence and then he croaked out a request for them to repeat the question. His voice was an instrument that sounded as if he had not used it for a very long time.

It had taken a very long time for the interviews to be recorded and filed. Kobus had watched his men being questioned and although they had not heard the command to start firing it was clear that there was a riot. This was something that could not be questioned. Hadn't everyone seen the mass of weapons that the rioters had accumulated?

Kobus was asked if he had given the order to start firing. He said that it was very difficult to say as they were being attacked. Everyone had seen the black man come out and he had ignored a specific order from Kobus. Kobus returned again and again to the same question — had they not seen the array of weapons that the rioters had used to threaten the police?

Besides he had a new recruit who had been driven out of his mind by the rioters. *Klein* Jannie would have to explain why he had started firing but the others were only following protocol. Kobus could lay a lot at the feet of *klein* Jannie as he very much doubted if the boy would be able to explain his own part in the fiasco.

Only the most experienced had crept amongst the dead and the dying to lay the false branches and stones at their hands. It was a question of belief, and it was, after all, a riot. Kobus was satisfied that he had done the job that he was appointed to do, protect the people from black terror.

After the endless questions, Kobus was at last allowed to return home. He was ordered to stay away and would be informed of his status in due course. Until such time as he heard from them, he was on gardening leave. He was under no circumstances to speak of this to anyone.

Eventually even the new commander could see Kobus' distress as if the tiredness hung around him like body odour. He said, 'You better go home Jonker,' and turned away as if Kobus no longer existed.

And as he walked up to the house the darkness enveloped him like a Brandt and cut him off from the rest of the world. It was late, very late and there was a dark stain in the road where the *kombi* had been parked. Even though this was a victory, it was soured by the memory of his son's pale face and his shrill, desperate voice.

He felt his fists curling and wanted even now in the dead hours to get the boy out of bed. Shake him until he understood. Until he became the son that Kobus deserved. Yet he could afford to let the boy grow calmer. He remained confident that he would be able to speak to the boy after a few days had passed. Make him see sense. Make him accept that the risks Ruben posed were too big.

But as his boy had left the study that day, like a broken string, he almost started up and had half called his name before Pinkie was in the doorway.

She was not smiling but held out a piece of paper. He was needed at the police station. There was an illegal funeral gathering in Langa and he was needed immediately. All thoughts of his son had been pushed away to one side. He was needed at another emergency and all thoughts of his son and Rueben had been banished for the day.

Finally reaching his own room as if after a hellish nightmare it was a dark testament that Marta was asleep. In the doorway he stopped realising that, despite his bone-weary tiredness, he did not want to go into the room yet. Although he was tired, he could not imagine laying his head on the pillow and sleeping.

The house was deadly silent. None of the usual creaking sounds could be heard. Away in the distance he could hear the occasional car but that was fleeting and felt completely disconnected from the house.

Sissie's room too was dark and there was no light coming from under the door. He tiptoed down the corridor to his study. The room where he'd often found solace in the last few weeks. He had a bottle of brandy in the bottom drawer. That is what he wanted above all else.

He opened the door quietly and reached around for the light switch. The room exploded into light which fell on the swinging body and Kobus stared right into the hanging bulging face of his beloved son.

Afterword

Although the Langa massacre did happen, this is a work of fiction.

At the end of 1984, I had just matriculated from secondary school and was undecided on the path that I wanted to take. In 1985, I began working in a toy shop in Uitenhage as a stop gap before I started my real career — whatever that would be.

One day I saw hundreds of people stream past carrying or dragging injured comrades. It was notable that every person I saw was black.

Earlier that day I had heard gun fire, but it had become so much part of our lives that there was nothing remarkable in that.

The steady stream of distressed and obviously seriously injured people increased until it was an unstoppable flow that would swamp the Uitenhage Provincial Hospital that was not very far from the shopping arcade where I worked.

Another notable point was the lack of emergency vehicles and their sirens as it was clear to me that something terrible had happened. Of course, these were the days before mobile phones and the internet; it would take many hours before some of the facts, blurred as they were, would emerge.

Then I can remember watching the news that night with my family as the full horror of what had happened came to light. And even though we did not, at that stage, get the whole truth, we did know that many had been killed and many hundreds very badly injured. We knew too that all of the injured and killed were black. I remember my mother, white as a ghost, saying, 'Oh no, not another Sharpeville.'

Martial law was swiftly imposed on Uitenhage and surrounding townships and for weeks and weeks we lived as if in a war zone.

It was not until years afterwards that the full truth came out and even then, the obfuscation had caused many of the true facts to be lost forever. It is true that the commanding officer kept the ambulances waiting in order to plant 'weapons' of stones and sticks next to the wounded, dying and dead. He did this in order to place the blame on the demonstrators (or rioters as the regime would call them).

Officially it was reported that twenty people were killed in the Langa Massacre that day, 21 March 1985, and many hundreds more injured, many with life changing injuries. The injured then had to go on living in an environment that was wholly unsuited to wheelchair users and those with missing limbs or impaired sight or hearing. Of course, there were injuries that could not be seen and would never be treated.

It was also with immense sadness and desperation that the demonstrators returned to a Langa that no longer existed. Their homes were systematically destroyed by a South African regime that was determined to erase Langa from the face of the earth. Interestingly, the South African regime did pay out a record sum of money to a young man that they put into a wheelchair that day. Then they wiped their hands of the whole affair and pretended that it never happened.

Government ministers and officials appeared on television after the massacre, all of them dressed in grey suits, all of them wearing dark sunglasses, all of them expressionless. Not one of them showed anything other than outrage that they were being called to task by the international community for protecting their country from terrorists. It was particularly pertinent that the South Africans watching the news during those days after the massacre were not able to see the eyes of their politicians as they hid anything remotely human behind sunglasses. Possibly they could not show the expressions of sympathy that they should, so they hid.

Also, the South African regime had a long history of dealing with these catastrophes. The Langa Massacre had been preceded by the Sharpeville Massacre which, poignantly, had also occurred on the 21st of March. That was in 1960, when over 250 people were killed or injured. Then followed the Soweto uprising in 1976, and so on and so on. By the time Langa happened, the regime had become well-rehearsed in crisis management.

After the Langa Shootings, the international community did act, and they imposed sanctions on South Africa.

Government-sanctioned racism will always throw up people like Danie Swanepoel and Kobus Jonker. In fact, neither of these characters came anywhere near the cruelty and inhumanity of men like Eugene de Kock, who formed a counter-insurgency agency called C10, later changed to C1.

I feel very strongly that politicians today should be looking very carefully at what happened in South Africa. It is, after all, recent history, not ancient history, and it shows what happens when public figures normalise racism. It shows what can happen when public figures vilify the 'other' in society. Before leaders and politicians urge their nations into racism and xenophobia, they should look carefully at what can happen. The truth is that the regime that governed South Africa gave people like Kobus and Danie permission to treat the black people of South Africa as if they were little more than animals. The result: mass killings and torture.

Nelson Mandela, when he came to power, knew that there could be no peace in South Africa unless the stories of the suffering could be told and understood and so he formed The Truth and Reconciliation Committee. This committee was only possible through the herculean efforts of people like Desmond Tutu.

There was an understanding in the new South Africa that although justice could never be fully delivered it was important to hear the truth. Desmond Tutu was given the role of trying to unravel the atrocities during The Truth and Reconciliation Committee hearings. What Tutu heard nearly broke him and the nation watched with horror as story after story was told — all of them tragic beyond words. I don't think that Mandela or any of the others that were involved with the committee realised the colossal number of horrific stories that would come out of apartheid. I don't think that the most imaginatively gifted writers amongst us could even for a minute have dreamed up the awful truth. Nothing that I have written here can come close.

The Langa Shootings have been with me since that terrible day in 1985 and I cannot stop thinking about it. I am hoping that the telling of this story will help to keep the memory of this truly tragic event alive and help to honour the memory of those innocents who were mowed down that day. The reason they were killed? They were black.

What the South African regime did and how they got away with it for so long is down to foreign governments saying one thing and doing another. The United States and the United Kingdom and many places in

Europe turned their faces away and allowed it to happen. For forty long and terrible years the National Party was able to oppress nearly forty million people while the whole world looked the other way.

I also believe that, while the black people of South Africa suffered immensely and the repercussions are felt even today and will still be felt for many years to come, there are other victims as well. I believe that the apartheid regime crushed the souls of all its people, both black and white. The white population became soulless in the face of the indoctrination of apartheid. The white people of South Africa were unable to see blacks as real people. That is why it has always been such a source of amazement and joy to me that so many people were able to come out from under the weight of apartheid.

They did not rush down into the pit of despair and become totally brutalised. The most famous figure is, of course, Nelson Mandela himself. I have, like many South Africans, listened to his speeches, heard forgiveness preached over and over again as he urged the amazing resilient people of South Africa to build the rainbow nation into a country of hope and beauty.

While Winston, Looksmart, Cleva and Gwala are fictions of my imagination, they do embody some of the truth that I do know of the people I met and lived with in South Africa. Kobus Jonker and his family too come from my imagination. However, as with all of the people in this book, there are parts of people that I do know embedded and melded together from what I understand South Africa to be. The truth of apartheid is that it makes victims of us all. Firstly, it makes tragedy on a Shakespearean scale for the victims of apartheid and there are too many to name in one little book. Secondly, it must also be noted that it makes victims of the perpetrators too, although they do not know that their humanity and souls are sucked out and replaced with a vacuum that can only be filled with fear and hate. Danie Swanepoel was created from my readings of the Kannemeyer Commission into the Langa Massacre and my readings about Eugene de Kock.

Many other aspects of this narrative are true. There were 'hit' squads operating in South Africa during the apartheid years, the most famous of which was the *Koevoets*. The word *koevoets* means crowbar and the word was supposed to indicate their approach to tackling terrorism. They were a counter-terrorist agency operating ostensibly out of South West Africa (now Namibia) which South Africa treated as part of its own territory. The *Koevoets* were responsible for hundreds of search-and-destroy missions, and they were accused of numerous atrocities. They operated outside the law and had special powers that allowed them to ignore the law of the land and make their own laws. Reading about their operations, it becomes hard to draw a line between their operations and those of criminal gangs and mafia type organisations.

The number of casualties they inflicted were truly staggering. Between 1979 and 1989, reported killings or captures numbered thousands. The unit captured 3,225 insurgents, many of whom were never heard of again. These organisations' activities were shrouded in secrecy, and it meant that the truth was never truly revealed. While teams like the A-team did exist in South Africa, it needs to be noted that many white, coloured and black people worked together to help stop the suffering.

The years leading up to the Langa Massacre were years of unrest and struggle for the black people of South Africa and there were a tiny number of white people who tried to assist. Many activists believed that they were getting the upper hand and they also believed that the Afrikaners' hold on the country was limited. They were not to know that it would be a further ten years before the Nationalist Party in South Africa would fall, and with it, apartheid. Ten years is a very long time and there were many more Winston stories during those years.

My family and I lived in a small valley called The Elands River Valley which I tried to describe here as honestly as I could. It was truly idyllic and growing up I was very privileged to be part of the life I describe for Winston. However, I had one huge advantage over Winston and his family and that was: I was white.

There was a tragic killing on one of the farms in my neighbourhood just like the one described where Winston's father loses his life. The farmer was ordered to pay the widow R7000.00 for the loss of her husband. He too, like Thienus van der Merwe, pleaded that he was being threatened by a black man with an axe. The truth of this story will never be told because there were only two witnesses and one of them is dead. The dispute was also over a piece of farm machinery. The fact is that during the dark days of apartheid, white people could and did kill black people with impunity.

Later, when I participated in the protest marches in 1993 and 1994, just before the white regime was finally brought to its knees — it was commonplace to be in a protest with 80,000 to 100,000 people — nearly every single one of those people were black. I was proud to be a tiny, tiny part of that protest and the memory of those days still brings me out in goosebumps, such was the excitement those marches produced. I suppose that it can be compared to the fall of the Berlin Wall.

I remember what it felt like marching within the depths of those hundreds of thousands. The hope that seemed to zing in the air as we marched and sang. Also, amongst hundreds of thousands there was safety, and we knew then that the police could not kill us all. Numbers finally dismantled apartheid.

I began then to create my character Winston and I hoped to invest in him and his friends the hope that we felt that day when 80,000 people in Port Elizabeth stood up and made the country change. All around the country similar marches were held. Cape Town, Pretoria, Durban and Bloemfontein, to name just a few. What was truly staggering was that many of these marches boldly strode into the heart of the Afrikaner heartlands.

Millions of black people marched for freedom and achieved it. If you have never been on a march with that many people you cannot know the force that those people carry with them merely by hoping. It can be, and was, a tangible thing. I found out that day that hope is stronger than anything else, and it is most certainly stronger than hatred. When we returned from our marches we put on the televisions and there all over the country were huge waves of people showing the country and the world that finally apartheid was beaten.

I remember, too, the day that we finally went to the polls in South Africa, chanting the refrain, 'one man, one vote.' Long lines of black people, jubilant and unafraid for the first time in their lives. We voted, all of us, and all around we could hear the voices of those people who had been lost in the struggle. Because of them, South Africa was able to come out from under the yoke of apartheid and live in a country that no longer discriminated against people because of the colour of their skin.

I remembered the wild stories of fear that the Afrikaner spread — the idea of *swart gevaar* (black danger) — and realised then in that voting queue that someone would have to tell the story of Langa. I have tried here as best I can.

I have already mentioned the Langa Massacre and the farm shooting of a labourer — these were all too real but there are some other real-life stories interwoven here. For example, Ivy Gcina whose four sons and husband were killed in the struggle fighting for liberation and freedom. It is true that she was not allowed out of her prison cell to attend their funerals. I remember going to a meeting where she was a guest in the 1990s. She was a wonderful woman, no bitterness, only concern for her fellow South Africans and their right to freedom.

Steven Biko, a black activist, who was murdered by the security police while being questioned at the Walmer Police Station in Port Elizabeth. I mention this man because the South African Police Commissioner commented on international television that the death of this man left him cold. This of a man who had never done anything criminal. This of a man who had small children and a wife. I include the cameo of this story — I do not do this man justice; he deserves a whole book to himself — but I mention it only because this demonstrates the kind of attitude that the apartheid government had towards black people. My story is not an exaggeration.

In the interest of fairness, I mention Helen Suzman, a white woman, who was the sole Member of Parliament for the Progressive Federal Party for thirteen years and went every day to parliament to be vilified, booed and subjected to the most awful abuse because she cared. She was a lone white, Jewish woman facing a crowd of hostile white men who saw her as no better than a traitor. And she did this for thirteen years all on her own. It is important to remember that not all white people were supporters of the regime. I could name many more here but perhaps that is for another story.

I ask readers to think about this: if a person can be racist, then surely it is not a long jump for that same person to be xenophobic or anti-Semitic, or sexist, or homophobic. These hatreds all band together and form an ugly dangerous thing. Hence the story of Ruben and Piet. All of these hatreds exist together and that had to be broken and it was.

Many homosexual people in South Africa suffered just as much as the black population. Finally, I would like to add a short note about the Aversion Project that was introduced in the South African Defence Force (SADF) which was initiated to help 'cure' homosexual men. Hence Ruben Ariel's fear of his conscription and his plans to leave the country.

The Aversion Project was a medical torture programme led by Dr Aubrey Levin during those apartheid years. The project identified gay soldiers and forced them to submit to "curing" their homosexuality. There was a very real danger for people like Ruben Ariel and Piet Jonker as they would have been 'called up' for national service. If found out they would have been submitted for the Aversion Project. Homosexuality was illegal in South Africa until 1993.

Ever since that warm, blustery, March Day, Thursday 21st of March 1985, I have been wanting to write this story. I've had many false starts and plenty of hand-wringing cuts and changes, but in the end, I am pleased that I have been able to write this book. It needed to be told.

I would like to add a note about the Black Lives Matter issue that is particularly pertinent at the moment. This is important as when we look at the history of the Langa Massacre — we must all, ordinary citizens and leaders alike, remember apartheid and what it allowed white supremacy to perpetuate. We must all stand up to racism before more black people are killed because of irrational hate. We must read and know the stories of the past in order to stop racism. Winston and his friends did not matter, and their lives were a forfeit because they were black.

Glossary

amandla	A chant used by activists as a rally call. It means 'power' and the response is *awetu* which means 'people'. The two shouted together means 'power to the people'.
awetu	See note above.
baas	boss
bakkie	pick-up truck
bedonnered	angry
blerry	South African colloquialism for 'bloody'
boetie	small brother
boomslang	tree snake
braai	barbecue
braaied	barbecued
buffel	An army vehicle designed to carry a small body of soldiers.
bundu	An Australian term used in South Africa to describe the bush veld.
COSATU	Congress of South African Trade Unions — the largest of South Africa's three trade unions.
cents	South African currency (coins)
doos	Literally means 'box' but is used as a derogatory term and insult, similar to the English equivalent 'cunt'.
donnerse	bloody, as in 'bloody idiot'
dorp	small town
Engelsman	Englishman
gevaar	danger
gogo	grandmother

hande on kop	hands on head
hayi	no
hemel	heaven
ja	yes
jammer	sorry
jy het gesê, jy het gesê	you said, you said
impi	young man
kaffir	A highly derogative term used to refer to black people in South Africa. Often used by white racists. Its literal meaning is heathen, which is something that white supremacists were trying to imply.
kaffir boeties	A term used to refer to white people who worked towards helping black people gain equal rights.
kaptein	captain
klein	small
kloof	valley
knobkerrie	fighting stick
koeksisters	similar to yum yums or sweet baked treats
kolonel	colonel
kom	come
kombi	a Volkswagen camper van
kommandant	commander
koper	copper
lappa	over there
luister	listen
luister jou domkop	listen you dumbo (*domkop* literally means dumb head)
mamas	mothers

melkhout	mile wood — shrubs or small trees
meneer	mister
moffie	a derogatory term for a gay man
naartjie	tangerine
niks	nothing
paw paw	papaya
polisie	police
polisie sentraal	police central
polisiestasie	police station
rand	South African currency (notes)
rooinek	red neck — a derogatory term used towards English men whose necks would go red in the African sun; first used in the Boer war
rusbank	bench
sersant	sergeant
seun	son
seun ons het kamers vir julle. Ek het die bed reg gemaak. Alles is reg.	Son, we have rooms for you. I made a bed for you. Everything is ready.
shebeen	an illegal drinking den
sissie	a girlie boy
stoep	veranda
swart	black
swart gevaar	black danger
takkies	trainers
toyi toyi	a high-kneed, foot stomping dance for activists
uitkyk	outlook or view

uMkhonto we Sizew	spear of the nation — the resistance army fighting the South African Defence Force
veld	the bush in South Africa
vierkleur	four colours — this was the name of the old South African flag used during the Apartheid years
voetsek	fuck off
voorkamer	front room
voortrekkers	pioneer men and women, usually of Dutch descent, who penetrated into the centre and north of South Africa
vrou	woman or wife
vroumens	women
vygies	Succulents that grow naturally in the veld. They bear beautiful, coloured flowers once a year. Often used as a water source as their leaves are fleshy and full of water.
wag 'n bietjie bush	a large thorny bush that holds on to skin and clothing, resulting in the name, 'wait a big'
wat is jou naam	what is your name
wunderkind	wonder child
weermag	army or the military in general
Xhosa	a South African cultural group and language

Made in the USA
Las Vegas, NV
28 June 2022

50836315R00155